T0024202

SPIRITS ABROAD

Also by Zen Cho

Cyberpunk: Malaysia (editor)
Sorcerer to the Crown
The True Queen
The Order of the Pure Moon Reflected in Water
Black Water Sister

ZEN CHO

SPIRITS ABROAD

STORIES

Small Beer Press
Easthampton, MA

This is a work of fiction. All characters and events portrayed in this book are either fictitious or used fictitiously.

Spirits Abroad: Stories copyright © 2021 by Zen Cho (zencho.org). All rights reserved. Page 342 is an extension of the copyright page.

Small Beer Press
150 Pleasant Street #306
Easthampton, MA 01027
smallbeerpress.com
weightlessbooks.com
bookmoonbooks.com
info@smallbeerpress.com

Distributed to the trade by Consortium.

Library of Congress Cataloging-in-Publication Data

Names: Cho, Zen, author.
Title: Spirits abroad and other stories / Zen Cho.
Description: First edition. | Easthampton, MA : Small Beer Press, [2021] |
  Summary: "Nineteen sparkling stories that weave between the lands of the
  living and the lands of the dead"-- Provided by publisher.
Identifiers: LCCN 2021001588 (print) | LCCN 2021001589 (ebook) | ISBN
  9781618731869 (paperback) | ISBN 9781618731876 (ebook)
Subjects: LCGFT: Short stories.
Classification: LCC PR6103.H6 S69 2021 (print) | LCC PR6103.H6 (ebook) |
  DDC 823/.92--dc23
LC record available at https://lccn.loc.gov/2021001588
LC ebook record available at https://lccn.loc.gov/2021001589

First edition 2 3 4 5 6 7 8 9

Set in Centaur 12 pt.
Cover illustration copyright © 2021 by Wesley Allsbrook (wesleyallsbrook.com).

Printed on 55# Natures Natural 30% PCR recycled paper by the Versa Press, East Peoria, IL.

Contents

Here

There

Elsewhere

To my parents
With all my love

Here

The First Witch
of Damansara

Vivian's late grandmother was a witch—which is just a way of saying she was a woman of unusual insight. Vivian, in contrast, had a mind like a high-tech blender. She was sharp and purposeful, but she did not understand magic.

This used to be a problem. Magic ran in the family. Even her mother's second cousin, who was adopted, did small spells on the side. She sold these from a stall in Kota Bharu. Her main wares were various types of fruit fried in batter, but if you bought five pisang or cempedak goreng, she threw in a jampi for free.

These embarrassing relatives became less of a problem after Vivian left Malaysia. In the modern Western country where she lived, the public toilets were clean, the newspapers were allowed to be as rude to the government as they liked, and nobody believed in magic except people in whom nobody believed. Even with a cooking appliance mind, Vivian understood that magic requires belief to thrive.

She called home rarely, and visited even less often. She was twenty-eight, engaged to a rational man, and employed as an accountant.

Vivian's Nai Nai would have said that she was attempting to deploy enchantments of her own—the fiancé, the ordinary hobbies, and the sensible office job were so many sigils to ward off chaos. It was not an ineffective magic. It worked—for a while.

There was just one moment, after she heard the news, when Vivian experienced a surge of unfilial exasperation.

"They could have call me on Skype," she said. "Call my hand-phone some more! What a waste of money."

"What's wrong?" said the fiancé. He plays the prince in this story: beautiful, supportive, and cast in an appropriately self-effacing role—just off-screen, on a white horse.

"My grandmother's passed away," said Vivian. "I'm supposed to go back."

Vivian was not a woman to hold a grudge. When she turned up at KLIA in harem trousers and a tank top it was not through malice aforethought, but because she had simply forgotten.

Her parents embraced her with sportsmanlike enthusiasm, but when this was done her mother pulled back and plucked at her tank top.

"Girl, what's this? You know Nai Nai won't like it."

Nai Nai had lived by a code of rigorous propriety. She had disap-proved of wearing black or navy blue at Chinese New Year, of white at weddings, and of spaghetti straps at all times. When they went out for dinner, even at the local restaurant where they sat outdoors and were accosted by stray cats requesting snacks, her grandchildren were required to change out of their ratty pasar malam T-shirts and faded shorts. She drew a delicate but significant distinction between flip-flops and sandals, singlets and strapless tops, soft cotton shorts and denim.

"Can see your bra," whispered Ma. "It's not so nice."

"That kind of pants," her dad said dubiously. "Don't know what Nai Nai will think of it."

"Nai Nai won't see them what," said Vivian, but this offended her parents. They sat in mutinous silence throughout the drive home.

Their terrace house was swarming with pregnant cats and black dogs.

"Only six dogs," said Vivian's mother when Vivian pointed this out. "Because got five cats. Your sister thought it's a good idea to have more dogs than cats."

"But why do we have so many cats?" said Vivian. "I thought you don't like to have animals in the house."

"Nai Nai collected the cats," said Vivian's sister. "She started before she passed away. Pregnant cats only."

"Wei Yi," said Vivian. "How are you?"

"I'm OK, Vivian," said Wei Yi. Her eyes glittered.

She'd stopped calling Vivian jie jie some time after Vivian left home. Vivian minded this less than the way she said "Vivian" as though it were a bad word.

But after all, Vivian reminded herself, Wei Yi was seventeen. She was practically legally required to be an arsehole.

"Why did Nai Nai want the pregnant cats?" Vivian tried to make her voice pleasant.

"Hai, don't need to talk so much," said their mother hastily. "Lin—Vivian so tired. Vivian, you go and change first, then we go for dinner. Papa will start complaining soon if not."

It was during an outing to a prayer goods store, while Vivian's mother was busy buying joss sticks, that her mother's friend turned to Vivian and said, "So a lot of things to do in your house now ah?"

Vivian was shy to say she knew nothing about what preparations were afoot. As her mother's eldest it would only have been right for her to have been her mother's first support in sorting out the funeral arrangements.

"No, we are having a very simple funeral," said Vivian. "Nai Nai didn't believe in religion so much."

This was not a lie. The brutal fact was that Nai Nai had been an atheist with animist leanings, in common with most witches. Vivian's parents preferred not to let this be known, less out of a concern that Nai Nai would be outed as a witch than because of the stale leftover fear that she would be considered a Communist.

"But what about the dog cat all that?" said Auntie Wendy. "Did it work? Did your sister manage to keep her in the coffin?"

Vivian's mind whirred to a stop. Then it started up again, buzzing louder than ever.

Ma was righteously indignant when Vivian reproached her.

"You live so long overseas, why you need to know?" said Ma. "Don't worry. Yi Yi is handling it. Probably Nai Nai was not serious anyway."

"Not serious about what?"

"Hai, these old people have their ideas," said Ma. "Nai Nai live in KL so long, she still want to go home. Not that I don't want to please her. If it was anything else . . . but even if she doesn't have pride for herself, I have pride for her!"

"Nai Nai wanted to be buried in China?" said Vivian, puzzled.

"China, what China! Your Nai Nai is from Penang lah," said Ma. "Your Yeh Yeh is also buried in Bukit Tambun there. But the way he treat Mother, I don't think they should be buried together."

Vivian began to understand. "But Ma, if she said she wanted to be with him—"

"It's not what she wants! It's just her idea of propriety," said Ma. "She thinks woman must always stay by the husband no matter what. I don't believe that! Nai Nai will be buried here and when her children and grandchildren pass on, we will be buried with her. It's more comfortable for her, right? To have her loved ones around her?"

"But if Nai Nai didn't think so?"

Ma's painted eyebrows drew together.

"Nai Nai is a very stubborn woman," she said.

Wei Yi was being especially teenaged that week. She went around with lightning frizzing her hair and stormclouds rumbling about her ears. Her clothes stood away from her body, stiff with electricity. The cats hissed and the dogs whined when she passed.

When she saw the paper offerings their mother had bought for Nai Nai, she threw a massive tantrum.

"What's this?" she said, picking up a paper polo shirt. "Where got Nai Nai wear this kind of thing?"

Ma looked embarrassed.

"The shop only had that," she said. "Don't be angry, girl. I bought some bag and shoe also. But you know Nai Nai was never the dressy kind."

"That's because she like to keep all her nice clothes," said Wei Yi. She cast a look of burning contempt at the paper handbag, printed in heedless disregard of intellectual property rights with the Gucci logo. "Looks like the pasar malam bag. And this slippers is like old man slippers. Nai Nai could put two of her feet in one slipper!"

"Like that she's less likely to hop away," Ma said thoughtlessly.

"Is that what you call respecting your mother-in-law?" shouted Wei Yi. "Hah, you wait until it's your turn! I'll know how to treat you then."

"Wei Yi, how can you talk to Ma like that?" said Vivian.

"You shut up your face!" Wei Yi snapped. She flounced out of the room.

"She never even see the house yet," sighed Ma. She had bought an elaborate palace fashioned out of gilt-edged pink paper, with embellished roofs and shuttered windows, and two dolls dressed in Tang dynasty attire prancing on a balcony. "Got two servants some more."

"She shouldn't talk to you like that," said Vivian.

She hadn't noticed any change in Ma's appearance before, but now the soft wrinkly skin under her chin and the pale brown spots on her arms reminded Vivian that she was getting old. Old people should be cared for.

She touched her mother on the arm. "I'll go scold her. Never mind, Ma. Girls this age are always one kind."

Ma smiled at Vivian.

"You were OK," she said. She tucked a lock of Vivian's hair behind her ear.

Old people should be grateful for affection. The sudden disturbing thought occurred to Vivian that no one had liked Nai Nai very much because she'd never submitted to being looked after.

Wei Yi was trying to free the dogs. She stood by the gate, holding it open and gesturing with one hand at the great outdoors.

"Go! Blackie, Guinness, Ah Hei, Si Hitam, Jackie, Bobby! Go, go!"

The dogs didn't seem that interested in the great outdoors. Ah Hei took a couple of tentative steps toward the gate, looked back at Wei Yi, changed her mind and sat down again.

"Jackie and Bobby?" said Vivian.

Wei Yi shot her a glare. "I ran out of ideas." The *so what?* was unspoken, but it didn't need to be said.

"Why these stupid dogs don't want to go," Wei Yi muttered. "When you open the gate to drive in or out, they go running everywhere. When you want them to chau, they don't want."

"They can tell you won't let them back in again," said Vivian.

She remembered when Wei Yi had been cute—as a little girl, with those pure single-lidded eyes and the doll-like lacquered bowl of hair. When had she turned into this creature? Hair at sevens and eights, the uneven fringe falling into malevolent eyes. Inappropriately tight Bermuda shorts worn below an unflatteringly loose plaid shirt.

At seven Wei Yi had been a being perfect in herself. At seventeen there was nothing that wasn't wrong about the way she moved in the world.

Vivian had been planning to tell her sister off, but the memory of that lovely child softened her voice. "Why you don't want the dogs anymore?"

"I want Nai Nai to win." Wei Yi slammed the gate shut.

"What, by having nice clothes when she's passed away?" said Vivian. "Winning or losing doesn't matter for Nai Nai anymore. What does it matter if she wears a polo shirt in the afterlife?"

Wei Yi's face crumpled. She clutched her fists in agony. The words broke from her in a roar.

"You're so stupid! You don't know anything!" She kicked the gate to relieve her feelings. "Nai Nai's brain works more than yours and she's dead! Do you even belong to this family?"

This was why Vivian had left. Magic lent itself to temperament.

"Maybe not," said Vivian.

~~~

When Vivian was angry she did it with the same single-minded energy she did everything else. This was why she decided to go wedding dress shopping in the week of her grandmother's funeral.

There were numerous practical justifications, actually. She went through them in her head as she drove past bridal studios where faceless mannequins struck poses in clouds of tulle.

"Cheaper to get it here than overseas. Not like I'm helping much at home what. Not like I was so close to Nai Nai."

She ended up staring mournfully at herself in the mirror, weighted down by satin and rhinestones. Did she want a veil? Did she like lace? Ball gown or mermaid shape?

She'd imagined her wedding dress as being white and long. She hadn't expected there to be so many permutations on a theme. She felt pinned in place by the choices available to her.

The shop assistant could tell her heart wasn't in it.

"Some ladies like other color better," said the shop assistant. "You want to try? We have blue, pink, peach, yellow—very nice color, very feminine."

"I thought usually white?"

"Some ladies don't like white because—you know—" The shop assistant lowered her voice, but she was too superstitious to say it outright. "It's related to a not so nice subject."

The words clanged in Vivian's ears. Briefly light-headed, she clutched at the back of a chair for balance. Her hands were freezing. In the mirror the white dress looked like a shroud. Her face hovering above it was the face of a mourner, or a ghost.

"Now that I've tried it, I'm not sure I like Western gown so much," said Vivian, speaking with difficulty.

"We have cheongsam or qun kua," said the shop assistant. "Very nice, very traditional. Miss is so slim, will suit the cheongsam."

The jolt of red brocade was a relief. Vivian took a dress with gold trimmings, the highest of high collars, and an even higher slit along the sides. It was as red as a blare of trumpets, as red as the pop of fireworks.

This fresh chili red had never suited her. In it she looked paler than ever, washed out by the vibrant shade. But the color was a protective charm. It laid monsters to rest. It shut out hungry ghosts. It frightened shadows back into the corners where they belonged.

Vivian crept home with her spoils. That night she slept and did not dream of anything.

The next morning she regretted the purchase. Her fiancé would think it was ridiculous. She couldn't wear a cheongsam down the aisle of an Anglican church. She would take it back to the boutique and return it. After all, the white satin mermaid dress had suited her. The sweetheart neckline was so much more flattering than a mandarin collar.

She shoved the cheongsam in a bag and tried to sneak out, but Wei Yi was sitting on the floor of the laundry room, in the way of her exit. She was surrounded by webs of filigreed red paper.

"What's this?" said Vivian.

"It's called paper cutting," said Wei Yi, not looking up. "You never see before meh?"

On the floor the paper cuttings unfurled. Some were disasters: a mutilated fish floated past like tumbleweed; a pair of flirtatious girls had been torn apart by an overly enthusiastic slash. But some of the pieces were astounding.

"Kwan Yin," said Vivian.

The folds in the goddess's robes had been rendered with extraordinary delicacy. Her eyes were gentle, her face double-chinned. Her halo was a red moon circled by ornate clouds.

"It's for Nai Nai," said Wei Yi. "Maybe Kwan Yin will have mercy on her even though she's so blasphemous."

"Shouldn't talk like that about the dead," said Vivian.

Wei Yi rolled her eyes, but the effort of her craft seemed to be absorbing all her evil energies. Her response was mild: "It's not disrespectful if it's true."

Her devotion touched Vivian. Surely not many seventeen-year-olds would spend so much time on so laborious a task. The sleet of impermanent art piled around her must have taken hours to produce.

"Did Nai Nai teach you how to do that?" Vivian said, trying to get back on friendlier ground.

Wei Yi's face spasmed.

"Nai Nai was a rubber tapper with seven children," she said. "She can't even read! You think what, she was so free she can do all these hobbies, is it? I learnt it from YouTube lah!"

She crumpled the paper she was working on and flung it down on the floor to join the flickering red mass.

"Oh, whatever!" said Vivian in the fullness of her heart.

She bought the whitest, fluffiest, sheeniest, most beaded dress she could find in the boutique. It was strapless and low-backed to boot. Nai Nai would have hated it.

That night Vivian dreamt of her grandmother.

Nai Nai had climbed out of her coffin where she had been lying in the living room. She was wearing a kebaya, with a white baju and a batik sarong wrapped around her hips. No modern creation this— the blouse was fastened not with buttons but with kerongsang, ornate gold brooches studded with pearls and rhinestones.

Nai Nai was struggling with the kerongsang. In her dream Vivian reached out to help her.

"I can do!" said Nai Nai crossly. "Don't so sibuk." She batted at the kerongsang with the slim brown hands that had been so deft in life.

"What's the matter? You want to take it off for what?" said Vivian in Hokkien.

"It's too nice to wear outside," Nai Nai complained. "When I was alive I used safety pins and it was enough. All this hassle just because I am like this. I didn't save Yeh Yeh's pension so you can spend on a carcass!"

"Why do you want to go outside?" Vivian took the bony arm. "Nai Nai, come, let's go back to sleep. It's so late already. Everybody is sleeping."

Nai Nai was a tiny old lady with a dandelion fluff of white hair standing out from her head. She looked nothing like the spotty, tubby, furiously awkward Wei Yi, but her expression suddenly showed Vivian what her sister would look like when she was old. The contemptuous exasperation was exactly the same.

"If it's not late, how can I go outside?" she said. "I have a long way to go. Hai!" She flung up her hands. "After they bury me, ask the priest to give you back the kerongsang."

She started hopping toward the door, her arms held rod-straight out in front of her. The sight was comic and horrible.

This was the secret the family had been hiding from Vivian. Nai Nai had become a kuang shi.

"Nai Nai," choked Vivian. "Please rest. You're so old already, shouldn't run around so much."

"Don't answer back!" shouted Nai Nai from the foyer. "Come and open the door for Nai Nai! Yeh Yeh will be angry. He cannot stand when people are late."

Vivian envisioned Nai Nai hopping out of the house—past the neighborhood park with its rustling bushes and creaking swings, past the neighbors' Myvis and Peroduas, through the toll while the attendant slumbered. She saw Nai Nai hopping along the curves of the Titiwangsa mountains, her halo of hair white against the bleeding red of the hills where the forests had peeled away to show the limestone. She saw Nai Nai passing oil palm plantations, their leaves dark glossy green under the brassy glare of sunshine—sleepy water buffalo flicking their tails in wide, hot fields—empty new terrace houses standing in white rows on bare hillsides. Up the long North-South Expressway, to her final home.

"Nai Nai," said Vivian. *Don't leave us,* she wanted to say.

"Complain, complain!" Nai Nai was slapping at the doorknob with her useless stiff hands.

"You can't go all that way," said Vivian. She had an inspiration. "Your sarong will come undone."

Whoever had laid Nai Nai out had dressed her like a true nyonya. The sarong was wound around her hips and tucked in at the waist, with no fastenings to hold it up.

"At my age, who cares," said Nai Nai, but this had clearly given her pause.

"Come back to sleep," coaxed Vivian. "I'll tell Ma. Bukit Tambun, right? I'll sort it out for you."

Nai Nai gave her a sharp look. "Can talk so sweetly but what does she do? Grandmother is being buried and she goes to buy a wedding dress!"

Vivian winced.

"The dress is not nice also," said Nai Nai. "What happened to the first dress? That was nice. Red is a happy color."

"I know Nai Nai feels it's pantang, but—"

"Pantang what pantang," snapped Nai Nai. Like all witches, she hated to be accused of superstition. "White is a boring color! Ah, when I got married everybody wanted to celebrate. We had two hundred guests and they all had chicken to eat. I looked so beautiful in my photo. And Yeh Yeh . . ."

Nai Nai sank into reminiscence.

"What about Yeh Yeh?" prompted Vivian.

"Yeh Yeh looked the same as always. Like a useless playboy," said Nai Nai. "He could only look nice and court girls."

"Then you want to be buried with him for what?"

"That's different," said Nai Nai. "Whether I'm a good wife doesn't have anything to do with what he was like."

As if galvanized by Vivian's resistance, she turned and made to hit the door again.

"If you listen to me, I'll take the dress back to the shop," said Vivian, driven by desperation.

Nai Nai paused. "You'll buy the pretty cheongsam?"

"If you want also I'll wear the kua," said Vivian recklessly.

She tried not to imagine what her fiancé would say when he saw the loose red jacket and long skirt, embroidered in gold and silver with bug-eyed dragons and insectoid phoenixes. And the three-quarter bell sleeves, all the better to show the wealth of the family in the gold bracelets stacked on the bride's wrists! How that would impress her future in-laws.

To her relief, Nai Nai said, "No lah! So old-fashioned. Cheongsam is nicer."

She started hopping back toward the living room.

Vivian trailed behind, feeling somehow as if she had been outmaneuvered.

"Nai Nai, do you really want to be buried in Penang?"

Nai Nai peered up with suspicion in her reddened eyes as Vivian helped her back into the coffin.

"You want to change your mind, is it?"

"No, no, I'll get the cheongsam. It'll be in my room by tomorrow, I promise."

Nai Nai smiled.

"You know why I wanted you all to call me Nai Nai?" she said before Vivian closed the coffin. "Even though Hokkien people call their grandmother Ah Ma?"

Vivian paused with her hand on the lid.

"In the movies, Nai Nai is always bad!"

Vivian woke up with her grandmother's growly cackle in her ears.

Wei Yi was in the middle of a meltdown when Vivian came downstairs for breakfast. Ma bristled with relief.

"Ah, your sister is here. She'll talk to you."

Wei Yi was sitting enthroned in incandescence, clutching a bread knife. A charred hunk of what used to be kaya toast sat on her plate. The *Star* newspaper next to it was crisping at the edges.

Vivian began to sweat. She thought about turning on the ceiling fan, but that might stoke the flames.

She pulled out a chair and picked up the jar of kaya as if nothing was happening. "What's up?"

Wei Yi turned hot coal eyes on Vivian.

"She doesn't want to kill the dogs wor," said Ma. "Angry already."

"So? Who ask you to kill the dogs in the first place?" said Vivian.

"Stupid," said Wei Yi. Her face was very pale, but her lips had the dull orange glow of heated metal. Fire breathed in her hair. A layer of ash lay on the crown of her head.

"Because of Nai Nai," Ma explained. "Wei Yi heard the blood of a black dog is good for Nai Nai's . . . condition."

"It's not right," said Wei Yi. "It's better for Nai Nai if—but you won't understand one."

Vivian spread a layer of kaya on her piece of bread before she answered. Her hands were shaking, but her voice was steady when she spoke.

"I think Ma is right. There's no need to kill any dogs. Nai Nai is not serious about being a kuang shi. She's just using it as an emotional blackmail." She paused for reflection. "And I think she's enjoying it also lah. You know Nai Nai was always very active. She likes to be up and about."

Wei Yi dropped her butter knife.

"Eh, how you know?" said Ma.

"She talked to me in my dream last night because she didn't like the wedding dress I bought," said Vivian.

Ma's eyes widened. "You went to buy your wedding dress when Nai Nai just pass away?"

"You saw Nai Nai?" cried Wei Yi. "What did she say?"

"She likes cheongsam better, and she wants to be buried in Penang," said Vivian. "So I'm going to buy cheongsam. Ma, should think about sending her back to Penang. When she got nothing to complain about she will settle down."

"Why she didn't talk to me?" said Wei Yi. Beads of molten metal ran down her face, leaving silver trails. "I do so many jampi and she never talk to me! It's not fair!"

Ma was torn between an urge to scold Vivian and the necessity of comforting Wei Yi. "Girl, don't cry— Vivian, so disrespectful, I'm surprise Nai Nai never scold you—"

"Yi Yi," said Vivian. "She didn't talk to you because in Nai Nai's eyes you are perfect already." As she said this, she realized it was true.

Wei Yi—awkward, furious, and objectionable in every way— was Nai Nai's ideal grandchild. There was no need to monitor or reprimand such a perfect heir. The surprise was that Nai Nai even thought it necessary to rise from the grave to order Vivian around, rather than just leaving the job to the next witch.

Of course, Nai Nai probably hadn't had the chance to train Wei Yi in the standards expected of a wedding in Nai Nai's family. The finer points of bridal fashion would certainly escape Wei Yi.

"Nai Nai only came back to scold people," said Vivian. "She doesn't need to scold you for anything."

The unnatural metallic sheen of Wei Yi's face went away. Her hair and eyes dimmed. Her mouth trembled.

Vivian expected a roar. Instead Wei Yi shoved her kaya toast away and laid her head on the table.

"I miss Nai Nai," she sobbed.

Ma got up and touched Vivian on the shoulder.

"I have to go buy thing," she whispered. "You cheer up your sister."

Wei Yi's skin was still hot when Vivian put her arm around her, but as Vivian held her Wei Yi's temperature declined, until she felt merely feverish. Her tears went from scalding to lukewarm.

"Nai Nai, Nai Nai," she wailed in that screechy show-off way Vivian had always hated. When they were growing up Vivian had not believed in Wei Yi's tears—they seemed no more than a show, put on to impress the grown-ups.

Vivian now realized that the grief was as real as the volume deliberate. Wei Yi did not cry like that simply because she was sad, but because she wanted someone to listen to her.

In the old days it had been a parent or a teacher's attention that she had sought. These howls were aimed directly at the all-too-responsive ears of their late grandmother.

"Wei Yi," said Vivian. "I've thought of what you can do for Nai Nai."

For once Wei Yi did not put Vivian's ideas to scorn. She seemed to have gone up in her sister's estimation for having seen Nai Nai's importunate specter.

Vivian had a feeling Nai Nai's witchery had gone into Wei Yi's paper cutting skills. YouTube couldn't explain the unreal speed with which she did it.

Vivian tried picking up Wei Yi's scissors and dropped them, yelping.

"What the—!" It had felt like an electric shock.

Wei Yi grabbed the scissors. "These are no good. I give you other ones to use."

Vivian got the task of cutting out the sarong—a large rectangular piece of paper to which Wei Yi would add the batik motifs later. When she was done Wei Yi took a look and pursed her lips. The last time Vivian had felt this small was when she failed her first driving test two minutes after getting into the car.

"OK ah?"

"Not bad," said Wei Yi unconvincingly. "Eh, you go help Ma do her whatever thing lah. I'll work on this first."

A couple of hours later she barged into Vivian's room. "Why you're here? Why you take so long? Come and see!"

Vivian got up sheepishly. "I thought you need some time to finish mah."

"Nonsense. Nai Nai going to be buried tomorrow, where got time to dilly-dally?" Wei Yi grasped her hand.

The paper dress was laid in crisp folds on the dining table. Wei Yi's scissors had rendered the delicate lace of the kebaya blouse with marvelous skill. Peacocks with uplifted wings and princely crowns draped their tails along the hems, strutted up the lapels, and curled coyly around the ends of the sleeves. The paper was chiffon-thin. A breath set it fluttering.

The skirt was made from a thicker, heavier cream paper. Wei Yi had cut blowsy peonies into the front and a contrasting grid pattern on the reverse. Vivian touched it in wonder, feeling the nubby texture of the paper under her fingertips.

"Do you think Nai Nai will like it?" said Wei Yi.

Vivian had to be honest. "The top is a bit see-through, no?"

"She'll have a singlet to wear underneath," said Wei Yi. "I left that for you to do. Very simple one. Just cut along the line only."

This was kindness, Wei Yi style.

"It's beautiful, Yi Yi," said Vivian. She felt awkward—they were not a family given to compliments—but once she'd started it was easy to go on. "It's so nice. Nai Nai will love it."

"Ah, don't need to say so much lah," Wei Yi scoffed. "'OK' enough already. I still haven't done shoe yet."

They burnt the beautiful cream kebaya as an offering to Nai Nai. It didn't go alone—Wei Yi had created four other outfits, working through the night. Samfu for everyday wear; an old-fashioned loose, long-sleeved cheongsam ("Nicer for older lady. Nai Nai is not a Shanghai cabaret singer"); a sarong for sleeping in; and a Punjabi suit of all things.

"Nai Nai used to like wearing it," said Wei Yi when Vivian expressed surprise. "Comfortable mah. Nai Nai likes this simple kind of thing to wear for every day."

"Four is not a good number," said Vivian. "Maybe should make extra sarong?"

"You forgot the kebaya. That's five," Wei Yi retorted. "Anyway she die already. What is there to be pantang about?"

They threw the more usual hell gold and paper mansion into the bonfire as well. The doll servants didn't burn well, but melted dramatically and stuck afterward.

Since they were doing the bonfire outside the house, on the public road, this concerned Vivian. She chipped doubtfully away at the mess of plastic.

"Don't worry," said Ma. "The servants have gone to Nai Nai already."

"I'm not worried about that," said Vivian. "I'm worried about MPPJ." She couldn't imagine the local authorities would be particularly pleased about the extra work they'd made for them.

"They're used to it lah," said Ma, dismissing the civil service with a wave of the hand.

They even burnt the fake Gucci bag and the polo shirt in the end.

"Nai Nai will find some use for it," said Wei Yi. "Maybe turn out she like that kind of style also."

She could afford to be magnanimous. Making the kebaya had relieved something in Wei Yi's heart. As she'd stood watch over the flames to make sure the demons didn't get their offerings to Nai Nai, there had been a serenity in her face.

As they moved back to the house, Vivian put her arm around her sister, wincing at the snap and hiss when her skin touched Wei Yi's. It felt like a static shock, only intensified by several orders of magnitude.

"OK?"

Wei Yi was fizzing with magic, but her eyes were calm and dark and altogether human.

"OK," replied the Witch of Damansara.

In Vivian's dream a moth came fluttering into the room. It alighted at the end of her bed and turned into Nai Nai.

Nai Nai was wearing a green-and-white-striped cotton sarong, tucked and knotted under her arms as if she were going to bed soon. Her hair smelled of Johnson & Johnson baby shampoo. Her face was white with bedak sejuk.

"Tell your mother the house is very beautiful," said Nai Nai. "The servants have already run away and got married, but it's not so bad. In hell it's not so dusty. Nothing to clean also."

"Nai Nai—"

"Ah Yi is very clever now, har?" said Nai Nai. "The demons looked at my nice things but when they saw her they immediately run away."

Vivian experienced a pang. She didn't say anything, but perhaps the dead understood these things. Or perhaps it was just that Nai Nai, with sixty-five years of mothering behind her, did not need to be told. She reached out and patted Vivian's hand.

"You are always so guai," said Nai Nai. "I'm not so worried about you."

This was a new idea to Vivian. She was unused to thinking of herself—magicless, intransigent—as the good kid in the family.

"But I went overseas," she said stupidly.

"You're always so clever to work hard. You don't make your mother and father worried," said Nai Nai. "Ah Yi ah. . . ." Nai Nai shook her head. "So stubborn! So naughty! If I don't take care sekali she burn down the house. That girl doesn't use her head. But she become a bit guai already. When she's older she won't be so free, won't have time to cause so much problems."

Vivian did not point out that age did not seem to have stopped Nai Nai. This would have been disrespectful. Instead she said, "Nai Nai, were you really a vampire? Or were you just pretending to turn into a kuang shi?"

"Hai, you think so fun to pretend to be a kuang shi?" said Nai Nai indignantly. "When you are old, you will find out how suffering it is. You think I have time to watch all the Hong Kong movies and learn how to be a vampire?"

So that was how she did it. The pale vampirish skin had probably been bedak sejuk as well. How Nai Nai had obtained bedak sejuk in the afterlife was a question better left unasked. Vivian had questions of more immediate interest anyway.

"If you stayed because you're worried about Wei Yi, can I return the cheongsam to the shop?"

Nai Nai bridled. "Oh, like that ah? Not proud of your culture, is it? If you want to wear the white dress, like a ghost, so ugly—"

"Ma wore a white dress on her wedding day. Everyone does it."

"Nai Nai give you my bedak sejuk and red lipstick lah. Then you can pretend to be kuang shi also!"

"I'll get another cheongsam," said Vivian. "Not that I don't want to wear cheongsam. I just don't like this one so much. It's too expensive."

"How much?"

Vivian told her.

"Wah, so much ah," said Nai Nai. "Like that you should just get it tailored. Don't need to buy from shop. Tailored is cheaper and nicer some more. The seamstress's phone number is in Nai Nai's old phonebook. Madam Teoh."

"I'll look," Vivian promised.

Nai Nai got up, stretching. "Must go now. Scared the demons will don't know do what if I leave the house so long. You must look after your sister, OK?"

Vivian, doubtful about how any attempt to look after Wei Yi was likely to be received, said, "Ah."

"Nai Nai already gave Ah Yi her legacy, but I'll give you yours now," said Nai Nai. "You're a good girl, Ah Lin. Nai Nai didn't have chance to talk to you so much when you were small. But I'm proud of you. Make sure the seamstress doesn't overcharge. If you tell Madam Teoh you're my granddaughter she'll give you discount."

"Thank you, Nai Nai," said Vivian, but she spoke to an empty room. The curtains flapped in Nai Nai's wake.

On the floor lay a pile of clothes. Moonlight-sheer chiffon, brown batik, maroon silk, and floral print cotton, and on top of this, glowing turquoise even in the pale light of the moon, the most gilded, spangled, intricately embroidered Punjabi suit Vivian had ever seen.

The Guest

Yiling was riding home on her motorcycle when she saw the cat. It was late evening and the air was thick with smells, but the scent of the cat rang out like the clang of a temple bell, cutting through the stench of exhaust and the oil-in-the-nose smell of fried food wafting from the roadside stalls.

Yiling turned off the road and parked her motorcycle on the grassy verge next to the stalls. She bought two pyramidal packets of nasi lemak, each neatly wrapped in banana leaf, and some kuih: the sticky green kind layered with white santan, and triangles of pink-and-white kuih lapis. She thought of buying a durian—she liked to entertain well and did not get the chance to do it often—but she already had too much to carry.

As she walked back to her motorcycle she scooped up the cat. It had been looking elsewhere, and by the time Yiling grasped it by the back of the neck it was too late for it to escape.

The cat's claws came out; it hissed in indignation. Yiling ignored it. She put it on her lap and steered her motorcycle one-handed for the rest of the ride home.

It was not really home. Her parents lived in another house with her two siblings. Yiling rented a room in a terrace house from an acquaintance of her grandmother's. The presence of the auntie went some way toward comforting her parents.

The auntie was not generous, and the rent was high considering Yiling only had a bedroom to herself—the auntie did not even like Yiling to cook in the kitchen, or to watch TV in the living room. But the auntie was not interested in Yiling's life and that suited Yiling.

She had never raised the issue of pets but would have been surprised if the auntie had welcomed the idea. Fortunately the auntie was not at home when Yiling got back, and she got the cat up the stairs without incident.

Her room was not big, but there wasn't much in it. It was made to look barer by the depressing quality of the light from the fluorescent lamp. The pale white light was unsteady as a drunken man and it gave everything a grayish, dirty look. This was even though everything in the room was very clean, from the scuffed parquet flooring to the pimpled whitewashed walls. Yiling had a bed, a cupboard for her clothes, and two chairs, one for herself and one for clients. She also had a small television which showed only three channels with any reliability.

When she set the cat down it began to explore, sniffing around the room. Yiling unwrapped one of the packets of nasi lemak and set it on the floor. She did not feel like going down the unlit stairs and through the dark abandoned house to the kitchen, so she sat on one of her chairs and ate her packet of nasi lemak with her hands. Her mother was nyonya, so she knew how to eat like this, using only her right hand to scoop up the food. From a corner of the room the cat watched her suspiciously, but after a while it came closer and started on its rice.

Yiling had never liked cats. Even as a small child having dinner at a restaurant with her family, she jumped and screamed whenever a stray cat brushed past her legs under the table. Her brother and sister had liked to feed the cats surreptitious scraps from the table, but Yiling used to draw her feet up to her chair and refuse to let them down until she felt safe from that soft tickle of cat fur.

This cat could not have appealed even to a cat lover. It had a gaunt, scheming look and could have done with at least three baths. One of its hind legs was injured and it limped as it walked. Fortunately there was nothing wrong with its eyes. The diseased strays of her youth had often had eye problems, and the dried liquid matting the fur around their filmy eyes had disgusted her more than anything else.

She was between jobs so that night she had nothing to do. She ate her kuih while watching TV. It was almost like being at home again: the buzz from the TV, the silence lying between her and the other living being in the room. The cat's silence was less heavy than her parents' silence, its breathing less of a repeating threat. That was an improvement on home.

She laid a sheet of plastic on the floor, and for every piece of kuih she ate, she put one piece down on the sheet. While she stared at the TV she could sense the cat coming close to her leg and nibbling daintily at the kuih.

Before she went to bed she took a duvet out of her closet, which she did not use because she never turned on the air conditioning. She folded the duvet in half and then in half again and placed it on the floor. It made a high, soft bed for any cats that might want one. She turned off the light and went to sleep without waiting to see if it was going to be used.

The next morning Yiling did not dare leave the door open for the cat in case it escaped. On the way out she told the auntie offhandedly that she had got a pet. She was out of the door before the auntie could begin to remonstrate.

Yiling held a diploma in business management from a local college. She worked at a small family-owned company that sold medicinal foot creams. Her precise role was not clear, but she did all sorts of things: kept the accounts, dealt with suppliers, and wrote marketing copy in Chinese, Malay, and English.

Shortly after she had got the job the owners had retired and their daughter had taken over the management of the company. She was not much older than Yiling. She had got an MBA from an overseas university and sometimes still sounded mildly Australian, especially when speaking to customers. She rebranded Yiling as a marketing executive, which would sound well if Yiling ever moved to another job.

The daughter had a serious, pale face with fine skin and straight eyebrows like bridges over the dark water of her eyes. Yiling was strangely disappointed when she brought her well-off young friends to the office and they had loud conversations about the size of a friend's engagement ring: "Must cost at least his three months' salary or he doesn't love you," the daughter had said. A bubble of high, meaningless laughter had drifted from her room.

Yiling had been living with the cat for two weeks when the memory of this incident came to her. Suddenly she felt sorry. It was unfair of her to think that because someone was beautiful, she must be interesting. Or that something must be interesting to her to be worthwhile. Really, she had this feeling because she had so little in her life. She clung onto this sense of superiority to give herself significance. But there was nothing to be proud of in being different. There was nothing special about being lonely.

Returning to her empty room had always reminded her of this fact, but somehow it did not bother her so much with the cat around. After three or four days she started leaving the bedroom door open. It was a gamble, but it paid off. The cat did not leave.

After a while when she came home she would see it curled up on top of the pillar next to the gate. When she got off her motorcycle to unlock the gate it would open one disdainful eye and peer at her, as if to say, "Oh, are you back?" Then it would jump off the wall and stalk into the house to make the point that it had not been waiting for her to return.

In this way affection returned to her life, so that the next time she met a client she was in a softened frame of mind. The client told a common story. She came, she said, because she had heard through a family friend that Yiling could do wonderful things. Her mother's friend had had trouble with her son and Yiling had been able to fix it. Now she, Priya, also had trouble with a man, but this was a boyfriend rather than a son.

The boyfriend had first been her coworker, but they had become close because they had so much in common. He was clever and ambitious; he had a sense of humor; he was the kindest, most giving person. In the beginning they were only friends, but it was no surprise that they should have fallen in love. Unfortunately the boyfriend already had a girlfriend. This was proving a minor obstacle to their romance.

"How come he don't want to break up with her?" said Yiling.

He wanted to, but things were complicated. It was a complicated relationship. Assuredly he and the girlfriend did not love each other, Priya said. He was always telling Priya about how the two of them fought, even before Priya had confessed her love to him. And the girlfriend—what a bitch, so heartless, so capricious it was difficult to see what had drawn him to her in the first place. She had no respect for his opinions, no interest in his ideas. She could not even fulfill him . . . you know . . . in *that* way. She could not make him happy.

And yet they were still together. Sometimes Priya's beloved would say he could not spend time with Priya because he had an appointment with the girlfriend. But he did not even like her! He longed to break up with her, but his parents were fond of her and would be heartbroken if he dumped her. Besides, there was the girlfriend to think of. For all her faults, she was still someone he cared for. He did not want to hurt her feelings. She was very stressed at work. If he broke it off now, it might tip her over the edge.

Yiling felt doubtful of her power to help in such a situation, but when Priya wiped her eyes and said, "I don't know what to do, I just want to be happy with him," she felt a startling surge of sympathy. What a fragile necessary thing love was. She told Priya she would try to help her, but Priya must bring her something that smelled of her boyfriend.

"I work primarily with smells," said Yiling. In fact she worked only with smells, but she felt pleased with the "primarily"—it had a crisp, businesslike, American feel to it.

When the consultation was over, Yiling let Priya out and went to find the cat. The cat was in the garden and withdrew when Yiling tried to pick it up. It refused to be conciliated even when Yiling tempted it with fried fish bought specially for the purpose. It eventually came back into the house but sat itself down next to the auntie in the living room to watch TV—the auntie had cable and had come to be on cordial terms with the cat.

Yiling left the door of her room open and went to bed feeling melancholy. She woke up in the middle of the night to a shadow hovering over her face. The only light in the room was from the streetlamp outside, filtered through the curtains. The windows were two dark glowing rectangles in the wall. In that non-light Yiling saw that the black blob was the cat, perched at the head of the bed and looking down at her. Yiling sat up and scratched behind the cat's ears and rubbed its face while the cat purred. After a while they both lay down and went to sleep.

The next time Priya came, Yiling decided to let the cat stay in the room for the meeting. After all there was no way she would be able to keep the resulting work from the cat. If it was complex, the job might take weeks.

The cat had fine manners. It pretended to sleep on its duvet throughout the interview.

Priya brought a football jersey that belonged to her boyfriend.

"It's not so easy to do anything when the smell is not so strong," said Yiling. Priya smiled in an embarrassed way.

"Hopefully it's strong enough," she said. "I never wash it since he wore it."

She handed Yiling the jersey. There was no "hopefully" about the odor that came off it. Yiling did not look at the cat because she was a professional and used to such things, but the temptation was strong.

Yiling was not about to ask how Priya had come to be in the possession of the boyfriend's worn football jersey, but Priya seemed to feel that it begged an explanation. There was one night, she said shyly, when the girlfriend was outstation and Priya and the boyfriend had gone for a date. They had stayed at a mamak stall till late, and he had insisted on seeing her home because he was a gentleman. And one thing had led to another. . . . Priya's parents lived in Ipoh and she had come to KL for work. She lived alone.

"Nowadays these things don't matter," said Yiling, thinking, they did matter if the man had another girlfriend.

"Yes, yes," said Priya. "We are both very modern about this kind of thing." But her smiling eyes looked uncertain.

"So," said Yiling. She shook out the jersey and the scent gusted out. It smelled of sweat. Under that lay the smell of good intentions, indecision. "What do you want me to do for you?"

"I want him to," said Priya. She hesitated.

"You want him to choose you, is it?" said Yiling. Priya looked pained. Of course she told herself that he had already chosen her, and it was only external factors—his parents, his tender heart, his girlfriend's late nights at the office—that kept him from declaring it to the world.

"I want him to be free to be with me," said Priya.

"Har," said Yiling. "Difficult."

But the girl was lonely. At least Yiling had the cat.

"I'll see what I can do," she said. "But no promises, OK?"

People had odd ideas about what she was able to do, but then, to be fair, her skill was not a conventional one. No one had ever heard of a smell magician, which was why her parents had not supported her in trying to make a career of it.

And even she was still in the process of figuring out what she could and could not do. She could craft things out of smells, but she could only make certain things. You could not make tomyam out of a block of pecorino cheese; similarly, you could not turn the smell of a philandering asshole into a loving boyfriend. She could reproduce a philandering asshole from the smell, but she did not think this was what Priya wanted.

Over the next few weeks she worked on the job in the evenings, after she had come home from work. The cat did not like the smell of the jersey and stayed away when Yiling was working, even though it was madly curious. Crouching on the floor like a tiny sphinx, it gazed at her as she moved her hands over the fabric, her eyes half-closed and her mouth murmuring snatches of spells.

When she had done all she thought she could do, she arranged another meeting with Priya.

Priya did not say anything at first when she came. She sat down on the other chair, opened her mouth, then put her hand over it. Her eyes went red.

"He's getting married to the girlfriend," she said. "It's over."

"That bastard," said Yiling.

"He's not a bastard," sobbed Priya. "It's his parents, they are forcing him to do this."

Yiling gave Priya the jersey. She had folded it and wrapped it in paper like something precious. She also gave Priya a piece of tissue paper.

Priya thanked her and blew her nose. She clutched the parcel as if her salvation lay in it. "What have you done with it?"

"I washed it," said Yiling. She tapped the parcel. "That's free, don't worry. I had to do laundry anyway.

"Ma'am," said Yiling. "I work very hard on this but I cannot do anything. When somebody is grown up already, they must make their own decision. I cannot change their mind for them."

Priya stared at her through eyelashes beaded with tears.

"But you helped my mother's friend," she cried. "You changed Vijay's mind—he went to America and he didn't want to come back."

"I brought back her son, but her son never went to America. Her son died," Yiling said. "I know this will sound very funny. But it is easy for me to make a person from a smell. When I give her back her son, he was the same person he used to be when he was alive. But your ex is still alive and he is already one kind of person. I cannot make a different kind of person from his smell. I cannot change this alive person's heart.

"I'm sorry," she said. "But I really spend so many hours on this. And I won't charge you. OK? You will move on. There is plenty of fish in the sea."

Priya flashed her a look of hatred.

"Everybody says that," she said. "But I only want one fish."

Apart from this outburst she was polite enough. After all, it would really have been fair for Yiling to charge her. She never made promises in terms of results. It was understood that the client took the risk.

When Priya had left, the cat said from behind Yiling's back, "That was generous of you."

Yiling had known that this must happen sooner or later. Even so, it was difficult to make herself turn around. In fact it was the hardest thing she had ever done. It was not that she was afraid, but that she was shy.

When she finally managed to turn around, she saw that the cat was blushing. This made things a bit more comfortable.

The cat had long hair, curling in a wonderfully pretty way at the ends. She had round dark eyes and skin the color of sandalwood. She was sitting in the bed and had covered herself with the blanket because she had no clothes. Yiling noted that she was Malay, but that would not be a problem. It was not like they could get married anyway.

Yiling sat back down on her chair. She felt oddly formal.

"Actually, Puan Thanga already paid me double to tell Priya her boyfriend is useless," she said. "She knew Priya from small. Her son Vijay used to date Priya in school. She said Priya only start liking this new guy after Vijay so-called went to America. Now he is back, Puan Thanga is hoping they will start to like each other again. She told me she always wanted a daughter, and when Priya and Vijay were going out she felt like Priya is her own daughter. She thinks they are perfect for each other."

"Sibuk," said the cat disapprovingly. "So busybody."

Yiling shrugged. It was in the nature of aunties to be busybodies.

"This Vijay is a good guy," said Yiling. "I can tell from his smell. I never remake a dead person unless I think they are a good person. Enough useless people in the world already."

"So you lied?" said the cat. "You could change the boyfriend's mind if you want?"

"I don't lie to my clients," said Yiling sternly. "Everything I said was true. But it's not my business if my clients want to pay me extra for doing something sensible."

She looked at the cat for a while, just for the pleasure of it, and the cat looked at her. The cat was still thin, but not as thin as she had been when Yiling had first taken her home.

"I'm sorry I kidnap you," said Yiling. The cat waved one elegant hand.

"Not to worry," she said. "I would have run away if I wanted to. But we must stop living like this. You don't eat properly. Hawker food is okay, but not every day. I can cook for you, I am a very good cook. It's good you like Malay food. We will move to our own apartment so that auntie cannot know all our business. She always come into this room in the afternoon to snoop around."

"Oh," said Yiling.

"Never mind, she never find out anything. You don't own anything interesting also," said the cat. "That's one more thing, you must have a nicer room. Living in one room like this, how to be comfortable? We will make sure you have an office for your work in our new place. I will set up the business for you. With your talent you don't have to only work for scheming aunties. If you advertise your talent better you can get more customers, earn more money."

"But an apartment will be expensive," said Yiling, because she could not think of anything better to say.

"No! One bedroom, one room for the office, kitchen and bathroom," said the cat. "We don't need so much to start with. Simple-simple enough already."

"One bedroom?" said Yiling.

The cat was surprised. She looked at her intently. Then she sat up, reached over, and took Yiling's hand.

"Of course," said the cat. "That's why I ran away from my parents' house. Somebody told my boss at work and I got fired and I panic and ran away. Ended up no money, no house, must sleep on the street. So I thought it was safer to be a cat. That's the only thing I can do. I'm not so clever as you, I cannot do all this spell or what. What happen to you?"

Yiling stared at their joined hands. She did magic and she liked girls. She lived alone because she was not the kind of daughter anyone would have asked for.

"Nothing happen," said Yiling.

She had just packed a bag one day, stepped out of her parents' house, and never gone back. There had been no precipitating event behind it, no big fight with her parents. She had not even had a girlfriend to leave for.

"Nothing happen," she said again. "I just don't like lying."

"Good," said the cat. "My name is Ada. You knew, right?" She did not mean her name.

"I always know who people are," said Yiling. "By their smell. That's the one thing nobody can lie about."

But Ada was not listening to this philosophizing. She was of a practical bent. She said, "But first, before we do all this thing, you must get me some clothes, OK, sayang?—Can I call you sayang?"

"Please," said Yiling. "Feel free."

The Fish Bowl

Su Yin was hiding the first time the fish spoke to her. It was three o'clock on a Thursday and she was at Puan Lai's house for maths teras tuition.

She did not have strong feelings about Puan Lai, but she liked the house. Between the entrance and living room there was an expanse of cool, white marble floor that would have been a hallway in a normal house. Puan Lai had dug out a hole in the floor and filled it with water. The pond was rectangular, like a swimming pool, but the water was green, swarming with koi and goldfish.

It had never been explained why they were there.

"Probably she rear them to sell," said Su Yin's mother. "Koi are very valuable, you know."

Puan Lai hadn't provided an explanation herself. As a teacher her style was direct and unfrivolous. She bombarded her students with exercises, leaving scarcely any time for questions, much less idle conversation.

For the past three Thursdays Su Yin had sat in an alcove by the pool while waiting for class to start, hidden from the front door by an extravagant potted palm. She passed the time watching the koi, golden and white and black, like splashes of paint curling in the water.

If she stared long enough she could feel her thoughts take on the measured glide of the fishes' bodies through the water. She felt as weightless as they must feel.

This mysterious peace was disturbed when the fish spoke.

"Eh, listen," said the fish. "I got secret to tell you."

Su Yin jumped. The voice had sounded clear and small in her right ear. She looked down into the water and saw a white koi, missing one eye.

"You want to hear or not?" said the koi.

Su Yin was going mad. Finally her mind was giving way. It was not as frightening as she'd thought it would be.

"Whether you want to listen or not, it's not my problem," said the koi. "I'm not the one missing out."

The koi's mouth opened and closed, an intermittent surprised O. Its white skin was so smooth it seemed scaleless. It would feel like silken tofu if you touched it. Seen from above, the fish's one eye looked heavy-lidded and wise.

"Are you a magical fish or a door-to-door salesman?" Su Yin whispered.

"Wah, still know how to joke people ah," said the koi. "You're correct. I'm magical. I can grant your any wish. That's my secret. Good or not?"

Su Yin no longer read much, but she used to like books. This was not unexpected.

"OK," she said. "So what?"

"You don't have to whisper," said the koi's voice in her mind. "You don't have to open your mouth. I can hear you screaming."

Su Yin got up, knocking her elbow against the potted palm. She walked to the living room, her face stiff.

That wasn't funny, she thought.

At this point she still thought it was her mind doing it, showing her magical talking fish. She thought it was the tiredness speaking.

Su Yin's parents went to bed at 11:30 every night. At midnight Su Yin put on a thin cardigan and walked soft-footed downstairs to the computer.

She used to play RPGs, but even with the volume turned down she worried that her avatars' thin battle cries and the muffled roaring of the dragons would reach through the ceiling and pierce her parents' sleep. And you had to save your game, and her younger brother played it as well, so the evidence of what she did was there, ripe for the picking if he ever felt like betrayal.

These days she made dolls. There were hundreds of doll makers online, on different themes. Doll makers for every movie you could think of, for bands, for books and TV shows. It was a simple pursuit, but you never ran out of variations.

There was something reassuring about it. You started out with a naked, bald body, featureless and innocent. Then you built it up into the approximation of a person, adding hair, eyes, clothes, shoes, a smile or frown.

When Su Yin was done she saved the graphic in a folder she'd squirrelled away inside five nested folders named things like "Nota_Bio_Encik's Cheah's class." She gave each doll a name: Esmeralda for a green-eyed girl with wild red hair; Jane for a quiet-looking one in a gingham dress, her eyes cast down.

When Su Yin finally went to bed her back was stiff and her feet were cold. From her bed she could see the glowing green face of the clock. It was 2:20 a.m. She would not sleep for at least another hour.

Wednesday was usually a good day. She had two tuition classes in the afternoon, but in the half-hour gap between them, her dad drove her to a nearby coffeehouse. They sat at a sticky enamel table and she ate her way through three plates of siu mai while Dad watched a Hong Kong variety show on the TV.

She never felt sleepy in the kopitiam, despite the dozy mid-afternoon feeling of the air and the somnolent hum of the ceiling fan. It was only when Dad had dropped her off at Puan Rosnah's and the lesson had started that she began to droop.

Su Yin no longer tried to fight it. She crossed her arms on the table and dropped her head.

Puan Rosnah was a nice older lady with a soft, creaky voice and a smile that crinkled the skin around her eyes. She never complained about the naps. She was not an especially good teacher, and tended to drone. It didn't matter because Su Yin also attended another, more effective BM tuition class. She didn't question why she had to have two classes for the same subject: she'd got a B in BM for UPSR four years ago.

After class the students milled in the garden outside Puan Rosnah's house, waiting for their parents to pick them up.

"Wah, relaxed ah you," said Cheryl Lau to Su Yin.

There was no decent way to fob Cheryl off. She insisted on talking to Su Yin. They'd used to be friends, back when they were rivals for top of the form. Now that Su Yin was out of the running she avoided Cheryl when she could, but Cheryl still sought her out.

"Can nap in class also," she said. "You study finish for the test already, is it?"

Su Yin's heart clenched. She said, "Hah? Sorry, didn't hear."

"You know, Puan Sharifah's test," said Cheryl. They were in different classes, but they shared teachers for a couple of subjects. Puan Sharifah was one of them. She taught history and was known for her total lack of mercy.

"Our class had the test already," said Cheryl. "Damn hard, man. Study like siao also still didn't know how to answer."

Su Yin couldn't ask when her class was going to have the test. That would show she hadn't been paying attention for weeks, maybe months.

"Is it? When was it?" she said.

"Tuesday," said Cheryl. "Sucks, man. Have to study the whole weekend. Your class test is on Friday, right?"

Su Yin dug her fingernails into her palm.

"Yah," she said. "I think so."

One day was not enough to study for a test, especially not one set by Puan Sharifah. The next day at school, Su Yin's classmates confirmed that it was going to be on Friday. Puan Sharifah had announced it three weeks ago. It would cover the five chapters they'd already been tested on in the last round of exams, and an additional three they'd studied since then.

Su Yin hadn't looked at her history textbook in months.

During the drive to Puan Lai's house, her dad said, "Why so quiet, girl? Thinking what?"

Su Yin came out of her bad dream.

"Nothing," she said. "Thinking about school only."

"My girl is so hardworking," crooned Ma.

"Don't need to overthink one lah," said Dad. "Do the work and listen to the teacher enough already. With your brain, like that can pass already."

Su Yin was half an hour early, and none of the other students were there when the maid let her in. She crawled into her hiding place.

Remembering the conversation in the car made her want to hurt herself. She was ready when the fish said, "Change your mind ah?"

It was the white koi, floating up out of the dark water like a ghost.

She said, "How you know?"

The koi clearly thought it beneath itself to answer such a stupid question. It waited in the water, silent.

"Can you make me pass?" Su Yin whispered.

"Cheh, that only? Very easy," said the koi.

"Not just pass," said Su Yin. "Do well. Get good marks."

"You want to get hundred?" said the koi.

That was pushing it.

"Seventy lah," said Su Yin. Even that would be a disappointment to her parents. It would be an improvement compared to what she'd got in the last round of exams, but her parents didn't know about those.

"Can," said the koi. "I get you seventy exactly. No need to worry. Puan Sharifah won't think you cheated. She'll be very happy. She'll think you buck up after the last exam."

Su Yin didn't ask how the koi knew she'd been worrying about that.

"One thing only," said the koi. "My payment."

"What is it?" said Su Yin.

The fish's mouth opened and closed. It was toothless like the mouth of a hungry baby, or the mouth of an old man chanting a mantra under his breath.

"I'm so hungry," it said.

Su Yin nodded.

"Put your hand here," said the fish.

Su Yin dipped her right arm into the water, flinching at the cold. The fish blinked its one wise eye and swam up to her. She closed her eyes. The sharp, sharp teeth closed over her flesh.

It had to be true that the fish was magic, because it stole her voice. She felt the scream tear her throat, but there was no sound. It didn't so much as ripple the water.

She snatched her arm out of the water, clutching it to her chest. The fish had bitten out a chunk of her forearm about the size of a fifty-sen coin. Blood ran down her arm and dripped onto her shorts. She held her arm, shuddering.

The world went fuzzy. The separate leaves of the palm merged into a green blob, as if she was seeing them through tears.

"Wait first," said the fish. "I'll take the blood away." Its voice in her head sounded drowsy, contented.

Answering her unasked question, it said, "No. It doesn't work without the pain."

By the time class started, the wound was already scabbing over, and her shorts were dry. The flesh of her arm felt raw and wet. She had to keep looking down to convince herself of the scab.

It was dark red and ugly on the inner side of her arm. The guy next to her flicked his eyes at it and looked away hastily. Unease pulled the air around him taut.

But Su Yin felt calm. The tension that had been lurking at the back of her head for months, ever since she'd seen the report card, had dissolved. She felt safe. Even sleepy. As if it was her who was cradled in the dark, cool water, enjoying the peace of a full belly, dreaming of blood.

At first Su Yin thought it hadn't worked. She opened the test paper and her mind went blank. The words on the page did not mean anything. Panic rose up from her belly.

She had to write something. She put the pen to paper.

It was as if someone had stabbed her in the arm. Su Yin's left hand flew to her mouth, pressing down the shout. She pulled up her sleeve. The scab on her right forearm was gone. The wound was open and bleeding, pus seeping from the edges. The skin around it was inflamed.

How had this happened? It had looked fine earlier. The scab had hardened overnight, was solid that morning.

Su Yin had faked a sneeze in the car going home from Puan Lai's the day before. Her mother had said accusingly, "Hah, sneezing already!" and insisted on her changing into something warm. This had given her the excuse to put on a long-sleeved T-shirt. Today she was wearing baju kurung, so the scab had escaped notice.

Nobody could miss it now. She looked around, but everyone's heads were bent over their desks. The teacher wasn't looking in her direction.

The blood was streaming down her arm. Would it drip on her hair if she raised her hand for attention? thought Su Yin wildly.

The blood dripping on her desk began to form into balls like spilt mercury. The red liquid balls rolled onto the test paper, where they grew spidery legs, transformed into letters, resolved into words, and arranged themselves in tidy sentences. When the blood sank into the paper it turned blue. The writing was Su Yin's own, the tails of the g's and y's flying off into space.

Su Yin's blood did the test for her. In a trance, she turned each page over as it filled up with words.

When the last drop of blood had jumped onto the page, the wound healed up again. It happened in a matter of seconds. The scab was dry by the time she passed up her paper.

The pain was a throbbing thing in her arm.

Puan Sharifah had an agonizing habit of announcing test results in descending order, starting from the highest mark. You had to walk all the way up to the front of the classroom to take your paper from her.

The practice would have caused Su Yin hideous anguish in earlier days. The only thing worse than not coming first was knowing that she hadn't come first. Nowadays it didn't bother her. Her name came so late that most people had lost interest by then.

This time her name was fourteenth in the list. When Puan Sharifah handed her the paper, she said, "Good. This is an improvement."

Puan Sharifah was sparing with her praise. Su Yin was so startled she didn't react, but when she was back at her seat she allowed herself the burst of pleasure. She had earned it.

Her mother was not so pleased.

"Seventy?" she said. "That's not 1A, right?"

"2A only," said Su Yin, knowing her mother knew this. "You need seventy-five for 1A."

Her mother pursed her lips.

"Girl, history is very important," she said. "After this, when you're doing STPM, you can drop the subject. But if the university sees you're not so good at history, they will think you're not so good at writing."

"Do you need Sejarah tuition?" said Su Yin's dad.

Nobody took tuition classes for history. The received wisdom was that you only had to memorize the textbooks to do well. Understanding was not required.

"Sejarah don't really have tuition one," Su Yin said. "Just have to study harder, I guess."

"Don't study hard. Study smart," said her dad. But the answer pleased him: she was showing the right spirit.

"You got any problem concentrating at school?" said her mother. "Is your teacher not so good? You know you can tell us if anything."

It was her chance. Su Yin almost told them.

The thought of the report card stopped her. She hadn't thrown it away because they might have seen it in the trash can. She couldn't put it in the underwear drawer, because her mom did her laundry and put her clothes away. She'd thought of hiding it under her mattress, but her mom might notice it when she was changing the bedclothes.

In the end Su Yin had stuck it between the pages of a form three geography reference book. She hadn't looked at it again.

If Su Yin told her parents, she would have to tell them about the report card. The lie would come out. They would cry.

"You didn't do well is one thing," they'd say. "Mummy and Daddy can help you if you have problem at school. But the fact you lie to us, Su Yin—that means we didn't bring you up properly."

She didn't say anything.

"If you need tuition, Mummy and Daddy will find for you," said her mother. "Never mind whether Sejarah tuition got or not. Teachers' salary is not very good also. Sure can find one who is willing to give tuition. Just need to pay only."

"Don't need," said Su Yin. "I can handle it."

After all, she wasn't on her own anymore.

Form three was the best year of Su Yin's life. People said form one and form two were the best years, because the workload was light and you didn't have to worry about exams. Form three meant the first big exams, PMR, and then it all went downhill from there.

But Su Yin had always enjoyed exams. She liked the run-up to them best: the last two weeks before the exams, when your vision narrowed and your world contracted to this one essential thing. You were let off doing chores; TV and Internet were banned; co-curricular activities came to a stop. You entered a monkish world, a sanctuary from ordinary life, where all that was required of you was that you study and make the grade.

And you did the exams and you passed and you felt a sense of accomplishment. Your parents were proud of you. This was your job. It was what you were there for.

She'd done very well in PMR, leaving aside the B in BM. She'd got an extra A for Chinese even though neither of her parents spoke Mandarin, and she hadn't had extra tuition. The tuition classes had only started in form four. Her parents had thought she could do with the help, since it was such a leap from form three to form four.

What Su Yin remembered of form three was a feeling of clarity. A sense of being capable of doing everything necessary.

It was funny. She could remember the fact of being happy. She knew intellectually that life had once been easy, that she had once known she could do things. But she no longer knew how that felt.

Now she lived on the edge of a volcano. Everything seemed fine aboveground, but panic slumbered underneath. At any time things could go horribly wrong.

As they did when Miss Yong gave up on her.

Miss Yong did this without ceremony. She took the grade seven repertoire book off the stand and said,

"This is pointless."

Su Yin's chin and shoulder hurt from holding the violin in place. She lowered her bow, not sure if she was supposed to stop playing.

"If you're not taking this seriously, better don't waste both our time," said Miss Yong. "You're not practicing. You think I cannot tell?"

Su Yin took her violin by the neck so she could roll her shoulders. She mustn't cry.

Miss Yong must have noticed her shock, because her face softened. She was a young woman with a temper, and many an exasperating student had felt the sharp side of her tongue, but they had always got along before. She had taught Su Yin since Su Yin started playing at the age of ten.

"Look, don't take this personally," said Miss Yong. "But might be better if you find another teacher. Maybe I have taught you so long, you are too used to me already. You're getting complacent. It's not that you don't have talent. But you cannot pass grade seven without practicing. How many times a week do you practice?"

Su Yin was silent. She rushed through her pieces every Saturday morning before she went to class.

It wasn't that she'd thought Miss Yong wouldn't notice. There was just so much going on. Violin hadn't been a priority.

"I thought so," said Miss Yong. "I'll talk to your mother. Don't look so upset. It's not the end of the world. If you start practicing now and you're disciplined, you can definitely pass your exam. But do you want to perform at the concert or not?"

The charity concert was in a fortnight. Su Yin was going to play one of her exam pieces. Her grandparents would be in town that weekend, and they were coming along with her parents to see her. They'd bought tickets weeks ago.

"Yes," said Su Yin. She heard her voice wobble.

"I'm not going to stop you," said Miss Yong. "But you're old enough to know whether you can do it or not. Do you think you're at a level where you can play for an audience? People are not going to be lenient, you know. I have a student, nine years old, this tall—" she sketched in the air a child the approximate size of a garden gnome— "and she's the same grade as you. She's been practicing every day for the concert. This year she's performed in public twice already."

"I can do it," whispered Su Yin. She cleared her throat. "I'll do it."

Miss Yong nodded, her mouth grim.

"Let's finish early today," she said. "I don't think you'll get much out of the class if we go on also."

"I need another wish," said Su Yin to the still water.

The white koi blinked a sleepy eye at her.

"Still want more?" it said. "One not enough meh?"

"One more only," said Su Yin.

She was seeing the world through a film of water. For a moment she thought she was in the pool, looking up through the green light at a girl with a huge pale face and puffy eyes. Then she was back inside her body, kneeling by the pool and dripping tears into the water.

"I will pay," she said.

"I was joking only," said the white koi. "No matter how much wishes you want also, I can grant. As long as got payment. You want what?"

"Let me play well at the concert," said Su Yin. "Don't need until like Yo Yo Ma like that. Decent can already."

She had not even been decent for the past few weeks. It wouldn't make sense to be brilliant. She had to hide.

"This will be more expensive, know," said the koi. "First time got discount. This time price is higher."

"Can," said Su Yin. "Anything also can."

This time she dipped both her arms into the water, up to the elbow. Her fingers brushed a passing goldfish. It shot off into the depths, a shivering gold droplet of alarm.

This time she kept her eyes open. The white koi's gummy mouth looked soft. When the mouth touched her skin, it looked as if it was covering her with little sucking kisses.

It felt as though hooks had sunk into her arm. They punctured the tender flesh of the inside of her elbow and tore their way through her skin, down to the wrists.

Su Yin managed to take her arm out of the pool to steady herself against the ledge, though her vision was going funny. Blood stained the water.

The koi had to do her other arm. It had to be slow. That was part of the magic.

The slower it was, the better she'd be. The pain made her safe. It would make her good enough.

On stage, Su Yin had a moment of terror. She touched her bow to the strings and a screechy hiss came out.

Her mother had put makeup on her, and her face felt heavy, unfamiliar. She cast a pleading look in the direction of the piano, though she could hardly see Miss Yong for the glare of the lights.

Miss Yong had the decency not to grimace. She nodded at Su Yin, lifted her hands from the keyboard, and prepared to start over again.

Su Yin had to perform. But nothing hurt.

She took down her violin, pretending to flip through her score. As she lifted her right hand to turn the page, the sleeve of her blouse fell away. The welts stood out, red on her skin.

She knew how she would do it.

She pulled the sleeves up to her elbows and nodded at Miss Yong. Miss Yong started playing the intro again. Su Yin touched the bow to the skin of her left arm.

The texture of the horsehair was hideous, dragged across raw flesh. But it sounded beautiful. A rich, round, woody sound unfurled from her bow.

There was a reason the fish had torn four lines down the length of her arm. Her fingers stayed on the fingerboard, dancing from string to string, but the strings were silent. Her bow scraped across the wounds on her arm, and the violin sang.

What did the audience see? Surely not the blood, dripping on the stage. It saw an ordinary girl, playing a piece competently.

Wrapped in the fish's enchantment, Su Yin was safe from being seen. She felt she could do anything.

"That was very good," said Miss Yong after the performance. "Finally thought you'd practice, hah?"

Su Yin's playing had been OK only for a grade seven student, but she could tell Miss Yong wanted to be encouraging. She nodded.

"Are you all right, Su Yin?" said Miss Yong. "You're a bit pale."

"I've been working hard," said Su Yin, and smiled at her distantly, ecstatically.

Su Yin was drooping over the table at Puan Rosnah's house, waiting for class to start and sleep to take over, when Cheryl pulled out a chair next to her.

"Eh," said Cheryl. She hesitated. "I want to talk to you. Are you free later?"

Su Yin stared at Cheryl for a dazed moment before the words registered.

She'd stopped doing the dolls—she'd only liked them because they kept her mind quiet, and nowadays the old buzzing thoughts no longer troubled her. But she still wasn't getting much sleep. These days she lay awake at night for hours, perfectly content, watching the patterns of light shiver and uncoil on her ceiling like ripples in a pool.

"Hah?" she said.

She didn't know what to say. She was free later. She never had anything important to do. She wasn't free later. Her dad was coming to pick her up, and then there would be dinner and homework and the latest Canto serial, and then the light dancing on the ceiling.

Cheryl was smiling, trying to convince Su Yin it was nothing serious. The smile was a trap.

"We so long never talk," Cheryl said. "What say we go kopitiam, have some snack, chat a bit? My mom can give you a ride home afterwards."

"Is this for, like, a CF thing?" said Su Yin. Cheryl had been irritating in the past about inviting Su Yin to Christian Fellowship meetings.

Cheryl looked relieved.

"Yah! Want or not? Promise I won't talk about it too long," she said. "Come lah."

"But my dad—"

Cheryl shoved her handphone into Su Yin's hand.

"Quickly call him before class starts," she said. "We'll walk over to the kopitiam after class. I told my mom to pick me up from there."

At the coffeehouse Cheryl bought some kuih and a Horlicks ais. Su Yin wasn't hungry, but she ordered bubur cha cha to be sociable. When it came she dipped her spoon in the thick soup and lifted it out again, watching the yam and sweet potato bob to the surface on the waves she created. Any moment now the axe was going to drop.

"Are you doing OK ah?" said Cheryl.

Su Yin tried to look surprised.

"Yah," she said. "Why?"

"Is everything OK at home?" said Cheryl. "With your parents all that."

"Everything's fine," said Su Yin.

"I know maybe, recently," said Cheryl. She was stirring her glass of Horlicks extra fast. "Like, maybe your studies have been a bit . . . how to say, you know, like, maybe they're not going so smoothly. But you know, it's no big deal, right? It's nothing so important. At the end of the day, it doesn't really matter. Right?"

"Is that right?" said Su Yin. Her plan had been to stay quiet, but some evil genius moved her to say: "What matters, then?"

"Oh, you know," said Cheryl.

Say God, thought Su Yin. *I dare you to say God.*

"Being happy," said Cheryl. "Family."

Something in Su Yin's chest came unstuck.

"What if they contradict?" she said. She regretted it the moment she said it.

"Su Yin, you are not doing OK," said Cheryl.

It was too late to deny it. Stupid, stupid to have said that—

"It's OK. I'm handling it," said Su Yin. "Like you said, doing badly in studies is not the end of the world."

"I didn't mean that," said Cheryl. She reached out too quickly for Su Yin to stop her, and flicked up her sleeve.

The red lines on her arm flared out before her sleeve slipped down again.

"You are not doing well," said Cheryl. "This is not right."

Su Yin said, "It helps."

She didn't know how to explain about the fish and the magic. About how giving something small and unimportant like pain meant you got back big things.

It looks worse than it is, she wanted to say. *It's worth it.*

"I don't know how to handle this kind of thing," said Cheryl. She sounded scared. "Su Yin, you need better help than this. Have you told your parents?"

Su Yin didn't need to answer that. She stared at her bubur cha cha. It would be cold if she ate it now.

"They should know," said Cheryl.

"You can't tell them!" said Su Yin.

"I have to tell somebody," said Cheryl. "You cannot go on like this. You think other people haven't noticed? I'm talking to you now because another guy in our tuition told me a few weeks ago you came in with a huge scar on your hand. You know when people start to gossip, this kind of story can spread very fast. Everyone at school knows why you don't wear short sleeve anymore. It's either your parents find out from me now, or a teacher tells them later."

Su Yin swallowed her heart back down her throat.

"The teachers know?" she said.

"It's only a matter of time," said Cheryl. "Everybody knows already."

That night Su Yin did not sleep.

When she saw her face in the pond again, it startled her. She had used to dislike her round face. She wasn't chubby, but she had a flat, broad peasant's face, full-cheeked.

Now her face had fined down. The cheeks were hollow. Her cheekbones stood out. Above them her narrow eyes were ringed with dark circles, panda-like.

She hadn't noticed how she'd changed. Even her parents, usually so attentive, had missed it. When you saw someone every day, you did not see them change, little by little.

Small things, given time, become mountains. Fish bones lodge in the throat and choke you.

She said to her reflection in the water: "I need help."

"What do you need?" said the white koi.

Su Yin thought about the hidden report card. The scars on her arms. Miss Yong dumping her as if six years counted for nothing. Cheryl's inexorable kindness. Her mother and father.

Su Yin's hands were shaking. She whispered: "Hide me. Can you do that?"

"For how long?" said the fish.

"Until it's over," said Su Yin.

"Are you willing to pay?" said the fish.

"Yes."

The fish's mouth opened and closed, opened and closed again.

This time there was no need for negotiation. In some mysterious way, Su Yin and the white koi wanted the same thing.

"Leave your clothes on the floor there," said the fish.

Su Yin took her clothes off. She knelt on the floor, wincing when the chill of the marble hit her skin. She reached out to the fish with bare arms.

The white koi's mouth opened wide. It was a black hole into which air and water flowed. What came out was transfigured, a substance entirely new.

What went in was hidden.

Su Yin put her hand into the koi's mouth. It was warm and wet, but not unpleasantly so. She put in the other arm and closed her eyes and lowered her head, and let herself be swallowed whole.

The koi's mouth was a dark place. Her body was being crushed, compacted, folded away. It hurt. But after this, Su Yin knew, there would be rest. After this, nothing.

The girl climbed out of the pond with jerky movements, as if she was so tired she had forgotten how to use her limbs. It took her a few tries to get out, collapsing on the marble floor. She lay limp as a landed fish on the edge of the pool, her hair unspooling in the water. Curious goldfish nibbled at the strands and swam away.

She got up, holding her body like someone learning an unfamiliar dance. The clothes were a puzzle, but she knew what they were supposed to look like. She worked at them until they looked right.

When she was done she walked out from behind the potted palm, leaving a trail of wet footprints behind her.

With every step her legs grew stronger. With every step her feet got more used to the ground.

The students waiting in the living room looked up at her approach. Their eyes widened.

"I fell in," said the girl.

First National Forum on the Position of Minorities in Malaysia

"Did you see the mak cik?" said Hasnah.

Esther was fiddling with the projector: it wouldn't project. It took a minute for Hasnah's words to filter past her worry.

"Mak cik?" She remembered a very old, very small woman in a dazzling baju kurung, wandering along the corridor outside the conference room. "The one with the pink tudung, is it?"

"She's here for the forum!" said Hasnah triumphantly.

"Kidding? I thought she was a guest at the hotel."

"She's the founder of some women's NGO here," said Hasnah. "The Amnesty guy invited her."

"Thank God for the Amnesty guy," said Esther.

The program timetable meant that they'd only had a week and a half to prepare for the Pahang forum. It had been a nightmarish 1.5 weeks for Esther, whose job was to make sure they had enough delegates at the forum, while avoiding the steely gaze of the mainstream media.

One night last week she'd woken herself up trying to invite delegates in her dreams. She'd lain dazed in her bed and heard a voice talking, and did not at first know it was herself: ". . . calling from API. API. The Asian Political Institute. No, not Bicycle, *Political*—yes, we're an NGO. We are organizing a forum on the position of minorities in Malaysia. Would your organization be interested in sending a representative?"

Thank God for the Amnesty guy. Esther had found his contact details in an obscure corner of the Amnesty International website.

She hadn't even known the guy before she phoned him up, but he'd dug up everyone with a modicum of civic sensibility in Kuantan.

The result seemed to be a huge number of uncles in batik shirts, but Esther wasn't complaining.

"We were chatting when she registered," said Hasnah. "She told me she's eighty-six years old."

"So old already still want to talk about human rights," said Intan. Intan was a long, bony piece of irony, with uncovered short hair and bored eyes. She directed the local branch of a major international nonprofit.

"Eh, don't so ageist," said Hasnah. "Old people also should exercise their right to participate in civil society."

"When I am old I won't care about this kind of thing anymore," said Intan. "Minority rights ke, religious freedom ke—all that, forget about it. I will be totally burn out. I'll go live in a fishing village in Terengganu and watch the penyu come out of the sea, and I'll never read the news."

"If by then this country is not fixed, then really no hope," said Hasnah somberly.

Hasnah was technically Esther's boss, but sometimes she made Esther feel old.

Intan pursed her mouth.

"Still got time," was all she said. "I'm not old yet."

"Ah!" said Esther. They all looked up at the screen.

The first PowerPoint slide said:

First National Forum on the
Position of Minorities in Malaysia

It was in English and Malay. Well, sort of Malay.

"'Forum pertama tentang posisi minoriti di Malaysia'?" said Intan, outraged. "What idiot did that translation?"

Of course Ming Jun came up just at that moment. Fortunately he was frowning at his BlackBerry and didn't hear her. Intan hit him on the arm.

"Eh, you. What is that, hah? You call that Bahasa Melayu?"

Ming Jun flicked his eyes up, still typing. He had the grace to look embarrassed when his eyes slid over the title.

"I couldn't find my Kamus Dewan that week," he said. "And after that, we already use it for the first few forums, so have to be consistent."

"Next time," said Intan, "go to bookshop and buy the damn dictionary."

At two o'clock the delegates started filtering into the conference room, greased into contentment by the free buffet lunch. Kuantan wasn't as fun as Melaka had been, with the delights of Jonker Street just down the road, but at least the food at this hotel was decent.

There were forty people today and five facilitators, which meant eight delegates per group—a good number for a roundtable discussion.

"I only have three Malay guys at my table," confided Murni. Esther nodded. She'd only met Murni that morning, when she introduced herself as the press officer of a Muslim feminist group.

"The Muslims don't like us and the feminists also don't like us," she'd told Esther.

"How many feminists?" Esther said now.

Murni laughed.

"Haven't find out yet," she said. "There's one lady from the Women's Society of Kuantan, wearing this sexy baju kebaya. Very tight! I have high hopes for her. Are you rapporteuring for me today?"

Esther shook her head. "I'm with Ming Jun. You know how fast he talks. I'm the fastest typist, so I'm the one who has to have hand pain."

Ming Jun's voice drifted over to them. He was talking to a grumpy-looking Chinese uncle in a green batik shirt. Ming Jun spoke fluent textbook Malay, but he'd studied eight years at the University of Minnesota before coming home, and it showed in his accent. Combined with his ultra-formal diction, the effect was outlandish.

"Sounds like RTM kan," said Murni. "Like the newscaster on the TV."

"Radio Televisyen Minneapolis?" whispered Esther. They both giggled.

"OK, tuan-tuan dan puan-puan," said Hasnah. "Thanks for coming. Just to confirm, yes, we are awarding certificates for attendance. . . ."

Something funny was happening at Esther's table. She couldn't work out what it was.

It had taken a while for the discussion to get off the ground, because the mak cik was at their table. Ming Jun had scarcely finished asking the first question on the list ("How would you define 'minority' in the Malaysian context?") when the old lady's hand shot up.

"Tuan Pengerusi," she said. "Mr. Chairman."

Esther smothered a shout of laughter under a coughing fit. Ming Jun blinked.

"Uh, yes, Datin Zainab?" he said.

"Assalamualaikum and good afternoon," she said to the table. She spoke the beautiful precise Malay of the schoolteacher: her cadences were a wonderful thing. "Thank you for inviting me to speak today. The chairman has asked a question. I would also like to ask a question. My question is, what is the meaning of 'context'?"

"Told you 'konteks' wasn't Malay," hissed Esther.

But apparently the question was rhetorical.

"When I was an MP near Raub in 1965, what was my context?" said the Datin. "My constituents were simple villagers. We had only one small primary school, no secondary school. The closest secondary school was miles away. I used to wake up at five a.m. and my driver and I would pick up the bright, ambitious children, and drive them to the secondary school in town. After that I went straight to work and I worked until six p.m. Then I went home and cooked dinner for my family and helped my children with their homework. At ten p.m. I went to bed, but then I would be woken up again. One of the villagers would come: 'Datin, my wife is ill, please can you send her to the doctor.' What was there to do? Who else had a car? I could only get the car out, wake up the driver and go out again. And the next morning, up again at five a.m.

"That was my context. To me, it was nothing hard. I didn't think I was suffering. It was my job. Now the politicians say they are very busy, oh, so many important things to do. But if they say they are too busy to help their constituents? I don't believe. It's whether you want to or not. That is what I believe."

Ming Jun's face was a sight to delight the heart of the wicked, but the seven other faces around the table were solemn and attentive. Polite murmurs rose in response.

"That's right."

"True, very true."

Ming Jun cleared his throat.

"Uh, thank you, Datin," he said. "That's a valuable contribution, thank you. But maybe we can focus on the issue of minorities, the definition of what is a minority."

Datin Zainab seemed pleased that he'd brought this up. She said, "Mr. Chairman, do you know what women are?"

"Um—"

"They are a majority! How many people in this world have a mother?" she said. "How many have a grandmother? All these mothers and grandmothers are women. Yet how are women treated? In my organization, we support women who need help. The ones who are too poor to buy their children milk. The ones whose husbands beat them. Women are treated like this. They are not a minority, but they are treated so badly. But women have an advantage that true minorities don't have. Women have the advantage of numbers. I believe that if we use our advantage and help each other, women can overcome the way society treats them. That is why I set up my organization."

"Nowadays seems to me women are treated better. Men are the ones who are bullied," muttered a man from St. John's Ambulance.

Datin Zainab put on a pair of spectacles that made her eyes enormous. She peered across the table. "What did encik say?"

The St. John's Ambulance man fell quiet.

It was the patience that impressed Esther. They'd had forums with Muslims, Christians, Buddhists, and Hindus seated around the same table. They'd had representatives from every political party going, including ones Esther had never heard of before. They'd had opinionated old judges, belligerent doctors, self-important businessmen, and earnest students bearing downy new mustaches and sociology textbooks.

Consequently they'd had noisy forums. At nearly every one, people had started talking over one another after the first five minutes had passed and they'd forgotten their manners.

But this table was dead quiet while Datin Zainab went on—and how she did go on. As the delegates listened in respectful silence, she told them about the work her organization did, just stopping short of sketching out their timetable and listing their daily meals. She recounted tales of the joys and tribulations of the women they helped. She discussed what it had been like to be a female MP in the '60s.

"R u getting everything?" Ming Jun texted Esther. "Gr8 stuff! Social history!"

Esther tapped the Dictaphone and nodded. Fortunately Datin Zainab spoke slowly, in passionate separate syllables, like a debater. Unlike normal people, she did not speak in fragments, but in whole considered sentences, exquisitely formed.

But when the Datin started to talk about the year she had been lost in the forest and her family had given her up for dead, Ming Jun's conscience seemed to trouble him. He turned to the man sitting next to him, a lawyer with an outspoken blog.

"What is encik's opinion? What do you think the government could do to protect minorities' rights?"

The lawyer had skin the color of sandalwood, a high-bridged nose, and deep-set eyes hooded by heavy eyelids. He opened his mouth and said in a strong Chinese accent, "Protect minorities' rights? First thing is to identify who is the minorities. In this country so many people complaining: I am the one who is bullied, no, I am the one who is suffering. Actually you know who is suffering? It's the invisible minority!"

Esther checked the delegate list. The man was named Abner Ignatius.

The rest of the table also seemed taken aback. But Ming Jun perked up. Sexuality rights hadn't come up in previous forums. People had been too busy arguing about race.

"Correct, correct. That's a very pertinent point," he said. "The minorities people cannot see. They are forgotten."

"The invisible minority also needs support," said a representative from Islamic Scholars of Pahang. "Just because our needs are not obvious, it does not mean the government should so easily ignore us."

He also spoke with a Chinese accent. In fact, his voice was exactly the same as Abner Ignatius's.

"Farid?" said the other representative of the Islamic Scholars of Pahang, staring. Farid ignored him.

"Where I live, the electricity supply is terrible," said Farid. "So unreliable! Like everybody else, we also like to listen to the radio. In the forest, the connection is so bad, only one channel is available! Hitz FM. This channel is for the younger people. If you don't like Rihanna, what are you going to do in the evening? Can the government tell me that?"

"And another thing," said Annabella Lim. Annabella ran a breast cancer support group, and spoke in a growly baritone. "The Internet is impossible! Cannot even watch one YouTube video before it dies out. Then you must wait half an hour before it comes back on. Today we are living in a knowledge economy! How is my community going to participate in the economy without Internet access?"

Ming Jun and Esther's fascinated eyes moved along the table to Datin Zainab. Her pink-scarved head was drooping. She had fallen asleep.

"But most important," said the secretary of the Pahang Consumer Association next to her. He was an elderly man, with fluffy white hair and skin so dark it was almost blue. His voice was the same as everyone else's at the table: a middle-aged Chinese man's voice.

"More important than anything else," he said. "My community does not have any schools. Puan Zainab talks about the school in her village. But we do not even have a primary school. We parents have to educate the children ourselves. The government should consider setting up special schools for our children. SJK (B)."

Datin Zainab stirred.

Esther had gone to a SJK (T), though attending a Tamil-medium primary school for six years hadn't helped her much—her Tamil was still terrible. She knew Chinese schools were SJK (C).

"What does the B stand for?" said Ming Jun.

The Datin had woken up and was looking around wildly.

"Chor Seng?" she said. She blinked, rubbed her eyes and woke up all the way. "Who called me Puan Zainab?"

Ming Jun looked worried. It would never do to offend an ex-MP.

"It's Datin Zainab, not Puan Zainab," he told the consumer association rep.

"Beg your pardon?" said the rep in a pleasant tenor. He didn't sound in the least Chinese.

"It doesn't matter," said Datin Zainab. She was looking—not at the consumer association rep, but at the empty space between him and Ming Jun. Her gaze was focused, almost as if there were a person there.

"That's what he called me when we first met," she said. To the air, she said, "Chor Seng, I'm a Datin now."

The Chinese man's voice said: "Bunian."

The voice came from no one's mouth. It came out of the air.

"What?" said Ming Jun.

"He said, the B stands for bunian," said the Datin. "You know orang bunian? They are a magical people. They live in the forest but you cannot see them, can hear them only. That is why they are called bunian. From bunyi—means sound."

"Ah, that makes sense," said Annabella Lim. Her voice was a normal throaty auntie's voice, more English educated than Chinese school. "I was wondering why everybody has the same voice."

Murmurs of agreement from the table. Everyone was looking relieved to have the mystery solved. Ming Jun looked bewildered.

"But orang bunian aren't real!" he said.

"Can tell you are a city boy," said Farid. "If you live near the jungle, you will realize that what is real and what is not real is not always clear. In the forest there is not a big gap between the two."

"Of course, it's all heathenish superstition," said the other Islamic Scholar.

"Khairul is right," said Farid. "It is all heathenish superstition. People who truly understand religion will not believe in this kind of thing."

"But you seem to believe orang bunian exist," said Ming Jun.

"Ah, it is very hard to have a true understanding of religion," said Farid reflectively.

"We are still working on it," Khairul agreed.

"This is ridiculous," said Ming Jun.

The air snorted. The Chinese man's voice said, "Oh yah, young man? Then my voice is coming from where, please tell me?"

Ming Jun glared at the delegates as if he thought one of them might be a ventriloquist. Of course, that was more likely than the idea that an orang bunian had actually turned up at their forum.

But the hotel did abut a jungle. Everybody knew what the jungle was like. It was not safe. There were mosquitoes and leeches, which were bad enough; there might be tigers, which were even worse; but worst of all—jungles were full of spirits.

"Why? I am not allowed to attend this forum, is it?" said the bodiless voice. "Aren't orang bunian also a minority? Don't we deserve the chance to fight for our rights? Nobody ever did a survey of our opinions. Nobody wants to know what we think. We are being marginalized!"

"But why are you a Chinese?" said the St. John's Ambulance man.

"What's that? First I'm not allowed to stand up for my community's rights. Suddenly I'm not allowed to be Chinese also?"

"No, my learned friend has raised a very good point," said Farid. "Orang bunian is a Malay folktale."

"We live in the same Malaysia as the rest of you," said the invisible man. "You look around you. Does everybody look the same race to you?"

"I am Chinese also. But I always heard that orang bunian are supposed to be devout Muslims," said Annabella Lim.

"This is what is wrong with our country!" Datin Zainab burst out. "You younger generation do not know how to accept. You don't know how to live together. In my day, whether somebody was Chinese, Malay, Indian, Orang Asal, Sikh, Kristang, anything—we didn't care. When we went to school together and played on the playground, do you think we chose our friends based on race? No. Muthu sat with Ah Ming, Ali played with Jaspreet. There was no division.

"Now people have grown intolerant. They only want to see their own race. The state of the country has become bad, very bad. I remember when I was a child, I used to play in the village with my friend Miriam, she was a Christian, and I would eat my lunch in her home. Yes! My parents didn't worry that they would serve me food that was not halal. We trusted her family and they trusted us. That was what it was like in the old days."

"That's right," said the lawyer. "Things were better then."

A haze of nostalgia settled over the table.

"I remember when I was young," said the consumer association rep. His eyes went dreamy behind the thick lenses of his spectacles. "Us estate kids used to play by the road after school, and the Malay boys would come up from the village on the bullock cart. They used to buy bags of kacang putih from the roadside stall and give them to us to eat."

"You young people don't know what it was like," said the lawyer to Ming Jun and Esther. "You see what we have come to—parading cow heads and attacking churches. In the seventies, our country was so beautiful."

"No, no," said the consumer association rep. "In the fifties, it was more beautiful."

"Looks like you all made a mess of it, then," said Ming Jun distinctly.

This was the American influence in him coming to the surface. Esther winced. Shocked silence reigned over the table.

"How are you humans bringing up your children?" said the orang bunian's voice. "My child would never talk to his elders like that."

Datin Zainab sat back and put her hand over her eyes.

"You have children?" said Khairul.

"How do you think orang bunian reproduce?" said the voice, with asperity. "I must say, Zainab, humans have become stupider since our time."

"It's the education system," said the Datin. Her eyes were still hidden. "The standards are falling."

This would be like a red flag to a bull. Esther knew she had to speak quickly before anyone got started on the inadequacies of the education system if she wanted an answer to the question that had been bothering her.

"Datin," she said. "How do you and the orang bunian know each other?"

"Eh, I have a name, please," said the irritable spirit. "Tan Chor Seng. But you young ciku must call me uncle lah."

Datin Zainab took her hand away from her face. Esther saw with horror that her eyes were wet.

"We met," she said, "a long, long time ago."

"It was not so long for me, Zainab," said the orang bunian.

"I have changed, I know," said the Datin.

"Not so much," said the voice. For once it was not so grumpy. "Voice is still the same."

"Ah, but when it comes to appearance!" said Datin Zainab. "I am a grandmother now. Hair no longer black. Wrinkles, hunched back. . . ."

"My eyesight was never very good," said the orang bunian. "My hearing only. First time I met you I thought, this woman has the most melodious voice I have ever heard. It is like the stars singing. Now I hear you again, that's still true."

Ming Jun was frowning down at his BlackBerry, his fingers flying. Esther was not surprised when her phone buzzed with a text message:

"R they flirting?!"

As the youngest people at the table, Ming Jun and Esther had to keep their speculation electronic. The delegates were older and did not feel the need to be quite so discreet.

"When you say you met," said the consumer association rep to the Datin, "met means dating or what?"

"None of your business," snapped the orang bunian's voice.

"Don't cry, mak cik," said Annabella Lim. She took a pack of tissues out of her handbag and passed them to the Datin. "What is wrong?"

Datin Zainab wiped her eyes.

"I have never told anybody," she said. "I was a young girl then. Thirty-five, thirty-six years old only. I liked to go hiking. My husband didn't like these strenuous activities. He liked staying home and watching TV. But he was always very supportive of my hobbies. We lived near the jungle and I used to go on walks by myself."

"Singing," said Chor Seng's voice. "She used to sing as she walked."

"I wanted to scare off any animals in case they wanted to bother me," the Datin explained.

"All of us orang bunian used to stop to listen when she sang," said Chor Seng. "I was also young in those days. I was impulsive. I heard her singing, but I wanted to know what her speaking voice sounded like. So one day when she was walking past my house I said hello to her."

"That is how it started," said the Datin. She looked down at her hands with their exquisitely manicured nails. "We were very young and foolish. When the child came . . . how could I explain that to my family? Chor Seng's family took me in. A whole year I was gone. I told my family I got lost in the forest but I didn't remember anything else. They took me to a bomoh and he told them a spirit enchanted me when I was out walking. He said the year had felt like only a few hours to me.

"Never waste your money on bomoh," Datin Zainab told Esther. "After this, I realized most of them are cheats. He didn't know anything about what happened to me. Guessing only."

"But you were married," said Khairul.

Datin Zainab glared at him.

"And you have never done anything wrong in your life?" she said. "It is for God to judge, not you. I regretted. You think I didn't regret?

But I suffered enough for my mistake. After that incident my husband did not let me go walking alone in the forest anymore. We moved when he got a new job, and I never heard my child again."

"You abandoned the baby?" said Farid.

"Encik," said the Datin with exaggerated patience. "If you know how I could have brought up an invisible child, please can you tell me. I am only a weak woman and I thought it might be difficult when it came to sending him to school. When he raised his hand, the teachers would not be able to see."

"Boon Yi takes after me more," Chor Seng's voice agreed. "His mother not so much."

Datin Zainab folded her hands.

"How is Boon Yi?" she said quietly.

"Doing well," said the orang bunian. "Studies hard. Good at writing but very lazy to do mathematics. I am raising him to be Muslim, like you asked. He goes to my neighbor's house twice a week to mengaji Quran."

"That is good," said Khairul, mollified.

"Nobody asked you, busybody," said the orang bunian's voice. "Boon Yi is very big now, very clever. Can understand a lot of things. He asks about you every day, Zainab. He wants to hear all the stories about you. He wishes he could know his mother."

"I left him my photo," said Datin Zainab. Annabella Lim pressed another tissue into her limp hand.

"Boon Yi is like me. His eyesight is not so good," said the orang bunian. "You know to us sound is more important. He has never heard your voice. That is why I came. His birthday is coming up soon—"

"February twenty-second," said Datin Zainab. "I always buy a birthday cake on that day. When my family asks, I tell them it is to celebrate the fact that even mistakes can have good consequences."

"I want to give him something meaningful for his birthday," said Chor Seng. "I want to give him the sound of your voice. That is why I came. Will you come with me to talk to him?"

"From here?" said Datin Zainab. She laughed a little. "Chor Seng, where you live is so deep in the jungle. How would I get there?"

"Walk," said Chor Seng, as if this was obvious. The table scoffed as one person.

"At her age!" said Annabella. "In this hot sun! Old lady like that, how to walk so far?"

"You are not being practical," said Farid. "You should have planned ahead."

"Orang bunian age more slowly than us," said Datin Zainab. "It is not his fault. But they are right, Chor Seng. My body cannot take it anymore."

There was a silence.

"I forgot that humans work differently," said Chor Seng. "I'm sorry. It is good that I did not tell Boon Yi. He won't be disappointed."

"Ne more of this n Im going 2 cry," texted Ming Jun to Esther.

Esther put her phone down on the table, feeling as depressed as everybody else looked.

Her eyes fell on the Dictaphone.

"There is no need to disappoint Boon Yi, Uncle," said Esther. "We have a Dictaphone here. If Datin records a message inside, Uncle can take it back to play for your son to hear. Come with me and we will do it outside in the corridor. In here it is too noisy. And while we are outside maybe Ming Jun can get on with the discussion. There's only fifteen minutes left, and we only covered five of the questions."

"Shit!"

"We'll record over that part," said Esther.

Outside in the corridor Esther tried to make herself scarce while Datin Zainab recorded her message, but she had to go over to help them find the "stop" button.

While she fiddled with the Dictaphone, a thought occurred to her. Esther said: "Uncle, if you came to get Datin's voice, why did you say all that about minority rights?"

"Our rights are also at stake what," said the orang bunian. "Cannot do two things at the same time meh? Let me tell you, girl. Life and politics is equally important. Cannot separate the two. Both also you must take seriously. What I said, you must remember to tell the government, OK?"

"OK," said Esther dubiously. She was going to warn him that going by previous record it didn't seem likely that the government would be interested in invisible minorities' rights, but Datin Zainab started speaking.

"Tell Boon Yi to study hard," said the Datin. "And tell him he must make sure to respect women and treat them with consideration. That is the best way to show respect to his mother. Tell him I always save one piece of the cake for him. Just in case. Tell him—"

"Why don't you come with me and tell him yourself?" said Chor Seng gently. "We are old already, Zainab. We don't have so many obligations anymore. Can't we please ourselves? You used to love the forest, remember? You could come back."

Datin Zainab paused.

"I have grandchildren," she said. "And I have my work with my women. I cannot simply go where I want. And I am old, Chor Seng. My bones like to have soft cushions to lie on. They like to be driven around in a Mercedes. If I'd stayed with you, back then . . . but I am too used to my lifestyle now. The jungle, romance—these things are for young people."

"Wrong," said Chor Seng. "Nobody can be too old for romance."

"It is rude to contradict a woman," said Datin Zainab.

"I'm just going to go to the toilet," said Esther. "The exit is over there—Uncle knows, right?"

But they were still there when Esther came back. Datin Zainab was standing by the doors at the end of the passage, talking softly. The blinding sunlight outside made a black silhouette of her body. Her arm was stretched out, the hand wrapped around air.

After a while her hand dropped to her side. The murmurs died down. She stood in the doorway for a long time, listening for the goodbye.

Odette

Odette's time for hope was short.

Early that morning, the first morning of the rest of her life, she'd gone out of her house to the end of the garden. The air was as pure as the breath that first animated the clay of Adam's flesh. She looked out over the island and saw no limitations.

But then she saw him—Uncle Andrew, in his polo shirt and khaki shorts, coming out for his daily morning walk. He pretended not to see her as he opened the gate and passed her by, but he knew she was there.

Odette realized her life had not changed after all. She would have to live with Uncle Andrew for the rest of her life.

He had only died the day before.

Uncle Andrew had insisted on being discharged from the hospital.

"If it is my time, I will die with dignity," he said. He spoke slowly, pausing between words to struggle for breath. "A Christian shouldn't be scared of death."

It wasn't Odette's place to disagree. Uncle Andrew's friends from church stepped in for her.

"Andrew, God helps those who help themselves," said Auntie Gladys. "You are still so young. Don't you think it's too soon? Let the doctors treat you."

"God can wait for a while," said Auntie Poh Eng. "He knows how much we all need you!"

All this was no less than what Uncle Andrew expected, but he was inflexible. "The doctors have had their chance. They poke me here, there, everywhere also, they still don't know how to cure me. God is calling me back to Him. I'm not so foolish as to put my faith in humans over God."

Auntie Poh Eng took Uncle Andrew's hand. Her eyes were full of tears.

"God has been good to let us have you for so long," she said.

Auntie Poh Eng was Odette's favorite of their church friends. Her only flaw was an unfailing affection for Uncle Andrew. But this was a flaw shared by all Uncle Andrew's friends. It was not Odette's place to complain.

Her place was by Uncle Andrew's side, except when she was in the laundry room, or the kitchen, or in the dining room polishing the heirloom silver. Just because Uncle Andrew was about to die didn't mean he was about to let standards slip. They had a cleaner who came in every day to go over the house, but the clothes Uncle Andrew wore and the food he ate had to come fresh from Odette's hands. As for the various antiques and other treasures Uncle Andrew had accumulated over the years, they could not of course be entrusted to a cleaner who only earned RM600 a month.

Uncle Andrew had collected enough that looking to the upkeep of his possessions, cooking for him, keeping him in clean clothes, and nursing him was too much for one person. Odette suggested that perhaps the cleaner could cook and do the laundry.

"Then I can put a hundred percent into looking after you and the house, Uncle."

"You should already be putting in hundred percent," said Uncle Andrew. "Who is paying for you to live? Not like you have so much to do. When Beatrice was alive she did all this and more. She didn't even have a degree, not like you. She never complained. You young people are spoilt. Given too much."

"Auntie Letchumi is a better cook than me. Maybe you'll feel like eating more, Uncle. It'll be good for your health."

"Instead of learning to cook better, you want to pay someone else to do," said Uncle Andrew. "You're useless! If not for my money

I don't know what you'd do—end up lying in the street like a tramp. I don't eat all this Indian food."

"If you don't want her to cook for you, what if we ask her to do the laundry? It will give me more time."

"What else are you doing with your life? Do you have a job? Do you have a husband? All you have to do is take care of your uncle who has done so much for you. Even that you don't want to do. I sacrifice for you and still you are so selfish."

Odette was of the unfortunate mold that does not grow less sensitive with time and use. She fell silent. Crying irritated Uncle Andrew to a fury. He took it as an unjustifiable assertion of self.

"After I die, your life will be very easy," said Uncle Andrew. "My time left here is short. But you can't even wait until God takes me." He coughed.

"I'm sorry, Uncle," said Odette.

"There's no use saying sorry," said Uncle Andrew. "You shouldn't be so selfish in the first place. If your hand causes you to sin, cut it off."

He banged the bedside table, but though Odette jumped she wasn't really scared. Five years ago the force of the blow would have rocked the table back and forth on its legs. Now Uncle Andrew was so weak it barely rattled the glass of water Odette had brought him. She watched the surface of the water tremble and go still, and hid a smile.

Uncle Andrew only spoke this way when they were alone. His friends did not see this side of him.

The friends watched Odette bring in meals, give Uncle Andrew his medicine, serve him hot drinks, fluff his pillow. They didn't see her change his bedsheets every day, bathe and dress him, do the laundry, eat only in the brief intervals granted her between chores—standing at the kitchen counter, stuffing the food into her mouth, dry-eyed.

Auntie Poh Eng told her: "You are taking Jesus' life as your model. Life is hard now, but God will reward you in the end."

Odette only shook her head. "I don't need His reward, Auntie."

After all, Uncle Andrew had always been so kind to her. He was known for this kindness. A pillar of the church, counsellor to his friends, benign dispenser of advice to their children.

It was all the more impressive in one who had done so well for himself. *Look at that beautiful house he lives in,* said his friends. *In the foothills overlooking the sea.* The only tragedy in Uncle Andrew's life was that he had no children of his own. But then, he had Odette.

To Odette his kindness had been wearyingly comprehensive. It had covered sending her to university, and insisting that she stay in his home for the duration of her course. He never asked for rent—she wouldn't have been able to pay it. In return for accommodation she did the household chores.

She hadn't minded staying at home for university. It meant living with Uncle Andrew, but she was used to that. The house was almost enough to make up for it.

It was the mansion of a nineteenth-century Peranakan merchant. Uncle Andrew liked to give out, and seemed to half-believe, that it had been in the family for generations, but he had bought it when he was in his forties from the businessman's great-grandson.

"Fella said he's an artist." Uncle Andrew snorted. "Cannot even hold on to the house his father gave him."

Whatever he had been, the great-grandson had had an eye for beauty. Upon Uncle Andrew's arrival the house was exquisitely pre-served. No incongruity had been permitted in it, no disruption to its elegant lines.

Uncle Andrew had improved the plumbing and installed air con-ditioners in every room. He filled the house with big ugly imitations of Western masterpieces, ludicrous photos of himself and Auntie Beatrice, and imposing jade sculptures he bought on trips to China ("I haggled them down to RM500 from RM3,000. These Chinamen will skin you if you don't watch out"). He replaced the Victorian tile flooring with marble, and brought in white leather sofas and glass coffee tables.

But the bones of the house shone through these embellishments. Odette loved the graceful shuttered windows, the intricate latticed vents, the pillars topped with carvings of cranes and fruit. The very gutters were wonderful because they fit so well with the building; they had that perfection that comes from being impeccably appropriate. The beauty and intricacy of the house was such that it could sustain even the incongruity of Uncle Andrew's additions and turn them into something marvelous.

The house was the only thing Odette loved. It was worth staying for.

She'd made the mistake of trying to leave once. Right after she graduated from university Auntie Beatrice died. It was sudden—cardiac arrest, the doctors said.

Odette understood that her aunt had finally given up.

She had not known Auntie Beatrice well, though they had lived under the same roof for many years. Auntie Beatrice had compacted herself so efficiently she seemed to take up no space in the world. Two days after her death Odette found herself struggling to remember what her aunt's face looked like.

Odette had started applying for jobs with a sense of foreboding.

When she was offered a teaching job, she was nonplussed. She had not really expected to get a job. But here it was, her ticket to another life. She would be teaching at a tuition center in Singapore— would be able to pay rent, feed herself, and live without reference to Uncle Andrew.

But there was the house. If Odette took the job, she would have to leave it. She would not see it again. Uncle Andrew had made it clear when she started university that she was not getting a degree so that she could enter the workforce.

"God has been generous," he said. "As long as I live, nobody else in the family will need to work."

Odette struggled with her decision for days. A week after she'd received the offer, she woke up suddenly in the middle of the night.

Uncle Andrew's bedroom was air-conditioned, but Odette wasn't allowed to turn on the air conditioner in hers—the expense of it. The windows were open, and outside the cicadas were shrieking insistently. The mosquito coil burning under her bed scented the air. Moonlight shone through the air vents high in the walls. Seeing the inky tracery of the shadows cast on the floor, Odette felt a shock of love.

In Singapore it would be an ugly little flat she lived in—bare of flourishes, with grilles on the windows and white fluorescent lighting. She would sit on a cheap sofa from IKEA and watch TV. She would have surrendered the glories of carved ivory and old rosewood armoires in favor of that cold idol, freedom.

Odette went back to sleep with her mind made up.

The next morning Uncle Andrew was waiting for Odette when she came back from the wet market with the groceries. A letter was on the table in front of him.

"All the money I spent on you, and you go and do this?" said Uncle Andrew. "I treat you like my own daughter. Fed you since you were small. Paid for you to go to uni. Someone like you, you think you would have this kind of lifestyle if I didn't pay for you?"

Odette's voice came out strangely calm. "I thought if I get a job, I can be less of a burden on you, Uncle."

"So clever to make excuses now, hah?" said Uncle Andrew. His face had gone dark red. He slammed the table. The letter fluttered. "Don't try to lie to me. You want to run off! Sick of listening to your uncle, is it?"

A prickling sensation spread up Odette's nose and behind her eyes. "I'm sorry I didn't tell you. I forgot."

"You think I'm stupid?" roared Uncle Andrew. "Useless! Idiot! If you're so rushed to get out of this house, get out! Go pack your things and get out! If you don't even know how to be grateful, why should I spend any more money on you? Go lah! Go!"

Odette was sobbing. "Uncle, I just wanted to contribute. I'm ashamed to keep taking your money. I'm an adult already."

"You think I'm the kind of person who won't support their own niece?" said Uncle Andrew. "My friends will be very surprised to hear that. You ask the church people, my staff. Everybody will say Andrew

Teoh isn't afraid to spend money on his family. You know better than all these people, is it?"

Odette shook her head. "I was going to reject the offer, Uncle."

"Nice story," said Uncle Andrew. "What for you go and apply then?"

The house gave her the right thing to say.

"I wanted to try," said Odette. "But when they offered, I knew I couldn't accept. I don't want to leave this house."

Uncle Andrew stared at her. The color in his face faded to pink.

"Hmph," he said. He crumpled the letter and threw it at her. It hit Odette on the shoulder and fell to the floor.

"I don't want to see that again," said Uncle Andrew. "Go put the food in the fridge."

After this, a merciful blankness descended on Odette. She felt nothing, and could even laugh at a couple of Uncle Andrew's jokes at dinner.

The next morning at church, Uncle Andrew sent Odette to the car a couple of times—first for a packet of tissues, then for a copy of a magazine he'd promised Auntie Gladys. When Odette came back with the *Reader's Digest*, Auntie Gladys said: "So guai your niece, Andrew. If my daughter was so helpful I'll be very happy."

"Beatrice and I did our best to bring her up," Uncle Andrew said. "But what's the most we can do, a childless couple like us?"

"You've done better than so many parents. Odette is lucky to have you all to look after her."

Uncle Andrew inclined his head. "As long as I'm alive, she'll always have a home."

They turned their eyes on Odette—Auntie Gladys's face distant and tender with thoughts of her daughter in America, Uncle Andrew looking just past Odette's ear. She smiled as expected.

When she got home she shut the door to her room and crawled into bed. Her body was sour with hatred. Her eyes burnt with tears.

The house absorbed them—weathered her storm—until she lay boneless on her bed and saw love shine through the vents, as it had done the night she decided to stay.

~~~

Odette had been young when her parents died. She didn't miss them as people—more as symbols of a warmth locked in the past, rendered forever inaccessible by their deaths.

Her mother's family were numerous, but lived in Indonesia. Though only a cousin of her father, Uncle Andrew staked his claim before any of her other relatives arrived on the scene. God had been good to them, he said, and he and Beatrice had never intended to waste their good fortune on themselves. Beatrice would enjoy having someone to fuss over. She regretted the fact that they had no children. Uncle Andrew made out that his wife had been the prime mover behind their offer to adopt Odette.

Even then Odette had found this hard to believe. Auntie Beatrice was the quietest woman she had ever met. She never looked up. She spoke in a whisper. It was hard to imagine her daring to want anything.

Uncle Andrew, on the other hand, impressed Odette with unfavorable force. She was still at an age where she only understood snatches of what grown-ups said to her. She watched his face instead of listening to his words, and what she saw worried her.

Two weeks after her parents' death, she was dozing in the back seat of his car as it wound up the hill toward his home.

She always remembered her first sight of the house. Auntie Beatrice had bored her and Uncle Andrew frightened her, but she knew the house to be a friend the moment she laid eyes on it.

How blue it had looked against the green velvet backdrop of the forest—the intense blue of the sea in paintings of summer days. The red tiles on its roof reflected the last of the setting sun; the lanterns hung under the eaves cast a golden glow over the deepening twilight. As she passed through its double doors, her skin prickled with the shivery, delightful excitement of being on holiday.

She was given a teak bed with a headboard carved with peacocks and white linen sheets. She slept soundly for the first time since her parents had died.

The house had been made to be loved, but what lived in it was not a real family.

Odette was the only person who knew what the house wanted. Uncle Andrew brooded over his possessions, indulged in tantrums, and tended his public persona as though it was a bonsai. Auntie Beatrice floated through the rooms, never denting a cushion or ruffling a rug.

But Odette divined the house's secrets. Nooks under staircases and crannies between sofas and walls, the perfect size for an eight-year-old to daydream in. Columns of light that moved around the house, picking whatever room suited their fancy. Wistful silences lying in wait in the concrete-floored courtyard, open to the sky.

She watched birds build their nests in the eaves and spiders construct webs in forgotten corners. She knew the moods of the house as well as she knew Uncle Andrew's.

This made her life easier, as Uncle Andrew's moods made her life harder. The house comforted her when Uncle Andrew tore up her homework, upbraided her for her stupidity and ugliness, told her she should have died when her parents did, that he never should have taken her in.

It was not so bad living with Uncle Andrew. Other children got beaten. Other children had nothing to eat. Uncle Andrew usually aimed to miss. He gave her food and clothing and even gifts at birthdays and Christmas. She didn't know how to articulate what was wrong until she heard a stranger's offhand remark.

"I always forget how beautiful your house is, Andrew," said one of his friends. "It's made for peace."

Odette looked past the friend at Uncle Andrew's smiling face. Uncle Andrew did not know or want peace, in a house made for peace. He desecrated it by living there. She had not hated him before that moment.

She didn't cry when Uncle Andrew told her she would have to find somewhere else to live.

"I looked after you long enough already," he said. "People your age are married, have their own house, children! I've done my part. If by now you haven't found a husband, you can only blame yourself."

Uncle Andrew was moving to Singapore.

"I have a lot of friends there, and I know the pastor of my new church," he told Auntie Poh Eng and the rest. "As a Christian in Malaysia, you never know . . . In Singapore the lifestyle is more convenient. An old man like me, I cannot be driving myself around forever. This Odette never learnt, she's too scared to go on the roads. In Singapore at least you can rely on public transport, not like here."

Odette had not been allowed to learn to drive. She was thirty-one and she had never had a job.

"Odette will like it," said Auntie Poh Eng, smiling at her. "Singapore is nice for young people. More fun, yes?"

"Ah, Odette won't be coming with me," said Uncle Andrew. "So boring for her to live with an old man. She's going to find her own place. These young people want to be independent. You give them your sweat and blood and at the end of the day, they go off and do what they want."

"That's the way of life," said Auntie Gladys. "But what are you going to do with the house, Andrew? Are you keeping it? It's been in your family for so long."

Uncle Andrew shook his head. "Selling. My grandfather would be upset, but things have changed since his day. A big old house, you must spend so much for upkeep. I'm not earning anymore. I don't want to worry about it in my old age. There's a developer who's very interested. Not many heritage buildings around that are so well-preserved. He wants to turn it into a hotel. The Mat Salleh like all this kind of thing."

Most of the friends nodded, but Auntie Poh Eng looked at Uncle Andrew as if for the first time her belief in him had wavered.

"You're selling to a developer?" she said. "To make it into a hotel?" But she remembered herself almost at once. "Of course most people cannot afford such a beautiful house. Maybe it's nice for them to have the chance to stay here also, even if it's for one or two nights only."

"I haven't answered the developer yet. I'm hoping to find someone who wants to live here," said Uncle Andrew smoothly. "It's very sad to have a home turned into something commercialized. Next best thing would be if the government buys it. Make it into a museum for everybody to visit."

Auntie Poh Eng beamed, her belief in Uncle Andrew restored.

"That would be perfect," she said.

It wasn't Odette's idea. She was standing in the kitchen wiping her hands when she saw a strand of hair on the countertop.

Hair in his food was the greatest sin anyone could commit against Uncle Andrew. Odette picked up the strand of hair and put it in the bin.

The idea was given to her.

Odette already knew Uncle Andrew's birthdate. It was easy to find out the time. He kept his birth certificate in the second drawer of the desk in his study, along with his passport and IC.

It was easy, too, to get strands of his hair. She peeled them off his pillows and dug them out of the drain in the shower. She was unflinching in her preparations. She gathered fingernail clippings and even saved a scab he'd picked at absently and discarded on one of the ugly coffee tables.

She'd never done magic before, but she knew how it was done. You went into all that was too close, too sticky, the things human beings didn't share with one another—that was what the hair and fingernails were for. You did it with strong love or strong hatred.

She poured malice into Uncle Andrew, a patient poison that impregnated the food he ate and released fumes into the air he breathed. And it worked. He sickened. His breath grew short and he could no longer enjoy his meals. He became thin and weak and his body was racked with pain.

The doctors said it was cancer, but Odette knew what was killing him. Sometimes she was even a little afraid of the house.

The manner in which Uncle Andrew chose to depart this life was appropriately Victorian. It was a still hot afternoon and Odette was refilling his glass of water when he opened his eyes and said: "Jesus is calling me."

Odette paused with the glass in her hand, unsure of how to respond.

"Do you want a drink, Uncle?" she ventured.

"Sit down, girl," snapped Uncle Andrew. "People are dying and you still want to do housework. Remember, Mary, not Martha, was praised by the Lord."

Odette sat down. Uncle Andrew was speaking, more to himself than to her.

"I'm still young. If not for this cancer, I could have been useful to my fellow men for many years. But His will be done. In Heaven," he added contemplatively, "I will see Beatrice again."

It wasn't clear whether the prospect gave him any pleasure.

Odette felt called upon to fill the gap left by the absence of his friends.

"Don't talk like that, Uncle," she said. "There's still hope. The doctor said—"

"Doctors! What do doctors know?" said Uncle Andrew. "Of course there's still hope. What is better than the hope of the Kingdom of Heaven? I have nothing to reproach myself with."

His wandering eyes settled on her with some of their former keenness.

"Nothing," he repeated. "Will you be able to give the account of yourself to Him that I will be able to give? Look into your conscience. Ask yourself."

Odette stayed silent, but she could not help a quick intake of breath then. She was so close.

"Hah," said Uncle Andrew triumphantly. "You see! Look to yourself! Look to yourself before it's too late!"

He didn't die then—only later, after his shouting had sent him into a coughing fit and Odette had given him water and been snarled at for spilling some on him. Finding fault with her put him in such a good mood that he went to sleep with little trouble after that. The next morning Odette found him cold in his bed.

~~~

When Uncle Andrew had realized he was dying he'd willed the house to the church. Odette would get a legacy—an annuity of RM8,000 a year.

"More than a lot of people earn by their own hard work," said Uncle Andrew. "You are lucky."

Odette agreed with Uncle Andrew that this was generous. She resented him no more for this than for anything else, though the bulk of his wealth would go to a successful nephew in Canada who hadn't visited in years.

"Jit Beng has children," said Uncle Andrew.

Jit Beng had an Ivy League degree and a big job in a multinational company. Uncle Andrew yearned over Jit Beng with a stifled affection he had never shown his wife or Odette.

Odette didn't care about the money. It was the house she wanted, and it was easy enough to alter the will. She was the one who had filled out the blanks while Uncle Andrew dictated. She'd bought the will-making kit for him from a bookshop. Uncle Andrew didn't believe in lawyers.

Nobody questioned the result. Everyone except Uncle Andrew had thought Odette should get the house. The church got the RM8,000 a year, a generous donation from a faithful servant of the Lord.

Even Jit Beng got something. Odette willed him a kamcheng, part of a nyonyaware set that had mostly been destroyed when Uncle Andrew had thrown the pieces at her for going to a friend's house after school. She swathed the kamcheng in layers of bubble wrap and posted it to Jit Beng herself.

After the funeral she came home and lay on the chaise lounge in the front hall, gazing up at the gorgeous wooden screens that softened the heat of the sun.

She would have the coffee tables removed. The gigantic TV, that would go. Maybe she could sell it. She'd already put most of the sculptures and paintings away when Uncle Andrew got too ill to come downstairs to see them, but there were a couple she liked and that she would keep.

She would clear away the clutter, give the house space. Let it breathe.

Her eyes were shut, but if she opened them she would see the light shining through her skin, like moonlight through the filigreed vents. For the first time in her life she gave herself up to happiness.

Uncle Andrew walked his usual route. Down the driveway, up the slope to the top of the hill, then back down again to the back gate, where he let himself in.

Odette had been standing by the pillars at the entrance, waiting for him. Her hand curled around a pillar, drawing strength from the house. Perhaps she hadn't really seen him, she told herself. He wouldn't come back. She had just imagined it.

She knew this was a lie. It was not a surprise to see him return. When he lifted the latch on the gate, the sunlight shone through his arm.

If he had been alive she would have felt the movement of air on her skin as he walked past her. He didn't so much as glance at her, though he knew she was there. Temper held him, its weight crumpling his forehead, pulling his mouth taut.

He would be silent for days, pointedly ignoring her in his pique. His anger would fill the house like dark, oily smoke. The stench would get into everything.

Life would be the same as it had always been.

Odette saw that the house needed Uncle Andrew more than it loved her. It needed him as much, perhaps, as she did. It would never let either of them go.

The harsh glare of the sun hurt her eyes. It was too hot to be outside. She let go of the pillar and saw that a splinter had driven itself into her palm.

She turned and went into the house. The shade enveloped her, cool as the air in a crypt. The doors swung shut, closing her in.

The House of Aunts

Dedicated to the women of my family.

The house stood back from the road in an orchard. In the orchard, monitor lizards the length of a man's arm stalked the branches of rambutan trees like tigers on the hunt. Behind the house was an abandoned rubber tree plantation, so proliferant with monkeys and leeches and spirits that it might as well have been a forest.

Inside the house lived the dead.

The first time she saw the boy across the classroom, Ah Lee knew she was in love because she tasted durian on her tongue. That was what happened—no poetry about it. She looked at a human boy one day and the creamy, rank richness of durian filled her mouth. For a moment the ghost of its stench staggered on the edge of her teeth, and then it vanished.

She had not tasted fruit since before the baby came. Since before she was dead.

After school she went home and asked the aunts about it.

"Ah Ma," she said, "can you taste anything besides people?"

It was evening—Ah Lee had had to stay late at school for marching drills—and the aunts were already cooking dinner. The scent of fried liver came from the wok wielded by Aunty Girl. It smelled exquisite, but where before the smell of fried garlic would have filled her mouth with saliva, now it was the liver that made Ah Lee's post-death nose sit up and take interest. It would have smelled even better raw.

"Har?" said Ah Ma, who was busy chopping ginger.

77

"I mean," said Ah Lee, "when you eat the ginger, can you taste it? Because I can't. I can only taste people. Everything else got no taste. Like drinking water only."

Disapproval rose from the aunts and floated just above their heads like a mist. The aunts avoided discussing their undeceased state. It was felt to be an indelicate subject. It was like talking about your bowel movements, or other people's adultery.

"Why do you ask this kind of question?" said Ah Ma.

"Better focus on your homework," said Tua Kim.

"I finished it already," said Ah Lee. "But why do you put in all the spices when you cook, then? If it doesn't make any difference?"

"It makes a difference," said Aunty Girl.

"Why do you even cook the people?" said Ah Lee. "They're nicest when they're raw."

"Ah girl," said Ah Ma, "you don't talk like that, please. We are not animals. Even if we are not alive, we are still human. As long as we are human we will eat like civilized people, not dogs in the forest. If you want to know why, that is why."

There was a silence. The liver sizzled on the pan. Ah Ma diced more ginger than anyone would need, even if they could taste it.

"Is that why Sa Ee Poh chops intestines and fries them in batter to make them look like yu char kuay?" asked Ah Lee.

"I ate fried bread sticks for breakfast every morning in my life," said Sa Ee Poh. "Just because I am like this doesn't mean I have to stop."

"Enough, enough," said Ah Chor. As the oldest of the aunts, she had the most authority. "No need to talk about this kind of thing. Ah Lee, come pick the roots off these tauge and don't talk so much."

The aunts had a horror of talking about death. In life this had been an understandable superstition, but it seemed peculiar to dislike the mention of death when you were dead.

Ah Lee kept running into the wall of the aunts' disapproval headfirst. They were a family who believed that there was a right way to do things, and consequently a right way to think. Ah Lee always seemed to be thinking wrong.

She could see that as her caretakers the aunts had a right to determine where she went and what she did. But she objected to their attempts to change what she thought. After all, none of them had died before the age of fifty-five, while she was stuck forever at sixteen.

"It's OK if I don't follow you a hundred percent," she told them one day in exasperation. "It's called a generation gap."

This came after Sa Ee Poh had spent half an hour marveling over her capacity for disagreement. In Sa Ee Poh's day, girls did not answer back. They listened to their elders, did their homework, came top in class, bought the groceries, washed the floor, and had enough time left over to learn to play the guzheng and volunteer for charity. When Sa Ee Poh had been a girl, she had positively delighted in submission. But children these days. . . .

Once an aunt got hold of an observation she did not let go of it until she had crunched its bones and sucked the marrow out, *and* saved the bones to make soup with later.

"Gap? What gap?" Sa Ee Poh said.

"It's a branded clothing," said Aunty Girl. She was the cool aunt. "American shop. They sell jeans, very expensive."

The aunts surveyed Ah Lee with gentle disappointment.

"Why do you care so much about brands?" said Ah Ma. "If you want clothes, Ah Ma can make clothes for you. Better than the clothes in the shop also."

So Ah Lee did not tell them about the boy. If the aunts could not handle her having thoughts, imagine how much worse they would be about her having feelings. Especially love—love, stealing into her life like a thief in the night, filling her dried-out heart and plumping it out.

Being a vampire was not so bad. It was like eating steak every day, but when steak was your favorite food in the world. It wasn't anything like the books and movies, though. In books and movies it seemed quite romantic to be a vampire, but Ah Lee and her aunts were clearly the wrong sort of people for the ruffled shirt and velvet jacket style of vampirism.

Undeath had not lent Ah Lee any mystical glamour. It had not imbued her with magical powers, gained her exotic new friends, or even done anything for her acne.

In fact Ah Lee's life had become more boring post-death than it had been pre-, because at least when she was alive she had had friends. Now she just had aunts. She still went to school, but she was advised against fraternizing with her schoolfellows for obvious reasons.

"Anyway, what is friends?" said the aunts. "Won't last one. Only family will be there for you at the end of the day."

The sayings of aunts filled her head till they poked out of her ears and nostrils.

Yet here came this boy one fine day, and suddenly her ears and nostrils were cleared. Her head was blown open. The sayings of the aunts fluttered away in the wind and dissolved with nothing to hold on to. Love was like swallowing a cili padi whole.

A classmate caught her staring at the boy the next day.

"Eh, see something very nice, is it?" said the classmate, her voice heavy with innuendo. She might as well have added, "Hur hur hur."

Fortunately Ah Lee did not have quick social reflexes. Her face remained expressionless. She said contemplatively, "I can't remember whether today is my turn to clean the window or not. Sorry, you say what ah? You think that guy looks very nice, is it?"

The classmate retreated, embarrassed.

"No lah, just joking only," she said.

"Who is that guy?" said Ah Lee, maintaining the facade of detachment. "Is he in our class? I never see him before."

"Blur lah you," said the classmate. "That one is Ridzual. He's new. He just move here from KL."

"He came to Lubuk Udang from KL?" said Ah Lee.

"I know, right?" said the classmate. This seemed an eccentric move to them both. Everyone had uncles and aunts, cousins, older brothers and sisters who lived in KL. Only grandparents stayed in Lubuk Udang. In three years, Ah Lee knew, none of the people sitting around her in the classroom would still be living there. Lubuk Udang was a place you moved away from when you were still young enough to have something to move for.

Fresh surprises awaited. The first time the boy opened his mouth in class, a strong Western accent came out. It said, "I don't know" in answer to the obvious question the Add Maths teacher had posed him, but it made even that confession of ignorance sound glamorous.

People said Ridzual had been at an international school in KL. The nearest international school to Lubuk Udang was in Penang, a whole state and strait away.

"He sounds like TV hor," said the classmate. "Apparently he was born in US."

Ridzual called natrium "sodium" and kalium "potassium." For the duration of his first week at school he wore dazzlingly white high-top leather sneakers instead of the whitewashed canvas shoes everyone else wore. The shoes didn't last long—they were really too cool to be regulation. But it didn't matter that Ridzual had to give them up to the discipline teacher a week after he had started. The aroma of leather hung around him forever after, even when he was only wearing Bata like the rest of the class.

Ah Lee had never been in love but she took to it like a natural despite her lack of practice. She spun secret fantasies about him: the things they would say to each other, the adventures they would have. She would reel off dazzling one-liners; he would gaze at her with intrigued longan seed eyes. She saw them sitting in a café unlike any kopitiam to be found in Lubuk Udang, with flowered wallpaper, tiny glossy mahogany tables, and brisk, friendly waitresses who took your orders down in a little notebook and did not shout in the direction of the kitchen, "Milo O satu!"

They would sit together at a table, Ridzual's curly head bent close to her smooth one. They would speak of serious things, but she would also make him laugh. Through this love she would be renewed, brilliant, special.

However lurid her fantasies got, her imagination never stretched beyond conversation. You could not imagine kissing a boy when you were never more than a room's width away from an aunt. Ah Lee's favorite time to dream was in that precious space of quiet between getting in bed and falling asleep. She could construct a pretty good Parisian café as she lay underneath her Donald Duck blanket. But cafés were one thing: kisses were another. No kiss could survive Ji Ee's snores from the mattress across the room.

It was no big deal. There was time enough to imagine the later stages of her romance—after all, she had not even got to the overtures. Ah Lee came from a family that believed in being prepared. While staring at the back of Ridzual's lovely head in class, she wove conversation openers, from the casual to the calculatedly cool.

She then made the fatal mistake of writing them down.

The aunts would have pulled it off if they had left everything to Ji Ee. In life Ji Ee had played the violin. She could have been a professional if her husband had not become envious and depressed, so that she had had to stop playing to keep him happy. She had not touched a violin since, but she still had the soul of an artist. It gave her sensibility.

She sat down next to Ah Lee one day and asked her what she was doing.

Ah Lee was trying to think of nonchalant ways to ask Ridzual what life meant to him.

"Bio homework," she said. She snapped her exercise book shut.

"Good, good," said Ji Ee. She looked dreamily into the distance.

They were sitting on the step outside the kitchen door. Behind them came the hiss and clang of Ah Chor making human stomach soup with bucketloads of pepper and coriander. In front of them stood the orchard.

It was one of those blindingly sunny days: the leaves of the trees shone with reflected sunlight, so bright that if you looked at them purple-green shapes remained imprinted on your eyes after you looked away. The heat was relieved by an occasional breeze that lifted the leaves and touched their faces like a caress.

A monitor lizard paused on the branch of a tree to look at them. It blinked and ran up the branch, out of sight.

"When you are young, you must focus," said Ji Ee. "You must pay attention at school, study hard and become clever. When you are young, that is when you have the best chance. And you are young now, in this modern day, when women can do everything. Can be doctor, can be lawyer. You know none of us went to university. Your Ah Chor wasn't allowed and when Ah Ma and Sa Ee Poh were young, during the war, everything was too kelam-kabut. I wasn't clever enough. Aunty Girl's family couldn't afford it, so she could only get a diploma.

"But you, Ah Lee, you have all the opportunities. We have lived so long, we have saved enough money. Maybe if you study hard, if you get a scholarship, you could even go to England like my uncle the doctor, your Tua Tiao Kong. Your English is so good. You have a good chance."

Ah Lee was used to such pep talks. The aunts never scolded; they did not believe in raising their voices. They only "told." The benefits of only ever being told and not scolded were obvious, but the disadvantage of it was that while people only scolded when you had done something wrong, the aunts got to tell all the time.

"I know, Ji Ee," Ah Lee said. "You all have told me before." In her daydream Ridzual had been on the point of tucking her hair behind her ear. She was impatient to return to it.

"You must not get distracted by anything," said Ji Ee. "There will be time for other things when you are older. There is so much time ahead of you. Right now you must focus on your studies. Then we can tell all the neighbors about our clever girl."

She put her soft hand on Ah Lee's arm and stroked it. Love came up the arm and melted Ah Lee's thorny teenaged heart. When Ji Ee said, "You'll listen to Ji Ee, yah?"

Ah Lee said pliantly, "Yes, Ji Ee."

So she never heard the rest of the talk, planned if Ah Lee had proved intransigent, which went into alarming detail about the inadvisability of youthful romance.

The way Ji Ee had two-stepped around the subject matter, Ah Lee would never have known what she was talking about if not for everyone else. All the other aunts believed in the forthright approach, and not one of them could keep a secret.

When Ah Lee came home from school the day after Ji Ee had given her little talk, Ah Chor looked up from the dining table and said, "Ah girl! Who is this Malay boy? What is he called already?" She turned to Ah Ma. "Ri—Li—Liwat or what?"

Ah Ma did not know any dirty words, and could not have told you what sodomy was if you'd asked her. She said unconcernedly, "Ridzwan, Ma. He is called Ridzwan. Isn't that right, Ah Lee?"

"Cannot marry a Malay," Ah Chor told Ah Lee. "They don't know how to treat their women."

Ah Lee was surfing the waves of outrage. She started to say, "You all read my diary?" Then she clamped her mouth shut in fury. Of course they had. She could just picture Ji Ee and Aunty Girl reading it out loud, translating the English and Malay to Hokkien as they went along for the benefit of Ah Chor and Ah Ma and Sa Ee Poh, who could not read. The aunts' conception of the right to privacy went far enough to allow you to close the toilet door when you were peeing, but no further.

"Ah Ma saw you when you were being born," Ah Ma said. No further explanation was required.

"Even if you think you will be so happy and the man is so good, you don't know what can happen," said Ah Chor. "Do you know or not, they can marry four wives? Malay men. . . ."

"Si Gu had four wives. He wasn't even Muslim," said Aunty Girl.

Ah Chor said repressively, "Your uncle was a very naughty boy."

"It wasn't four wives, not four wives," said Ah Ma. "Only one wife. The others were girlfriends only."

"The laksa lady cannot even count as girlfriend," sniffed Sa Ee Poh. "Remember how she threw a bowl of laksa in his face when he told her he wasn't going to marry her? Even a laksa lady can put on airs like that."

"She asked him to pay for it some more!" said Ah Ma. She realized they were enjoying reminiscing about her naughty brother's adventures rather too much, and changed her face to look serious. "Ah Lee, this is what men are like."

"Not all men," said Ji Ee.

"Yes, all men," said Sa Ee Poh.

"Only bad men," said Ah Ma. "But when you are young you cannot tell whether a man is a good man or a bad man yet. You are too small. Now you must focus on your studies. Don't think about this Ridzwan."

"His name," said Ah Lee, "is *Ridzual.*"

She stormed out of the kitchen.

From that day there was no respite for her. The aunts abounded in stories of bad men and the bad things they had done to good women.

"Look at your great-grandfather," said Aunty Girl.

"Shouldn't speak ill of the dead," said Ah Ma piously. "He was your grandfather, Ah Girl. You should show respect."

"No need to respect That Man," said Ah Chor, who had been That Man's wife.

"This is what happens when you marry too young," she told Ah Lee. "That Man didn't even deserve to be called husband. I was only nineteen when I had my third child, your Sa Ee Poh, and already he had a second wife."

"She lived in Ipoh," Sa Ee Poh confirmed.

"When I found out, I told him, if you don't stop seeing her, I will take my children and go," said Ah Chor. "He promised he wouldn't see her again. But all along after that, little did I know he was going back and forth between me and that other woman! My fourth child is the same age as her second child. He didn't know how to feel shame! Never mind my heart. At least if she didn't have children nobody would know. But he didn't even care enough to save my face."

Ah Ma was uncomfortable. "Ma, so long ago . . . it's not good to speak bad of other people."

"Ah Lee must know so she won't make the same mistake," said Ah Chor. "He didn't even support the second wife properly, so she came to me asking for money. When I saw her with the baby, I packed up and brought all my children here. Don't think this was your grandfather's house! He was rich before he lost it all in gambling, but this was my parents' home. His creditors couldn't touch this. All this was my land. If That Man came on it without my permission, I could call the police on him."

Ah Lee was interested despite herself. "Did you ever see him again?"

"Of course," said Ah Chor. "Where do you think your four other great-uncles and great-aunts came from?"

"Ma says too much. Shouldn't talk about such things," said Ah Ma to Sa Ee Poh, but Sa Ee Poh only laughed.

"We all know this story already," she said. "Let Ah Lee listen. Maybe she will learn something also."

"But you said if he came on your land you would call the police," Ah Lee said to Ah Chor.

"Oh, he was my husband, after all," said Ah Chor. "I didn't let him live here. Only visit. I told him, you can come and stay for good only after you get rid of that woman. But he didn't, so even after he asked and asked, I never went back to him.

"It wasn't easy, you know or not? Raising eight children with no husband. Lucky my mother was there to help me. That's why you cannot think about this kind of thing at your age—men, romance. It's too early."

"But Ah Ma married Ah Kong when she was sixteen," Ah Lee objected. "I'm going to be seventeen already."

"That's not the same," said Sa Ee Poh.

Ah Ma stared at her hands on the table.

"You forget, girl," said Ji Ee gently. "There was a war then."

Ji Ee's husband wouldn't let her play the violin, an iniquity long known to Ah Lee. Curiously, if anything was going to stop Ah Lee's wayward heart from loving Ridzual, it was Ji Ee's patience when she talked about Ji Tiao.

"He was a good husband. Men have their little ways. They have their likes and dislikes. As long as they are responsible, as long as they look after you and the children, there's no harm in letting them have their way."

Ah Lee was less impressed by the wickedness of Sa Ee Poh's husband. Sa Ee Poh was the only one who spoke about her husband with the complacency of someone who had asked more of love and always received it. But she still complained about her husband's vegetarianism.

"Sa Tiao Kong being a vegetarian doesn't sound so bad," Ah Lee objected. "How was that suffering for you?"

"You think what? I had to be vegetarian also!" Sa Ee Poh retorted. "You think he cooked for himself? I cooked for the two of us. Vegetarian a few times a year or for a few months, I don't mind. Vegetarian all the time . . . for the rest of my life I never tasted garlic or onion!"

Ah Ma kept the story about her marriage for the right time. One night Ah Lee's evening hunt had taken longer than usual, so she got home late and only managed to finish her Add Maths homework after eleven. She was feeling creaky-jointed and lonely as she got ready for bed in a house full of night sounds. The beam of light under Ah Ma's door came as a pleasant surprise.

She poked her head into Ah Ma's room. "Not sleeping yet, Ah Ma?"

Ah Ma was lying propped up on the pillows, her eyes half-closed, but when Ah Lee spoke she sat bolt upright.

"No! Cannot sleep," she said in a blatant lie. "Brushed your teeth already? Come sit down next to Ah Ma."

Ah Lee climbed into bed to the soft melody of Ah Ma's fussing: "Come under the blanket, you'll get cold. Let Ah Ma feel your hands. Ah, see lah, so cold! Next time you mustn't go out until so late. Not good to work so late at night. Why don't you want to eat dinner with us?"

"I like to have fresh meat sometimes," said Ah Lee.

"Then don't be so picky. Ah Ma always tells you, eat the first man you see."

"I did, Ah Ma," Ah Lee protested. Now that she was under the blanket with Ah Ma's bony arm around her and Ah Ma's warm chest against her cheek, she felt drowsy, protected. "The guy had a motor-bike. Didn't know how to get rid of it."

"So how? Did you manage to get rid of it in the end?"

"Yes. Flew out of town and dumped it in the middle of an oil palm plantation. No bloodstains, and I took off the license plate."

Ah Ma tsked.

"So difficult," she said. "Next time just eat with us. We all have hunted for you already. And we are older than you so we know which people are the nicest to eat."

"OK, OK," mumbled Ah Lee.

They sat in silence for a while. Ah Lee half-shut her eyes to keep out the light from the lamp on the bedside table. Through the slits of her eyes she could see Ah Ma's reading glasses and the container in which she kept her false teeth. The teeth floated in cloudy water, yellowed by coffee and blood.

The cicadas screeched. The ceiling fan hummed to itself. The air was cool enough that the breeze it created was a pleasure rather than the necessity it usually was. Ah Lee forgot the persistent sense of irritation she had had since the aunts had found her diary, which had felt as if she had sand in her underwear. She was almost asleep when Ah Ma spoke.

"Do you know why I married your Ah Kong?" she said.

Embarrassment woke Ah Lee up.

"Don't know," said Ah Lee. An expectant pause ensued. Ah Ma was waiting for a better attempt at an answer. "Er . . . you loved him?"

"Where got?" said Ah Ma. "I was sixteen, a little girl only. How to know what is love yet? Ah Ma washed your backside when you were a baby. Now that is love."

"That's different," said Ah Lee. "You wouldn't marry someone just because they didn't mind washing your backside."

"Don't answer back to your elders," said Ah Ma. "No, I married him because of the war. The Japanese soldiers used to come to every-one's houses looking for young girls. So Ah Chor cut our hair and put us in our brothers' clothes. It worked with Sa Ee Poh because she was younger and skinny, but you know when Ah Ma was young Ah

Ma was so chubby-chubby. Even wearing boys' clothes, I still looked like a girl.

"When the soldiers came Ah Chor would tell us to run to the forest behind the house and hide there until the soldiers went away. So horrible! Must lie in the mud. Cannot move even with mosquitoes biting your body. When I came back to the house my face looked like it had pimples all over it because of the mosquito bites, and my legs were covered with leeches. I had to sit down in the kitchen and Ah Chor would put salt on them, but you cannot take them off with your hand, you know? Must wait until they drop off. Then when they came off, my legs would bleed everywhere. So horrible."

"That's why you never let me play in the forest," said Ah Lee. "Because you don't like leeches."

Ah Ma nodded.

"One day some soldiers came without warning to our house. I was in the kitchen cutting ubi kayu. Those days we had nothing much to eat, only tapioca that we grew ourselves. There was no time to run out to the forest, so I just tried to make myself look small, bent my head over the chopping board. Your Ah Chor was so scared, she offered them all the food: do you want Nescafé, do you want biscuit, this lah, that lah. And she talked. Usually when the soldiers came we didn't talk so much. Scared they think we asked questions because we were spies or what. But Ah Chor didn't want them to look at me, so she kept talking. Did they like Malaya? How was Japan like, not so hot? Her Japanese was not so good but she used every word she knew. When she ran out of words she knew, she repeated everything she'd already said.

"But the soldiers kept looking over at me. I was so scared I cut my finger instead of the ubi and the blood went all over the tapioca. And I didn't even make a sound. The soldiers drank coffee. They talked to Ah Chor, very friendly. Then they finally got up to go. Suddenly their captain turned around and pointed at me. He said, "'Can we have that tapioca?'

"All along they were looking at the ubi kayu on the shelf above my head! We gave them all the ubi we harvested from our own plants, even though we went hungry for the next few days. Your great-grandfather said Ah Chor should have given me away instead."

"That wasn't very nice of him," said Ah Lee.

"Men cannot stand having empty stomachs," said Ah Ma. "After that your great-grandparents were very anxious to see me married. When your Ah Kong came to lodge with us he was already quite old—thirty-eight years old—and we only knew him a few weeks before he asked to marry me. But he was a teacher and an educated man and the Japanese respected him, so my mother and father said yes."

A hush. Ah Lee said into it, "He wasn't so bad, was he?" She remembered her grandfather as a benign figure, distant, but kindly enough when he was reminded of your existence.

"Your Ah Kong was a good father," said Ah Ma. "All his students at his school looked up to him. Even the Japanese could see that he had a good character. And he knew how to be polite. He never said a bad word to me.

"But when a girl marries so young, to someone so much older . . . and he was educated, and I couldn't even read. I could hold a pen but I could only draw pictures with it. Ah girl, you must never tell anybody this. But your Ah Kong did not respect me. Without love you can live a happy life. Love is something that will come after you live together with your husband, after you have children together. But a woman should not marry where there is no respect. Respect is the most important thing.

"So you must study hard and go to university. Now, at your age, is not the time to look at boys. Understand or not?"

"Yes," said Ah Lee. But the mutinous thought rumbled to the surface of her mind: *They're the ones who don't understand.*

When she was a child Ah Lee had often wondered whether adults could read her mind. They seemed to have an uncanny ability to tell what she was thinking at any given moment. Ah Ma evinced this telepathy now: "Ah, you're angry already," she said. "Don't think so much. Listen to Ah Ma and do what you're told. Now give me a kiss and go to bed."

~~~

In the end it was not even Ah Lee's doing. Suddenly, easily, without any need for imaginary cafés or prepared lines scribbled in exercise books, Ah Lee became friends with Ridzual.

It was because of Thursdays. Ji Ee and Aunty Girl were the only two of the aunts who could drive, so it was their job to pick Ah Lee up from school. But they had line dancing every Thursday, and so they were an hour late.

Ah Lee usually waited for them in the canteen, doing home-work if she felt like it and daydreaming if she didn't. In the middle of the day there weren't many people around, and it was pleasant, even quiet. It smelled of grease, heated metal from the car park, and the freshly washed flesh of the afternoon session kids waiting for school to start.

The background hum of talk and the hiss of oil in frying pans made Ah Lee feel secure. She liked the feeling of being idle while others were busy, alone when others were talking.

It was at this peaceful moment, while Ah Lee was following a drop of condensation on her glass of iced soybean milk with a finger and thinking about nothing much, that Ridzual tapped her on the shoulder. He said, "Tamadun Awal, right?"

And that was how she met him. The boy who gave her back her sense of taste.

He dropped his schoolbag on the floor and sat on the bench next to her with an admirable lack of self-consciousness.

"Your name is Eng Ah Lee? Don't worry, I'm not a stalker. I know 'cos I was checking out all our team members in class. I'm using this project as an exercise to get to know people. My name's Ridzual, I'm new. So what do you think of early civilizations? I don't know shit about them."

Despite her many fantasies, Ah Lee had not seriously considered ever actually talking to Ridzual. She waited for her throat to close and her muscles to freeze. But she found herself speaking naturally, as if to a friend whom she had known forever.

"It's OK. I like this kind of thing," she said. "Anyway, at least it's not Persatuan Penulis or whatever."

"Hah! Don't even say that," said Ridzual. "No, that's true. At least with Tamadun Awal maybe we can dress up like ancient Egyptians or something. I think I'd look good in eyeliner."

"Nanti kena rotan by the discipline teacher then you know," said Ah Lee. "You know Puan Aminah doesn't even let us wear colored watches. Must be black, plain black strap." She showed him the watch she was wearing. "Metal watch also cannot. Too gaya konon."

"Wah lau," said Ridzual. He said it in a toneless accent Ah Lee found peculiarly charming. "I think that woman is jealous. Like when she confiscated my shoes. She couldn't stand looking at them, just got too jealous of my style."

It would have been obnoxious if he had been serious. But Ridzual wore a perpetual embarrassed smile, an uncertainty around the eyes, that made it obvious that the hot air was just joking. Ah Lee liked vulnerability in a human, and she warmed to this.

"She took your shoes?" she said. They both looked down at his feet, now encased in boring white canvas. "Never give back meh?"

"I never saw them again," said Ridzual. "I think she's wearing them now. Sometimes if you look closely you can see the white flash under the hem of her baju.

"Discipline teachers cannot stand me," he said mournfully. "I remind them of what they can never achieve. At my last school there was one teacher like that. Encik Velu. He used to chase me around the school with a rotan. He said it's because I ponteng or I made rude gestures at the teacher or I kencing in the beaker or some garbage like that. But he couldn't fool me. I knew it was because he wished he was like me when he was young, one million years ago."

"You peed in the beaker?" said Ah Lee.

"Only once," said Ridzual modestly. "It was for science. I wanted to titrat it but the kimia teacher stop me before I can do it."

"International school got discipline teacher meh?" said Ah Lee.

"What makes you think I went to international school?" said Ridzual.

Ah Lee went pink.

"Your slang," she said. "You talk like Mat Salleh."

"Oh, that," said Ridzual. It was his turn to look embarrassed. "That's called a Bangsar accent. But don't hold it against me. I'm trying to be a Lubuk Udangite. A good prawn."

"I've lived in Lubuk Udang my whole life," said Ah Lee.

"Right? What should I do to become a good Lubuk Udangite?"

"Don't call us prawns," said Ah Lee.

Ah Lee had not had a friend to spend break with since she'd started at that school. She did not eat during break. It had seemed simpler to avoid the crowd at the canteen and find some out-of-the-way spot on the school grounds where she could read.

Of course, it had been different before she was dead. But that was before, in another life—and more importantly, at a different school.

Now that she and Ridzual were friends, Ah Lee bought a bag of keropok lekor in the canteen every day and ate them while Ridzual wolfed down a bowl of tomyam noodles.

She had loved the chewy fried fish sticks in life. Now she was dead they tasted of nothing. She ate slowly and threw the remaining keropok away when break was over. She felt bad about the waste of it—heart-pain, the aunts would have said. Ah Lee's upbringing had trained her to a mindful parsimony, so that it did almost feel like a physical pain to see the fish sticks tumbling into the bin.

She asked Tua Kim if she would disguise some innards for her to take to school.

Tua Kim considered her for a moment in silence. Then she said, "I'll deep-fry them. They'll look like chicken nugget."

She turned back to her washing.

"Er, Tua Kim," said Ah Lee. "Um, don't tell the others, OK or not? Ah Chor and Ah Ma and all of them. Ah Ma will scold me for eating fried things. She'll say I'll get pimples."

When Ah Lee saw Tua Kim's face she felt foolish for the lie.

"This is because of your friend," Tua Kim said, in the tone of one pointing out an obvious fact to a dim person.

Ah Lee looked down at her feet. Her smallest toes curled in embarrassment.

"I'm shy to be the one not eating," she mumbled. "People like to eat together."

"You need your own friends," said Tua Kim. When Ah Lee peeked up she saw that Tua Kim's face had not softened. She spoke almost sternly. It was not kindness in her face, but understanding.

"You need your own thing," said Tua Kim. "Something that's nothing to do with your family. You feel this especially when you're young, but even for old people it's important. Some people don't understand this kind of thing. So it's better not to talk so much about it."

She wiped her hand on a dishcloth and started putting the clean dishes back in the cupboard. "I'll put your snack in your backpack in the morning. Other people don't need to see."

"Thank you, Tua Kim," said Ah Lee.

She had never thanked an aunt for anything before. It was understood that they would do things for her, that that was the way the world worked. She did not need to thank them any more than trees thanked the sun for shining or the earth thanked the clouds for rain. Ah Lee was not sure the aunts would have understood or even registered any attempt on her part to express gratitude for the many ways in which they cared for her.

It made her feel funny to say the words—stripped, somehow. Skinless and shy. To say it was to contemplate a world in which the aunts did not look after her.

Tua Kim only inclined her head slightly to show she had heard. She made no other response. That was one thing you could rely on Tua Kim for. She had a sense of the appropriateness of things.

The next day at school Ah Lee opened her plastic container and almost felt normal, eating fried kidney nuggets as if she were any ordinary kid at school. Ridzual sneaked looks at the nuggets as he was eating his tomyam noodles. When he had finished his noodles, he said casually, "What's that?"

Ah Lee had expected this. Food was for sharing. If she had been human she would have responded to his interest by offering him a nugget.

This simple unthinking generosity had been put beyond her power after her death—one reason why she had not bothered with friends until Ridzual. Fortunately there was a simple way of avoiding awkwardness.

"Pork," she said. She ate another nugget.

"I've always wondered what pork tastes like," said Ridzual to the air.

"I've always thought it's very important to respect other people's religion," said Ah Lee to the nuggets.

"What is life if you don't taste everything that the world has to offer?" said Ridzual.

"In this country we must accept other people's customs," said Ah Lee. "Not just tolerate, but respect. That is how to live together."

Ridzual laughed and gave up.

"If you don't want to share your nugget, say lah," he said. "Why so shy to admit you're greedy?"

"Who's greedy now?" said Ah Lee. "One bowl of tomyam, how many otak-otak—tak cukup ke? Your mother and father don't feed you?"

"I'm a man! Men need nutrition, OK," said Ridzual with dignity. Ah Lee made jeering noises through a mouthful of nugget.

Of course perfect happiness could not be allowed to continue without an aunt stepping in to intervene. If anyone had ever dared to suggest to the aunts that children should be allowed to make their own mistakes and learn from them, it would have horrified the aunts.

Ah Lee was doing her chemistry homework in the kitchen one afternoon when Aunty Girl said,

"Wah, studies so funny meh? Why are you smiling?"

Ah Lee started. She had been thinking about her conversation with Ridzual about nuggets, but she hadn't realized she was smiling.

"Nothing," she said.

"Must be that small boy," said Ji Ee.

"No!" said Ah Lee a little too loudly. "Everything is Ridzual this, Ridzual that. You think that's the only thing I think about, is it?"

Before this outburst, the aunts had been absorbed in their usual afternoon task of preparing dinner and had only been making chat for the sake of it. They squatted over their buckets of viscera, sorting the nice bits of the human innards (the intestines, the liver, the kidneys, the heart, the lungs) from the less nice bits (the spleen, the gallbladder, the esophagus).

Now the aunts were all interested. Aunty Girl even washed her bloody hands and came to sit at the table with Ah Lee.

"Who's this Ridzual?" said Ah Chor.

"She's talking about that Malay boy, Ma," said Ah Ma. "What's his name again—Ridzwan?"

"Oh, Ridzwan," said Ah Chor. "Why, Ah Lee still likes this Ridzwan? I thought that was all finished already!"

"Ah Lee doesn't so easily forget," Ji Ee chided.

"That's right," said Aunty Girl. "She doesn't stop liking things so fast. Remember when she was small, she liked that English show, what was it called"—she switched to English for the title—"'My Little Horsie.' She had all those horse toys, with the long hair and the stars on the backside. She liked it for two years! From four until six."

"It's because she has a good memory," said Ji Ee.

"Children usually don't remember things for so long," Ah Ma agreed. "Ah Lee only. Never forgets anything!"

"Men are not like My Little Heh Bee," said Ah Chor reprovingly. "There's no problem with liking little heh bee for a long time. But Ah Chor has already told you, so many problems come if you like a man."

"You should use your good memory to remember what is in your textbooks, not for remembering your boyfriend," said Sa Ee Poh.

"He is not my boyfriend," said Ah Lee. "We are just friends. Can't I have friends?"

"Ah Lee, friends are not a problem," said Ji Ee.

"No, you cannot have friends," said Ah Ma.

"Ma," Ji Ee protested. "You let me have friends when I was Ah Lee's age. There's nothing wrong with boy friends—not sweethearts, not at this age, but boy friends are OK. That's normal."

"Your time was different," said Ah Ma. "Ah Lee is not like you. Ah Lee is not normal."

She looked up at Ah Lee.

"Ah Lee, you are not like any of us," she said. "When we were young we could have boy friends."

"We couldn't," said Sa Ee Poh. "Not you and me. Never mind sweethearts. Ma didn't even allow us just to be friends with boys."

"Yes, I never let you," Ah Chor agreed. "After a certain age, it doesn't look nice for a good girl to be around boys too much."

Ah Ma ignored them.

"When we were older we could get married, and everybody could come to our wedding," she said. "There was nothing to hide. It's not the same for you.

"Ah Ma wants you to get married someday. Ah Ma wants you to graduate from university. Maybe you will never have children, but you can be a good scholar and have a good job. Other people will admire you. Your husband will respect you.

"But for this to happen, people cannot know. You must be very careful. You have to go to school so you can study, but you must make sure people don't remember you. No friends. Don't talk too much to teachers. You remember we all told you this before you started school again."

Ah Lee remembered. She stared at her exercise book. Ridzual had written "What does any of it MEAN?" at the bottom of the page. She had whited it out with liquid eraser, but the words showed through after the white fluid had dried.

"If you are friends with Ridzual that is even worse than if you like him," said Ah Ma tenderly. "You must not go around with him anymore."

"Don't do it suddenly," said Ji Ee. "Slowly just become more distant. Don't drop him immediately, but don't need to talk to him so much. He will get the hint."

"Things will change in the future," said Aunty Girl. "When you are older, at university, it'll be easier to hide. You can have friends there. But this place is too small. Everybody knows everybody's business. It's better to keep to yourself."

"There's no need to be so sad, girl," said Sa Ee Poh. "Even if you hurt his feelings, he won't remember you after a while. Young people recover very fast."

I will remember, thought Ah Lee. She did not want to cry because the aunts made such a fuss when you cried. She gulped and squeezed her pen and looked at Tua Kim.

Tua Kim was sorting through the slippery organs, listening to the conversation but not part of it. She said, eyes still on the bucket, "Every woman has secrets."

"Hah! Very true," said Aunty Girl. "When you get married, you won't be the only bride who knows something the groom doesn't know. Cousin Kah Hoe didn't even know his wife was pregnant until she had the baby six months after the wedding."

"He never found out who the father was also," said Sa Ee Poh.

"Shh! Eh, enough!" said Ah Chor, scandalized. "Shouldn't talk about such things."

"Don't listen to your naughty aunties," Ah Ma told Ah Lee.

How could you die and not be old enough to hear about pre-marital sex? How could you die and still not be allowed to fall in love or be honest? Surely not everything had to wait for university and a good job. Passion and truth had to trump even those things.

Still, it wasn't a conscious decision on Ah Lee's part to rebel. She was not even thinking about the many-aunted lecture when the urge to candor came to her.

It was a Thursday again, Ji Ee and Aunty Girl's line dancing day, and Ah Lee and Ridzual were hanging around waiting for their respective rides home. They had found the perfect width of concrete ledge to sit on next to the monsoon drain outside their school. From here they had an unobstructed view of the road, and a big leafy flame-of-the-forest provided dappled shade.

It was so sunny the whole world gave off a metallic glare. Ah Lee and Ridzual sat on their ledge, squinting at the road.

Ah Lee surprised herself when she said, "Ridzual, do you have any secrets?"

Once it was out she felt a great sense of relief. She knew she wanted to tell him. She was sick of keeping everything important to herself, hidden away from the piercing gaze of the aunts.

"Yah," said Ridzual slowly. "Yes. Funny you should say that. I've been thinking I should tell you one of them."

Ah Lee was nonplussed.

"Oh, but I was going to tell you—" she said. "Um, never mind."

"Oh, if you were going to say something, then you should say first," said Ridzual.

"No, it's OK, you go first," said Ah Lee.

"My secret isn't very interesting," said Ridzual. "You say first lah."

"My one is very interesting," said Ah Lee firmly. "It'll take long time to tell. You go first."

"Cannot," said Ridzual. He got up off the ledge, fell into a squat, bent his head and put his hands in his hair.

Ah Lee started to feel worried. She had never seen Ridzual act like this before. Something seemed really wrong. Maybe something bad had happened at home. She got up and touched his shoulder.

"Eh, why like this? What's wrong?"

"My life," moaned Ridzual.

Ah Lee felt relieved. If Ridzual was in a good enough mood to whine then he was manageable.

"Eh! Merajuk already," she said. "Don't need to sulk like that. How old are you?"

When Ridzual lifted his head she saw his eyes were wet.

"It's no big deal," he said. "It's nothing to you. There's nothing wrong. I just like you, that's all. That's my big secret. Probably you know already, probably it is very obvious. You want you laugh lah. But it's the first time I've ever been in l-love, so sorry if I want to make a big fuss about it."

He shoved his head under his arm and sniffed.

Ah Lee did not know what face to make.

"Oh," she said foolishly. "Oh—but—"

Ridzual threw up his hand.

"It's OK!" he said. "Don't say! I know the answer. I've embarrassed myself enough. Out of the kindness of your heart, can you please don't say anything?"

"But I—"

"For five minutes!" said Ridzual. "In five minutes my dignity will return. Just leave me in peace to enjoy my misery for five minutes, OK?"

Ah Lee began to frown.

"Don't need to be so drama," she said. "You think this is Cantonese serial or what? I had something to tell you too, remember?"

There was a pause in which Ridzual did not move or even show that he had heard. Then he rubbed his eyes. He rearranged his limbs, sat down on the ledge, and looked at her.

"Sorry," he said. "That wasn't so gallant of me."

"No," Ah Lee agreed. "Not gallant langsung."

"I'm not so good at this love declaration stuff," said Ridzual.

"Yah, true."

"You don't have to agree when I kutuk myself!" said Ridzual. He gave her the sweetest half-smile. His eyes were red and his lashes were still wet.

"What did you want to tell me?" he said.

"I—" said Ah Lee.

She found she could not do it. It was absurd. She had promised herself that she would tell him that she liked him, and not just as a friend. She *liked him* liked him.

It had seemed so easy five minutes ago. It ought to be even easier now. She had only to say, "I like you back." But what if Ridzual didn't believe her? What if he thought she was saying it to comfort him? What if, once she said it, he revealed that he had just been joking about liking her? Could she stand to give so much of herself away?

The words stuck in her throat. She said: "I—"

Through a process of thought even she did not understand, she swerved and went for what felt like the less difficult truth. She said: "I'm a vampire."

It was not the most intelligent thing she had ever done.

"What?" said Ridzual.

"That's why you can't share my nuggets," Ah Lee said wildly. "They're not not-halal because they're made of pork. They're not halal because they're made of human."

At first Ridzual looked as if he might believe her. He looked at her for a long time, his mouth grim. His eyebrows knitted, his mouth twisted—then his face cleared and he laughed.

"You're such a freak," said Ridzual. "You're the weirdest person I know. Is that how you always try to change the subject in an awkward situation? "'Scuse me, sir, your fly is undone. But don't worry about it, I'm a werewolf!'"

He rubbed his eyes.

"Sorry ya," he said. "I'll be normal again soon."

Ah Lee should have been relieved, or maybe touched, or any one of a number of benign emotions. Instead she felt vexed. You told someone the biggest secret you had and they didn't even take you seriously!

"You know, everything is not about you," she snapped. "I don't say things just because of you. Men!"

She changed to show him. It was always too easy to change when she was angry.

What was she thinking? she asked herself later. She knew that love was supposed to make you act funny, but she did not know that it could actually deprive you of all common sense. Or kindness. It was not kind to show that to a human.

What Ridzual saw was a cold, gray face, a face incontrovertibly dead. The features were Ah Lee's own everyday features, but the skin did not have the comforting human glow—the flush in the cheek, the sweat on the upper lip. The texture of it was such that it did not even look like skin. Her face looked like it was made of plastic.

The long, black hair hung around the face lankly. The eyes were white. When her mouth opened, a musty inorganic smell gusted out.

The tongue was bright red, the color of fresh arterial blood, and it was too long.

The teeth were perfectly ordinary.

Maybe a part of her was hoping that he wouldn't be horrified, that he would still like her. Most of her was the sensible Ah Lee she had always been, however, so it was with resignation that she watched Ridzual step back, drop his schoolbag, whimper and turn and run.

She watched him run down the road, his limbs flailing and growing smaller. When he reached the junction at the end of the road, he stopped and doubled over. He would be bathed in sweat—the sun was unforgiving today, and Ridzual always skipped PE class. He paused and Ah Lee could almost see him wonder whether he should scrape up his dignity and come back to the forgiving shade, or keep jogging and probably have sunstroke.

She felt her tragedy crust over with awkwardness.

"Why this kind of thing always happen to me?" said Ah Lee miserably.

But then, thank all the gods that ever were, Ji Ee's small brown Proton turned into the road. In five minutes Ah Lee would be able to get into the car and pretend she didn't see Ridzual walking back to their spot next to the monsoon drain, his hand shielding his eyes, his eyes not looking in her direction.

Ah Lee could not bear to ask Tua Kim to stop making her fried human nuggets. The first day after her confession she took them to the canteen as usual.

But then it was an agony to be sitting alone. It took so long to chew each nugget when she wasn't using her mouth for talking. She caught glimpses of Ridzual through the crowd, queueing up for his tomyam and awkwardly not looking at anyone because he didn't have any friends except her. The nuggets tasted like paper. It was as if she was eating human food.

After that she avoided the canteen. Behind one of the school blocks there was a narrow channel that ran between the building and

the wall that surrounded the school grounds. It had become a reposi-
tory for unwanted things: buckets of dried paint were lined up along
the wall, and broken old furniture came here to die. Ah Lee fit right
in. Here she could sit and read in peace, just as she had done before
she'd ever become friends with Ridzual.

A week after her life was ruined—five long, dreary days during
which she and Ridzual carefully ignored each other at school—she
had only got seven pages into her book. She was reading the eighth
page at break, the words flying out of her mind the minute they
entered through her eyes, when Ridzual said, "Good book?"

Ah Lee jumped and punched Ridzual in the chin.

"Ow!" said Ridzual.

"What lah you, coming out of nowhere like that," Ah Lee
snapped, to cover her relief.

"Sorry lah," said Ridzual in a mild complaining tone. He rubbed
his jaw. "What is this, WWF? Man, you have a strong right hook."

Awkwardness rose like a wall between them.

"It's because I did taekwando since I was small," said Ah Lee
flatly. "Not because I died."

Ridzual looked around for a chair, but failed to locate one. In a
government school, chairs only got rejected from classroom duty for a
real fault, such as having a hole in the middle of the seat, or being in
several pieces. He sat down on the ground instead.

"I didn't even know such things were real," he whispered. He did
not look up at her. "How did you become a—a—"

"Vampire?" said Ah Lee.

"Is that what you call it?" said Ridzual. "Isn't that a bit different?"

Ah Lee said, "You want to say it? You want to tell me what am I?"

Ah Lee never said the true term herself.

"Vampire" was safe. "Vampire" was like Dracula, like goofy old
black-and-white films, like pale ang moh boys who swooned over
long-haired girls. Vampire was funny, or sexy, depending on which
movie you watched.

The right word was not funny. It was not sexy. Most of all, it
was not safe.

Ridzual had a boyish disregard for subtextual cues. He did not seem to notice how wound up Ah Lee was. He said, softly, as if he were speaking to himself, "You know, I like you. I really like you."

"Har," said Ah Lee noncommittally.

"I've really never liked anyone as much as I like you," said Ridzual. "In my life. Not even as a, a girl. I've never even had a friend I liked as much as you.

"When I'm with you I feel like life is exciting. Like everything has an interesting secret behind it, like nothing is normal or boring. That's how you make me feel. Not even by doing anything. Just when I'm hanging out with you."

Ah Lee said in a stifled voice, "That's how I feel when I'm with you too."

Ridzual reached down into his pocket.

"That's why you deserve this," he said.

Ah Lee had just enough time to register that he had a long, rusty nail in his hand when Ridzual flung himself at her, aiming the nail at her throat.

When you are dead, certain things stop mattering as much as they do to the living. Time, weight, pain all lose some of their meaning.

The protein-rich diet and frequent exercise while chasing down prey are also excellent for the muscles.

Ah Lee caught Ridzual's lunging body and threw him with no trouble.

While he lay on the ground, stunned, she slipped the nail out from between his fingers.

"What's this?" she shouted. "What's this? You're trying to play the fool, is it?"

She felt as if the top of her head had come off.

Ridzual looked terrified.

"I was—I was—"

"What?" roared Ah Lee.

"I just—" Then Ridzual said, in one breath, "I Googled and it said if I put a nail in your neck you would stop being a hantu and become a beautiful woman, and I thought maybe then we could be together, but turn out I wasn't fast enough, I'm sorry—"

"How dare you?" gasped Ah Lee.

"I just wanted to save you, OK!" Ridzual rubbed his eyes. "I'm sorry I couldn't make it in time."

"Who do you think you're talking to?" said Ah Lee. "There is no Ah Lee the vampire and Ah Lee your friend—the girl who used to be your friend. I am just one person. If you make me not a vampire anymore, doesn't mean we can be—be dating. If you make me not a vampire anymore, means there is no me anymore. You understand?"

She threw the nail on the ground. She wasn't quite angry enough to aim it at Ridzual, but it pleased her in a horrible way when he flinched.

"And one more thing," said Ah Lee. "I am already a beautiful woman, dungu!"

She stomped off without looking back.

Ah Lee felt strong and brave all day, big with her righteous anger like a balloon full of air. It took her through the rest of the school day and the ride home.

When she took off her shoes at the front door, the air hit her nose, crowded with homey smells: coriander and hong yu and the stale scent of clean blankets. The balloon popped. Ah Lee drew in a huge breath and expelled it as a sob.

She sat down on the sofa in the living room and wept for half an hour.

"Girl, what's the matter?" said Ji Ee.

"What's happening?" said Ah Chor.

"Hao ah," said Ah Ma. "Crying!"

"Crying?" said Ah Chor. "Ah Lee is crying?"

"You're crying, is it?" said Sa Ee Poh.

The diagnosis bounced from aunt to aunt, each aunt repeating it to another for certainty.

"So old already still crying!" said Ah Chor.

"Nobody has died. Your stomach is not empty. What is there to cry about?" said Sa Ee Poh.

"Ah girl, don't cry lah, ah girl," said Ji Ee.

"Teacher scolded you, is it?" said Ah Ma. "Or is it because Ji Ee and Aunty Girl were late when they picked you up from school?"

"Ah, that's it, late!" said Ah Chor sternly. "Always late! What's the use of all this line dancing? Now you are late to pick Ah Lee up and you have made her cry."

"She is so big already. I thought she can look after herself for an hour," said Aunty Girl, but she spoke with contrition, conscious that she was in the wrong.

"Ah girl, don't cry," said Ji Ee. "Ji Ee won't be late anymore. We don't need to go dancing. Ah, so old already, we won't miss it!"

Ah Lee loved that Ji Ee and Aunty Girl danced. Her voice pushed through the terrible loneliness that locked her throat and said, "It's not that!"

"What is it?" said Aunty Girl.

"I never believed in all this dancing thing," said Ah Chor. "In my time girls didn't put themselves up there on the stage for people to look at it. It's not so nice."

"Ma, their dancing is not like cabaret," said Sa Ee Poh. "It is exercise, like taichi or aerobic. Anyway the girls are so big already. Why not let them do it?"

"Ah Lee says it's not that anyway," said Ah Ma. "What is it, girl?"

But Ah Lee couldn't say.

Tua Kim was the only one who had stayed in the kitchen when Ah Lee started crying. Now the sound of the running tap stopped and she came into the room, wiping her hands on a rag. A momentary lull had fallen as the aunts waited for Ah Lee to reply, so everyone heard Tua Kim when she spoke, even though her voice was as quiet as it always was.

"What did the boy do?" said Tua Kim.

The silence flattened out and grew solid.

In the hush, Tua Kim sat down on the sofa next to Ah Lee and put her arm around her. The aunts were not from a generation that hugged. Tua Kim did it in a detached, almost a clinical way. In the same way the aunts had picked Ah Lee up and carried her when she was too exhausted to walk, those first few hours after she died.

"Tell Tua Kim," said Tua Kim.

So she did.

Ah Lee went to bed feeling pleasantly hollow and tired from crying so much. Her eyes were red and the skin around her nostrils was rough, but she felt clean and quiet inside. Aunt after aunt came into her room on some pretext, to lay their soft, wrinkled hands on her head and make sure her blanket was tucked around her properly. She slept like the virtuous dead, dreamless and innocent.

The next morning she felt newly minted, born again. She walked past Ridzual's desk without a tremor, and went home feeling almost happy, feeling like maybe she could get over him and it would be OK someday.

It would start hurting again soon. The sense of invulnerability wouldn't last forever. The aunts would stop spoiling her and start chiding her for still being upset about it. But someday she'd stop being upset, stop missing Ridzual at all, and when she was done with school she would go to university far away from Lubuk Udang, and maybe there she'd meet someone nicer than Ridzual.

She needed quiet to study Add Maths, so instead of working in the kitchen as usual, she sat down in her room and buried herself in exercises until the light turned. She switched on her desk lamp, and the action made her aware of a quietness in the house.

She got up and walked through the silent, dark house, wondering. There was no one in the kitchen. The living room was empty. It was six-thirty, past the hour when Sa Ee Poh's favorite Cantonese serial would have begun—and yet the house was auntless.

They must have gone out hunting, though it was late for that. Ah Lee herself preferred to hunt at night, under the cover of darkness, but the aunts did not even think you should laugh loudly before going to bed, or it would give you nightmares. Hunting was considered far too stimulating an activity to engage in so close to bedtime. They preferred to hunt in the afternoon, when the household chores were done and the humans were dozy.

It was strange that they had all gone out at the same time. Even on the rare occasion that the aunts went out hunting in a body, one of them usually stayed at home—often Tua Kim, because Tua Kim disliked the mess and exertion of hunting. Somebody had to make sure Ah Lee fed herself and did her homework. Somebody had to look after her.

With that thought, Ah Lee knew where the aunts had gone.

She didn't bother going back to her room to turn off the lights, or changing out of her pasar malam T-shirt and faded gray shorts, or putting on shoes. She burst through the back door and leapt straight out into the evening sky.

Most of the time Ah Lee was a girl. Her body and her mind were more used to it. Being in vampire mode made her uncomfortable. She avoided it as much as she could.

But whenever she slipped into it, it was like putting on a pair of slippers after a long day of standing in high heels, like stepping out of a ferociously air-conditioned room into the welcoming warmth of the outside world.

Her whole self relaxed. Her body became a weapon: smells grew sharp, her vision cleared. Ordinary thoughts were big, vague clouds, too complicated and light to bother about, and through the clouds thrust the one vital thing, red and pulsing like a fresh bruise—hunger.

Hovering above Lubuk Udang, she became invisible. The dying sunlight shone through her bones. The scents of the town floated up to her: a woman's jasmine-scented hair, the stink of the underarms of a tired hawker stallholder, the smell of someone's earwax. Anything else, anything not human, smelled pale in comparison, like water, but she could distinguish those scents if she concentrated hard enough, pulling them up from beneath the textured smells of humans.

The aunts would smell of nothing. But she knew Ridzual's scent. She sorted through the scents coming to her on the wind; his wasn't there. It might be too late already. How long had it been since they'd

left? And once Ridzual was meat she wouldn't be able to find him—
he wouldn't smell of himself anymore. He would just smell of food.

She dove through the sky, following her nose.

The sky was going gray and the sunlight was fading when Ridzual
left school. His dad would be busy getting dinner ready and his mom
was outstation, so he'd told his dad he would cycle home. It would
take half an hour, but the air was soft and humid in the evening, cool
enough to cycle.

He hated koku, but he'd stayed for the extra few hours of marching in his Scout uniform, sweating under the blistering sun in a desperate attempt to fit in. It was probably worth it. If he didn't go, he
would probably fit in even less, whereas at least now people knew who
he was. Last week one guy had even thwacked him on the back in a
friendly way, yelling, "Oi! What's up, Mohsein?"

Of course, he had then had to explain that he wasn't Mohsein,
which had dampened the atmosphere of warmth and camaraderie
slightly. But they had recognized the name when he said, "I'm Ridzual," or at least they had said, "Oh, Ridzwan, is it?"

Maybe he wasn't friends the way the other guys were with each
other. Maybe they didn't shout, "Oi, macha!" when they saw him, or
request that he "relaklah, brother!" or imply heartily that he was gay
in some sort of macho bonding ritual.

But Ridzual had never been the kind of guy who attracted that
response from his fellow guys, and he was OK with that. He flew
under the radar enough that he'd never been bullied. People let him
do his own thing, and that was all he wanted. He hadn't even really
noticed not having friends. In KL he'd hung out with his cousins, who
were used to him being the weird one and didn't hold it against him,
and here in Lubuk Udang there was Ah Lee.

Had been. There had been Ah Lee.

His brain had successfully been avoiding the subject of her for
all of ten minutes, but now it slid back down the old path. He kept
forgetting and thinking of her as his friend, as the girl he'd fallen in

love with. And if you thought of her as a human being, it was horrific what he had done to her. He had been a prize asshole, an unmitigated jerk.

But before he could begin beating himself up for messing up the best thing that had ever happened to him, he'd remember that face she'd turned to him. And that made him not know how to feel again. That face had not been human. Kindness wasn't a thing that lived in the same world as that face.

He'd been having nightmares ever since he saw it. The teeth, he'd think in the dream, struggling in the grip of terror, the teeth.

That was the scariest thing. The one mad, inexplicable thing in the whole mad, inexplicable situation that got to him.

How come there wasn't anything wrong with her teeth?

They had been perfectly human teeth. Even, rounded at the edges, slightly yellow.

He had to stop thinking about this. There was nothing he could do about it. Maybe she wasn't a vampire. Maybe she was deluded and he'd been hallucinating. Or maybe she was a vampire, but she wouldn't kill and eat him as long as he left her alone. She knew he wouldn't tell anyone. Who could he tell? Who believed in vampires anyway?

"Stupid," said Ridzual aloud. The word wasn't "vampire." "Vampire" wasn't scary enough to describe the thing he'd seen. It was like calling a toyol a pixie.

"Not vampire," said Ridzual. "The word is 'pontianak.'"

The problem with Ridzual was that he was a city boy. He'd grown up watching Japanese superhero TV shows and reading Archie comics. He hadn't really known his grandparents—they'd died when he was too little to hold conversations, much less be told scary stories.

So he knew nothing.

He didn't recognize the scent that sprang out of the evening then, though he registered it as something floral. It reminded him of Ah Lee: it smelled of her. It was funny that it had never occurred to him that Ah Lee might use perfume.

He'd cycled on a little further when he heard the baby crying. A long wail, followed by a piteous sob-sob-sob that pierced the heart. It was startling how close it was—practically next to his ear. He braked by the side of the road and got off his bike.

It was an odd place for a baby to be. He was standing on the edge of a car park. Across the road was a row of shoplots, their signs still lit up, but the entrances a line of closed gray faces.

The car park was an expanse of orange earth, dusty and crumbling and covered with weeds. It was fenced with rusting wire, and shrubs ran along its periphery. There weren't many cars parked there, and the booth at the entrance was dark.

The falling light turned the place eerie. It was the kind of place where you could get done for khalwat, or be murdered, depending on who else was around.

It was the kind of place where you could dump a baby, if you needed to.

He'd read about baby-dumping in the newspapers. But you never thought you'd encounter such things yourself. And not in such a place as this, surely—a nice small town? This wasn't KL.

Who would dump a baby? said a voice in Ridzual's head. Someone young, who wasn't supposed to be doing anything that would lead to a baby in the first place. Someone scared.

He parked his bike on the pavement and walked into the car park. The floral scent grew stronger, though there weren't any flowers around that he could see—only the bushes, strung out around the car park like a salad God had started eating and left forgotten on His plate.

The baby would be somewhere in there, probably. But he couldn't seem to work out where. The farther he walked in what he thought was the direction of the sound, the softer the baby's cries got.

It was getting darker. The world was a pale purply-blue, and the moon showed clear in the sky. The car park was full of dark shapes—empty cars, rustling bushes. The cicadas were screaming their heads off, and the baby was getting so soft he could hardly hear it through the insects—but it was still crying, a long, drawn-out wail, trailing off in a hopeless series of hiccups.

He was terrified, but if he was scared, how would an abandoned baby feel?

He found something behind the next bush. It wasn't a baby, though. It was an old lady, lying crumpled on the ground in a pathetic heap of batik and gray hair.

"Shit," said Ridzual without thinking. He bent down and reached out to touch the lady's shoulder: "Sorry, mak cik. Are you OK?"

The face the mak cik turned to him was a normal mak cik face. She was a Chinese lady with fluffy white hair and a mole on her left cheek. She looked like any other auntie you might see at the pasar basah. Her teeth were perfectly ordinary. She was dead.

Ridzual stumbled back. He was shaking so hard his teeth rattled in his head.

Teeth! Of course there was nothing wrong with the teeth. Teeth was vampires. Pontianak didn't pierce the neck with fangs. They didn't drink your blood.

The mak cik held her hands out to Ridzual, as if she was going to hug him, pet his hair. Her hands were small and delicate. The fingernails were long, curving, and yellow—and blunt.

It would take a long time for those fingernails to pierce his belly, to scoop out the intestines. It would hurt.

The others came out of the bushes one by one. They were all little old ladies—little old Chinese ladies in those Chinese old lady clothes that looked like pajamas. All with long, blunt fingernails. All dead.

All hungry.

"No," someone whimpered. Ridzual thought of the baby before realizing it was his own voice. "No, no, please, no—"

He turned and went running, crashing through the bushes. Somewhere in the distance a baby was screaming breathlessly, but he knew the wail was issuing from six dry old dead mouths, and it grew softer and softer the closer they were.

His chest was a great flame of pain. He banged his hand against the side-mirror of a car and knew it would hurt later (if there was a later), but it felt like nothing now. He couldn't hear the baby anymore.

A weight hit him in the back and he went down, sobbing. The fingernails dug into his side. Cold, musty breath gusted on to his ear.

He was going to die. He was sorry for everything. The fingernails cut into his skin, raising welts, and he opened his mouth to scream.

The next minute his mouth was full of earth and pebbles. Something had hit the creature on his back a full-body blow, the impact driving Ridzual's face into the ground. The pontianak rolled off his back, ripping his T-shirt in the process.

They must be fighting over him. There wasn't enough of him to go around, even if they were small. Old ladies didn't usually have much of an appetite, but pontianak were probably different. He had a second while they were distracted, but no more. He struggled to his feet, willing his limbs to move.

It came as something of a surprise to hear one of the pontianak saying, in an angry mak cik croak, "Ah girl, what you doing here? You go home right now! So late already!"

He should run.

He turned around slowly.

It was Ah Lee, glaring at the old lady who had been about to eat him.

"Who ask you to eat my schoolmate?" she said shrilly. "How'm I suppose to go back to school now? So lose face!"

The pontianak crowded around. Weirdly, they had lost all their eldritch horror: they looked like ordinary mak ciks now. They were definitely talking like aunties, in indignant high-pitched Hokkien.

"And what are you doing?" snapped Ah Lee.

"Me? What am I doing? What are you doing?" said Ridzual.

"Standing around like this! You want to be eaten, is it?" said Ah Lee.

"No!" said Ridzual.

"Go away," said Ah Lee.

Ridzual had one last chance. He didn't understand everything that had just happened—in fact, it would be more accurate to say that he didn't understand anything that had just happened. But she'd saved his life, and not, it appeared, because she wanted to eat him herself.

You wouldn't save someone's life if you were a monster, would you?

You wouldn't save someone if you thought they were a monster.

"Ah Lee," said Ridzual. "We need to talk."

"Not now," said Ah Lee. Her voice was a door closing. "I need to talk to my family."

The last he saw of her, in that dwindling light, was her gallant back moving away from him, and the cloud of aunts drawing in around her.

Ah Lee decided to try something new.

In the morning she waited outside the school gate until Ridzual arrived. When his parents' car had driven off, she said, "Let's go."

They couldn't go to a kopitiam or mamak restaurant in their school uniforms, so they went to a nearby park. It was early, cool enough to walk. They didn't talk much on the way.

There were a couple of people in the park—an uncle and an auntie, walking in circles with serious, intent looks on their faces. But the kids' playground was empty and they settled down on the swings there.

Ridzual broke the silence first.

"What happened last night, after I went?"

"Oh. Nothing much," said Ah Lee.

"Was it—" Ridzual hesitated. "Did they—?"

Ah Lee stared at him mutely.

Dealing with the aunts had actually been less difficult than she had expected. They had told her off for not staying home and doing her homework, but it was a half-hearted telling off. The aunts knew they had forfeited the moral high ground by trying to eat her classmate. Ah Lee had listened without saying a word to their unconvinced lectures as they flew home.

At the door, she had turned and said to the aunts: "We are not dogs in the forest."

She had gone straight to bed without speaking to anybody.

She felt guilty about it in the morning—she had said too much. The aunts had already known that they'd overstepped the line, broken the rules by which they operated. The aunts seemed to feel equally ashamed, tiptoeing around her at breakfast.

She had kissed Ah Ma with special tenderness before leaving for school, particularly as she was already planning to ponteng and knew how shocked the aunts would be at that. Non-attendance at school would probably seem a worse crime to them than eating humans.

She didn't know how to explain any of this to Ridzual. It all seemed too complicated.

"Did you have to fight, or—I don't know—something?" said Ridzual. Ah Lee could tell that he was already feeling foolish about having asked. "I mean—never mind."

He paused.

"Do you really eat people?"

"Not really people," said Ah Lee. "Only their, you know, their usus, all that. Their entrails." She tapped her belly. "We don't like all the other parts."

Ridzual screwed up his mouth. But he only said: "Thanks for not eating me. And not letting those others eat me."

Ah Lee shrugged. "Usually they won't eat you anyway. We don't eat people we know. They all were just angry only."

Ridzual looked down at his feet. He was scratching shapes in the sand with the toe of one shoe.

"You guys can't eat anything else?" he said. "Like, animal intestines?"

"No."

"Do you eat good people as well, or only bad people, or—?"

"We don't eat women," said Ah Lee. "And we don't eat people we know. That's all. I don't pick and choose, depending if I like your face or I don't like your face so much."

"Not women?" said Ridzual. "I didn't realize vampires did affirmative action."

"It's already suffering enough to be a woman," Ah Lee recited. "Don't need people to eat you some more."

This was Ah Chor's line, but the aunts were unanimous on this. Hadn't Ah Ma told Ah Lee how she had cried whenever she gave birth to a daughter, because she knew what sorrow lay in her future?

"After all there's enough men around," added Ah Lee.

Ridzual grinned, but he looked a little sick.

"Doesn't it bother you?" he said. "At all?"

Ah Lee stared into the distance. It was hard to explain. She had felt differently about these things when she was living.

"I know what you are trying to say," she said. "But it's like animals."

"You feel it's like eating animals?"

"No!" said Ah Lee. "It's like *I'm* the animal now. After I die I kind of became an animal. When I'm hungry, when I eat, there's no feeling. Afterwards maybe some feeling, I feel a bit bad. But that's why we don't simply just eat people. We process them first. My aunties like to make pepper soup. You know too thor t'ng? Pig stomach soup? Like that, but not with pig stomach."

"Oh," said Ridzual faintly. "Wait, all those old ladies last night—they're your aunties?"

"One is my grandma and one is my great-grandma," said Ah Lee. "The others are my aunties. But don't you think it's a bit weird if there's so many vampire in a small town like this and they don't know each other?"

Ridzual opened his mouth. Then he closed it, his throat working.

"That's definitely weird," he said in a strangled voice.

"Anyway, don't worry about my aunties. They won't eat you," said Ah Lee. "I told them already. And I won't eat you. Never never."

"I know," said Ridzual.

Ah Lee looked at the ground. She felt her eyes start to prickle, so she said it quickly.

"Are you going to try to nail me?"

She was startled and not a little offended when Ridzual started chortling.

"What's so funny?" Ah Lee demanded.

"Er," said Ridzual. "It's an American thing. Maybe I'll tell you some day."

"This is suppose to be serious!" said Ah Lee.

"Sorry, sorry." Ridzual wiped his eyes. "I'm not going to nail you. No."

Saying it seemed to sober him up.

"I'm sorry I tried it," he said.

"Thank you," said Ah Lee. Now the next thing. "You don't have to be friends with me anymore. I won't be offended. I'll understand."

She had to say it. Then it would be done, finished, and they could both go back to their respective lives with all of this behind them.

"It was kind of worth it." Ah Lee kept her eyes on the ground. She would be too shy to say it if she looked at Ridzual. "Ever since I became like this, I didn't really have friends. It was a bit lonely. So it was nice having you."

"I don't want to be friends with you," said Ridzual.

Ah Lee had expected this answer, but she was still taken aback by how much it hurt to hear it. She had been sad about him enough, she told herself sternly. All the aunts had said that.

"Don't waste so many tears on one man," they had scolded, as if it would have been all right to spread out the tears over several men, but not to allocate so many to only one person.

Ah Lee, having been brought up to hate waste, agreed with them. She locked her hands together and blinked furiously. Her chest ached.

"OK," she said.

Ridzual touched her hand. Ah Lee clenched it into a fist so he couldn't take it, but then he tried to pry her fingers apart one by one. Of course it didn't work. Ah Lee started giggling.

"Ah, I give up," said Ridzual, exasperated. "I'm a moron to try to fight a pontianak. But look, 'I don't want to be your friend' doesn't mean 'I don't want to hang out with you'. There can be another meaning."

"What other meaning?" said Ah Lee. She looked up when he didn't answer.

Ridzual was looking at her with a kind of glow in his eyes. It was the way her mother and father used to look at her, back when she was alive, before all the bad things had happened—as if she was something special. Something precious. Ah Lee's ex-boyfriend had never looked at her like that.

Ridzual had always had this look, Ah Lee realized. He had always looked at her as if she was the sunrise after a long, dark night.

"Oh," said Ah Lee.

"You don't have to not want to be my friend back," said Ridzual.

Ah Lee hesitated. But there was a perfect way to say yes and still sound cool.

"I don't mind," she said.

Ridzual turned his face away, but he was too slow. Ah Lee already knew he was beaming. She reached out and took his hand, encountering less trouble than he had done.

"OK," said Ridzual. "That works."

They smiled stupidly for a while, shedding radiance on the slide and sandbox, showering incidental romance on the speed-walking uncle and auntie.

"Only one thing," said Ah Lee.

"Oh, there's something else on top of the vampire mak cik and the human pig stomach soup?" said Ridzual. "What more is there? I have to fight a werewolf first before I can date you, is it?"

"No lah, there's no such thing as werewolf," said Ah Lee. "It's a small thing only. But—'vampire' is OK. The other word, please don't use. Is that OK?"

"Why?" said Ridzual.

"It's not such a nice word," said Ah Lee.

"OK," said Ridzual. "OK."

Then he said, "Can I use it one last time?"

Ah Lee nodded. She knew what was coming.

"Will you tell me how you became a pontianak?"

Sitting there with him in the park, Ah Lee told him. She had not told anyone else the story before. He didn't let go of her hand.

Her grandmother watched her being born. Her grandmother watched her die.

Who died in childbirth in the twenty-first century? It didn't happen. Not if you were middle class in Malaysia. Not if you'd followed the rules and paid attention at school and listened to your parents.

Not if you'd been a good girl.

By the time her parents had suspected, it hadn't been too late. That was the thing. The worst thing—worse than being dumped by the boy who'd given her the baby, though that had felt terrible when it'd happened.

But it was nowhere near as bad as her parents' carefully expressionless faces, as they had gone from day to day pretending nothing was happening. The day she fainted because she'd thrown up all her breakfast and had hidden in her room and refused to eat—they hadn't said anything. When she choked on her food because things tasted different now she was pregnant, they didn't say anything. She stopped going to school. Her parents stopped talking to her. Her world contracted.

It was like being invisible. It was as if she had died and no one had noticed.

Months of it, months of feeling sad and ashamed, but now that it had become serious enough that even her parents could not ignore it, now that she was in the hospital and somebody was looking after her, Ah Lee did not feel free, or relieved.

She felt angry. She resented her parents wildly for breaking their promise that they would protect her, for failing to love her no matter what.

And still she was sorry that the secret had to come out—the baby had to come out—and they would lose face. She wished she could be dying in some less embarrassing way. She could have drowned in a monsoon drain. She could have been run over by a car.

She felt bad for them. But she wished they would stop hanging over her bed and crying.

"I'm sorry, girl. Mummy's so sorry, girl."

Sorry no cure, Ah Lee wanted to say.

After a while it stopped. Somebody took her parents away. Ah Lee regretted her silent fury. She missed them. Somebody was doing something pointless down there. She was bleeding.

When she died someone was holding her hand. Not a mother or a father, with their enormous burden of expectation. Someone calmer, their hands softer, wrinklier-skinned. At the very last moment Ah Lee opened her eyes and saw her grandmother, waiting for her.

After death:

The scent of frangipani—the stench of decay—revenge a red flame at the heart.

Her hair whipped against her face, smelling of the mulch in a graveyard. Her nails were long and yellow. Her body was free. She got up on the bed and nothing hurt.

She had lost all sense of the disgusting. She had bled so much that she would never flinch from blood again. She was made for tearing out kidneys, feasting on livers, pulling out strings of intestines. It would never again be her own blood that was spilt, her insides that were pulled inside out.

She flew down the corridors of the hospital and there was no pain—or rather, everything was pain, but it spun outward, knocking people over, ripping heads off. Blood sprayed on the walls. People were screaming.

Someone grabbed the wrists of the hurricane. Someone slapped the face of the typhoon.

"Enough! Stop now!" The voice was as familiar to her as her mother's. She would have killed anyone else, but the voice brought her down.

"Angry already, har?" said the voice.

"Just because you're angry doesn't mean everybody else must suffer!" scolded another voice.

Blood was rolling down from her eyes. She blinked, but her eyes stung.

The world was a smear. She couldn't see a thing.

"Quieting down already."

"Can listen now."

"Can see now."

"Close your eyes, Ah Lee."

"Close your eyes, girl."

Someone brushed a damp cloth over her eyelids. When she opened her eyes, she saw who it was.

"No need to cry," said Ah Ma. "No need for all this. Come, we are going somewhere else. Then you can lie down, rest first. You'll feel nicer after that."

"Where are we going?" said Ah Lee. Her voice came out in a hoarse whisper, scraping her throat. It was sore from the screaming. "Where's Mummy and Daddy?"

"Mummy and Daddy have to look after your brothers and sister," said an old lady in a baju kebaya. Ah Lee had never seen her before, but she leant her head trustingly against the old lady's chest when the old lady picked her up.

She felt as tired as if she had just been born.

"What about the baby?" she whispered.

"The baby's gone," said Ah Chor. It was the first time they met. "Don't worry. We'll look after you now."

"Ji Ee?" said Ah Lee blearily, as her eyes began to pick out familiar faces. "Tua Kim? Aunty Girl?"

"I don't have children," said Ji Ee.

"My children are all grown up," said Tua Kim.

"How to let you go alone?" said Aunty Girl. "Now you don't need to worry. We'll be with you."

There was something to tell them.

"Ah Ma," said Ah Lee.

"Yes, girl?"

Shame washed over her. It had been bad enough with her parents. How could you tell your grandmother something like this?

"The baby," she said. "The father. I didn't purposely—at the start, I wasn't thinking about all that. I just liked him. We were dating, and it just happened. When I found out I was pregnant, I didn't know what to do. I was scared to tell anybody. And then, Mummy and Daddy—"

She didn't know what to say about that worst betrayal. She still felt sorry. She had not had the chance to apologize, to explain.

"Can you tell them?" she said. "Tell them it was an accident. I didn't purposely—I didn't think. I didn't think this would happen. Tell them I'm sorry."

They were walking down the hospital corridor. Ah Chor cradled Ah Lee to her chest, stepping over the bodies.

"Ah Ma already said there's no need to cry," said Ah Ma. "It's not your fault. Your Mummy and Daddy should have looked after you. Ah Ma tried to teach your Mummy to bring up her children right, but there's no need to be so strict. You are her daughter, whether you are good or naughty. Ah Ma should have explained."

"We all should be saying sorry," said Sa Ee Poh. She didn't mean just the aunts. "You are only a child."

"Never mind. It's over already," said Ah Chor. "Don't worry about it anymore."

When they reached the stairwell at the end of the corridor, Ah Lee was already half asleep. When they smashed through the glass and jumped out the window, seven floors up, she was sleeping. She didn't feel the night wind on her skin, or see the starlight on the aunts' faces.

When she woke up she was a new person. She was dead, but she wasn't alone. There was nothing to be scared of in this new life. With six aunts behind you, you can be anything.

Balik Kampung

There were a lot of unexpected things about being dead. The traffic was one of them.

Time passed differently here in the netherworld, so Lydia might have been perched on the back of her cheap motorcycle, clinging to her demon, for hours or years or centuries. Every once in an eon they moved about three centimeters along. The light of the living world shone maddeningly at the end of the tunnel, not so very far away from them—but the intervening space was crammed full of hungry ghosts, using every form of transport they could beg, borrow, or steal for their trip up north for the Festival.

"Can't believe the traffic is so bad," she said to her demon. "It's halfway through the month already!"

"You should see this road on the first day," said her demon. "The queue goes all the way back. Like this is not so bad."

Since the dead were only allowed into the living world for one month in each year, the time was precious. Lydia was only so late because nobody had been burning hell money for her, and it had been a struggle to get together the funds to buy some form of transport.

She'd only managed to get the bike by promising to be bonded to a hell official for the next year. It was what they called a kapcai—a small, aged Honda of the kind hawkers took their kids to school on and Mat Rempits raced with. Fortunately her demon was as bony as most demons were, and didn't take up much space.

The demon had been another surprise. It had appeared the day she arrived in the netherworld. At first she had been too stunned by grief, too numbed by strangeness, to question the tangle-haired creature who followed her around hell. By the time she got around to questioning it, she'd grown used to its unvarying calm, its voice that was like the echo of the voice inside her own head. Its answer felt like something she had already known.

"I am your personal agony," it said.

"What agony?" said Lydia.

"You'll figure it out when you understand why are you a hungry ghost," said the demon.

Hungry ghosts were the spirits of the unfortunate, unlamented dead: those who were killed violently; who died burdened by unfulfilled longings; who had been greedy or ungenerous in life; who were forgotten by their living. It was obvious to Lydia which category she fell into.

"I don't care about my parents anymore," she said to her demon.

It wasn't bravado. Lydia had long made her peace with the fact that she was not the daughter her parents had wanted, and they were not flexible enough people to love her in spite of it. Stuck in the traffic jam, she thought not of them but of Wei Kiat.

Thinking about him and their home in Penang made the wait easier. The tunnel leading up to the human world wasn't the most pleasant place to while away a few hours. The rock walls were painted with the inventive torments to which the wicked dead were subjected—disrespectful sons and daughters having their tongues torn out; incompetent physicians being chopped to pieces; litterers being made to kneel on spikes; cursers of the wind being bitten by grasshoppers and kicked by donkeys.

Around Lydia the other hungry ghosts were discussing what they would do once they were out.

"Bastard, if the fella knew how to do his job I won't be dead now. I'm gonna find his clinic and then that guy better watch out. He better get used to killing his patients."

"It's not like RM5 is such a big deal. It's just annoying, you know? I was dying also she couldn't bring herself to pay me back. Maybe it's too much to possess somebody for that, but if not it's gonna keep bothering me lor."

"Yah, go for the Christians. The less superstitious the better. They're not prepared because they don't believe in hantu all that. Muslim also can, I guess, but I prefer to possess Chinese, feels more comfortable . . . Anyway, have you ever met a skeptic Melayu?"

"No lah, I'm not gonna do all this possessing stuff. Die already, no point holding grudges. I'm gonna go home, see how my relatives are doing, smell my ah ma's rendang."

"You're going home to see your family, is it?" said one of the older ghosts to Lydia. She was traveling by bullock cart, and spoke a Hokkien so strangely accented that Lydia struggled to follow it.

"Yes," said Lydia. "What about you, auntie?"

"Hai, I'm too old to have relatives to visit," said the ghost. "I have some great-great-grandchildren in Muar, but they all speak Mandarin and play their iPhones only. Nowadays I only go to the living world to see the shows."

"Auntie must find the shows very different," said Lydia. "Even when I was small I remember there were more operas, puppet shows, that kind of thing. These days you only see girls in miniskirts singing Cantopop."

The antique ghost lowered her voice to a confidential whisper.

"I don't mind the Cantopop girls," she said. "After all, the weather is so hot. Why shouldn't they wear something cooling?"

"That's very open-minded of you, auntie."

"Just because you're dead doesn't mean you can't be flexible," said the old woman. "So you're visiting your family har? Where do your parents live?"

"My husband, auntie," said Lydia. "He's in Penang."

In Penang. As she sat there in the stinking dark, her arms wrapped around her personal agony, a vision of the small terrace house she and Wei Kiat had lived in together rose up before Lydia. The low gate, with the patches of rust where the gray paint was peeling away; the narrow front yard Lydia had populated with potted bougainvilleas. She'd had them in every conceivable hue: magenta, rose pink, peach, lilac, deep purple, white. Every day she'd come home from work and exult over the wash of color spread out before her front door.

She saw her house so clearly she could almost feel the grainy texture of the grille swinging open under her hand. Their living room was floored in fake marble, dim and cool even on the hottest of days. Lydia had furnished it with old-fashioned cane chairs and rag rugs. Wei Kiat had admired her taste.

"You should be an artist," he'd told her. "You look at things so differently."

She was always finding out delightful new things about herself with Wei Kiat. He saw in her depths her parents would never have seen, talents and virtues unsuspected even by herself.

She knew she could not expect her home to have stayed the same while she was dead, but there would be a profound comfort simply in seeing it again, in feeling the tiles cool against her bare feet, and smelling the air in her house: a smell that was a mix of old newspapers, clean laundry, and the curry perpetually being cooked next door.

"We'll have to come out at KL," the demon said. "That's the only exit for Malaysia."

Which was why she'd needed the motorcycle. The dead were disappointingly limited. It was no more possible for her to fly herself to Penang than it would have been when she was alive.

At least, Lydia reflected, the demon knew how to ride a motorbike. She'd never ridden a motorcycle in her life—her parents had thought it unsafe, and Wei Kiat had driven her everywhere in his Chevrolet—but the demon piloted their vehicle with consummate ease.

When they finally emerged into the living world, somewhere behind KL Sentral, it was several hours past sunset. The lights of KL were blinding after the dim red caverns of hell. The starless vault of the night sky seemed too big. Lydia hunched down behind the demon as if it could protect her.

"Hopefully we missed rush hour," said the demon. "Jam out of hell, jam out of KL, everywhere also jam jam jam. If the government stop playing the fool and improve our public transport we won't have this problem."

"Do we have to stay here?" said Lydia. She'd grown up in KL, but she felt no nostalgia for the city. The constant honking of car horns made her flinch. The living, bustling around her, smelt too strongly and felt too sad.

"You don't want to visit your parents?" said the demon. "We can drop by TTDI first."

Lydia shook her head, her hair brushing against the back of the demon's polo shirt.

"Home," she said.

The farther they got from KL, the less populated the roads were. The glow of the orange streetlights on the unfolding measures of asphalt, so infinitely familiar, calmed Lydia down.

"When are we reaching ah?" she said.

"You know how long it takes," said the demon. "You sure or not you want to go?"

"What else do people do when they have holiday, aside from balik kampung?"

"You don't want to find out how you died meh?"

Lydia didn't remember how she had died. She hadn't tried to recover the memory. She didn't want to be like other hungry ghosts, clinging to historic grievances, hagridden by old sorrows. As in life, she had managed to get by in hell by sheer discipline: focusing on survival, hope, the image stored inside her of the red-tiled roof of her home, glowing in the sunshine.

"It's not important," she said.

"If you don't even know where you're coming from, how can you understand where you're going?"

"Eh, are you my demon or my feng shui master? Can you please concentrate on the road?"

"It's not like it makes any difference if we have an accident," said the demon grumpily, but it shut up.

~~~

The demon insisted on stopping off at Kampar. "We should try the curry chicken bread. It's very famous."

"We don't need to eat or pee," said Lydia. "Stop for what?"

"After you're dead for a while you won't need to act human anymore, but you haven't adjusted yet," said the demon. "Might as well eat. You've never had curry chicken bread before. Remember what the auntie said. Dead also still can be flexible."

"Easy for her to say! She got nobody to visit," snapped Lydia. "I only have fifteen days. And I might have to waste time trying to find Wei Kiat."

"Wei Kiat is not going anywhere," said the demon, unmoved. "Come lah, let's make you less hungry."

Since they could hardly stride into a restaurant to order the world-famous Kampar curry chicken bread, it was necessary to hang around the restaurant kitchen and dive at the dishes before they were carried out to the living punters. This made Lydia uncomfortable.

"They can still eat," the demon said. "It's not like we're stealing. We only eat the *spirit* of the food."

"It feels weird," said Lydia. Being a spirit gave her a weird double vision. On one level, in the material world, the plate of chicken bread her demon had despoiled was perfect, unmarred. In the spiritual world, half of the bun had been removed and the curry was leaking out the side. "Can't we just go outside and eat the offerings?"

As was usual during the Festival, there were offerings of food laid at the roadside: small piles of rice and fruit and lit incense set out by devotees.

The demon was offended. "Fine," it said. "If you want to have cold rice instead of chicken curry, suit yourself."

"Maybe I will!"

"Hungry ghosts I've heard of before," said the demon, "but I didn't know got such thing as *dieting* ghosts."

It was when they were walking back to the motorbike that they heard the unmistakable sound of the Hungry Ghost Festival being celebrated by the living: the strains of Cantopop, blaring at top volume out of doors at ten o'clock in the evening.

"We might as well check it out," said the demon. "What else do people do when they have a holiday?"

Lydia pretended not to hear it, but she found herself drifting toward the light and noise.

The Festival tents had taken over a whole road. A huge effigy of the King of Hades dominated one tent, flanked by effigies of the guardians of the underworld. An urn full of joss-sticks sent up curls of scented smoke before his stern blue visage.

The tents bustled with people, both living and dead. Food was set out for the ghosts, a much more attractive array of dishes than the roadside plates of rice. Lydia took a pink rice cake. As she drew back from the table she almost upset another ghost's plastic cup of orange cordial.

"Sorry," she said.

"No problem," said the ghost. He was struggling to balance a paper plate loaded with food and his cordial. "You're only eating so little ah? There's a suckling pig at the other table there."

Lydia was going to say she wasn't hungry, but realized in time how stupid that would sound. "Is it? I'll go find it. Thank you, uncle."

"That's right," said the uncle. "Not like when we're alive, can celebrate New Year, Thaipusam, Hari Raya, Mooncake Festival, all that. Now we only get one holiday a year. Better make the most of it!"

Everyone seemed uncommonly cheerful—the dead stocking up on provisions, the living praying at the various altars. Lydia hadn't even known she'd grown so used to the hangdog looks of the other ghosts and the bureaucratic indifference of the hell officials. Despite her sense of urgency, her mood began to lighten under the influence of the atmosphere.

She only glanced at the stage set up at the end of the road, but it was enough to tell her that the show would have pleased the open-minded bullock cart auntie. The girls onstage would not have looked out of place at a beach, except for their go-go boots.

As at every ko tai she'd seen in life, the front row of seats was reserved for the ghosts. The only difference now was that she could see the occupants.

But the focus of interest seemed to be somewhere else. She followed the crowd to another tent, where a man in robes was blessing the living. She was about to move away again when the man turned and looked straight at her and the other hungry ghosts watching.

"Sorry ah, good brothers," he said. "I'm almost finished here. Let me drink some water first and I'll be ready."

"He's a medium," said Lydia's demon. "Why don't you talk to him?"

"I thought only the living liked to consult mediums," said Lydia. "Send messages to their relatives all that. Spirits talk to medium for what?"

While she was speaking a queue of hungry ghosts had formed behind her. Lydia paused, embarrassed.

"You think what?" said the demon. "For the same reason lah."

"Good evening, sister," said the medium. The beads of sweat on his forehead and upper lip gleamed in the fluorescent light, but he smiled at Lydia with genuine friendliness. "Have you eaten?"

Lydia nodded. "The food is very good."

"The Festival committee is run by the local hawkers," said the medium. "So the catering is not bad. How can I help you, sister?"

Lydia had to pause to formulate her question. Despite growing up in KL she only spoke enough Cantonese to order food and watch subtitled Hong Kong dramas. Her parents had spoken Hokkien, and living in Penang had meant that what little Cantonese she had was rusty.

The sentence she produced wasn't the sentence she'd expected. She opened her mouth and heard herself say: "How did I die?"

The medium blinked. "You don't know meh?"

"I don't remember," said Lydia. "Can't you tell me?"

The medium looked confused. He took off his spectacles and polished them before putting them back on.

"Sorry ah, sister," he said. "Usually the living come and ask me questions. The good brothers and sisters just send messages. Advice, life lessons, that kind of thing. You are the ones with the wisdom what."

"I was only late twenties when I died," said Lydia. "It was recently only. I haven't had much time to become wise yet."

"Ah," said the medium. He scratched his head. "If sister gives me your name I will try to find out for you how you passed on. I'll look tomorrow."

"By tomorrow I won't be in Kampar already," said Lydia. Frustration surged in her. She should never have stopped to talk. Every minute she spent here was a minute she could have used to get to Wei Kiat. And she hadn't even asked the right question. "Never mind. Sorry to waste your time, sifu."

"That is not a problem," said the medium. "To contact you is very easy. I am a medium. That's my specialty. You will know what I find out. That one at least I can promise."

"Thank you," said Lydia. She started to get up, but the medium stopped her.

"Wait a minute, good sister," he said. "I have a question for you, if you don't mind."

"I don't have any advice for anybody," said Lydia.

"No, no," said the medium. He looked embarrassed. "I just want to know, what's your birth date?"

The sifu's eyes unfocused, his face twitching. The light of transcendent enlightenment filled his face. His mouth fell open. From the dark depths of his throat issued an awful bellow: "Eight two one one!"

Even in her impatience this surprised a laugh out of Lydia.

"*Oh*, 4D," she said. "So people can buy lottery tickets, right?"

"Chinese like to gamble too much," said the demon disapprovingly.

The sifu was still shouting numbers to an attentive crowd when they walked away from the lights and smells of the festival.

The demon had parked the motorcycle next to a drain inhabited by bullfrogs, and their importunate moos filled the night air as the strains of Cantopop died out.

"Can we go now?" said Lydia, but suddenly, for no reason, she was afraid.

What would she find when they arrived in Penang? If Wei Kiat no longer lived at their house it would be difficult to find him. He might not even be in Penang anymore. And if he was, would he be different?

The living world seemed suddenly strange, quick-moving, unknowable. Lydia wished the sky was not so large. She wished, for the first time, that she was still safe within the caverns of the netherworld, protected by the rock ceiling from change and inconstancy.

"You'd better sleep first," said her demon. "If not, you'll be tired. We can leave in the morning."

"I'm *dead*," said Lydia.

"Then there's no better time to rest, no?"

The sky was brightening when they set off again, and dawn crept over the country as they sped along the North-South Expressway. Lydia kept dropping off, her face smushed against the demon's bony back.

Every once in a while she would open her eyes to the landscape of the annual journeys of her childhood. The dark green sea of oil palm trees; massy white cumulus clouds in a harsh blue sky; the narrow barren boles of abandoned rubber tree plantations; the occasional water buffalo standing patiently by the road. They zoomed past orange earth stripped clean and leveled flat, waiting for development; temples with elegant roofs curving toward the sky, roof tiles blinding in the sunlight; billboards advertising herbal supplements and massage chairs.

The shape of the green-furred mountains against the sky brought back an unpleasant memory—the first time she remembered really seeing them and noticing their beauty. She'd been eight, and she'd wanted to ask her parents why some of the mountains were red on the inside and some white, but they were fighting in a whisper, believing her asleep.

"I told you to ask for discount. These people want to make the sale, ask only they will give you one."

"Haiyah, bought already," Lydia's father had said. "At most also won't save more than RM100 lah. What for heart-pain over a small thing like that?"

"For you maybe it's not much. Easy lah you, every day come home at five. I'm the one who has to do OT, pay for Lydia's tuition, everything. At the end of the day still I'm the one cooking dinner. For some people it's very easy!"

"If it's so difficult marrying a civil servant, why didn't you marry some tycoon?"

"I'm just stupid lah," Lydia's mother had snarled. "That's why, no?"

Lydia had hunkered down in the back seat, making herself small. It had seemed politic to continue being asleep—absent, unhearing.

"What's wrong?" said the demon.

"Just remembering," said Lydia. She told the demon about it. "Dunno why I'm so upset also. They all fought all the time anyway. But Chinese New Year was the worst because they had to be in the same car for five hours."

"Aiyah," said the demon. "Be more xiaoshun lah. Your parents what."

Lydia experienced an unfamiliar spike of outrage. "Aren't you supposed to be my personal agony? Whose side are you on?"

"Of course I'm sympathetic," said demon. "But you're dead liao mah. Your parents also were suffering. Angry for what now?"

Somewhere past the Kedah-Perak border, the demon went off-route. Lydia only woke when the bike started jolting over uneven ground.

They were riding over a dirt track in an abandoned patch of oil palm plantation merging into secondary jungle. It was hot and very, very still.

"What's happening?" Inarticulate fury rose in Lydia. "Bastard, always delay, here delay there. You don't realize my time got limit, is it? You think I sold off a year of death to a hell official just to cuti-cuti Malaysia? Where are we going?"

"I'm taking you to the place where you died," said the demon.

They only stopped when they were deep enough that they could no longer hear the noise of traffic from the highway. A heaped black pile of oil palm fruit sat rotting by the path. A lizard ran over the ground by Lydia's feet, lifted its head as if it heard something, and hurried on.

The demon squatted by a tree and looked at Lydia as if it was waiting for something.

"Why—" Lydia realized she was crying, but it was only her demon, after all, only her personal agony whom she had carried ever since she left the living world, only the part of herself she knew best, and she plowed on: "Why everything has to be some kind of life lesson? I don't need to know what. It's done already. This's supposed to be a vacation. I'm not trying to find myself or what. I just want to relax and see my husband. What's so wrong I cannot do that?"

"What's your agony, Lydia?" said the demon.

"My parents lah!" wailed Lydia. "Ask me something I don't know! My parents give me headache my whole life. Even after I die also I still have to deal with them. But I can't forgive, OK? You think I didn't try? I wanted to be a good daughter. I sent them money everything. But you can't control how you feel."

"You're wrong, Lydia."

"What do you know? You're just a demon," said Lydia. "You can't force yourself to love somebody."

"Not that," said the demon. "You're wrong about the agony. Look around. You sure you can't remember?"

Lydia looked, but the tears in her eyes had turned the world into a brilliant blur. Shapes lost their meaning. She only saw blotches of vivid green, black shadow, blinding patches of sunlight.

"I don't *know*," she started to say, but she felt a warmth in her hand. She looked down.

An orange light was kindling within her palm. As she watched, the flame crept outward, forming a thin ring of fire. Within it unfolded a scrap of paper. The fire flickered out.

It was a newspaper clipping, its edges burnt black. Lydia had never received a burnt offering before, but she remembered the kind uncle's face, turned to her in puzzlement. The medium in Kampar. He had sent her a message after all.

At first she thought he'd wasted his time. She couldn't read it. It was a Chinese newspaper clipping, and Lydia had gone to a government school. Her Malay was pretty good, her written Chinese nonexistent. But she didn't need it in order to understand the picture.

It was a picture of Wei Kiat. She recognized him at once, even though he'd ducked his head to hide his face from the camera. The photograph was familiar—the stern figures of police officers flanking the sullen convict emerging from the courtroom. She'd seen dozens of such pictures in the newspapers in the course of her life. She'd never known anyone in them before.

"You want me to translate?" said the demon.

Lydia shook her head.

"Do you remember now?" said the demon.

She looked around that buzzing, empty space. The only noise was the whirr of insects' wings. You wouldn't hear anything from the road.

It was a good place to have done it.

"No," she said, but there was a hollowness inside her that contradicted the denial. The knowledge settled into her. Lydia knew how it had come to be that she was dead.

She sat down.

"Why did he kill me?" she said.

"I don't know," said the demon.

"I thought he loved me."

"Yah."

"I loved him so much."

"Yah."

Lydia stared at her hands. "My family was so . . . like that . . . I thought I was so lucky to find Wei Kiat. He was my chance. Before him I never knew what it's like to be happy." She looked up. "You really don't know ah?"

"I don't have any answers," said the demon.

"You know how to ride motorbike and read Chinese."

"I'm what you need to find your hunger," said the demon. "Doesn't mean I know anything important. I'm just your sadness. I'm just the fact your true love betrayed you."

"You didn't have to say it like *that*," said Lydia.

She sat with her head bowed, weighed down with grief, and it seemed as if a very long time had passed when the demon's voice broke in on her sorrow. It was as if the voice were merely another strand of her own thoughts, a song playing soothingly at the back of her head. It said: "Now you know. What does it matter? In the next life you won't remember this sadness. You're already dead. Let go lah your attachments."

Lydia lifted her weary head. "Why are you saying all these pointless things to me?"

The demon fell silent. Then it said, "What do you want to do now, Lydia?"

Lydia scrubbed her eyes, but instead of a scathing rejoinder, what sprung to mind was a vision of the sea. A blue-gray expanse seen over the low wall that bordered Gurney Drive. The waves glinting so brightly in the sun that they almost seemed made of metal. Around the bay the dark green hills rising, and against them the prosaic white and gray forms of condominiums and office buildings.

She saw her bougainvilleas crowded together in her little garden, their delicate petals shivering at the touch of the breeze. Her heart clenched and relaxed.

"I want to go home," she said.

"Penang?"

"Yah," said Lydia. The bougainvilleas, and the sea.

"Not a bad idea," said the demon. "They should still be celebrating the Festival. Penangites really know how to layan ghosts. At least the food will be good."

"Is food the only thing you think about?" said Lydia.

"Somebody has to remember you're a *hungry* ghost," said the demon with dignity.

It was getting on for the evening by the time they got to Penang Bridge. The time of what her mother called falling light, the sky a mellow orange-tinged gray, the harsh light of the sun softened by dusk. Over the demon's shoulder Lydia could see the lights running along the bridge, the red taillights of the cars drawing away, the dark mass of the island rising ahead of them. And on the further shore, the lights of home.

~~~~~~~~~~

There

~~~~~~~~~~

One-Day Travelcard
for Fairyland

Two hours into the siege, Adeline's nerve broke.

"Where's the Maggi mee?" she said. She tore open the packet of instant noodles with the viciousness of a stray dog.

"Eh, that's our provisions leh," Hui Ann protested. "Cannot simply eat!"

"I need a snack," said Adeline. "Cannot tahan. I gotta do something or I'm gonna freak out."

"Can't you just sing a song or something," Hui Ann began to say, but their argument was interrupted by an explosion.

Everyone flung themselves flat. Hui Ann knocked her forehead against the stone floor and felt woozy for a moment. But she scrambled up again. This was no time to lie on the floor cowering for her life.

"They're coming in," wailed somebody, but one of the boys raised his hand.

"It's my firecracker," he said. "I dropped it outside when we were running here. Must be they picked it up and figured out how to use it. I brought it from home."

"Har," said Hui Ann blankly. "Is that even legal?"

Mun Kit, that was his name. "I thought because I won't be home for Chinese New Year mah," he explained. "Don't worry. No way it'll get through the door. It's a cheap one only. I bought it for RM2 from the kedai runcit."

"You should have told the kedai runcit guy firecrackers are banned in Malaysia," said Adeline.

"I was going to play in UK what, not Malaysia," argued Mun Kit. "Anyway, the firecrackers all got wet when we got off the bus yesterday. I'm surprised they even got it to work. I bet you the others won't go off."

He seemed to be right. They waited another half an hour, their hearts in their throats, but there were no more explosions. In fact there was no noise whatsoever.

You could almost have imagined there was nothing beyond the door, and they were hiding in the library for no reason.

Almost.

Outside, the fairies waited.

It had been drizzling when they arrived in England. The air outside the airport had been cold beyond belief, but the bus had been warm— not an honest, sticky heat, but a stultifying man-made warmth that smelled of dusty upholstery.

The drive along the winding country roads had been brutal. Dark hedges had risen on both sides of the bus as it burrowed deeper into the countryside. Once in a while the leaf-walls dropped away and Hui Ann got a glimpse of near-fluorescent green fields, smeared with rain.

She sat huddled in her scratchy new coat, feeling sicker and sicker.

When she staggered out of the bus, she'd begun to regret that she'd ever thought of going overseas to do her A-levels. Her parents had agreed because they'd thought it would help her get into a good university.

Currer Brundall College had seemed like the ideal school. Seventy percent of their student population was international, fifty percent Asian. The principal visited Kuala Lumpur every year and understood Hui Ann's parents perfectly.

"There's practically no crime in the area," he assured them. "We're right out in the countryside. The worse thing that happens is mobile phone theft in the school."

"Hui Ann is very careful with her things," said her parents.

They'd seen her off at the airport in a spirit of optimism, but this was forgotten in nausea and fatigue by the time Hui Ann had her first look at the school. It was a seventeenth-century manor house and it rose out of the green fields and gray skies like a tombstone.

But it wasn't the school that had turned out to be dangerous. What was really to blame was her own stupid two feet.

They'd taken refuge in the library because it used to be a chapel. It was Adeline who thought of it, when the fairies started bubbling into the main hall from the chimney.

Hui Ann had been too busy shouting to think. She'd strained her back pushing the sofas against the door and strained her temper trying to get everyone else to help, and it seemed outrageous to her that all their efforts should have been foiled by a chimney.

"What for go and put a freaking hole in the ceiling?" she was yelling. "What kind of stupid idea is that?"

She took off her shoe and threw it at a fairy. Adeline only got her attention when she snatched Hui Ann's other shoe out of her hand.

"Because they're fallen angels," Adeline was saying urgently. "Not a hundred percent fallen, but they're the ones who stop halfway between demons and angels. That's why they really don't like all the heaven stuff."

"What're you talking about?"

"You know the statue of the dead guy in the library?" said Adeline. "It's a tomb! They buried the guy underneath."

"Yer, I don't need to know that!" Hui Ann had just thought it was a statue. "Who buries people inside a building? A school some more!"

"It wasn't a school back then. It was a house," said Adeline. "Back then the library was a chapel. The family used to pray there. Hui Ann, that means it's a holy place. Fairies won't go there! Like vampires and holy water, you know?"

Behind them a boy screamed and fell to his knees, his head bristling with fairies. Someone had broken a window, and a group of kids was tussling amidst the broken glass, trying to get out. One girl, fleeing, tripped over a chair leg and went down shrieking as the fairies converged on her.

Hui Ann didn't need to think twice.

"Fall back!" she shouted. "Run! Go to the library! We'll fight them off there!"

Hui Ann had noticed Adeline on the first day, during the English test. Her pen had run out of ink, and Adeline was sitting next to her.

Adeline had a pale, soft-chinned face and furious red eyes with hardly anything in the way of eyelashes. She looked like a Chinese vampire reborn as a seventeen-year-old girl. She was the last person Hui Ann would have wanted to disturb during a test, but she was the only one whose attention Hui Ann could catch without disrupting the entire class—and she had four extra pens lined up on her desk.

Hui Ann reached out. She lost her nerve just before she would have made contact with Adeline's shoulder, and touched the back of her chair instead.

"Eh, 'scuse."

Adeline frowned at her.

"Can you borrow me one of your pens?" said Hui Ann.

The glower intensified. "Black or blue?"

For a moment Hui Ann quailed. But Adeline was referring to nothing more sinister than ink.

"Oh, anything—blue—no, black—sorry, anything—" She retreated to her desk, clutching the pen and covered in embarrassment.

She breezed through the multiple-choice section, but the essay question had her stumped. It asked her to describe her home.

An image of her house rose up before her, a semi-detached. Nothing like the houses here: strange narrow rectangles with windows like eyes, colored brick red and brown as in children's drawings of houses.

Her house was sort of beige and it had a bulgy bit at the side where her parents had added an extension. There was a balcony on the second floor, but they hardly ever used it because who would want to sit outside in the heat?

There was nothing much to describe in this. Hui Ann fiddled with the cap on the pen, frowning in thought.

This was when she broke scary Adeline's pen.

They brought the dead fairy to the library with them. Adeline kicked up a stink when she cottoned on.

"What's that doing here?" she said.

The fairy lay in a shoebox Hui Ann had scrounged from her luggage. Its eyes were shut, but its skin was so translucent, like that of a young tadpole, that you could see through the lids to the eyeballs. They'd covered its body with a tea towel, to show respect.

"Why, what's wrong with it?" said Hui Ann.

"What's the point of seeking sanctuary in a sacred place if you bring unsacred stuff in?" said Adeline. "It's gonna spoil the holiness!"

"It's dead liao, it can't be unsacred," snapped Hui Ann. "Who made you the boss of holiness? If that guy doesn't mind, why should you?" She jerked a thumb at the statue of the dead person.

It was true Sir Thomas Elphinstone didn't seem to have noticed the fairy. His statue slumbered undisturbed, its hands folded in eternal prayer.

He probably liked having another dead person around. The years must have felt very long when his only company had been students falling asleep on their textbooks and teachers telling kids off for whispering.

"Anyway, you shouldn't speak ill of the dead," said Hui Ann. "'Specially when it's our fault they're dead."

Adeline's shoulders slumped. "Why didn't you leave it for the other fairies? For all you know they're attacking us because they want the body."

"Doesn't seem right to do it like that," said Hui Ann. "Leave it in the middle of all the fighting. I want to pass it back to them, but we have to figure out how to communicate first."

Adeline gazed down at the dead fairy. "I can speak four dialects, but none of them is fairy language."

"If they're British fairies, should be they can speak English what," said Hui Ann. "If they don't speak English, must be they don't speak human language at all."

Nothing the fairies said was comprehensible. Most of them spoke in nature sounds, like a New Age music CD—donkey squeals, feline hisses, wind-howl, ocean-roar, and fire-crackle. But some of them spoke machine as well, in siren shrieks, fire alarm wails, engine growls, and dial-up burbles.

Their faces—when they had faces—moved as if they were talking, but they didn't use words.

And yet there was meaning there. Even now, when it was quiet, the silence on the other side of the door was the silence of still muddy water, full of life and growth. On the other side of the library door, a hundred conversations were happening.

She hadn't meant to kill the fairy. It was because of the pen.

You could still write with it—Hui Ann had only snapped the clip off—but this didn't make her feel any better about it. It had been a beautiful pen: the Pilot G-1 gel ink rollerball in lush deep blue, with a perfect 0.7 millimeter tip. Bereft of its clip, it looked noseless and ineffective.

She didn't have the nerve to tell Adeline when she found her after the test.

"How'd you find it?" she said instead.

"OK lah," said Adeline in an unexpectedly mild voice. She sounded pleased that Hui Ann had talked to her, though she looked as angry as ever. "Hopefully won't have to take the extra tuition. I tuition until want to die already. I came here 'cos I thought UK don't have."

"Tuition sucks," Hui Ann agreed. "What do we have next?"

"Free period, I think," said Adeline. She unfolded the schedule they'd been given. "Dinner served from six to seven in the canteen."

Guilt rid Hui Ann of shyness.

"You want to go find the canteen?" she suggested. "It's early, but we can check out the rest of the campus also."

She could work up the courage to tell Adeline about the pen on the way. The broken-off clip poked her palm in silent reproof as they walked out of the exam hall.

Adeline surprised Hui Ann by being easy to talk to. She was extremely religious.

"I gave up prawns to thank God for making my parents send me to UK," Adeline said. "But I was thinking of sacrificing something else. My cousin works here and he says British food doesn't really have prawn one."

Hui Ann didn't see the logic in this. "But if they don't serve prawn then it's easier to not eat prawn."

"It's not supposed to be easy," said Adeline severely. "It's supposed to be hard. That's the whole point. Why will God care if you sacrifice something you don't miss?"

Hui Ann wasn't sure why God would care even if you sacrificed something you would miss, but she refrained from saying this. She didn't feel like getting embroiled in a theological debate. The sunlight was fading even though it was only mid-afternoon—and they were lost.

Grass rolled away on either side of them. There were a few buildings around, but none of them looked like canteens.

"Where are we ah?" Hui Ann asked.

Adeline produced a map from the depths of her puffy jacket. "Boys' dorms, I think. Canteen is all the way on the other side. We're wrong already." She pointed at the map. "Look, there's a gate here. If we go out and walk round to the front gate, should be faster to get to the canteen."

The front gate opened on to the main road, which meandered through a minute village made up of fifteen houses and a post office before joining into the highway that had brought them here from Manchester Airport.

The back gate led to plain old countryside. Apart from the school, there was no sign of human habitation for miles.

Hui Ann had grown up in a suburb. The rolling fields were the loneliest thing she'd ever seen.

"Feels so ulu, hor." Adeline craned her head to look at the sky. "I wonder if there'll be a lot of stars at night."

Adeline thought the stars were seraphim and the twinkling came from the continuous flutter of their six wings. "They use two to hide their face, two to hide their feet, and two to fly."

"Why don't they just use all six to fly?"

"Must menutup aurat mah," said Adeline. "If Muslims must be modest, what more angels."

She had a lot of weird ideas of this kind. Adeline's parents were fantastically rich—"Our house got seven car and two security guard"—but she didn't see much of them.

"When the Currer Brundall principal asked them what grades I got in my SPM mock exam, they couldn't even answer. Not like it was hard to remember also. It was all As."

This level of parental detachment struck Hui Ann as improbable, but not unattractive. "If my parents had that much money they'd install a microchip in my skull so they can track me wherever I go."

"Sounds worse than mine," said Adeline doubtfully.

"No, they're OK," said Hui Ann. "I just wish they're a bit more laidback."

She rolled the pen clip in her hand. She should say now, get it over with, before she and Adeline became friends. They would be friends by the time they got to the front gate. If she stayed silent till then about her crime, Adeline would never know. Hui Ann would keep the pen forever and never mention it. Their friendship would be founded on a lie.

Maybe years from now Adeline would get married and Hui Ann would be her bridesmaid, large and blowsy in blue chiffon, dripping sentimental tears into her peonies. Throughout the beautiful wedding, while Adeline smiled her naked lashless smile, the sharp edges of the clip would be notching red marks in Hui Ann's palm.

"Thanks for borrowing me your pen," she said abruptly.

Adeline looked relieved. She'd obviously been wondering whether she was going to get it back. "That's OK!"

"I'm really sorry, though," Hui Ann rushed on. "I was fidgeting during the test and I just—"

She opened her hand and showed Adeline the clipless cap.

"Sorry," said Hui Ann.

Adeline took the pen, her eyebrows drawing downward. If Adeline's resting expression was anger, distress seemed to translate on her face to incandescent fury. Hui Ann was already embarrassed, and the livid look on Adeline's face shook her. She stepped back.

Her left foot went into a hollow. There was a high-pitched inorganic squeal, like the whine of rusty hinges. Hui Ann reached out, flailing, and her foot slid. She felt something snap beneath her shoe, like a twig.

The squeal cut off.

"Eh, you OK or not?" said Adeline, grabbing her. "Why you jump here, jump there like that?"

Hui Ann hesitated. "You looked kinda mad."

"It's just the clip! Who cares?" said Adeline. "My face looks like this all the time! It doesn't mean anything."

"Sorry."

"No lah, it's OK." Adeline shoved the pen into her jeans pocket and sighed. "I'm used to it. My mom always says I should smile more."

Hui Ann shrugged, still embarrassed. She cast around for something else to talk about.

"Did you hear some noise just now?" she said.

"Like a squeak, right?" said Adeline. "Did you step on something?"

Hui Ann eased her left foot out of the hollow. "I think I felt something down there."

She looked down.

In the hollow, barely to be seen in the evening half-light, was the fairy. Its eyes were still open—black, glassy eyes, like the eyes of a stunned mouse. Ichor pooled beneath its body.

It was dying.

She had killed it.

The next morning it was raining, and the fairies stood in serried ranks before the front gate.

They were of varying heights and colors, but none of them were higher than Hui Ann's knee. Some of them were humanoid, but with the radiant hair, bug eyes, and tiny faces of anime characters. Some of them looked like animals, but they stood upright on their hind legs, wore silks and brocades, and clutched bows and arrows in their paws.

Some of them didn't have facial features, human or otherwise. Some of them had too many facial features.

Hui Ann had finished breakfast and was coming out of the canteen with the other kids when they all saw the fairies. Everyone stopped in their tracks and stared.

"What do they want?" whispered Adeline.

"They want to kill us, probably," Hui Ann said, but she didn't speak softly enough. The group stirred.

"What are they?" said a boy.

"Fairies lah then!"

"What should we do?"

Hui Ann said briefly: "Chau."

When the group took flight, so did the fairies. Lifting from the ground in a body, like a flock of enraged birds, they hurtled over the gate.

The kids had tried to barricade themselves in the main hall, and this had worked until the fairies came down that damned chimney. The teachers were nowhere to be seen, but a piece of paper was pinned to the door of the Pastoral Care office. On it, hastily scrawled, were the words:

They don't like iron or running water
Don't understand thoughts, only feelings

> *They can sense your emotions*
> *They can die*
> *They have short attention spans*
> GOOD LUCK
> *WE ARE SORRY*

"If only we had a hose," said Adeline.

"Teachers," said Hui Ann. "Even when they're escaping, they can't resist. Die die also must try to teach you."

Adeline shuddered. "Let's not talk about dying."

To Hui Ann's relief nobody had blamed her for the fact that they were being attacked by an army of enraged pixies. Instead the other kids seemed to have concluded that since she was the only one who'd managed to kill a fairy, she probably knew what she was doing. They'd followed her willingly enough to the library, and now it was her they trusted to come up with a plan to fend off the fairies.

"They can't be that powerful, right?" said Mun Kit. He glanced at Hui Ann for confirmation. "If not, how come you step on one already it can die?"

The shame had been forgotten amidst other concerns, but it washed over Hui Ann now. She saw again the dead fairy lying curled up in the hollow, the life seeping out of its crushed body.

"I think it was hibernating," she said.

"We shouldn't just sit here waiting for them to come in," said a Singaporean girl with the strange-looking but mundane-sounding name of E-Qing. "We should go outside."

"But how're you gonna deal with the fairies?"

E-Qing shrugged. "They're so much smaller than us. So long as we're prepared, I don't think it's a problem. We can't wait here forever. Not like we can live on Maggi mee and sambal indefinitely."

"People brought sambal?" Hui Ann noticed people hastily squirreling away jars of dark red paste. "You brought that all the way from home? Eh, here in England they also got food one, you know or not?"

"I don't like fish and chip," said one of the sambal smugglers defiantly.

"I went to the sports hall and got this," said E-Qing. She cast a shimmering array of weaponry on the floor—fencing epees, bows and arrows. Hui Ann's eyes widened despite herself.

"Wow," she said. "My old school just had footballs only."

"The arrows are tipped with metal," said E-Qing briskly. Her hairtie was the exact same shade of lilac as her shoelaces; you wouldn't think she was the kind of girl who would take so readily to war. "And the swords are made of steel, of course."

"I brought seaweed snacks from home," chimed in another kid. "Seaweed got iron, right?"

"I don't think the teachers meant that kind of iron," said Hui Ann.

"We'll go out the window and come round to the front," said E-Qing. "Because all the fairies are watching the library door, they won't be expecting us. We'll take them by surprise."

Adeline was looking worried.

"It's a bad idea," she said. "Hui Ann, don't let them go."

E-Qing just about held herself back from rolling her eyes. Hui Ann noticed she was also wearing lilac eyeshadow.

"No offense," said E-Qing. "But Hui Ann's not even a prefect."

It wasn't like Hui Ann had even had the good sense to keep them out of this mess in the first place.

"You all go lah," she said. "But be careful, OK?"

It was her week for bad decisions, so Hui Ann shouldn't have been surprised when the screaming started on the other side of the library door. It was all of a piece with that stupid pen.

Adeline tried to stop her from opening the door. "E-Qing they all have swords and they can't even handle the fairies. What can we do?"

"Wait here while they all are being slaughtered outside?"

"Yah, I guess that's not a good idea also," Adeline conceded. "But if you open the door and the fairies come in, what's your plan?"

"They won't come in," said Hui Ann. "You're the one who said what. It used to be a chapel. They don't like religion."

Adeline's face crumpled. "Hui Ann, don't you know I just made that up! I was desperate!"

"Me also," Hui Ann told her. "Not to worry. I'll come up with something. Give me the shoebox."

In spite of her confidence her heart was banging against her ribcage when she flung the doors open and looked out into the corridor.

The air was thick with fairies. She couldn't even see if E-Qing and the kids who had gone with her were there. It was like walking into a swarm of bees.

As she watched in horror, the swarm reshaped itself into something even less credible.

"It's like Power Ranger," breathed Mun Kit.

The fairies were forming a gigantic fairy. It was like a warped cheerleading routine on a tiny scale. The small bodies piled on top of one another, fists grasping wings, legs wrapping around necks, needle-sharp teeth sinking into limbs. The surging interconnected mass developed legs, a torso, arms, and finally, a face, blooming out of the chaos.

It was Hui Ann's own face staring back at her.

"Like the Wizard of Oz," said Mun Kit.

With a sudden inexplicable access of understanding, like the clarity that comes in dreams, Hui Ann saw what was happening.

"Stop it!" she said.

"I know, right," whispered Adeline. "It's horrible!"

"No, not the fairies—well, yalah, the fairies also—but I was talking to *him*. Mun Kit, stop thinking!"

Maybe killing the fairy meant Hui Ann understood them better. Maybe that was how you joined their fellowship. That was why they had chosen to reproduce the shape of her face—death formed a bond between them.

"You thought it, right?" said Hui Ann. "Before you said it. You thought, 'Wouldn't it be cool if they joined together like Power Ranger to make one huge fairy.' Right?"

Mun Kit stammered, "I don't know! I wasn't really thinking!"

"You were thinking! You don't need words to think! Pictures count."

Fairies didn't need words. Words got in the way. Words were a human thing. Fairies thought in pictures. No—they thought in feelings. No—

Feelings thought them.

The landscape has feelings. Wind can be angry and skies can be cheerful. The sun is kind or cruel, as the mood takes it. The moon mourns. Nothing is detached from emotion but God.

Hui Ann looked into the strange little faces, unhuman, unanimal, unvegetable, unmineral. The fairies were made of strong, strong feeling. All the stronger because it was not like the feelings of human beings, diluted by thought.

The world didn't think. Its feelings unfolded naturally from the deep places of the earth and the distant reaches of heaven.

The fairies were rage and fear and fascination, all mixed up in a thick fog.

If they were made from feeling, then feeling could conquer them.

She looked down and saw black bits of paper on the floor. It took her a moment to recognize them as shredded nori, strewn on the floor by E-Qing's misguided warriors, as if trace amounts of iron might actually hold off a fairy army.

Hui Ann knelt down.

"What're you doing?" said Adeline.

Hui Ann was thinking boredom.

Her fingers fitted the bits of nori together as if they were pieces of a jigsaw puzzle. Watching them, she built up the heaviest, dampest, stuffiest mass of boredom there ever was.

The library was a good room to do it in. Centuries of tedium had soaked into the walls. The boredom of students puzzling over their books, and before that, the boredom of the small congregation, gathered to pray.

Hui Ann hoped they'd been preached dull sermons.

She felt her eyes begin irresistibly to close as the boredom sank into her. She pressed her fingers against the floor to steady herself, and let her mind leap out into the world.

Hui Ann tasted the boredom of people waiting at traffic lights, people sitting in offices, people pretending to be interested at business meetings, people pretending to be interested in bed. People dosing themselves with tedium in front of TVs and computers. Tourists gazing blankly at great works of art. Powerful leaders yawning in the middle of their own improbable promises. Management consultants bored of spreadsheets and astronauts bored of outer space.

The boredom flowed out of Hui Ann into the library and out into the corridor. It would flood the school grounds. It would roll through the sports hall, the lecture theater, the hostels, the village's fifteen houses and post office. When the tide receded, the fairies would be gone.

Adeline gasped. Hui Ann opened her eyes.

The air was clear. E-Qing and a few other kids were slumped on the floor, but they were alive.

"Oh," said Hui Ann, still glazed over with ennui.

The sun shone in through a window, casting a trembling bar of light on the wall. It was the first sun she'd seen since coming to England.

The teachers returned with disappointing promptness. The school had hardly been fairy-free for a day before the first adult was sighted, pootling shamefacedly into view in a red Mini.

They hustled everyone back into class immediately. Some of the kids found this a letdown. They'd been looking forward to living wild and battling fairies.

"So childish," said Adeline. "They all were talking about going to town on Wednesday and getting iron things. Golf clubs and things like that."

Hui Ann grinned. "Bet E-Qing wrote the shopping list."

"She finds fairies more interesting than A-levels," Adeline agreed. "Ridiculous. It's not like the fairies are coming back what."

"You never know."

"But they took their guy away already," argued Adeline.

This was true. Adeline had been clutching the shoebox, petrified, as Hui Ann sank into her trance of boredom, but not a single fairy had touched her. They'd melted away into the air with many jeers and siren shrieks. Adeline had only thought to look down when they'd vanished. The shoebox was empty.

"They're still out there," said Hui Ann. "I think they'll come back. Too many teenagers here. We're too excitable. Everywhere else is . . . boring." Hui Ann shrugged uncomfortably. "I think we called them here."

"By killing the fairy, you mean?"

"No, all of them," said Hui Ann. "Fairies in general. Fairies don't exist, right? Not in the modern world anyway. Not in cities or suburbs. Not even in the countryside. I mean, look at it." She gestured at the rolling green fields. "There's nowhere to hide. No mystery.

"I've been thinking. It doesn't make sense that I stepped on a fairy the minute we walked out that day. You'd think it wouldn't be so easy to find them. But maybe—maybe fairies are everywhere, because they're made of everything. But you can't see them unless you call them. Maybe we called them to us."

"But why us?" Adeline said.

"I don't know," Hui Ann admitted. "Teenagers have too many feelings, I guess."

"That's true," said Adeline. "I'm pretty mysterious. Half the time even I don't know what I'm thinking."

She looked thoughtful, but what she said next surprised Hui Ann. "I hope they all didn't eat the dead one or what, after they took it away."

"Maybe that's what it would have wanted," said Hui Ann. Guilt clanged in her chest. She would never be free of it, she realized. This was something you could not fix. Hui Ann felt very old; she felt she had begun to grow up.

"Maybe," said Adeline kindly, but she didn't sound convinced.

起狮，行礼
(Rising Lion—
The Lion Bows)

The hotel was not like any hotel Jia Qi had seen before. There was no drive swooping around a fountain featuring little peeing babies, no glass doors opening onto a golden lobby lit by chandeliers, no men in white gloves to hold the doors for you.

Perhaps English hotels were different. This one was a blocky old building made of weathered gray stone and covered with ivy. It looked like it should come equipped with knights and pointy-hatted ladies. The manager who came out to greet them looked incongruously modern in comparison—he wore a suit and a bright red tie, but no gloves. His name was Nick.

"Thanks for coming," he said to Tiong Han. Tiong Han was technically the president of the troupe. "The guests are really excited about the performance, really excited. So am I. I've never seen a lion dance performance before. It'll add a touch of culture to the night. Whoops! Need help with that?"

He was already moving forward to help Simon unload the lion head from the taxi, but Coco stepped in front of him before he could touch it.

Coco had been with the troupe for six years. She had never been their official president because she preferred not to deal with technicalities; it gave her more time to actually lead the troupe.

"Are Mr. and Mrs. Yu around?" she said.

It was Mr. Yu who had emailed them to ask if they would perform at a Christmas party that was being held at his hotel. It was a new hotel and this was the first big event they were hosting, so he was willing to pay them a generous fee. They had agreed that the troupe would perform before and after dinner. There were also going to be fireworks, and a disco.

Sensibly, Mr. Yu and Mrs. Yu had stayed indoors, but they were very hospitable when the cold, disheveled troupe poured into the lobby.

"We've got Chinese food, Chinese decorations, lanterns, fireworks," said Nick. "It's all been done up to theme. The company does a lot of business out in China, so they were very keen when we suggested a China night. When we heard about you we thought, well, that's ideal! We're so pleased you could make it all the way out here."

"Very pleased," said Mr. Yu in English. In Cantonese, he said: "*The ghost is in the upstairs cupboard.*"

"Thank you, we're looking forward to it," said Coco to Nick. To Mr. Yu: "*What kind of ghost is it?*"

Mr. Yu hesitated. Mrs. Yu had been overseeing Simon and Tiong Han as they carried the equipment in, but now she turned and said: "Nick, there is a drum. Will there be space in the dining room?"

"There's a drum? How big is—oh," Nick said, as the drum emerged from the front door. "We definitely haven't left enough space for that. I didn't know there'd be a drum."

"We thought they will use recordings," said Mrs. Yu. This was such a blatant fib that Jia Qi was surprised when Nick only said, "We'll have to clear some space, then. Let's see if we can jam it in the passage from the kitchen. You'll have to tell us whether that'll work."

Tiong Han glanced at Coco, who nodded. He left with Nick and the others followed, their arms full of cymbals, gongs, and cabbages.

Jia Qi stayed with Coco. Even after four months with the troupe, she was still too new to be much help with the setting up, and she wanted to know about the ghost.

Coco had told Jia Qi about the lion dance troupe's occasional secret assignments after she'd been coming to their meetings for a couple of months. It was earlier than Coco would usually have told a new member, but Jia Qi thought Coco felt a bond with her, as the only other girl in the troupe and the only other person capable of going ten minutes without talking about video games.

Besides, it had become obvious, even in that short period of time, that Jia Qi ate, slept, and dreamt lion dance. She was a quiet girl with an unfashionable accent, and British student culture had come as a shock to her system. She was ferociously homesick, she could not drink, and she only did well in classes where she was not required to speak.

The troupe did not seem to notice her quietness. They gave her something concrete to work at and never said anything she did not understand. She found refuge in their unfussy acceptance and reassuring Chineseness.

So she trekked out to Crusoe College for practice sessions every Wednesday. Her lion dance T-shirt went through so many washes that the rearing lion printed on the back faded from black to a patchy gray, and it became difficult to read the words *Christminster University Lion Dance Troupe* on the back even if you could read traditional Chinese. She learnt to relax her knees in the desired horse-riding stance so she felt hardly any pain at all for at least five minutes. During tedious lectures, she tapped out the rhythms of the cymbals on her desk.

When Coco told her the truth, she found it easy to believe. She demanded no proof. Jia Qi had already known that there was something magical about lion dance.

Mr. Yu told them about the ghost on the way upstairs, speaking low-voiced in Cantonese.

"Nick bought it with the business's money. Without our knowledge," he said. "We hired him because we thought he would understand the British customers better. I suppose it's not his fault. He was very happy about it. He said it was a bargain to get an antique like that in such good condition. He took it well when we told him no more antiques, but he refuses to get rid of this one. He says it adds to the character of the hotel. Matches the surroundings." Mr. Yu looked outraged at the thought. "I can tell you that's not true," he added.

"The rest of the surroundings aren't haunted. We got priests to bless the house before we moved in. No ghosts left anywhere, knock wood."

Jia Qi automatically rapped the banister along with Mr. Yu, but Coco was British and did not hold with superstitions. She was only interested in real ghosts.

"How old is the building?" she said.

"It was built in the 1970s," said Mr. Yu. You could tell from the disapproval in his voice that he thought this plenty old already. "The people who built it were interested in history. This is the recreation of some earl's house in Shropshire."

"Wow," said Coco. "They must have had a lot of money."

"Hnh," said Mr. Yu. "Gwailo have no sense. They treat the past like it's just an old movie. Like it's not serious."

The room he took them to looked like an ordinary hotel room, brightly lit and carpeted in beige, with two white beds and Van Gogh prints on the wall. Coco peered in.

"Where is it?"

"Oh, it isn't here," said Mr. Yu. "This is where you can wait before your performance. We try not to go to . . . the other room. That's down the corridor. The third door on your right, number eighty-eight."

"Wah, good number," said Jia Qi without thinking.

Mr. Yu's face turned suddenly stormy.

"I *know*," he said.

The others laughed when Jia Qi told them about the room number, except for Alec. Performances always made Alec stressed. If he had his way they would only ever have hunted ghosts, which at least didn't expose you in all your inadequacy to an audience. But as Coco and Simon and Tiong Han pointed out, what sort of a lion dance troupe didn't give performances?

"It would piss me off too," Alec said. "Why did they put it in that room? Why not put it in forty-four?"

"Nick did it, apparently," said Coco in English. Her accent went funny when she spoke to British people, but when she was with the troupe the familiar Cantonese tones reentered her voice. "Mr. Yu said when Nick found out about eights being lucky, he thought he could pretty it up and make it into a kind of special suite, charge couples more for it. It's larger than the other rooms as well."

"Now only the ghost gets to enjoy the space," said Tiong Han.

"Yeah, Mr. Yu said it comes out and stands around sometimes," said Coco. "They can't rent the room out. Even Nick feels it. He'll come out all covered in sweat, complaining that the heater in the room is broken."

"Hah," said Simon. "Funny. Ghosts usually make a place colder."

"What is it?" said Alec. "The haunted thing, I mean."

"Cabinet," said Coco. There was a groan from the troupe.

"I hate haunted cabinets," said Tiong Han. "Worse than haunted beds."

"Yah, those doors," said Simon. He winced at some unpleasant memory. "Cabinet door almost took off the lion's horn once. And Alec's hand," he added as an afterthought.

"Worse than chairs," said Tiong Han.

"No, chairs can be even worse," said Coco. "This was before your time, but once a sofa bed almost killed our lion. We had to bring in the Buddha."

"Oh, sofas are different from chairs," Tiong Han. "Sofas are super bad."

"Why are ghosts so nasty one?" said Jia Qi, breaking into the stream of spectral reminiscence.

Coco shrugged. "They can be horrible. It's actually really dangerous sometimes. Once you start a routine, you can't be sure it'll be OK until the lion's eaten the ghost."

"If you were dead you wouldn't feel like being nice to people what," Tiong Han pointed out.

"But weren't any of them good people before they died?" said Jia Qi.

Coco and Tiong Han exchanged a glance.

"We usually don't wait to find out," said Coco.

"So we attack first and ask questions later?" said Jia Qi. She was shocked. "Like that, of course the ghosts are not good mood!"

"If we wait for them to show if they're nice or not nice first, we'd be dead lah," said Tiong Han. "Ninety-nine percent of the ghosts I've met are all not nice. Very violent."

"They're not meant to be here, Jia Qi," said Coco. "It's really a kindness to let the lion eat them."

Simon had a less spiritual view of things.

"Lion's got to eat something," he said. "Cabbage not enough."

"Come on," said Alec abruptly. They could all tell he'd been working himself up over the performance to come. It was going to be a whopper of a performance—outdoors in the middle of winter, on unfamiliar ground. And it was to involve what, for the troupe, passed for acrobatics. Alec stood up. "Let's gao dim the ghost first and get it over with."

"So you can have plenty of time to worry about the performance?" said Coco. She patted his shoulder. "It'll be fine."

"We should have practiced more," muttered Alec as they filed out of the room.

"It'll be fine."

They were all so casual about the ghost that Jia Qi didn't even feel nervous. She'd never seen a ghost before, much less tried to lion-dance one out of existence. But there didn't appear to be anything to be nervous about when she first saw Room 88.

It was at least twice the size of the room where they'd been put, and furnished in an Oriental style. Rich red hangings draped over the windows. The bedspread was silk and had golden pop-eyed dragons embroidered all over it. Above the bed there was a large painting of a geisha with a parasol standing at the entrance of a Japanese house. Big red and gold vases stood in the corners of the room, containing plastic branches with pink cloth cherry blossoms.

The cumulative effect was awful. The only genuinely beautiful thing in the room was the cabinet. It was a rich dark brown, the sheen of the lacquered wood undulled by age. On its doors were gilded panels with the usual pictures of houses, mountains, clouds, trees. The shapes of the trees were like the shape of an old woman's body when she stands up and stretches her back, like the shape of slender ghosts with arms reaching out to embrace the living. The humans in the panels were incidental, quaint: peasants carrying buckets on both ends of poles slung over their shoulders, aristocrats standing in affected poses outside squat houses with flick-eared roofs, and processions of scholars on bridges arching over a dark river.

Looking at the cabinet gave Jia Qi a creepy feeling up and down her back, but she couldn't tell whether there was anything paranormal about it. Coco gave the woodwork a quick professional look-over, then she got down to business.

She tapped the rim of the drum twice, sharply, with the drumstick. Jia Qi raised her cymbals.

"Remember ah," Tiong Han told her, before she and Coco went in. He already had the shaggy sequined trousers on, halfway through his transformation into the lion's hindquarters. "No chiang chiang until the lion comes in. Follow the signal."

Now the drum gave voice to a deep rumbling. It was the sound of the stomach of a lion just waking from sleep to hunger. The lion came staggering into the room, blinking.

Jia Qi could still see Tiong Han and Simon's legs under the lion's head. The lion always started off as human. In the beginning you could tell it was paint and wood and paper and cloth. At the start it was only a show.

The head darted around, the mouth clacking, as the lion sniffed the air. Jia Qi found herself falling headfirst into the dance. Simon was their best dancer and the movements of the head were lovely, each clearly defined, but following each other with perfect timing, describing a fluid narrative in the air. The lion jumped, nosed the bed, and peered under the table, always casting glances at the cabinet over its shoulder.

Finally it minced over to the cabinet. When it was nearly on it, it paused and looked straight at Coco, blinking twice. This was the signal.

Coco and Jia Qi charged thunderously into 起狮, the Rising Lion. The lion rose and shook its horned head. 行礼—the lion bowed.

The troupe had agreed on the routine before the performance, but as a cymbalist Jia Qi did not need to remember any of it. She followed the beat of the drum, and every step came as a fresh wonder to her.

As the lion danced, an enchantment began to fall on the room. It was as though the dance had made the years turn over on themselves all at once, so that the dust of centuries began to settle on the furniture in a matter of minutes. Outlines grew hazy and the room grew dark, matching the blue-black evening sky outside. Only the cabinet glowed golden, the figures on its doors standing out in sharp relief, so vivid that they seemed about to move. And the lion—

The lion blazed through the room. Jia Qi knew its legs were Simon's and Tiong Han's legs, working in unison. She knew the tossing head and blinking eyes were operated by human hands. And yet she did not know it. The lion had changed; it was not human anymore. The spirit that slumbered in the lion head had awakened. It was a single, strange, live creature, and the beat of the drum was the beat of its heart.

The pictures on the cabinet's face came alive. A peasant put his buckets down and rolled his shoulders. The aristocrats giggled and flirted, passing each other jars of rice wine. The scholars found good spots on the riverbank and settled down to read or make up poetry.

The cabinet began to shake. Its doors rattled. Jia Qi closed her eyes in terror. With her eyes closed, she was in a thudding, crashing world, all cymbals and drum. She could feel the lion move around the room, its heavy footsteps dancing closer and closer to the cabinet. A gust of wind on her face meant that the lion had just swept past her. It would be opening its mouth, it would be rising over the cabinet, ready to devour, ready to swallow the ghost back into the darkness whence it came—

There was a shriek and a thud. Simon said, "Eh, si gina lai!"

Jia Qi's eyes snapped open just in time for her to see the cabinet jump a whole two inches off the ground. It resettled on the ground with a thump that she felt in her feet. The lion was gaping, Simon goggling through the open mouth. The lion's back deflated as Tiong Han crawled out from under the train to stare at what had come out of the cabinet.

It was indeed a child. A curly-haired black boy, about ten years old. He blinked sleepily and did not seem to know they were there at first. Then he opened his eyes wide.

"Where did *you* come from?" he said.

George had not heard of Malaysia. They drew him a map by committee.

"Is Laos between Myanmar and Vietnam? It is, right?" said Tiong Han.

"I don't think Hong Kong is so high up," said Coco, leaning over his shoulder. "And your proportions are all wrong! Singapore's not bigger than Hong Kong!"

"In ego it is," said Tiong Han, who was from Johor.

"See," said Simon to George. "It's on the end of Asia. Half is a peninsula. The other half is stuck to Indonesia."

The little boy bent his head over the map. It was touching to see how seriously he studied the scrawled picture. Tiong Han was studying architecture but that was apparently no guarantee of his draftsmanship.

"The Golden Khersonese," said George softly.

"No, no, Ma-lay-sia," said Tiong Han.

"Where are you from, George?" said Jia Qi.

"I would say nineteenth century, going from the clothes," said Coco. "Or maybe late 1700s. I'm not very good at telling this kind of thing."

"I was brought to this country when I was a little boy," said George. "My father was a king in Africa, but he lost his kingdom to the British soldiers. He gave me to one of the soldiers so that I would be safe, and so I could be educated, and learn to be a Christian. A captain of the Navy brought me to England with him when he returned home."

He recited this as if it were a story he had heard many times.

"Oh," said Simon. "So you're adopted by a British?"

George's forehead wrinkled.

"Your new mother and father are English now?" said Coco.

"I am sorry. I'm afraid I don't quite understand," said George.

"Who do you live with, George?" said Jia Qi.

The child brightened, looking relieved to be asked a question he could answer. "When I was alive, I lived with my master, Captain Joseph Pennywhite, and my mistress, his wife," he said. "Now I am dead, I live there."

He pointed.

They stared at the cabinet. George was gazing at the map.

"Are you all from this . . . Malaysia?" he said.

"Almost," said Simon. "Me, Tiong Han, and Jia Qi are. Alec is from Hong Kong and Coco is from here."

"My parents are from Hong Kong," said Coco. "But all my friends are Malaysian. Alec and I are like honorary Malaysians."

"And you are all together," said George.

"Yah," said Simon. "The lion dance troupe has always been like that. We tried to diversify but the ang moh—I mean, the Westerners —don't really feel so comfortable. Because usually when a Westerner comes to a training session, he ends up being the only one. It's a bit lonely for them."

George was fiddling with the edge of the paper they'd drawn the map on. He didn't say anything, but Jia Qi felt she could see right through his head into his thoughts.

She touched his shoulder.

"Do you like fireworks?" she asked.

Alec let George hold the stick to which they'd tied a head of cabbage. They were the only ones staying in the hotel room: the others trooped down the stairs, Coco holding the lion's head and Simon and Tiong Han carrying the drum. Their room overlooked the courtyard where the performance was to take place. The partygoers were already spilling out of the dining room, bringing the smell of alcohol and food with them into the cold night air.

Past the courtyard were fields of grass as far as the eye could see, no buildings to interrupt the flat, rolling vastness. In the daytime it would have been pretty; at night, there was something frightening about those looming fields.

The sky in the countryside seemed larger than it was in town. Jia Qi craned her head, shivering as the air hit her bare neck. Above her a handful of stars glowed white around a yellow moon.

"I thought there are more stars in the country," said Jia Qi.

"England's too cloudy," said Coco. She rapped the side of the drum. The lion's head snapped up. It blinked. The dance was on.

Their audience seemed eager to be pleased—Jia Qi had never felt more grateful for the existence of alcohol—but she could still sense Coco tensing as they reached the dénouement. A stick emerged from one of the windows and the cabbage dropped down. It bounced a few times as George waggled the stick to make sure everyone in the audience had noticed it.

The lion dropped into a crouch, shaking its behind in anticipation.

Why did lions like eating cabbage? Perhaps, being magical creatures, they could taste metaphor, and eating cabbage was like having the golden flavor of prosperity lying on their tongue. Lions were also fond of wine, but this was an inclination that did not require explanation.

Jia Qi wimped out and closed her eyes at the pivotal moment. When she opened them the lion was standing upright, the cabbage right next to its gaping maw. Inside the lion, Simon had managed to climb onto Tiong Han's shoulders.

The audience broke out into impressed applause. Jia Qi clanged as hard as she could, her hands aching from clutching the cymbals too hard. The lion wobbled—*please don't let Tiong Han lose his grip, don't let Simon slip*—the lion's head lunged forward, the cabbage vanished, and the tower of lion collapsed, but in a way that almost looked purposeful. The next moment the lion was itself again, Simon and Tiong Han back in control.

The lion staggered. The cabbage was not suiting its stomach. Why did lions have such delicate stomachs? Jia Qi understood the artistic usefulness of a storytelling device that enabled things to be thrown out of the lion's mouth to an appreciative crowd, but it still seemed funny to her that so many lion dance routines revolved around vomit.

Traditionally one showered the audience with shredded greens, indicating that it was now covered with prosperity, but there was a risk with this audience that it might just think it had been covered with cabbage. The troupe had therefore come up with an alternative. Jia Qi had suggested it, and she swelled with pride as the gold chocolate coins filled the air, accompanied by the laughter and cheering of the crowd.

"Wah, close one," said Tiong Han afterward. "Simon almost fell, man. I thought habislah, sure die already."

"I don't think the audience noticed," said Jia Qi.

Alec dismissed the audience with a wave of his hand. "The audience doesn't know how to see what's right or what's wrong. We are the ones who know whether it was good or not," he said. "What did you think, George?"

George's eyes were shining.

"It was the most wonderful thing I have ever seen," he said.

"George is your number one fan," said Coco to Simon.

"You were also very good," Simon told him solemnly.

"Yah, good cabbage-holding," said Tiong Han. George glowed.

"It wasn't bad lah," Alec conceded. "Apart from the slip, not bad. Eh, did you keep any of those chocolate coins?"

They ate the chocolate coins while watching the fireworks. George was enthralled—he barely glanced at the chocolate when it was offered.

"Thank you, but I don't do that anymore," he said.

Jia Qi withdrew into her hoodie, crimping her sleeves closed with her fingers so the air would not come in.

"Are you cold?" whispered George. Jia Qi nodded. "Here, take my hand."

"Oh," said Jia Qi. "You're so warm!"

George was watching the sky. Red sparks bloomed against the clouds, were reflected in his enchanted eyes.

"It's always been warm," he said. "Since I died."

They were packing away the equipment when Jia Qi said, "What are we going to do about George?"

The troupe stopped and looked at one another.

"We can't take him away from here," said Coco. "Ghosts have to stay with the object they're haunting."

"Then?" said Jia Qi. Her chest felt tight. "We just leave him here, is it? Never mind that this small kid is lonely. It's none of our business also."

No response, though everyone looked uncomfortable. Jia Qi plowed on. "Like that we might as well finish the job. Go back to the room and make sure the lion eats him this time. Otherwise we've just left it dangling."

"Oh, we can't do that," Coco exclaimed, almost involuntarily.

"*You* said they all are not meant to be here," said Jia Qi. She hardly recognized her own voice. "At least if the lion eats him then he's free. Maybe he can go to heaven, or be reborn, or—"

"Jia Qi, spirits don't go free after they get eaten," said Alec.

"Oh," said Jia Qi, taken aback. "What happens to them?"

"What d'you think happens after a lion eats you?" said Tiong Han.

"Digested," said Simon briefly.

"Yes," said Coco. She seemed embarrassed. "Sorry, Jia Qi, I should have explained that to you in the beginning. We're not priests. We're just an extermination service."

"Doesn't seem so right to eat George," said Simon. "He's smaller than my little brother also."

"But if we all leave him stuck here, what we gonna tell Mr. Yu?" said Jia Qi.

From Tiong Han's face it was clear he had been hoping to avoid this question.

"I thought if we just left, maybe he won't notice," he ventured.

Coco rounded on him. "Tiong Han! He paid us an extra hundred pounds for the ghostbusting! You weren't going to tell him we didn't do it?"

"OK, OK, fine," said Tiong Han. He looked wistful: their lion head was becoming somewhat tattered in its old age, and he'd been eyeing new ones on the Internet. "But you tell him, can or not? I feel shy. They gave us free dinner some more."

"I will tell him," said Jia Qi.

Mr. Yu was not pleased. "Lion dance is supposed to get rid of evil spirits. Why should I hire you if you're not going to bring good luck?"

"He's nine or ten only," said Simon. "He can't be an evil spirit at that age, right? Naughty at the very most."

"Mr. Yu, the ghost is a child," said Jia Qi. "How is he going to bring bad luck?"

"Yah, he can't even drive," said Tiong Han helpfully.

"Old or young, ghosts are bad for business," said Mr. Yu. "You can't have this kind of supernatural thing in the hospitality industry. People go to hotels to relax, not to pretend they are in a horror movie. I'll have to get a priest in—or burn the cabinet—"

A cry of protest rose from the troupe.

"You can't do that!" said Coco.

"Mr. Yu," said Jia Qi. "Give us the cabinet. We'll get rid of it for you."

"We will?" said Tiong Han.

Mr. Yu hesitated. "What will I tell Nick?"

"Tell him we stole it," said Jia Qi recklessly.

"Oh no, don't say that," said Tiong Han. "Say you lost it."

"We can't take the cabinet," whispered Alec. "Where are we going to keep it?"

Jia Qi left the others to argue it out between themselves. She had more important things to worry about.

The air in the hotel room was cold. The lights took a while to brighten after she flipped the switch, and in their dim glow the cabinet looked like nothing more than a dead piece of wood. Maybe George wasn't there anymore?

But when Jia Qi knelt down and asked her question, she felt the room grow warm. A breath of humid air brushed her cheek. George was sitting on the floor next to her.

"Could I help with the dance again? If I came with you?" he said. "Tiong Han said I held the cabbage well."

"Of course. You can do other things also if you like," said Jia Qi. "We'll teach you how to play the cymbals. And—" George was probably too small to be the lion. "And you can learn how to be the Buddha. You'll be the youngest member of the troupe ever."

"Would I be a member of the troupe?" said George, wide-eyed.

"You won't be on the mailing list," said Jia Qi. "But yah. Only if you want lah."

"Oh *yes*," said George.

There wasn't any space left in the back of the van, so they put the cabinet on the back seat. Jia Qi sat next to it, promising to make sure it didn't fall over. The rest of the troupe sat in the front and talked all the way back, but in the back it was quiet and stiflingly warm. Jia Qi felt herself blinking, her eyelids trying to gum her eyes shut.

The drive back seemed longer than the drive to the hotel had been. They went deeper and deeper into the darkness, hedges rising up outside the window and falling away, the country a slumbering mystery behind them. Jia Qi stretched out an arm across the front of the cabinet. It would wake her up if it so much as wobbled. She could let herself drift.

As sleep veiled her eyes, she felt a small, warm hand grasp hers. She slept and dreamt of sunshine; she dreamt of home.

七星鼓
(Seven Star Drum)

"When Boris was a kid," said Coco, "he was scared of everything."

Boris had been born with an extra membrane around his brain that filtered in things other people didn't see.

This was not unheard of. Everybody knows somebody who can see ghosts. But Boris's peculiar tragedy was that his parents were skeptics. Marvelously, incredibly, they did not believe in spirits.

It was not just that they did not pray. Boris's parents used to go jungle-trekking during their holidays. They were the kind of people who kicked tree stumps and shouted at the wind without fear of retaliation. They spoke openly of death as something that happened to everyone—something that would, one day, happen to them and people they knew.

This is all right, unless you are a child who sees ghosts. And Boris saw all kinds of ghosts. His eyes did not discriminate. He saw red-eyed, white-faced, long-tongued vampires, hopping horribly, reaching out for him with sharp-nailed hands. He saw pontianak and langsuir and toyol and penanggalan, orang minyak, hantu tetek, hantu kum-kum, evil genies, plain old dead people.

Even the quiet ones were terrifying, with their sad eyes and transparent bodies. They were so hungry.

Every ghost wanted something from Boris. Usually they wanted his entrails.

As a small child Boris started at everything. He was afraid of shadows and the dark, of loud noises, of whispers, of people with red faces, of cats and dogs, of old people and babies. He could not sleep if it was raining. He threw tantrums if he was forced to go to the bathroom alone.

This was irritating for his parents. Boris withdrew into himself. People started wondering if there was something, you know, *funny* about him. They felt sorry for his parents, though it was Boris who was suffering, prey to the whims of the ubiquitous underworld.

In the picture on the lion dance troupe's website, Boris looks strong and cheerful. His forehead is beaded with sweat from a training session. His lean arms hoist the lion head high in the air. He smiles fearlessly into the camera.

You can tell that here is a young man who has found a destiny to push him forward. He has the sunny conviction of one secure in the knowledge of what he is meant for.

But peel off the layers of time, roll him back to the child he was. Boris never got very large or tall, and he's never quite lost the frown that drew his eyebrows together. With not too strenuous an effort of the imagination you can see in the dauntless lion dancer the child's skinny legs pitted with scabs, the hunched shoulders, the small, guarded face.

He could easily have lived out his life with those hunched shoulders, pursued by the unfulfillable longings of the dead and spiritous, if not for the discovery.

It had happened when he was seven. It was Chinese New Year and for once his parents hadn't gone hiking on some spirit-soaked mountain. They were in Ipoh, where Boris's grandmother lived. His parents were buying kuih from a streetside hawker stall when Boris realized there was a man at the end of the street whom he should not look at.

Boris had learnt not to seem frightened no matter how much his heart shook and his breath stuttered. But his eyes stopped seeing; his mouth went dry. Because he refused to turn around he was not sure what the man looked like, but out of the corner of his eyes he saw the inhuman blue tufts of hair. He smelt the stale exhalations of the undead.

He must be calm. The man had not yet realized that Boris could see him.

Seeing ghosts was not really the problem. The problem was when they looked back.

"Ma," he whimpered.

Boris's tough, hearty parents ignored him.

"I'm getting the pisang goreng," said his mother. "You know your favorite? You wait first lah. Mummy will get for you."

Boris could not help himself. He looked.

He was wrong after all. It was only shaped like a man. When you had a proper look at it, it was not very like.

The thing looked back.

Nobody told Boris what happened when ghosts realize you can see them, but he knew it on a bone-deep level. He had escaped horror many times in his short life, but somehow he knew this time was different.

The thing started moving toward him, in a spiky, mechanical shamble. Boris could not move or cry out, though doing that had saved him before. He was frozen. He knew his doom was upon him, that fate was about to touch him on the face.

That was when he heard the drum.

The thing paused and raised its many-eyed head.

The lion came flaming down the road, attended by golden clashings.

"Ah!" said the hawker stall auntie, pleased.

"Aiyoh," said Boris's parents, dismayed—just when they'd thought they'd be able for once to have an afternoon out without an exhibition from Boris.

They looked at Boris and, seeing his still face, thought him struck with terror.

It was a great emotion that held Boris in its grasp, but for once it was not fear.

The lion was gold and red and silver; its head was white-furred like the face of a kind grandfather; the bounce of its feet was like the dance of sunlight on water. Its sequined body twinkled in the lights from the hawker stalls. The sky was blue with evening, but the lion was bright as the day.

When it landed in front of him, his mother put a hand on Boris's shoulder, to reassure her always-frightened son.

But Boris looked up into the lion's round glass eyes and what he felt was love. The lion's hinged mouth dropped open. The antennae on its snout quivered. Its hot, stinking breath brushed his cheek.

Boris knew, for the first time in his life, that he was safe. For once the membrane showed him something worth seeing—the fact that the lion was real. He saw the muscles rippling underneath its fur-lined scaly hide. He saw the pulse throbbed out by the drum shake the lion's flanks.

Under the clanging of the cymbals, he heard the ghost chitter with fear.

When the lion reared on its back legs and leaped forward, when its massive jaws closed around the ghost, it was only doing what Boris had expected it to do.

The other people on the street saw the lion eat air. Boris saw the lion's first snap crush the ghost's leg.

The lion bowed its head, blinking at a gourd quietly placed on the ground by a troupe member. A second snap.

One way of seeing: a human hand reached out from the lion's mouth and grabbed the gourd. You could only see it if you were close to the lion, and only from a certain angle. It was so swift you could almost believe the lion had done it itself.

Another way of seeing, just as true: the lion swallowed the ghost. It snatched the gourd by the neck and chugged its contents down. It dropped the gourd and raised its shaggy head in triumph, shaking its rear, puffed up with pride.

"See what I did?" it would have said, if lions spoke human languages. "I have kept everyone safe."

But lions don't talk—or roar, for that matter. They let their hearts speak for them.

As the lion pranced away down the road, the drum and the cymbals following, Boris disentangled his hand from his mother's and walked to the spot where the ghost had been slaughtered.

The lion hadn't cleaned its plate. A great brown slug glared up at Boris from the ground. Bizarrely for a slug, it had six staring red eyes, and a lot of blue hair.

"Eeyer," said Boris's mother. "Don't be scared, boy, come here and take Mummy's hand. Insect is more scared of you. Boris, what are you doing!"

Boris squashed the slug under his heel.

The viscera of the slug was corrosive. Smeared on the road, it created the smallest of potholes. Boris inspected the underside of his shoe. There didn't seem to be much shoe left, so he decided to take it off.

His mother could never understand what had happened to that shoe, and she never knew what happened to her son, either. He became outgoing and unflappable. He stared fearlessly into the corners of houses, went to sleep the minute his head hit the pillow, seemed to enjoy horror movies as if they were comedies.

At ten, he started to train with a local lion dance troupe. He went on with it when he went overseas to study, and founded a troupe at university.

"Otherwise I'll have nothing on my CV," he said when people asked, but really it was his favorite thing to do.

It was an expensive hobby, however. Lion heads cost a few hundred pounds; the large drum costs more; and all these things must be replaced as they are worn down over time.

The university paid out a little to support cultural diversity, but it wasn't enough. People are happy to shell out to have a lion dance inaugurate their shop or bless their wedding. They pay even more to have the skeletons cleaned out of their closets. Nobody likes having a ghost in the house.

"And that's how the troupe ended up ghostbusting," said Coco. "It's a good story, right?"

"What happened to Boris?" said Jia Qi.

"Oh, he's working at Goldman Sachs now," said Coco. "I see him sometimes when I go to London. He wants to be a millionaire by the time he's thirty."

This seemed to Jia Qi a somewhat disappointing ending to the story. "Does he still do lion dance?"

"He gets about four hours of sleep a night," said Coco. "I don't think he does much of anything besides work. Anyway, the last time I saw him Boris said he wasn't into it anymore."

"Lion dance for fun, OK," Boris had said. "To kill the hantu, not so much anymore lah."

"But that's why you got into it, isn't it?" said Coco.

"Yes, but," said Boris. His eyes went filmy and distant—though maybe that was just the redness of sleep deprivation.

"Actually, no," he said. "I started because of love. I really love that lion. You ask me if I love my girlfriend more than that lion, I also won't know how to answer you. And you know the story about the origins of the lion dance? Why they all started doing it in ancient China?"

"They wanted to get rid of the Nian, didn't they?" said Coco, who had read the Wikipedia page. "This monster came to the village and the lion fought it off."

"That's one story," said Boris. "But the other story is, maybe the lion is the Nian. You look at the lion. It doesn't look much like real lion, right? Where got real lion got horn? Maybe the Nian has horn. In the end maybe it's the same thing.

"Somehow doesn't seem right," said Boris, "getting the lion to eat spirit. It's like cannibal, right? That's why I stopped."

Coco shrugged. "Fish feed is made of fish."

"You ask me if I love my mother as much as that lion, I don't know if I would say yes or not," was all Boris would say.

But to be fair to Boris, he was pretty drunk at the time.

The Mystery of
the Suet Swain

Belinda was having boy problems again.

"How?" She'd unboxed the iPhone and laid it on her desk. They both regarded it as if it was a snake.

"I don't know what to do," said Belinda. "I told Euric to take it back. But he said if I give him back he'll sell it on eBay."

"Give back and let him sell on eBay lah," said Sham.

"But that'll hurt his feelings," said Belinda.

Sham snorted.

Belinda and Sham were best friends. On Sham's side, this was because she did not have any other friends. Belinda's reasons were more mysterious.

They'd met at the Malaysian Society freshers' tea party in their first week at Cambridge. Sham had been filling a backpack with Walkers crisps from the table of refreshments when Belinda had said to her: "I'm so sorry! I took the last prawn cocktail. But I didn't eat much. You want?"

Sham had looked down her impressive length of nose at Belinda. Belinda had glowed back, offering the packet of crisps with one trusting hand. She bore an extraordinary resemblance to a Shih Tzu puppy.

"I find prawn cocktail revolting," Sham informed her. "You can keep it."

Belinda had put her hand on her chest.

"Xing hao!" she'd said.

Belinda made a great best friend: she was considerate, humble, and infinitely anxious to please. But the same characteristics sometimes made her tiring.

"I don't know why you're so concerned about Euric," said Sham. "He's a dick."

"But he's my friend."

"Just because people want you to be their girlfriend doesn't mean they are your friend," said Sham. "This is, what, the fourth unwanted present this year?"

"The others were from other people," said Belinda. "This is the first thing Euric give me."

"But isn't he the one who printed out a picture of you and stuck it on his bolster?" said Sham. She paused. "Wait a minute, isn't he the guy who told you he has wet dreams about you?"

"That make me very uncomfortable," admitted Belinda.

"Give the thing back," said Sham. "If you don't nip this in the bud, next thing you know, the presents will be flooding through your door."

Outside the window there was a tinkling noise, followed by a dull thud.

They were two floors up. On the ledge outside lay a necklace, glinting in the orange lamplight. There was a note attached to it:

For the most beautiful girl in the world—Belinda.

"Oh my God," said Belinda.

"Next thing you know, bags of money will be falling out of the sky into my lap," said Sham hopefully, but nothing happened.

Belinda was training Sham to be normal. Her first step had been to create a Facebook account for Sham.

"How can you live without Facebook?" Belinda had marveled. "How d'you keep in touch with everybody back home?"

"I don't have an 'everybody,'" said Sham.

"If you want to meet people here you have to have an account," said Belinda, ignoring the fact that Sham had never expressed an interest in meeting people. "Anyway, I put all our photos up there, so you gotta log on to see."

Belinda loved having photographs taken of her and was constantly coaxing Sham into self-portraits. It was all right for Belinda. She came out looking twice as cute as in real life. In photos Sham was mostly nose and acne. Her face, lurking behind all of this, looked like an enraged hawk's.

But Facebook turned out to be more fun than Sham had expected. By scrolling through her feed for fifteen minutes every other night, she extracted more information about her compatriots than the sociable Belinda had any idea of.

"Hui Fern used to date Josiah back when they were at sec school," she told Belinda.

"Kidding? But Hui Fern and Josiah are so different!"

"She reminds him of his mother. He's still in love with her, but nowadays Hui Fern tells people she has no idea what she was thinking when she was going out with him," said Sham.

Belinda was round-eyed. "How you know all this stuff?"

Sham steepled her hands. "It would spoil the fun if I told you my methods."

"You FB stalk them, is it," said Belinda wisely.

"Hui Fern's put Josiah on limited profile. He always comments on photos posted by mutual friends where Hui Fern's been tagged, but you never see him commenting on her wall," said Sham. "Josiah has long conversations with his mother in the comments to his status updates, and his mom 'likes' all his pictures. She's an obstetrician with a perm. Hui Fern is a medic with curly hair. It's elementary, my dear Belinda."

"Stalker."

"It's not about the availability of the raw data, but the quality of the analysis," said Sham, with dignity.

She was browsing Facebook when she saw the pictures. They were of Belinda, and had been posted by a name Sham didn't recognize.

That in itself would have been nothing unusual. Belinda had tons of friends Sham didn't know. But there was something strange about these photographs.

The first picture in the album was of Belinda standing on one leg, flamingo-like, outside Sainsbury's, chatting to the *Big Issue* seller. The next was of Belinda playing Frisbee, frozen in mid-air. Another was of Belinda with a group of friends, walking out of the law faculty.

These were all taken from a distance. Belinda didn't seem to be aware that she was being photographed—she had a preferred angle for photos, one that made her face look sharper and her eyes larger. She hadn't arranged her face in these pictures.

It got weirder. Here was Belinda applying eyeliner in the bathroom. Belinda's hair spilling over her arm as she drowsed in bed, a textbook propped on her stomach. Belinda studying with her elbows on her desk, her room lit only by the table lamp. It looked like the picture had been taken from outside her window.

The window which was two floors up. The ledge was wide enough for a pigeon or a necklace, but not to support a human being with a camera.

Sham lifted her hands from the keyboard and touched her neck. Her hands were freezing cold.

"Sham, do you know where the necklace is?" said Belinda.

She had begged Sham to keep it. "What if I lose it before we figure out who it's from? I bet it's super expensive."

"If you lose it, so what?" Sham had said. "It's not like you paid for it what."

But Belinda had insisted, so Sham had taken the necklace. She'd put it in a box under her bed, behind the eleven toilet-paper rolls her mother had given her when she'd left home to go overseas.

Sham lived up the steep slope of a hill, half an hour's walk from Belinda's college, and it looked like Belinda had run all the way. She was panting, looking so discombobulated that Sham didn't even scold her for coming into the room with her shoes on.

"You found out who gave it, is it?" Sham said.

"No," said Belinda. She put her arms around herself.

Sham pulled the box out from under her bed, saying, "If you're cold, turn on the heater lah."

She opened the box. There was nothing inside it.

"Huh," Sham said. "I know I put it in here."

"Are you sure?" said Belinda. "Are you sure I passed it to you? Did I just keep it? You sure you remember or not?"

"You know I have an eidetic memory," said Sham.

"Then how did this happen?" said Belinda. She opened her bag and took out the necklace.

It glittered like ice in her hand.

"I found it in my closet," said Belinda. "You know how one of my closets, you open it and there's my sink inside? This morning this was hanging over the mirror. And got note."

The note said: *It's for YOU.*

"Creepy," said Sham.

"How?" wailed Belinda. "What should I do?"

Sham was not well equipped for this kind of situation. The division of labor in their friendship meant that Belinda did the cooking and feelings, and Sham did the cynicism and proofreading.

What would Belinda do?

"Take off your shoes and sit down," said Sham. "I'll make Milo."

She didn't have condensed milk, so it wasn't quite as good as home Milo. Still, there was nothing as comforting. Sham waited till Belinda had gulped down a mouthful and was beginning to look less wild-eyed. Then she announced:

"I know the answer to this mystery."

"What?"

"A bedder has fallen in love with you," said Sham. "Who else could get in?"

"Porter," Belinda pointed out. "They have all the keys."

"OK, a bedder or a porter has fallen in love with you," said Sham. "This is progress. We've narrowed the field down from everyone to two groups of people, both of whom you should be able to identify. You don't like this theory?"

Belinda hesitated.

"Lately sometimes I've been seeing, like, as if got something outside my window," she said.

If Belinda was being obscure, it showed she was frightened of what clarity could bring. Belinda seemed to think that using tactful words for unfortunate things could make unpleasantness go away. The tactic had not worked with the eleven boys unrequitedly in love with her, but she kept trying—as did they.

"A face," whispered Belinda. "Sometimes I see it at night."

"Who is it?" said Sham.

"Cannot see," said Belinda. "Can see face only, out of the corner of my eye. But when I look, he's gone. As if—as if he just vanish like that."

"A bedder, a porter, or a night-shift window cleaner is in love with you," said Sham. She sighed. "Your mom would be disappointed. Should've stuck to ensnaring Econs PhDs."

"Don't joke!" said Belinda. She put her mug down and drew her sleeve across her eyes. "It's not funny!"

"Cry for what?" said Sham. "Did I say it was funny? Of course it's not your fault whether some new idiot starts to like you. But don't you wish it was just Euric Liew and Harminder Singh? You look at those guys' physiques, no way they're gonna be able to get up the side of a building."

Belinda started laughing through her tears. Sham handed her a tissue.

"Don't freak out first," Sham said. "I got something worse to show you."

To her relief, Belinda didn't freak out when she saw the Facebook pictures. She seemed sunk in the calm of despair.

"Who is this guy?" she said.

"Don't know what kind of name is this," said Sham, peering at the screen. "He's called Bullet Sri Kaya. He's friends with all the Malaysians, see."

They scrolled through his friends list. Bullet Sri Kaya seemed to be acquainted with every Malaysian at Cambridge.

"Bullet must be a flower name," said Belinda. "Where got parents give such name, right? Is he our year? I haven't seen him around."

"I think you have seen him," said Sham. "I think he's the face outside your window. How else can he get these photos?"

"But how did he get there?" said Belinda. "And some of these photos, it's impossible, nobody could have get them. When I'm wearing my makeup, nobody is there! And the bathroom got no window!"

"Don't freak out first," said Sham again.

"You got *more* to show me?"

"No," said Sham. "Don't freak out, 'cos I'm gonna fix it."

There had to be things they could do about Bullet Sri Kaya. Official things. Sham didn't like to ask Belinda, because Belinda wasn't very good at law and it stressed her out when people assumed she knew anything about it just because she was studying it. But there had to be some kind of law against hanging around outside strangers' windows taking photos of them and putting them up on Facebook.

She would figure out what the offence was that they were going to charge him with later. First she had to find out who this guy was.

It was strange that Belinda had never met him. She knew everybody in the claustrophobic core of the Malaysian student community, and everybody seemed to know Bullet. Sham studied his Facebook profile picture, but it was unhelpful: a dimly-lit artsy shot of a guy with a baseball cap drawn low over his eyes.

Out of the shadow veiling his face, his teeth gleamed in a yellow-white smile.

The next day in the chemistry-department lounge, Sham put her hand on the back of Khoo May Ling's chair and said,

"Do you know this guy called Bullet Sri Kaya?"

May Ling jumped. Sham had once sat next to May Ling for the duration of three lectures without saying a word. It took a lot to make Sham feel awkward, but it seemed May Ling was more sensitive. She'd avoided Sham from that day onward.

But she was a nice girl. After a moment of astonishment, she pulled herself together and said, "Oh, hi, Shamini. Sorry, what did you say about Bullet?"

"Is his real name Bullet?" said Sham. She sat down.

"No lah, must be his real name is something else, right?" said May Ling. "But he asks everybody to call him Bullet. Alwyn is at his college. He says even their supervisor calls him Bullet."

"He's doing engineering?" said Sham. "Which year is he?"

"Same year as us," said May Ling. "You really don't know him?"

It was as if Sham had confessed to never having heard of David Beckham, or Siti Nurhaliza.

"Is he very popular?" said Sham.

"No lah, it's not that," said May Ling. Sham took mental note of the second of hesitation before she'd spoken. "But he's everywhere. He's at all the Malaysian Society things."

"Maybe I just never notice him," said Sham.

"He's a loud guy. Hard to miss. Don't you go to a lot of the events? Me and Alwyn always see you there with Belinda. Eh—" she leaned closer—"is Belinda going out with Euric?"

"Do you think Euric and Belinda should get together?" said Sham.

May Ling blinked. "He's a nice guy."

"Is Bullet a nice guy?" said Sham.

"Yes," said May Ling. "Very friendly."

But there was that hesitation again. Sham pressed her advantage.

"Sometimes too friendly?" she suggested.

"He's kind of a buaya," May Ling admitted. "But he's OK lah. Means well."

Bullet was chasing four different girls at the last count, was adopted "big brother" to another three. ("All skinny Chinese chicks," said someone, with a knowing look.) He was a regular participant in the engineers' weekly online gaming sessions. Everyone Sham spoke to had heard of him, and everyone had an opinion.

"He's funny," said Alwyn. "Wouldn't say we're BFF lah, but we're close enough. He's close to a lot of people."

"Wah, Bullet really likes girls, man," sniggered Rohan. "I've met some gatal guys, but that bugger is like king of the hamsap lo."

"He's a hero to the engineers," said Ambika. She snorted. "Mascot for all desperate single guys everywhere."

"That guy is dangerous," said Fairuz.

"Dangerous?" said Sham.

Fairuz was a tiny, pretty, soft-voiced girl with a round face framed by a gauzy tudung. The way she pressed her lips together did not make her look any fiercer, but her voice was grim.

"My mother always told me, don't trust men who don't respect boundaries," said Fairuz. "Bullet tu, either he doesn't know or he doesn't care what is boundaries. Men like that is dangerous."

Fairuz was only half right, thought Sham. It wasn't just men who didn't understand boundaries that were the problem. What made them dangerous was the people who found their lack of understanding funny, endearing, normal. The danger lay in everyone else.

"I know a secret about Bullet Sri Kaya," said Sham.

Belinda had crawled under her desk to search for something. Sham could only see the upturned soles of her feet, clad in polka-dot socks. The socks quivered.

"Not sure I want to know Bullet's secrets," said Belinda.

"Since he knows so much about you, better know as much about him as you can," said Sham. "That's called strategy. Ignoring him won't make him go away."

"But—"

"I see you still have Euric's iPhone," Sham observed. "Gonna give it back to him?"

Belinda emerged from under the desk. She looked rueful. "OK, OK. What's the secret?"

"I talked to a few people about Bullet," said Sham. "It's like everybody knows him except us. Bit weird, right? I thought you knew all the Malaysians. You even know the postgrads who have kids and live out in Grantchester. Party Malaysian, hermit Malaysian, hangs out with Mat Salleh only Malaysian . . . whoever they are also you know.

"But not Bullet. Everybody else, seniors and juniors also—if they haven't talked to him, they've heard of him. And to us it's like he didn't exist until you got the necklace. What happened to that, by the way?"

"I threw it in the Cam," said Belinda.

"Thought you were going to give to Oxfam?"

"I did," said Belinda. "It came back."

"Did throwing it in the river work?"

Belinda got up and opened the door to her sink. For reasons that were unclear to them, her sink was nestled inside a closet in her room.

At the bottom of the sink lay the necklace, coiled around the drain like an evil, sparkling worm.

"I threw it in the Cam on Thursday evening. Friday morning open the door to brush my teeth and here it is," said Belinda. "I haven't touch it since then."

"Good move. It's probably all gross from the Cam," said Sham. "Who knows what goes in there. Drunk people puke and whatnot."

Belinda shut the door on the sink. "What was the secret you were talking about?"

"When I heard Alwyn Goh was at the same college as this mysterious Bullet, I thought why not give him a visit," said Sham. "Alwyn is a bit weird, you know? He hangs his matriculation photo over his bed."

"How you know?"

"Facebook, duh," said Sham. "May Ling is a serial self-photographer and she often uses Alwyn's room as a backdrop. Me and Alwyn had a very nice chat. He's a gentleman. Pretended he wasn't weirded out by my visit."

"Yah, have you even talked to him since first year?" said Belinda.

"I asked to pinjam his notes on Professor Delmann's supervision. That was my excuse for the visit," said Sham. "But I'm obviously smarter than him, so it's not like it was a very good excuse."

"What did you find out?"

"From his notes? Nothing," said Sham. "That guy's heading for a 2:2 if he doesn't buck up. But it was still useful to see them. You know I like to keep an eye on the competition."

Belinda huffed; the word "kiasu" hung in the air. Sham ignored it.

"Plus I found out Bullet Sri Kaya wasn't in their college's matriculation photo," she said.

"What does that mean?" said Belinda.

"Doesn't mean anything," said Sham. "He could have been sick, or late, or forgot. But it makes you wonder, right? So I went to their college's admin office and asked about Bullet Sri Kaya. He's not registered as a student there."

"Maybe you got the name wrong?" said Belinda. "How can he not be a student? Alwyn and May Ling know him."

"I'm not sure anybody knows him," said Sham.

Belinda sighed. "My mother always says, one day I'll be old and I'll miss having all these boys chase after me."

"It's OK to be angry," said Sham. "You didn't ask for this also."

Belinda was blinking rapidly.

"I'm not angry, though," she said. "I'm scared."

"That's OK also," said Sham. "I got enough anger to cover two people. I can borrow you some."

Belinda smiled in a crinkly fragile way, a crepe-paper smile. She shook herself like a dog after a bath and got up.

"One more try and then I'll make dinner," she said. "You don't mind waiting?"

"What are you looking for anyway?"

"Malaysia Night T-shirt," said Belinda. "You know I'm helping backstage, and Jin wants the crew to wear the official T-shirt."

To forestall Sham saying something pointed about Jin's ego, Belinda hurried on: "The T-shirt design is really nice actually. It's off-white with hearts on the top here, near the shoulder. Quite stylo. But I don't know where it went. Are you very hungry?"

"I can wait," said Sham graciously.

~~~

The next time Sham saw Belinda she knew something had happened. Would it never stop? Did Bullet Sri Kaya not have anything to do besides stalk girls? Did he not have supervisions to keep up with and lectures to nap through, like everybody else?

"What's the matter?"

"You're wrong about Bullet," said Belinda. "He's definitely a student. Maybe May Ling got it wrong. Must be Bullet's at a different college from Alwyn."

"Why?"

"He emailed me, and he's got a Cambridge address," said Belinda. "You know that T-shirt I lost? He said I forgot to take it when the Malaysia Night committee was handing them out. So he took it. But he no chance to pass to me, so he put it in my pigeonhole."

Sham took the T-shirt from her.

"I didn't forget," said Belinda with quiet certainty. "I took it from Chia Wen and came home and put it in the drawer. I remember I put it just on top of my Hello Kitty T-shirt—what, what?"

"Ugh!" Sham dropped the T-shirt. "It's—"

The T-shirt unfolded to show a great stain across the front.

"Oh," said Belinda, sounding like she was going to cry. But Sham snatched the T-shirt up and rubbed her finger on the stain.

"No, it's OK! Don't stress! It's oil only. Look." She sniffed her finger. "Smells familiar—oh, it's palm oil. That's all it is."

"OK," said Belinda. She sat down shakily. "OK."

"All it needs is some detergent," said Sham. "We should get our minds out of the gutter."

Belinda tried to smile. "Is he still posting pictures on Facebook?"

Sham nodded. She was tracking the impossible pictures Bullet put up of Belinda and taking screenshots so they had a record.

"What do you want to do, Belinda?"

Belinda held up her hands and shrugged, a little despairing movement of the shoulders. *What's there to do?* her shoulders said.

"If he's really a student, we can report him to the uni," said Sham.

"Do you think that'll work?" Belinda was trying to sound normal, but her breath was coming in funny hitching gasps, and her nose was turning red. "Will that make him stop?"

Sham was not by rule a toucher, but she put her arm around Belinda. Belinda's thin shoulders jerked under her arm.

"I should—" said Belinda. "I should have—"

"Should have what?" said Sham. "Calm down."

"I should have said yes to somebody," gulped Belinda. "One of the eleven boys. I should have said I'd go out with one of them. B-but I didn't like them that way. I d-d-didn't ask them to like me also."

"Who said you did?"

"Feels like I'm being punished," sobbed Belinda. "Because I didn't say yes to any of them. Bullet was sent to punish me."

"This is what comes of being religious," Sham told her. "You all think everything that happens is because God wants to teach you something or other. Sometimes things just happen lah."

"Who is Bullet, then?" said Belinda. "How come he can do all this thing—the necklace and the photos? What is he? You don't know!"

"You think I don't know?" snapped Sham.

She didn't; she hadn't a clue. But if Belinda was scared, then somebody had to be angry for her. If Belinda didn't understand what was happening, Sham would pretend she did.

"He's an asshole, that's what he is," said Sham, and as she was saying it her eyes fell on the T-shirt. The grease stain on it made her mind suddenly light up.

Sham was desperate. She would never have believed what she was thinking at any other time. The fact that she turned out to be right she could only ascribe, later, to Divine Providence: Belinda's God stepping in and helping out for once.

"And he's something else also," said Sham.

The next day she persuaded Alwyn to let her into his college's computer room. She checked all the computers and found nothing.

She refused to feel foolish. She had to try everything.

"You all only have one computer room?" she said.

"Yah," said Alwyn. "Eh, no—actually there's another one at T staircase. Nobody really uses it. Why?"

"The printer here is not working," lied Sham. "We better go to the other one."

The second computer room was in the basement. Small and windowless, it might as well have been a converted dungeon for all its cheeriness and warmth. The computer she was looking for was in an especially dark corner of the room.

Of course this was where he'd have done it. The perfect den for the perfect stalker.

"Shamini," said Alwyn, as Sham bent over the keyboard. He looked awkward. "Look, I know this is going to sound kind of per-asan. But I really like May Ling. I mean, we're pretty serious. And I think you're a nice girl, but—"

"But you always thought I was a lesbian," Sham finished. She stood up. "Don't worry, Alwyn. I'm not trying to court you or what. Just trying to find out something."

Alwyn's mouth was open. "Are you?"

"Yah. I might make it my fallback if the scientist thing doesn't work out," said Sham. "Become PI instead."

"No, I mean, are you really, um, a lesbian?" said Alwyn.

"Oh, that," said Sham. "Yah, but didn't you know already?"

"Everybody says, but—" Alwyn clamped his mouth shut. Even his pimples looked embarrassed.

Sham took pity on him.

"Thanks, Alwyn," she said. "You've been very helpful. I won't waste any more of your time."

Sham's chance landed in her lap.

"Rohan and Wei Na want me to come for dinner on Friday," said Belinda.

They were meant to be going to a play on Friday. Belinda's New Year resolution had been to make an effort to keep up with the local drama scene. ("What if the next John Cleese is here, right now, and we miss him?" said Belinda. "We missed the last John Cleese and we're doing OK," said Sham.)

But Sham didn't mind tagging along. Belinda went in for Beckett and Brecht; Sham preferred musicals.

"Tell them we're going for the Narnia musical," said Sham.

"I did, but they insisted. I told them if we came we'll be late, and they said never mind, they'll wait for us to eat." Belinda paused. "I'm scared Bullet's going to be there."

"Did they say he's coming?"

"No-o. But Rohan said, 'If you don't come, the cook will be very disappointed.' It was just the way he look at me. He and Bullet suppose to be super close, right, you said?" Belinda flushed. "I'm becoming really paranoid."

"It's not paranoia if they're really out to get you," said Sham absently. "Belinda. If Bullet's gonna be there, you have to go."

"Why?"

"Because you have to tell him no to his face," said Sham. "I tell you, that's the only way to get rid of this kind of guy."

Belinda's mouth twisted. "What if it doesn't work?"

"You try first. If it doesn't work, I'll get rid of him some other way," said Sham. "Tell them we're coming."

Dinner did not get off to a promising start. Rohan dropped a pan of vegetables on the floor when he saw Sham.

"Shit! Where's Belinda?" he said.

"Your carpet is burning," Sham said to Wei Na, whose room it was.

"Rohan!" wailed Wei Na.

"That's gonna cost you," Sham observed, enjoying a pleasant sense of schadenfreude. "My college fine me £50 once just because I leave an electric fan in the room outside term-time. Burnt carpet will probably cost a million."

"Where's Belinda?" said Rohan. "Shit! You weren't even invited, and now Belinda's not here pulak—"

"She just went toilet," said Sham. "But sorry, I interrupted. You were saying how you didn't invite me?"

"Ignore Rohan. He's so stressed about this veg he doesn't know what he's saying," said Wei Na smoothly.

Rohan grasped at the excuse. "Yah, I burnt the cabbage."

"Don't worry," said Wei Na. "That's the only thing he made. The other things not he cook one."

"Oh right?" said Sham. "You cooked the rest, is it?"

Wei Na had the grace to look uncomfortable.

"No, no," she said. "We got an actual good cook to make. You'll see in a minute. Er—I'll go get the rice cooker from the kitchen."

"There's someone else coming for dinner?" said Sham to Rohan. "Thought you all only."

Rohan's eyes slid over her.

"Got another friend," he mumbled.

Sham felt a draft. The door shut behind her. Rohan's face brightened.

"Belinda! Sit down," he said. "How was the show? Good thing you came, man. I'm starving!"

"Sorry," said Belinda. "You all didn't have to wait."

"Have to wait," said a deep voice. Not Wei Na's voice. Not the voice of anyone they knew. "You're the whole reason we're here."

Sham turned around and saw the creature that called itself Bullet Sri Kaya.

It was shaped like a man. Not a bad-looking man, with curly hair and skin a few shades lighter than Sham's. He would have looked human if not for two things.

His whole body was covered with a thin layer of grease. His skin glowed. A buttery film submerged his eyes. Oil shone in the part in his hair. As he walked across the room towards Belinda, the grease marked dark footprints on the carpet.

The other thing was that he was nude.

Sham caught his arm before he could get to Belinda where she sat petrified. The flesh was slippery and horribly warm, the texture more like plastic than human skin. Sham was shuddering, but she forced herself to grasp his wrist and pull him down to the floor next to her.

"Come, sit here," she said brightly. "Tell me about yourself. I've heard so much about you."

"Can't believe you all haven't met Bullet before," said Wei Na, coming into the room with the rice cooker. "He's everywhere!"

"Seems like it," said Sham. The muscles in Bullet's arm were moving as if they each had a mind of their own, pushing against her hand. She bared her teeth at the thing.

"I didn't know UK also got things like you," she said.

"You know what I am," said Bullet. His blank eyes swiveled around to Belinda. "You also, darling?"

Belinda looked like she was going to throw up.

"Orang minyak," said Sham. She was so terrified she could barely hear what she was saying, but she kept talking to distract him. "The saddest ghost. The most loserish hantu. At least give us hantu tetek lah. Even that is more scary."

Bullet ignored her. His eyes were fixed on Belinda.

"Don't worry," he said. There was something funny about the timbre of his voice. If you closed your eyes, you couldn't tell where in the room it was coming from. It seemed to well from the walls and seep into the spaces inside your head.

"You can see me now," said Bullet to Belinda. "But not for long. When I touch your eyes, you will forget. I will look like a human to you. Like they all—they don't see anything funny."

Rohan and Wei Na were moving around the room with plates of curry and vegetables and rice. They seemed oblivious to the conversation.

"They have oil in their eyes and ears, but it didn't hurt them," said Bullet. "They're very happy. You don't have to be scared."

Sham let go of Bullet and got up. He didn't seem to notice.

"You can be happy too," said Bullet. "We can be together, darling. I came all the way here for you."

"One thing only I want to know," said Sham. She took a bottle out of her bag and twisted the cap off carefully, to avoid any liquid splashing out. "How did you find Belinda?"

"Facebook," said Bullet. "She is the sixteenth most beautiful girl I ever saw."

"All the hantu are online now eh," said Sham.

"I bought my flight here online also," said Bullet. "AirAsia X sale. Very cheap only."

"And what happened to the first fifteen most beautiful girls?" said Sham.

Bullet smiled. Even his teeth were oily. A shining bead of grease rolled out of his mouth and slid down his chin.

"I found them," he said.

Sham had to move quickly, but there was something to be done first. She said:

"I think Belinda has something to say to you."

Belinda's mouth worked. She shook her head slightly, her eyes fixed on Sham's in mute appeal.

"I could tell you," said Sham. "But it needs to come from her."

Belinda cleared her throat.

"I-I think you're a creep," she said. "And I want you to leave me alone!"

She gave Sham a delighted, unbelieving look. She had never said anything like this to any of her suitors before.

"You won't feel like that after I've touched you," said Bullet. He smiled.

Sham nodded.

"Thought you'd say something like that," she said.

She upended the bottle over his head.

The smell was awful, the scream Bullet let out even worse. Where the liquid had splashed his hair, it turned into black grease. His face blurred. His head started collapsing, his features folding in on themselves.

He pushed up off the floor and staggered towards Sham. He reached out, but the flesh on his arms was already melting away, revealing bone, until that too liquefied and dripped on the floor.

"Bitch," he said out of a misshapen mouth. It was probably a fitting word for him to die on.

His dissolution left a foul-smelling pool of grease on the carpet.

Sham was conscious of a sense of relief. She hadn't been sure the dispersant would have any effect on Bullet. It was good that it had worked.

She stared at the stain until Rohan's voice jolted her out of her daze.

"Shit!" said Rohan. "What the hell happened?"

Sham's face felt stiff. She looked down and realized Belinda was holding her hand. When Bullet had started screaming, Belinda had sprung up. Sham had thought she was going to run away, but she'd come closer instead.

"What's all that shit on the floor?" said Rohan.

"Somebody else's problem," said Belinda. "Come on, Sham. Let's go back."

Sham's hands were trembling, but Belinda's hand around hers was still and warm.

"Next time," Sham said, "you save the day."

"I know," said Belinda. "Thanks, Sham."

Prudence and the Dragon

There was a dragon in town.

Statues all over the city climbed off their pedestals and went walking about. The Winston Churchill from Parliament Square gave an interview to the BBC, still squinting as if the wind were blowing in its eyes. The statue was appropriately witty, but did not seem to remember anything about World War II. It did, however, have a lot to say about pigeons.

Silver griffins bowled down the streets of the City, tripping up lawyers and outraging bankers, and Winged Victory on the Arch finished her yawn and dropped her arms.

The pigeons grew human bodies, all of which wore suits from Austin Reed. They marched in their thousands into architects' firms, university admissions offices, food consultancy businesses, struggling non-profits; they stole colleagues' lunches and strewed cubicles with green-gray feathers. Despite these minor eccentricities they made excellent workers: they had a firm grasp of commercial realities and never went on Facebook.

For several days every Tesco in the country stocked only pomegranates and nothing else. If you ate the seeds from one of these you vanished and your soul was dispatched to Hades. There was a rash of deaths before anyone realized.

The buses of London turned into giant cats—tigers and leopards and jaguars with hollow bodies in which passengers sat. You could still use your Oyster card on them, but bus usage dropped: the seats were soft and pink and sucked at you in a disturbingly organic way when you sat down, and the buses were given to stopping in the middle of the road to quarrel with one another.

Meanwhile the dragon coiled itself around the tip of the Gherkin and brooded over the city.

Where Prudence came from, spirits were an everyday thing. You knew they were there and you acknowledged them when necessary. You set out the bunga melur for Dato Gong when you were going to build a house, asked permission of the grandfathers and grandmothers before you took a shit in the jungle. You apologized to tree stumps if you kicked them accidentally, and made sure the dead were fed well in the seventh month of the year.

In Britain people were far too sophisticated to pray to their spirits. Instead they wrote articles about them. The broadsheets did serious-minded comment pieces about how the dragon was a metaphor for the Labour party in exile from Whitehall. Thaumatologists were quoted as explaining that the mere presence of the dragon increased atmospheric magic levels and that was why clothes in Primark were now labelled things like "Made by enslaved goblins in Fairyland."

The tabloids wanted to know whether the dragon was receiving benefits. The gossip magazines claimed to have found a woman who was bearing the dragon's baby. The fashion magazines did spreads on draconic style. This apparently consisted of gaunt models with sunken eyes, swathed in clouds of chiffon and arranged in awkwardly erotic positions on piles of gold coins.

Because Prudence Ong never read newspapers or watched British TV, she maintained a spotlessly pure ignorance of the dragon throughout. She encountered the dragon in a rather more traditional setting. She met him down the pub.

Historically, it was the Sorcerer Royal who performed the role of human-dragon liaison, but nobody had been appointed to that office for the past couple of centuries. So it was the mayor who had to take the dragon to the pub, even though he would have preferred to stay in his office and worry about public transport.

He took the dragon to a pub on Lamb's Conduit Street, where the dragon would not meet anyone the mayor knew. Everyone knew what the dragon's visit was for, and while the mayor could think of several people he would like to have removed to another dimension, a dragon seemed too blunt and indiscriminate a tool to do it with.

In his human form the dragon was a man—imperially slim, with glowing blue-black skin and startlingly pale eyes. He was wearing a heather-gray suit and shining leather shoes. He was exquisite, so much so that when he paused at the entrance of the pub he drew a gasp from the people in it. The men gazed hungrily at him; the women touched their hair.

He didn't seem to notice the sensation he'd caused.

"It's considered terribly gauche now to obtain a maiden without first asking her if she wants to be obtained," he was saying to the mayor. "I assure you, the maiden's consent is paramount."

"That's good to hear," said the mayor. He was thinking about bicycle lanes.

But he roused himself as they waited at the bar for their drinks. "Of course one would never wish to discard the noble old traditions for no good reason. But it does seem likely that there would be some outcry if there was any incident of—any sort of—anything that might possibly be construed as, er, snatching, if you understand me."

"Oh no," said the dragon. He was gazing around the pub with interest, like an alien at the Grand Prix. It wasn't clear whether he meant that there would be no such incident, or whether he was saying that he didn't understand the mayor. The mayor did not get the opportunity to clarify, because just then the dragon froze like a dog that had smelled a squirrel. He was staring over the mayor's shoulder.

The mayor followed the dragon's gaze to a group sitting at the other end of the room. The attraction was obvious: at the table sat a young woman of dazzling beauty. She was so beautiful even the mayor felt his heart wobble in his chest. But he was a married man and still recovering from his most recent extramarital scandal. He said to the dragon:

"Shall we find a seat?"

They sat next to the girl, of course. The dragon lost no time. He leaned over to the next table. The flowerlike face turned to him.

"Excuse me," said the dragon. "What is the name of your charming friend?"

"Who?" said the beautiful girl. "You mean Prudence?"

It was only at this point that the mayor noticed the beautiful girl's friend. She was a small round-faced woman. Usually she would have been brown, but just then she was almost fluorescent pink. An empty pint glass sat in front of her.

"Yes?" said Prudence.

She was feeling cross. Alcohol did not suit her and she did not like pubs. She was only there because Pik Mun had asked. Prudence had ordered cider because she did not think it was worth paying £2 for orange juice transferred from a carton to a pint glass, but she was beginning to regret it. Twin tentacles of a headache were slithering along her temples and would soon meet in the middle of her forehead.

She looked at the men who had spoken to Pik Mun. One of them was an intimidatingly beautiful model type in a suit, and the other was a podgy white man with a sort of nose.

The nose-possessing white man blurted, "What, her?"

"Prudence," murmured the model, as if he were tasting the word and finding it delicious. "It's so nice to meet you. My name is Zheng Yi."

"Oh," said Prudence. She was puzzled. "Why are you named like that?"

"Prudence!" hissed Pik Mun. She smiled at the dragon. "Sorry, my friend's had a little too much to drink."

"I told you already I don't need a whole pint," grumbled Prudence.

"Could I have your number?" said Zheng Yi.

Prudence knew the answer to this one.

"No," she said. "I don't even know you."

She turned her back on him.

On the way home Pik Mun expostulated with her. "I can't believe you just turned him down like that! And you were so rude to him!"

"It's not like he's my friend what," said Prudence. "I don't like strangers who think it's OK to talk to you. If I wanted to talk to them we would be friends already."

"He was just being friendly," said Pik Mun. She sighed. "And he was so cute!"

The unfair thing about Pik Mun was that she was intelligent as well as stop-you-dead-in-your-tracks beautiful. She was creative, generous, and lively. She danced, painted, wrote poetry, sold her knit creations to raise funds for asylum seekers, and she had a fan club of boys who followed her around and made her bad birthday cakes by committee.

These days she went by the name Angela, but when Prudence had first met her in Standard One, at the age of seven, her name had been Pik Mun. Most of the people who knew them found it inexplicable that Angela chose to keep Prudence around, considering that the only book Prudence ever read was Cheese and Onion and she thought flamenco was a kind of bird.

But Prudence was the only one among Angela's friends who still called her Pik Mun. Angela valued history.

She also loved Prudence and wanted her to be happy. She said, "He seems so interesting. He had a Chinese name leh, even though he was so dark skinned. Aren't you curious to find out why?"

"You know I am not really curious one," said Prudence. She reached up and knocked one of the jaguar's vertebrae. The jaguar coughed and started inching towards the pavement.

"You asked him if he was mixed in the pub what," Angela pointed out.

"Hah?" said Prudence.

"You know, when you asked about his name," said Angela.

"Oh, that," said Prudence: but it was her stop.

"You better not regret ah," said Angela as Prudence stepped out of the bus. "If you change your mind, remember we can always try to Google him, OK!"

So the chance to mention it to Angela passed. But Prudence wondered about it as she walked home. The reason why she had asked the model type about his name was because when she was small, she used to daydream about marrying the pirate Zheng Yi and sailing the waves as an indomitable pirate queen. Zheng Yi had remained her ideal boyfriend until she turned twelve, when she put away childish things. In Prudence's world, childish things included boyfriends.

Angela would have found that bit of history interesting, but Prudence would probably forget to tell her the next time they saw each other. Prudence shrugged the shoulders of her mind. It was just a coincidence anyway.

On Monday morning Prudence opened her eyes knowing something was different. Zheng Yi smiled at her.

"Good morning, Prudence," said Zheng Yi.

Prudence screamed and leapt out of bed.

"Aaaaah!" She picked up the nearest thing to hand and threw the bottle of moisturiser at him. "Aaaaah!" She threw the alarm clock.

Zheng Yi put his hands behind his head and leaned back against the pillows. He was in a black suit with a plum-colored shirt and silver cuff links, but at least he'd had the manners to take his shoes off.

"Come live with me and be my love," he said.

"Aaaah!" A hardcover cookery book winged its way through the air. "Get out or I'll call the police!"

"You can't," said Zheng Yi. Sure enough, Prudence's mobile phone was nowhere to be found, though she was certain she'd left it on the bedside table before going to sleep the night before. She looked around for the telephone but that had vanished as well. It had turned into a ferret and escaped out of the window during the night, but Prudence didn't learn about this until much later.

Nothing magical had happened to the mobile phone. It was sitting in Zheng Yi's left pocket.

"You have no reason to fear me," said Zheng Yi. "I won't do anything to you against your will. I'm just making you an offer."

Prudence stopped throwing things. She glared at him suspiciously.

"What?" said Zheng Yi.

"What's wrong with your teeth?"

Had his teeth really looked like opals? The next time Zheng Yi smiled they were normal teeth, very white against his dark skin.

"Come away with me," said Zheng Yi. "I will show you sorcerous wonders, the likes of which you have never imagined. You will learn how to put your hand into fire and grasp its beating heart. You will speak to fairies, and they will speak back if they know what's good for them. I will teach you the secrets of the moon and the language of the stars."

Prudence threw the hairdryer at him.

"I'm not interested in astronomy!" she snapped.

The alarm clock had dropped behind the bed, but now it started ringing.

"Oh crap," said Prudence. She rushed out of the room.

When she came back in she was brushing her teeth. She tugged at Zheng Yi's shoulder with one hand.

"Get up," she said. "You can go to the living room, whatever, I don't care. I need to change. Late for school already!"

The living room and kitchen were open plan because there was not enough space for them to be separate rooms. There were four pieces of toast in the toaster. Prudence was conscious of her duties as a host even when her guest was an importunate model with the name of a pirate.

When Prudence came back in, Zheng Yi was inspecting the stethoscope on the dining table.

"What is this?" he said.

"Don't play with my stethoscope!" said Prudence. She picked up a sheaf of notes on the colon. "You can have toast and kaya. After that must go already. I got to go for lecture, and you can't get out of the building without the keys. How'd you get in anyway?"

Zheng Yi gave her a long look.

"I'm a dragon," he said. His eyes contained galaxies.

Unfortunately the comets and nebulae were wasted on Prudence. She was taking the kaya and butter out of the fridge.

"Where got such thing?" she scoffed. "In my country this we call stalker."

"You are amusing," said Zheng Yi. "Has it not occurred to you to be frightened of me at all?"

"You said I don't need to be scared of you what," said Prudence. "No?"

"Usually people don't believe me when I say that," said Zheng Yi pensively. "Humans are so narrow-minded. A little fire-breathing, a few maidens here and there, and suddenly you're not to be trusted."

Prudence was only listening to about forty percent of what Zheng Yi was saying, which was good because Zheng Yi only meant forty percent of anything he said. She lobbed the jar of kaya at him, and he caught it.

"No need to talk so much," she said. "Spread your own kaya."

Angela had saved a seat in the lecture theater for Prudence. It was next to the aisle, but by the time Prudence had opened her folder and uncapped her pen, this was no longer the case. She looked up to find Zheng Yi sitting next to her.

"Oh my gosh," whispered Angela. "He's a medic too? He's a bit old to be a student, right?"

Prudence had parted from Zheng Yi on her doorstep. She narrowed her eyes at him. If Zheng Yi had not been far too elegant to grin, she would have sworn that that was what he was doing.

"No," said Zheng Yi. "We came from her flat."

Angela's eyes went round.

"We had a business breakfast," said Prudence, glaring at him. "Zheng Yi is going to be my—my—"

"Everything," said Zheng Yi.

Angela laid a hand on Prudence's arm. She looked a little faint. "Don't you think this is moving too fast? You only met day before yesterday!"

"Pik Mun, he's right there. Whisper also he can hear," said Prudence. "Zheng Yi is just saying that he is going to be doing everything for me. He is my personal assistant."

"Huh?" said Angela.

"Is that a yes?" said Zheng Yi.

"He's a management consultant," said Prudence, inventing wildly. "But he's thinking of changing career to become doctor. We bump into each other on the street yesterday and he ask me if he can shadow me, so I said OK lor, provided he help me with stuff."

"Like what kind of stuff?" said Angela.

"Like taking notes," said Prudence. "You know I find it hard to concentrate on what the lecturer's speaking when I'm writing." She shoved a notebook and pen at Zheng Yi. "Nah. You take notes."

She waited till the lecture had started and Angela had turned her attention elsewhere. Then she hissed, "And no, that is not a yes!"

Zheng Yi was taking notes of the lecture with surprising diligence. He paused in the middle of a sentence to turn limpid sad eyes on her.

"I ask for your sake as much as mine," he said. "To refuse would be to miss the opportunity of a lifetime. Any magician would give his left eye for what I'm offering you. Really, you'll regret it tremendously if you say no."

"I don't even know what's the question you're asking!"

"Perhaps over time you will figure it out," said Zheng Yi. He turned back to his notes.

"What's that mean?" said Prudence, but Zheng Yi raised his finger to his lips.

"Shh, she's listing the various drugs for treatment," he said. "This is important stuff."

He was right, which was a pity, as Prudence was not going to have any record of it. This became apparent when Zheng Yi handed her his notes.

"What's this?" said Prudence.

"It's the notes of the lecture you asked me to take," said Zheng Yi.

"I can't read this," said Prudence. She could not even look at the symbols for long without feeling uncomfortable. The symbols seemed to writhe on the page.

"It's written in Draconic Runes," said Zheng Yi. "Much more interesting than any human language. Each ideogram is itself a poem on the qualities of each drug your teacher discussed, echoing the structure of each sentence, which discusses the same subject but reveals new layers of meaning and context underpinning your teacher's every utterance, and every sentence joins together into a giant ideogram, an uber-ideogram if you will, the significance of which is, 'I love Pru—'"

"Can't you write in English?" said Prudence.

"No," said Zheng Yi.

Another thing Zheng Yi could not do was take hints. He stopped sleeping on the bed after Prudence explained that this could only lead to grievous bodily harm, but he did not go away.

Fortunately he was good at cooking. And he would have watered the tomato plants every day, except that this had two results: first, the tomatoes thrived; second, they grew faces and began to talk. Prudence asked him to stop because she didn't like the way their eyes followed her around the flat, but after that the tomatoes stopped meeting her eyes and started weeping and begging for mercy whenever Zheng Yi came by their pot.

He was a difficult person to manage.

Also Prudence suspected that Angela was beginning to see through her ruse.

"Does he live here?" said Angela. She had come over for a cookout on Friday night, as was their tradition.

"No," said Prudence. "Why you ask?"

Angela looked at the sofa she was sitting on. "Then why got blanket and pillow here one?"

"I like to lie down when I watch TV," said Prudence.

"He's not actually doing work experience, right?"

"Yes," said Prudence. "I mean, no. I mean, he is! Why are you asking?"

Angela cast a glance towards the kitchen area, where Zheng Yi was bending over a bubbling pot of something or other. She leaned closer. "Your tomato got face! And I found this on your bathroom floor!"

She held up what looked like a chip of black marble, cut marvelously thin and translucent, with veins of gold running through it. Colors shifted on its smooth surface, as they do on an opal when you turn it this way and that in the light. Prudence was reminded of teeth.

She took it from Angela. It was less brittle than she thought it would be, bending like a thin sheet of plastic when she folded it.

"I think it's a scale," said Angela. "Like fish scale. I think your personal assistant is the dragon."

Prudence gave her a blank look.

"Hah, don't tell me you don't even know about the dragon," said Angela.

Prudence tried to look intelligent. It didn't work.

"Prudence!" said Angela. "Don't you even read the *Evening Standard*? Ah, don't answer. This is what happens when you only read textbook. The dragon came to London, what, a few weeks ago? Something like that. It comes to London every 100-200 years or so. The British say it comes to choose a maiden and then it takes the maiden away to live in this other dimension where the dragons live. Forever!"

Prudence thought about this.

"What for?" she said.

"How I know?" said Angela. "Got a lot of theory but nobody knows for sure. The dragons don't explain. People say maybe having a human helps the dragon to do its magic spells. But you don't know, Prudence. Maybe they eat the humans."

"Zheng Yi can't be a dragon lah," said Prudence. "Number one, he looks like human. Number two, he likes kaya toast. If you eat kaya toast, what for you want to eat human?"

"Then the tomatoes leh?"

"Hmm," said Prudence.

"What explanation do you have for a random guy who just shows up one day and follows you around?" said Angela.

"I thought maybe he's homeless," said Prudence.

"Prudence—" Angela dropped her hands in her lap. "OK. All that never mind. But tell me honestly, OK? Do you like him? As in, *like* him-like him?"

"No," said Prudence. "I don't even like him with one like."

"I heard that," said Zheng Yi from the kitchen.

"Then are you just going to let him hang around?"

"How to make him go away? When I try to call police I only get the Worshipful Company of Glaziers receptionist," said Prudence. "But never mind. I sleep with baseball bat one side, kitchen knife on the other side. And you know I do tae kwan do."

"I also heard that," said Zheng Yi.

"Good!" said Prudence.

Angela still looked worried.

"At least you'll tell me if you are going to another dimension, right?" she said. "You know we booked the bed-and-breakfast in Lake District already."

"I'm not going anywhere," said Prudence.

"I live in hope," said Zheng Yi, coming to the table. He laid a crockpot of stew on the table.

With a supernatural effort at politeness, Angela said, "Oh, that smells delicious. What is it?"

"Potatoes, carrots, swede, some grated apple for sweetness, fairies for protein. But only non-sentient ones," said Zheng Yi reassuringly. "Fairies are terribly good for you."

They were also quite crunchy, and froze well.

Prudence was by nature an incurious person, but she did find herself wondering about Zheng Yi. Dragon or no dragon, having him around did not change Prudence's life appreciably. She taught the tomatoes to sing songs so they would not get bored when she was away. She went to the hospital and for her lectures. Zheng Yi followed her around when she did not object and went about his own mysterious affairs the rest of the time.

They were grocery shopping at Sainsbury's one day when Prudence said abruptly, "How come dragons need maidens?"

Zheng Yi paused in the act of picking up a Basics bag of Onions of Forgetting.

"So you agree that I'm a dragon?" he said.

"I didn't say that," said Prudence quickly.

"One keeps explaining to humans, but they never believe one," said Zheng Yi. "It's a very simple reason. It just gets lonely. After thousands of years alone in a cave, one longs for companionship."

"Why don't you hang out with the other dragons?"

"Other dragons are bastards," said Zheng Yi. "I moved out of my mother's cave after my mother tried to rip my guts out."

"Oh."

"Granted, I had tried to steal her Tiara of Clairvoyance," said Zheng Yi. "Bad idea. Never try to steal anything shiny from a dragon."

"Not to say I believe you," said Prudence. "But say you are a dragon. Why choose me for what?"

Zheng Yi stopped in the middle of the aisle to take her hand. They were standing between the pasta and the coffee. His eyes were the deepest bluey-green. Prudence had seen that color only once before, out of a train window in Japan, speeding past mountain rivers which had taken on the color of the dark green pine forests around them.

Zheng Yi spoke in a low, velvety voice:

"You," he said, "are tremendously funny."

Prudence jerked her hand away.

"Must get some rice," she said. "We're running out."

It was all fine and good when Zheng Yi was just making himself useful, but then he became a problem. The problem was, Angela fell in love with him.

Prudence was not very good at this sort of thing. She did not really understand feelings, so it puzzled her when Angela began to act funny.

Angela started having other things to do on Friday night. Friday night cookouts were not a sacred tradition; they were allowed to miss Fridays if they had stuff on. But three Fridays passed by and Angela was busy every week.

Of course they still saw each other, at lectures and lunch and so on, but she was different then as well. They would be talking naturally, laughing away as they had always done, and then Prudence would say something about the food in her freezer and Angela's face would just change. Prudence did not need to be sensitive to notice change in a face she had known for so long, though she did not understand what it meant.

It was worst when Zheng Yi was around. Then Angela was outrageously rude to Zheng Yi, but at the same time he was the only one she had any attention for. She had no time to speak to Prudence.

Perhaps the fight was inevitable. Yet Prudence felt she might somehow have avoided it, if only she were not such a tactless person. She had not even meant what she was saying. They were in a park eating sandwiches after lectures and before clinics, and talking about babies. Angela was a great one for baby-watching.

"That's a pretty one," she said, waving her ciabatta at a little curly-haired brown baby. "I think I would like my baby to have curly hair."

"Where got Chinese got curly hair?" said Prudence.

"I'll just have to marry somebody non-Chinese lor," said Angela. Prudence hmm-ed.

"I don't mind," said Angela. "My parents are quite chilling about this kind of thing. My auntie got marry a Mat Salleh. Blue eyes, blond hair, everything."

"Mat Salleh are OK," said Prudence. "It's when they're not-Chinese, not-Mat Salleh. Then you see whether your parents are chilling or not. Especially if darker skin."

Angela made a face. "True."

They lapsed into silence, Angela considering the merits of each passing baby, and Prudence struggling with her baguette. Despite four years in a sandwich-eating country, she had yet to master this tricky form of food. Her chicken mayonnaise was starting to drip out the other end.

"I think I will name my baby Tristram," said Angela.

"Very posh," said Prudence. Perhaps if she started eating from the other end? But then the chicken mayo started coming out of both ends. It was difficult to know what to do.

"Don't you like Tristram?"

"It's a bit hard to pronounce," said Prudence. She caught a piece of chicken before it could make a break for it, and put it in her mouth. "And maybe the other kids will make fun."

"What you want to name your kids?"

"I don't want children," said Prudence. "OK, OK, but if I have to, I wouldn't name something like Tristram. If I have children already they will probably be bullied."

"Why?"

"Because they'll be mixed mah," said Prudence. "Not so many people are half-reptile." She was too much entangled in mayo-smeared disaster to observe Angela's expression or to notice the way she said, "Oh."

Prudence managed to get the remainder of the baguette in her mouth and chewed, feeling relieved. Next time she would get sushi to go.

"Are you and Zheng Yi together?" said Angela in a low voice.

"Ngah? Ngro." Prudence swallowed.

"No," she repeated. The past five minutes replayed themselves in her head. She had not really been listening to what she had been saying. For some unaccountable reason her cheeks felt hot.

"No lah," said Prudence. What a ridiculous thing to have said! What could have possessed her to say it? Such things did happen. You said something meaningless, for no reason, to fill the air with noise. It was just embarrassing when other people noticed it. The only thing to do was to pile more noise on top of it until it was forgotten.

"Why so curious? You're interested, is it?" she said jokingly. "You can have him if you want. I don't want him."

Angela's face closed up, like a gate clanging shut. The voice that came out of that taut pale face was like a stranger's.

"Well, that's a remarkably stupid thing to say," said Angela. "Even for you. And not like you're known for saying clever things like that."

Prudence had never seen Angela's face so mean. She managed to get out, "What?"

"You know I like him!" shouted Angela. "You pretend like you're so blur but actually you just pretend because it makes things easier for you! If you're blur then easy lah, you don't have to see anything you don't want to see, you don't have to do anything you don't want to do. People will accommodate you because you are so naive konon. You think it's cute, is it? Maybe you think you've fooled everybody. Maybe you've even fooled yourself. But you don't think you've fooled me."

She stood up. In the way of Angela, she did not even have any crumbs on her lap to brush off. She looked Prudence up and down, and for the first time Prudence was acutely conscious of the bits of bread and mayo stains on her jeans, of the width of her thighs, of the depressing lankness of her hair. Her hoodie did not look good on her; her face was too big. The whole world could see this.

"Just remember this," said Angela. "I don't need anybody's leftovers. And I especially don't need yours."

She stormed off.

Prudence put her hand on her chest. To her surprise, it was still whole.

Mostly Prudence felt bewildered. She was confused enough that when Angela didn't meet her at the station, she simply got on the train to Oxenholme by herself. It didn't occur to her to call the B&B and cancel the room they had booked for a week.

She had made it clear to Zheng Yi that he was not to come along. She hadn't said so in so many words, because Zheng Yi had an inconvenient way of ignoring direct orders, but he had instructions to look after the tomato plants and use up the food in the fridge.

When she looked around and saw him in the seat next to her, she was not surprised, or even annoyed. It seemed quite natural for him to be there.

Zheng Yi did not say anything. He took her hand. Prudence nodded and turned to look out of the window at the countryside flowing past. The green fields, the little red houses in the distance, the gentle gray sky above. Angela loved this kind of scenery: "The English countryside is so romantic," she liked to say. Prudence's face felt numb.

Angela was not at Oxenholme station either. Perhaps she would be at the B&B. There was no harm in going. They had booked it already.

When Angela was not at the B&B, and Prudence came to the awful realization that she was not going to come, that this was serious, that they were fighting and perhaps they would never be friends again, she turned to Zheng Yi.

"Might as well go for a walk," she said. "Get to know the area a bit."

She only started crying when they were safely away from the village.

If Prudence was confused, Zheng Yi was in an even worse state. He had been looking at Prudence the whole time with the expression of a dog who does not understand why you won't play fetch with it. This expression intensified with Prudence's tears, with an added dimension of panic. Now he looked like a dog who is worried that you might be thinking of throwing the stick away altogether.

"What are you doing?" he said.

"Seventeen years!" said Prudence. "We've been friends for seventeen years. That's how old some people are! Some people have only lived seventeen years!"

"I don't understand," said Zheng Yi.

"Pik Mun never didn't friend me before," wailed Prudence. "Why-why-why she doesn't like me anymore?"

"What is that coming out of your eyes?" said Zheng Yi. He looked closer. "And your nose?"

"What?" said Prudence. She touched her face, and her hands came away wet, but they were not any alarming color. "It's water. I'm crying, you doink! You've never seen tears before?"

She had not meant it seriously, but for the first time since Prudence had met him, Zheng Yi looked shy.

"Never," he said. "I've never actually had a human. You're my first."

"This dragon bullshit again!" Prudence rounded on him. "Can you stop talking nonsense? Pik Mun doesn't want to friend me any more and you can still talk cock like this!"

"I am a dragon," said Zheng Yi. "You know that."

"I don't know anything!" snapped Prudence. She turned and made to stomp away. However she had not been looking where she was going for quite some time. She found herself stomping right into a river.

It was too late to stop by the time she realized. The ground was muddy and treacherous—it had just rained. She slid down the bank, and the water came up and hugged her close. It was freezing cold, and the force of it swept her along the course of the river with dizzying speed. She pushed both her arms straight out and kicked.

Don't panic, she thought. *Must stay calm.* Swimming couldn't be that hard; you just kept moving and somehow that made it so you didn't sink—but she was sinking. And she couldn't breathe. Everything was a white swirl, and the roaring in her ears made it difficult to think. She was drowning—she had to stop drowning—

Stay still, said Zheng Yi's voice. She heard it as if he was speaking directly into her ear. *Stop fighting me. You're safe.*

The water trembled with the words.

Everything came together, the disparate elements of air and water and sound reconfiguring themselves into a logical pattern. The river turned from chaos into one long smooth curve, and Prudence was locked safely in its heart. She was not being battered anymore, not being flung about by the untamed force of the river. She was inside the river. The river was the dragon. She was sitting on a fixed place and she was moving, but in the way that you are moving when you sit in a plane—there is the forward motion of something larger than you that you scarcely feel.

She put out her hand and touched river water, cold as winter. She put out her hand and touched warm pulsing flesh. She was sitting in the dragon's mouth. She could see daylight through the gaps between his teeth. Magic clogged her nose and tingled on her skin.

The river and the dragon spat her out on the bank, and when the river receded it left the dragon. Prudence saw through bleary eyes a long, gleaming black creature like an overgrown gecko. When she blinked, Zheng Yi was human-shaped again.

"You see?" said Zheng Yi, looking smugger than anything that isn't a cat should be able to look.

"Can't see anything," Prudence managed to croak, before a fit of coughing overtook her.

"I am a dragon," said Zheng Yi superfluously. "Now will you come away with me?"

Zheng Yi helped Prudence sit up, but there was still a pressure in her chest. She pressed her hand against her chest to relieve it. The wail burst out of her startled throat.

"Shut up! I say no means no already! You don't know how to listen meh? Go away!"

"What?" said Zheng Yi, but Prudence was sobbing.

"You shouldn't make fun of people," she hiccuped. "You shouldn't invite people when you don't want them to come."

"What's this?" said Zheng Yi. His voice had gone all soft. Prudence felt embarrassed and hid her face, but she was soaking wet and it wasn't all that pleasant. She looked for somewhere else to hide her face and found a convenient expanse of warm fabric right next to her. Unfortunately this turned out to be Zheng Yi's shoulder, and dragon or not, he understood enough about human norms to take this as an indication that he should put his arms around her.

"I want you to come," said Zheng Yi. "Why would I ask you if not? Why would I go to all this trouble?"

"Don't simply hug people," grumbled Prudence, but only half-heartedly. It was difficult to tell someone not to hug you when you were busy wiping your nose on their sleeve.

"Why wouldn't I want you?" said Zheng Yi.

"You always laugh at me," said Prudence.

"When do I ever laugh at you?"

"You said I'm funny!" said Prudence.

"Oh, that. You are," said Zheng Yi. "Terribly."

This was the most he would ever say. As dragons go Zheng Yi was actually quite good at feelings that weren't goldlust, but he would never understand that he had to explain that when you are a dragon, and thousands of years old, most things become boring. The most wonderful thing anything can be is amusing. It was his way of telling her that he was madly in love with her.

"I bet you don't think I'm pretty," said Prudence, who was in a mood for self-pity.

"Oh, no," Zheng Yi agreed.

"I don't even know why you want me to go with you then," said Prudence.

Zheng Yi seemed puzzled. "But I've told you so many times."

"Anyway," said Prudence. "We can't go anywhere. I haven't finish med school yet. And after that I still want to get a job and work a few years in UK first."

"I don't mind staying in your dimension for a few years," Zheng Yi conceded. "Not more than a thousand or so, mind. I'd want to get back to the cave after a couple of millennia."

"Hah!" said Prudence. "I'll be dead by then lah. Don't you know anything about humans?" She stretched within the confines of Zheng Yi's arms, and noticed something.

"I'm not wet," she remarked. Even her canvas trainers were dry. Even her socks. The tips of her fingers were warm.

"Don't you know anything about dragons?" said Zheng Yi.

Well, it was like having any other kind of roommate. Zheng Yi looked human most of the time anyway.

"What about the time the dragon was seen drinking up half the Serpentine and the *Daily Mail* said he should be deported back to where he came from?" said Angela.

"He was hungover! I made beef stew, and you know I don't drink. So he had to drink up the rest of the red wine," said Prudence. "Anyway, the *Daily Mail* says that about everybody."

"True," said Angela.

It was a relief to have made up with Angela. It turned out that the falling out, like everything else, was really Zheng Yi's fault. A few days after they had returned from the Lake District, Angela had come to visit. She brought pandan-flavored cupcakes with gula melaka icing that she'd made, and they talked as if nothing had happened, until Angela said suddenly, "I don't even like him. He's not even my type. I don't know what happened."

"Oh," said Prudence, in a voice full of cupcake.

"No, that's a lie," said Angela. "I think I know what happened. It's not a good excuse, though."

Prudence swallowed.

"It's OK, we don't have to talk about it," she said quickly. She did not want to talk about feelings. To have Angela back and pretend that nothing had happened was her idea of a happy ending.

"I think," said Angela, "it's because he was glamouring super hard. I really never felt like that before. It was like when he was around I couldn't think. And then when you all went away, it was like a cloud went away. Suddenly I could see clearly again."

"You think it was magic?" said Prudence.

"Oh, I wouldn't accuse your boyfriend just based on what I think," said Angela. "I went to a thaumaturge and she confirmed my magic levels were super high. I don't have any talent myself, so she say probably I kena secondary glamour."

"But why would Zheng Yi want to glamour you?" said Prudence. Angela thwapped her on the back of the head.

"You never listen. I got secondary glamour. It was a side-effect of hanging out with you. He was glamouring to impress you lah. Did it work?"

Prudence tilted her head from side to side. Her thoughts shot around and bumped into each other inside her skull, as lively as ever.

"I think I can think. Don't feel like there's any cloud," said Prudence. "But Pik Mun, sorry. What did you call Zheng Yi?"

"What?" said Angela. "'Your boyfriend,' is it?"

"Oh," said Prudence. So that was what it was.

The Perseverance
of Angela's Past Life

Angela was stalking herself.

She was packing for Japan, and she had better things to worry about than doppelgangers, so she was trying to pretend her self wasn't there.

She thought she would probably need one pair of formal shoes, but she couldn't decide whether she should pack the new fancy shoes—which were beautiful and appropriate, but untried—or the old stalwart black peeptoes. They were a little manky, but they had seen her through May Balls and medsoc dinners alike.

"Bring both," said her old self.

Her old self could not enter the room without Angela's permission. She hovered at the window, peering in.

Angela was not going to invite her in. It was a cold night, but the dead don't feel the cold.

"I'm traveling light," said Angela. She set the new shoes down and picked up the old pair. What did it matter if they were scuffed? They had never let her down before. "I'm not bringing you also. All the more I shouldn't be bringing extra shoes."

"What lah, not bringing me," said her old self. "I'm part of you what."

The thaumaturge had confirmed this.

The problem was that Angela's best friend was dating a dragon. Initially Angela hadn't noticed any side-effects. Just the usual sort of thing. Outrage that her best friend was no longer as available as she used to be, that Angela was no longer the first person she called when she wanted to watch a musical or go to the park.

But these were ordinary incidents of the readjustment of a best friendship. Angela had got over it in time.

She was having difficulty getting over being split into two people, though.

"Considering you're in constant contact with a dragon, it's no surprise that your blood magic levels are so high," the thaumaturge had said. "But they're not at a level where I would usually be concerned about the impact on your health. You'd be surprised at the human body's tolerance for atmospheric magic. You hear of people living on the border of Fairyland all their lives and never coming to any harm of it. Their children are all engineers and accountants."

Angela cast a sideways glance at the girl who had followed her to the clinic.

"What about her, then?" she said.

"Eh, I have a name, OK," said the girl. "Pik Mun."

"That's *my* name," said Angela to the thaumaturge. "That's my self, actually. She's me. That's not normal, is it?"

"Yes, well," said the thaumaturge. "As I said, your blood magic levels are in the normal range, but I'm afraid you seem abnormally susceptible to thaumaturgical influence. Have you noticed any other symptoms of disproportionate magic uptake?"

"Besides suddenly having an evil twin, you mean?"

"I'm not evil," said Pik Mun belligerently. "I'm just you."

The thaumaturge politely ignored their bickering.

"Waking up several feet above your bed, for example," she said. "Sleep flying is a very common symptom. Or transmutations of ordinary household objects into magical creatures, or vice versa."

"Vice versa?"

"I had a patient with a similar complaint, whose main symptom was the ability to see pixies in her garden," said the thaumaturge. "Unfortunately her other symptom was the ability to turn pixies into spoons. She found it very distressing. She had to sell up and move when the pixies declared war. You could hardly blame them, of course."

"No," said Angela. "This is the only symptom I've noticed. How come my best friend isn't showing any signs of magic absorption? She's the one who's going out with the magical dragon."

"From what you've told me, it sounds like she's immune to magic," said the thaumaturge. "That's probably why you were drawn to each other. Magic often likes to work that way."

She pulled a sympathetic face. She was really a very pretty woman, with pale brown skin, short hair in lots of springy curls, and a charming sprinkle of freckles on her nose.

She'd offered no remedies, however, save for suggesting that Angela remove herself from the source of exposure.

Angela wasn't going to stop hanging out with her best friend just because doing so literally split her in two. But a language camp in Japan had sounded like the ideal opportunity to reduce her blood magic levels and try to get some thinking space, away from her pestersome other self.

She had to leave for Heathrow early the next morning. Angela finished packing, ignoring the heckling from the window, and got to bed by eleven. But it took her a long time to fall asleep.

She shouldn't have looked up her thaumaturge on Facebook. She'd done it because she was wondering about her name. Misola: such a pretty name. If she hadn't looked her up she wouldn't have found out that Misola was dating a woman.

Particularly susceptible, indeed.

"You're so scared for what?" said the voice at the window.

"Can you please go away or not?" said Angela. She rolled over and buried her face under a pillow.

In Japan they put her in a sleek grey building on top of a hill. Below it lay the city, nestled in the green cup of a valley which poured out a brilliant blue sea.

It was summer and the air was as close and sticky as it would have been back home in Malaysia. The nearest convenience store was

45 minutes' walk away, along a path winding past houses and rows of vending machines down the hill.

The hostel was sonorously empty. Angela and the other English teachers were the only ones staying there. In the mornings they taught English lessons; in the afternoons they learnt Japanese. The day finished at four and after that Angela was free.

There was something magical about that hill, but it was a magic that had nothing to do with dragons or pixies or doppelgangers. It breathed from the trees and the silence and the early morning mist.

Up here, Angela thought, she would escape herself.

"Sometimes past selves come back to seek closure," the thaumaturge had explained. "They're not unlike real ghosts. They hang around because of unfinished business. Was there any trauma—any unanswered questions—associated with that time of your life?"

Angela hadn't been sure what to say.

Like everyone else, she had improved beyond recognition after secondary school. She'd benefited from the usual remedies for unattractiveness: self-confidence, freedom from school uniforms, and a decent haircut. She'd discovered that she was sociable, competent, and interested in other people. Her twenties had been a dream of pleasantness, and that was even though she'd spent most of it at clinical school.

But her adolescence hadn't been unhappy either. It had just been normal. Being twenty-five was a lot better than being fifteen, but wasn't that true for everyone?

The name change had been a purely pragmatic decision. She'd started going by Angela in her first year at uni, to make it easier on British tutors who stumbled over her real name. It had stuck. There was no denying "Angela" was more euphonious than "Pik Mun."

She wasn't running away from anything in her past. She'd lived through her past, hadn't she? She'd been Pik Mun already. What was wrong with being Angela now?

A sign outside the hostel asked you politely to close the gate after entering or leaving "so the wild boars will not enter."

If you walked around with food at night the wild boars came out. Despite their wildness they were not aggressive—one of the other teachers had managed to take a picture of one before it fled.

Angela took to striding around the park with fragrant boxes of takeaway in plastic bags banging against her knee. She did it out of competitiveness as much as anything else. She was the only one of the teachers not to have seen a wild boar.

She was eating chicken karaage in the park when it happened. She speared a piece of fried chicken with a chopstick and looked up. The boar was right in front of her.

It was smaller than she'd expected, about the size of a collie, with longish dark fur and amber eyes.

Moving slowly, Angela fumbled around in her bag until she felt her camera. She took a photo of the boar one-handed, the chicken wobbling on her chopstick.

She'd forgotten to turn off the flash. It went off like a bolt of lightning. Angela started and dropped her chicken. The boar scooped it up neatly.

"Wah, flash some more," it said in a muffled voice. It swallowed. "You not scared meh? The zoo always say don't use flash when you take photo."

"You—you can talk?" stammered Angela, until she realized that it was her own voice that had spoken.

"Yah, it's me," said the boar. "Pig Mun." It snorted with pleasure.

"You're a wild boar now?" said Angela. "How come you're a wild boar? I thought you're suppose to be me!"

Angela had never seen a boar shrug before, but the image was not as jarring as she would've thought. All those anthropomorphized Disney animals she'd watched in childhood had obviously left their mark.

"I don't like planes," said Pig Mun.

"I got over that already," said Angela.

"No, we didn't," said Pig Mun. "You still don't like planes. You just put up with it. Since I can do magic, I might as well use another route what, right?"

"You keep following me for what?" said Angela. "Can't you go back to where you belong?"

"That's nice," said Pig Mun. "You sound like BNP like that. I have a valid three-month visa, OK. You should know what. You applied for it."

"You know what I mean," snapped Angela. "Back to the past."

"I don't belong in the past," said Pig Mun.

"Where, then?"

Angela recoiled, but not far enough. Pig Mun's bristly snout brushed her chest.

"There," said Pig Mun. "Inside you."

"No," said Angela. "No, no, no. I've *been* you already. What's your problem? I'm grown up now! Not even our parents want me to be a kid anymore!"

"I don't want you to go back to being me," said Pig Mun. She didn't say what she did want, but she didn't need to. After all, they were the same person—even if one of them was a wild boar.

"Isn't everybody embarrassed about their teenage selves?" said Angela. "What's wrong with that?"

"Everything is wrong," said Pig Mun. "If you're the teenage self."

Angela smashed the plastic cover down onto her bento and shoved it into the plastic bag. She got up. "Well, who ask you to come back anyway?"

"You lah!" Pig Mun shouted behind her. "You asked. You're me, remember?"

It wasn't that Angela disliked Pik Mun. They would have got along in other circumstances. If they had met as separate people, for instance. She wouldn't have noticed the width of her hips, the roll of fat at her belly, the daikon thighs. The accent and awkwardness would have endeared Pik Mun to her.

That sort of thing was all right on other people. But if you'd managed to grow out of that awkward stage and shed the accent and even worked off the fat, then fate shoving all of that back onto you just seemed petty.

Angela refused to go back to that. What she liked about being an adult was being able to control her life.

This was why she agreed to go to the Obon festival celebrations with the other English teachers when the Japanese students invited them. Anyone would think that Angela would avoid something as magical as the celebration of a festival, in a season as heavy with humid, thunderous magic as the tropical summer.

But it was the sort of thing she would have gone in for with enthusiasm if she were not being pursued by her dead teenage self. She wouldn't let herself be constrained by the shadow of Pik Mun.

The Obon festival turned out to be like a carnival. Angela drank half a pint of beer, and the world lit up. She floated along in her borrowed yukata, feeling beautiful and attachless, smiling beatifically upon the crowd.

It was all reassuringly human. There were alleys of stalls selling delightful-smelling food. The stream of humanity was not offensive and sour tempered, as humanity taken in the mass tends to be, but beautiful and individual—exquisite girls and boys in yukata; parents with toddlers on their shoulders; old people strolling along, arm in arm with their children.

There was a high wooden platform reared up in the middle of the field, on top of which there was a band and a very enthusiastic emcee. When Angela got close enough she realized the people encircling the platform were dancing.

"Come and dance," said her students.

"Oh, no," said Angela, hanging back. She'd bought some takoyaki to offset the half-pint of beer, and her hands were sticky with grease and mayonnaise.

It was a simple routine, a bit like line dancing—repeated movements of the head and hands and feet, nothing fancy with the hips. The dance was led by a group of older women wearing blue-and-white yukata: they danced with the focus of surgeons carrying out a delicate operation, with the superhuman intensity of star ballerinas.

Angela was so charmed she let herself be bullied into joining, despite her sticky hands and bonito-flaked mouth. She was craning her head to try to see what the nearest Japanese auntie was doing, when Pik Mun's face hove into view.

"Argh!" said Angela.

"I didn't know you're into this kind of thing," said Pik Mun. "I thought we hated dancing."

"I told you, I've grown out of all that," said Angela. "Dancing is fun. Especially if you're a bit drunk."

"Become like a Mat Salleh already, huh," said Pik Mun.

She was wearing the unflattering turquoise pinafore and white shirt of the Malaysian secondary school uniform. It didn't suit her. It looked especially incongruous because she was dancing as well, with mechanical perfection, never putting a step wrong.

"How come you know how to do that?" said Angela, trying to watch Pik Mun's feet while clapping her hands and bobbing her head in the prescribed pattern.

"Don't you know what this festival is?" said Pik Mun. "You didn't even ask what it's all about before you happy-happy put on your Japanese baju and join in? Angela, what happened to your curiosity? You think you know everything, is it? Grown-ups are so dungu!"

It was the first time Pik Mun had ever addressed her as Angela. It was the first time she'd really scolded her, though Angela had told her off plenty of times.

They fell quiet. The music went on. People's voices bounced off their bubble of awkwardness.

"Soran, soran!" roared the crowd, following the lead of the singer on the platform.

Angela and Pik Mun kept dancing, moving in their circle with clockwork regularity.

"Sorry," said Pik Mun.

"They told me there'll be dancing and fireworks," said Angela. "I thought it was just for fun."

"It's the Hungry Ghost Festival," said Pik Mun, not unkindly. "Japanese is a bit different; they have it at a different time because they don't follow the lunar calendar. What lah you."

"Oh," said Angela. She looked around. "This is nicer than our celebrations."

Traditionally, of course, the Hungry Ghost Festival had been celebrated with Cantonese opera performances to entertain the returning dead. Nowadays people put miniskirted girls on open-air stages to belt out raucous Cantopop. It was like any other concert, except the first line of chairs was left empty for the ghosts.

"Here everybody gets to join," said Angela.

"Back home everybody gets to join," said Pik Mun. "If they don't want to listen also, they can't get away from it. Hah! Remember when Dad called the police and tried to get them to ask the temple people to turn down the volume, and the police told him he should pray to the gods and say sorry for offending the dead?"

Angela laughed at the memory.

"Dad was so angry," she said. "He went around talking bad about the festival to everybody at church."

"Even our relatives started avoiding him," said Pik Mun. "I remember Ji Ee Poh pulled me into the kitchen and said, 'Hai, your father, making life very difficult for we all. Ever since he convert to Christianity he become so intolerant. Don't believe in ghosts is one thing, but why talk bad about them some more? That is just asking for trouble.'"

"It's not the Christianity," said Angela. "I think Dad was always a bit like that. From young also."

"Dad is too extreme," said Pik Mun. "He should be more flexible."

"Me also," said Angela.

"Yah," said Pik Mun. "Us also."

Angela's Japanese language class went on a trip to Kyoto. They visited temples and had dinner on the river, in a barge hung with round orange lanterns.

Dinner was extravagant, with the severe delicacy of Japanese food: fish, tofu, and vegetables sitting in their separate compartments. There was also nabe in bubbling hot pots distributed along the table.

The other students drank beer. Angela stuck to tea.

Angela ate half her fish and stopped to look out at the river. If you ate slowly your stomach got used to the food and you felt full earlier. It was a good way to avoid overeating.

The river was worth looking at. It had still been light when they'd got on the barge, but night had fallen with tropical swiftness. They weren't the only barge on the river; there were several others, similarly outfitted, and the orange light from the lanterns trembling on the black waters was beautiful. In the distance the mountains were a dark forested mystery.

Were there tengu brooding in those trees? Before she'd been split into two, Angela had known magic was real, but she hadn't thought about it as something that applied to herself. Some people courted that kind of thing—went to bomoh for charms and love potions, studied spells, prayed to the spirits of the earth and air and water.

Angela had never even watched *Charmed*. Being a doctor seemed a much more concrete way of working miracles.

But now she was only half a person, anything seemed possible. Tengu might come flying out of their mountain fastnesses, the wind from their wings snuffing out the lanterns. River dragons might raise gleaming horse-like heads out of the waters around them. She might discover something new about herself at the august age of twenty-five.

A sigh rose from the other diners. "Ah!"

"What is it?" said Angela to her neighbor.

"The birds are fishing—look!" The neighbor pointed with her chopsticks.

Angela could only see flashes of light in the darkness. The flame of a torch lit the face of an old man, laboring in the bow of a boat on the other side of the river. She couldn't see any birds.

She turned, wanting to ask her neighbor where the birds were and what they were doing, but as she did so she saw Pik Mun out of the corner of her eye.

Pik Mun was in the water, dog-paddling calmly along the side of the boat.

"How long have you been there?" said Angela.

"Long enough," said Pik Mun. "You finish your dinner yet or not? You took half an hour to eat that fish."

There was quite a lot of food left in Angela's lacquer box.

"Yeah, done already," she said. "Nowadays I only eat till seventy percent full."

Pik Mun was so outraged she missed a stroke. She went down and came up with a mouthful of water, spluttering. "What's this seventy percent? If you sit for exam and get seventy percent, that's not even a 1A!"

"Seventy percent is a First," said Angela.

"OK. OK. I see how it is," said Pik Mun coldly. "Your standards have gone down. This is called life experience, is it?"

"My standards haven't gone down," said Angela. "They're just different."

"If it was me I would have eaten all," said Pik Mun. "Except the enoki mushrooms—"

"—because they taste funny," Angela agreed.

"At least you remember that," said Pik Mun. "Tired lah."

"I'm not surprised; you've been swimming so long."

"Tired of you lah!" said Pik Mun. "You forgot what it's like to be me, is it? Don't you miss me at all?"

She looked wistful.

"I don't know if I miss you," Angela said. "You're a lot wiser than I actually was at fifteen. I was pretty stupid as a teenager."

"That's what you think now," said Pik Mun. "You didn't think so then. You should be kinder to yourself."

"I didn't finish yet," Angela chided her. "I said, you're a lot wiser than I was when I was an annoying teenager. So I guess I should listen to you. You want a hand up?"

Pik Mun stopped paddling. For a moment she floated in the water, suspended.

"You sure?" said Pik Mun.

"Yes," said Angela.

"If you take my hand it'll change you," said Pik Mun. "You made me go away for a reason, you know. If I come back you might remember stuff you want to forget."

Angela held out her hand. Pik Mun took it.

As Pik Mun climbed in their hands became one. Her elbows locked into Angela's elbows, her knees into Angela's knees. Angela's hips widened. Her face got rounder. The flesh under her chin pouched out. Her vision blurred.

She blinked, and then she could see clearly again. She was solid, weighted to the deck by her new substantiality.

Pik Mun was more pugnacious than her, not as well-groomed, rougher-edged. Angela was Pik Mun with all the unevenness sanded off. But she needed to have a surface that could catch on things. She needed to be capable of friction.

She looked down at the river. The orange light showed Angela her reflection, hazy and dark. Pik Mun smiled back at her from the water.

Somebody touched their arm.

"Are you OK?" said Angela's neighbor. "You almost fell in!"

"I'm OK," said Angela. She smiled at the girl.

The girl blushed.

Angela's stomach growled. She turned back to the table. "Good food, eh?"

"Yeah, really good," said the girl. She looked away, then back, then away again. She was smiling despite her discomfiture, smiling helplessly, almost against her will.

Now that's called charisma, said Pik Mun approvingly inside Angela's head.

Angela ate all of the fish. It was delicious.

Pik Mun had been keeping a secret for Angela.

It was silly to have kicked up so much of a fuss over it. Nobody cared nowadays, did they? OK, so Angela's family would probably care, but that hadn't been the reason why she'd tried to ignore it for ten years.

The reason had been embarrassment.

Picture Pik Mun, fifteen years old, not yet Angela, not yet beautiful. She's in love with her best friend and it's leading her down perilous paths. For example, the one that ends in her kissing the best friend, on a hot afternoon after school.

Pik Mun had known immediately that it had been the wrong thing to do.

"Never mind," she said, but Prudence was already talking.

"What's wrong with you?" said Prudence.

"Nothing," said Pik Mun. "It was just a—I don't know. Never mind! Forget about it."

"Do you *like* me?" said Prudence, in dawning horror. "Do you, like, have a crush on me?"

"No, no, no," said Pik Mun. Each "no" sounded less convinced than the last. "I'm sorry. I shouldn't have did that."

"It's like kissing my *sister*," said Prudence. She had never been a tactful girl.

"You don't even have a sister!"

"Why did you do that?" said Prudence. "Are you . . ." she lowered her voice. "Are you a gay?"

Pik Mun's eyes prickled.

"But you were dating that guy," said Prudence. "The prefect. Were you using him to hide the fact you're gay?"

"I'm not gay!" said Pik Mun.

"Then?" said Prudence.

"I liked Kenrick," said Pik Mun. But she'd stopped liking him. She'd started liking Prudence instead. That had been unexpected. "I wasn't faking it. I stopped liking him because he started talking about football all the time. Doesn't mean I never liked him."

"So do you like girl or boy?" said Prudence.

"I don't know," said Pik Mun. She hesitated. "Both?"

"Where got people like both one?" said Prudence. At that point, her parents' green Kancil had driven into the school car park. Prudence got up.

"Pik Mun, you must figure yourself out," she said. "Think about it and let me know when you decide. Call my home phone if you want to talk. But don't like me, OK?"

"Not like I choose to like you also," said Pik Mun.

"Choose to stop," said Prudence firmly. "I like you very much as friend, but this whole crush thing is a bit weird."

Pik Mun's crush had been smothered by the embarrassment. It went out without a whimper. And she hadn't liked another girl for ten years.

It was a long time to be hiding from yourself, and a stupid reason for doing it. But youth was for doing stupid things in anyway.

And Angela was still young.

It was almost lonely without Pik Mun around. Angela could talk to herself, of course, but it wasn't quite the same.

She called Prudence instead.

"I'm Facebooking my thaumaturge," she said.

"Why?" said Prudence.

Angela hesitated. But ten years was a long time to pretend something wasn't there.

"She's super my type," said Angela. "Got girlfriend already, but girlfriend doesn't mean married, right?"

The line crackled. Angela's chest seized up.

Prudence said, horrified, "Angela! That's so bad! Don't go stealing people's woman!"

"Joking only lah," said Angela.

"If you want, I can introduce people to you," said Prudence. "Girl or boy also can. You specify. But don't go and chase other people's girlfriend. Hmph. After you stay in Japan you become so immoral."

Angela was smiling. "I put on weight also," she said.

"Is it?" said Prudence. "Don't eat so much takoyaki. Eat more seaweed. That one not fattening."

"I think it suits me," said Angela.

"Oh? Then forget about the seaweed lah," said Prudence. "So long as you're OK with yourself. Are you OK with yourself, Pik Mun?"

"Yah, think so," said Angela.

"Good," said Prudence. That pretty much seemed to cover it.

If At First You Don't Succeed, Try, Try Again

The first thousand years

It was time. Byam was as ready as it would ever be.

As a matter of fact, it had been ready to ascend some 300 years ago. But the laws of heaven cannot be defied. If you drop a stone, it will fall to the ground—it will not fly up to the sky. If you try to become a dragon before your thousandth birthday, you will fall flat on your face, and all the other spirits of the five elements will laugh at you.

These are the laws of heaven.

But Byam had been patient. Now it would be rewarded.

It slithered out of the lake it had occupied for the past 100 years. The western shore had recently been settled by humans, and the banks had become cluttered with humans' usual mess—houses, cultivated fields, bits of pottery that poked Byam in the side.

But the eastern side was still reserved to beasts and spirits. There was plenty of space for an imugi to take off.

The mountains around the lake said hello to Byam. (It was always safer to be polite to an imugi, since you never knew when it might turn into a dragon.) The sky above them was a pure light blue, dotted with clouds like white jade.

Byam's heart rose. It launched itself into the air, the sun warm on its back.

I deserve this. All those years studying in dank caves, chanting sutras, striving to understand the Way . . .

For the first half-millennium or so, Byam could be confident of finding the solitude necessary for study. But more recently, there seemed to be more and more humans everywhere.

Humans weren't all bad. You couldn't meditate your way through every doctrinal puzzle, and that was where monks proved useful. Of course, even the most enlightened monk was wont to be alarmed by the sudden appearance of a giant snake wanting to know what they thought of the Sage's comments on water. Still, you could usually extract some guidance from them, once they stopped screaming.

But spending too much time near humans was risky. If one saw you during your ascension, that could ruin everything. Byam would have moved when the humans settled by the lake, if not for the ample supply of cows and pigs and goats in the area. (Byam had grown tired of seafood.)

It wasn't always good to have such abundance close to hand, though. Byam had been studying extra hard for the past decade in preparation for its ascension. Just last month, it had been startled from a marathon meditation session by an enormous growl.

Byam had looked around wildly. For a moment it thought it had been set upon, maybe by a wicked imugi—the kind so embittered by failure it pretended not to care about the Way, or the cintamani, or even becoming a dragon. But there was no one around, only a few fish beating a hasty retreat.

Then, another growl. It was coming from Byam's own stomach. Byam recollected that it hadn't eaten in about five years.

Some imugi fasted to increase their spiritual powers. But when Byam tried to get back to meditating, it didn't work. Its stomach kept making weird gurgling noises. All the fish had been scared off, so Byam popped out of the water, looking for a snack.

A herd of cows was grazing by the bank, as though they were waiting for Byam.

It only intended to eat one cow. It wanted to keep sharp for its ascension. Dragons probably didn't eat much. All the dragons Byam had ever seen were svelte, with perfect scales, shining talons, silky beards.

Unfortunately Byam wasn't a dragon yet. It was hungry, and the cows smelled *so* good. Byam had one, and then another, and then a third, telling itself each time that *this* cow would be the last. Before it knew it, almost the whole herd was gone.

Byam cringed remembering this, but then put the memory away. Today was the day that would change everything. After today, Byam would be transformed. It would have a wish-fulfilling gem of its own—the glorious cintamani, which manifested all desires, cured afflictions, purified souls and water alike.

So high up, the air was thin, and Byam had to work harder to keep afloat. The clouds brushed its face damply. And—Byam's heart beat faster—wasn't that winking light ahead the glitter of a jewel?

Byam turned for its last look at the earth as an imugi. The lake shone in the sun. It had been cold, and miserable, and lonely, full of venomous water snakes that bit Byam's tail. Byam had been dying to get away from it.

But now, it felt a swell of affection. When it returned as a dragon, it would bless the lake. Fish would overflow its banks. The cows and pigs and goats would multiply beyond counting. The crops would spring out of the earth in their multitudes . . .

A thin screechy noise was coming from the lake. When Byam squinted, it saw a group of little creatures on the western bank. Humans.

One of them was shaking a fist at the sky. "Fuck you, imugi!"

"Oh shit," said Byam.

"Yeah, I see you! You think you got away with it? Well, you thought wrong!"

Byam lunged upwards, but it was too late. Gravity set its teeth in its tail and tugged.

It wasn't just one human shouting, it was all of them. A chorus of insults rose on the wind:

"Worm! Legless centipede! Son of a bitch! You look like fermented soybeans and you smell even worse!"

Byam strained every muscle, fighting the pull of the earth. If only it had hawk's claws to grasp the clouds with, or stag's antlers to pierce the sky . . .

But Byam wasn't a dragon yet.

The last thing it heard as it plunged through the freezing waters of the lake was a human voice shrieking:

"Serves you right for eating our cows!"

The second thousand years

If you wanted to be a dragon, dumb perseverance wasn't enough. You had to have a strategy.

Humans had proliferated, so Byam retreated to the ocean. It was harder to get texts in the sea, but technically you didn't need texts to study the Way, since it was inherent in the order of all things. (Anyway, sometimes you could steal scriptures off a turtle on a pilgrimage, or go onshore to ransack a monastery.)

But you had to get out of the water in order to ascend. It was impossible to exclude the possibility of being seen by humans, even in the middle of the ocean. It didn't seem to bother them that they couldn't breathe underwater; they still launched themselves onto the waves on rickety assemblages of dismembered trees. It was as if they couldn't wait to get on to their next lives.

That was fine. If Byam couldn't depend on the absence of humans, it would use their presence to its advantage.

It was heaven's will that Byam should have failed the last time; if heaven wasn't ready to accept Byam, nothing could change that, no matter how diligently it studied or how much it longed to ascend.

As in all things, however, when it came to ascending, how you were seen mattered just as much as what you did. It hadn't helped back then that the lake humans had named Byam for what it was: no dragon, but an imugi, a degraded being no better than the crawling beasts of the earth.

But if, as Byam flashed across the sky, a witness saw a dragon . . . that was another matter. Heaven wasn't immune to the pressures of public perception. It would *have* to recognize Byam then.

The spirits of the wind and water were too hard to bluff; fish were too self-absorbed; and there was no hope of hoodwinking the sea dragons. But humans had bad eyesight and a tendency to see things that weren't there. Their capacity for self-deception was Byam's best bet.

It chose a good point in the sky, high enough that it would have enough cloud matter to work with, but not so high that the humans wouldn't be able to see it. Then it got to work.

It labored at night, using its head to push together masses of cloud and its tail to work the fine detail. Byam didn't just want the design to look like a dragon. Byam wanted it to be beautiful—as beautiful as the dragon Byam was going to be.

Making the sculpture was harder than Byam expected. Cloud was an intransigent medium. Wisps kept drifting off when Byam wasn't looking. It couldn't get the horns straight, and the whiskers were wonky.

Sometimes Byam felt like giving up. How could it make a dragon when it didn't even know how to be one?

To conquer self-doubt, it chanted the aphorisms of the wise:

Nobody becomes a dragon overnight.

Real dragons keep going.

A dragon is only an imugi that didn't give up.

It took 100 years longer than Byam had anticipated before the cloud was finished.

It looked like a dragon, caught as it sped across the sky to its rightful place in the heavens. In moonlight it shone like mother of pearl. Under the sun it would glitter with all the colors of the rainbow.

As Byam put its final touches on the cloud, it felt both pride and a sense of anticlimax. Even loss. Soon Byam would ascend—and then what would happen to its creation? It would dissipate, or dissolve into rain, like any other cloud.

Byam managed to find a monk who knew about shipping routes and was willing to dish in exchange for not being eaten. And then it was ready. As dawn unfolded across the sky on an auspicious day, Byam took its position behind its dragon-cloud.

All it needed was a single human to look up and exclaim at what they saw. A fleet of merchant vessels was due to come this way. Among all those humans, there had to be one sailor with his eyes on the sky—a witness open to wonder, prepared to see a dragon rising to glory.

"Hey, Captain," said the lookout. "You see that?"

"What is it? A sail?"

"No." The lookout squinted at the sky. "That cloud up there, look. The one with all the colors."

"Oh wow!" said the captain. "Good spot! That's something special, for sure. It's a good omen!"

He clapped the lookout on the back, turning to the rest of the crew. "Great news, men! Heaven smiles upon us. Today is our day!"

Everyone was busy with preparations, but a dutiful cheer rose from the ship.

The lookout was still staring upwards.

"It's an interesting shape," he said thoughtfully. "Don't you think it looks like a . . ."

"Like what?" said the captain.

"Like, um . . ." The lookout frowned, snapping his fingers. "What do you call them? Forget my own head next! It looks like a—it's on the tip of my tongue. I've been at sea for too long. Like a, you know—"

Byam couldn't take it anymore.

"*Dragon!*" it wailed in agony.

An imugi has enormous lungs. Byam's voice rolled across the sky like thunder, its breath scattering the clouds—and blowing its creation to shreds.

"Horse!" said the lookout triumphantly. "It looks like a horse!"

"No no no," said Byam. It scrambled to reassemble its sculpture, but the cloud matter was already melting away upon the winds.

"Thunder from a clear sky!" said the captain. "Is that a good sign or a bad sign?"

The lookout frowned. "You're too superstitious, Captain—hey!" He perked up, snatching up a telescope. "Captain, there they are!"

Byam had been so focused on the first ship that it hadn't seen the merchant fleet coming. Then it was too busy trying to salvage its dragon-cloud to pay attention to what was going on below.

It was distantly aware of fighting between the ships, of arrows flying, of the screams of sailors as they were struck down. But it was preoccupied by the enormity of what had happened to it—the loss of hundreds of years of steady, hopeful work.

It wasn't too late. Byam could fix the cloud. Tomorrow it would try again—

"Ah," said the pirate captain, looking up from the business of slaughter. "An imugi! It's good luck after all. One last push, men! They can't hold out for long!"

It would have been easier if Byam could tell itself the humans had sabotaged it out of spite. But it knew they hadn't. As Byam tumbled out of the sky, it was the impartiality of their judgment that stung the most.

The third thousand years

Dragons enjoyed sharing advice about how they'd gotten where they were. They said it helped to visualise the success you desired.

"Envision yourself with those horns, those whiskers, three claws and a thumb, basking in the glow of your own cintamani," urged the Dragon King of the East Sea in his popular memoir *Sixty Thousand Records of a Floating Life*. "Close your eyes. You are the master of the elements! A twitch of your whisker and the skies open. At your command, blessings—or vengeance—pour forth upon all creatures under heaven! Just imagine!"

When Byam was low at heart, it imagined.

It got fed up with the sea: turtles kept chasing it around, and whale song disrupted its sleep. It moved inland and found a quiet cave where it could study the Way undisturbed. The cave didn't smell great, but it meant Byam never had to go far for food, so long as it didn't mind bat. (Byam came to mind bat.) Byam focused on the future.

This time, there would be no messing around with dragon-clouds. Byam had learned from its mistakes. There was no tricking heaven. This time it would present itself at the gates with its record of honest toil and hope to be deemed worthy of admission.

It should have been nervous, but in fact it was calm as it prepared for what it hoped would be its final attempt. Certainty glowed in its stomach like a swallowed ember.

It had been a long time since Byam had left its cave, which it had chosen because it was up among the mountains, far from any human settlement. Still, Byam intended to minimize any chance of disaster. It was going to shoot straight for the skies, making sure it was exposed to the judgment of the world for as brief a time as possible.

But the brightness outside took it aback. Its eyes weren't used to the sun's glare anymore. When Byam raised its head, it got caught in a sort of horrible basket, full of whispering voices. A storm of ticklish green scraps whirled around it.

It reared back, hissing, before it recognized what had attacked it. Byam had forgotten about trees.

It leapt into the air, shaken. To have forgotten *trees* . . . Byam had not realized it had been so long.

Its unease faded as it rose ever higher. The crisp airs of heaven blew away disquiet. Ahead, the clouds glowed as though they reflected the light of the Way.

Leslie almost missed it.

She never usually did this kind of thing. She was indoorsy the way some people were outdoorsy, as attached to her sofa as others were to endorphins and bragging about their marathon times. She'd never thought of herself as someone who hiked.

But she hadn't thought of herself as someone who'd fail her PhD or get dumped by her boyfriend for her best friend. The past year had blown the bottom out of her ideas about herself.

She paused to drink some water and heave for breath. The view was spectacular. It seemed meaningless.

She was higher up than she'd thought. What if she took the wrong step? Would it hurt much to fall? Everyone would think it was an accident . . .

She shook herself, horrified. She wouldn't do anything stupid, Leslie told herself. To distract herself, she took out her phone, but that proved a bad idea: this was the point at which she would have texted Jung-wook before.

She could take a selfie. That's what people did when they went hiking, right? Posted proof they'd done it. She raised her phone, switching the camera to front-facing mode.

She saw a flash in the corner of the screen. It was sunlight glinting off scales.

Leslie's mouth fell open. It wasn't—it *couldn't* be. She hadn't even known they were found in America.

The camera went off. Leslie whirled around, but the sky was empty. It was nowhere to be seen.

But someone up there was looking out for Leslie after all, because when she looked back at her phone, she saw that she'd caught it. It was there. It had happened. There was Leslie, looking dopey with her red face and her hair a mess and her mouth half-open—and in the background, arced across the sky like a rainbow, was her miracle. Her own personal sign from heaven that things were going to be OK.

> **leshangry** Nature is amazing! #imugi #이무기
> #sighting #blessed #여행스타그램 #자연
> #등산 #nature #hiking #wanderlust #gooutside
> #snakesofinstagram

The turning of the worm

"Dr. Han?" said the novice. "Yeah, her office is just through there."

Sure enough, the name was inscribed on the door in the new script the humans used now: *Dr. Leslie Han.* Byam's nemesis.

Its most *recent* nemesis. If it had been only one offence, Byam wouldn't even be here. It was the whole of Byam's long miserable history with humans that had brought it to this point.

It made itself invisible and passed through the door.

The monk was sitting at a desk, frowning over a text. Byam was not good at distinguishing one human from another, but this particular human's face was branded in its memory.

It felt a surge of relief.

Even with the supernatural powers accumulated in the course of three millennia of studying the Way, it had taken Byam a while to figure out how to shapeshift. The legs had been the most difficult part. Byam kept giving itself tiger feet, the kind dragons had.

It could have concealed the feet under its skirts, since no celestial fairy ever appeared in anything less than three layers of silk. But Byam wouldn't have it. It was pathetic, this harking back to its stupid dreams. It had worked at the spell until the feet came right. If Byam wasn't becoming a dragon, it would not lower itself to imitation. No part of it would bear any of the nine resemblances.

But there were consolations available to imugi who reconciled themselves to their fate. Like revenge.

The human was perhaps a little older than when Byam had last seen her. But she was still alive—alive enough to suffer when Byam devoured her.

Byam let its invisibility fall away. It spread its hands, the better to show off its magnificent sleeves.

It was the human's job that had given Byam the idea. Leslie Han was an academic, which appeared to be a type of monk. Monks were the most relatable kind of human, for like imugi, they desired one thing most in life: to ascend to a higher plane of existence.

"Leslie," crooned Byam in the dulcet tones of a celestial fairy. "How would you like to go to heaven?"

The monk screamed and fell out of her chair.

When nothing else happened, Byam floated over to the desk, peering down at the monk.

"What are you doing down there?" began Byam, but then the text the monk had been studying caught its eye.

"Oh my God, you're—" The monk rubbed her eyes. "I didn't think celestial fairies descended anymore! Did you—were you offering to take me to heaven?"

Byam wasn't listening. The monk had to repeat herself before it looked up from the book.

"This is a text on the Way," said Byam. It looked around the monk's office. There were rows and rows of books. Byam said slowly, "These are *all* about the Way."

The monk looked puzzled. "No, they're about astrophysics. I'm a researcher. I study the evolution of galaxies."

Maybe Byam had been dumb enough to believe it might some day become a dragon, but it knew an exegesis of the Way when it saw one. There were hundreds of such books here—more commentaries than Byam had seen in one place in its entire lifetime.

It wasn't going to repeat its mistakes. Ascension, transcendence, turning into a dragon—that wasn't happening for Byam. Heaven had made that clear.

But you couldn't study something for 3,000 years without becoming interested in it for its own sake.

"Tell me about your research," said Byam.

"What you said just now," said the monk. "Did you not—"

Byam showed its teeth.

"My research!" said the monk. "Let me tell you about it."

Byam had planned to eat the monk when she was done. But it turned out the evolution of galaxies was an extremely complicated matter. The monk had not explained even half of what Byam wanted to know by the time the moon rose.

The monk took out a glowing box and looked at it. "It's so late!"

"Why did you stop?" said Byam.

"I need to sleep," said the monk. She bent over the desk. Byam wondered if this was a good moment to eat her, but then the monk turned and held out a sheaf of paper.

"What is this?"

"Extra reading," said the monk. "You can come back tomorrow if you've got questions. My office hours are three to four p.m. on Wednesdays and Thursdays."

She paused, her eyes full of wonder. She was looking at Byam as though it was special.

"But you can come anytime," said the monk.

~~~

Byam did the reading. It went back again the next day. And the next.

It was easier to make sense of the texts with the monk's help. Byam had never had anyone to talk to about the Way before. Its past visits with monks didn't count—Leslie screamed much less than the others. She answered Byam's questions as though she enjoyed them, whereas the others had always made it clear they couldn't wait for Byam to leave.

"I like teaching," she said when Byam remarked upon this. "I'm surprised I've got anything to teach you, though. I'd've thought you'd know all this stuff already."

"No," said Byam. It looked down at the diagram Leslie was explaining for the third time. Byam still didn't get it. But if there was one thing Byam was good at, it was trying again and again.

Well. That *had* been its greatest strength. Now, who knew?

"It's OK," said Leslie. "You know things I don't."

"Hm." Byam wasn't so sure.

Leslie touched its shoulder.

"It's impressive," she said. "That you're so open to learning new things. If I were a celestial fairy, there's no way I'd work so hard. I'd just lie around getting drunk and eating peaches all day."

"You have a skewed image of the life of a celestial fairy," said Byam.

But it did feel better. No one had ever called it hardworking before. It was a new experience, feeling validated. Byam found it liked it.

Studying with Leslie involved many new experiences. Leslie was a great proponent of what she called fresh air. She dragged Byam out of the office regularly so they could inhale as much of it as possible.

"But there's air *inside*," objected Byam.

"It's not the same," said Leslie. "Don't you get a little stir-crazy when you haven't seen the sun in a while?"

Byam remembered the shock of emerging from its cave for the first time in 800 years.

"Yes," it admitted.

Leslie was particularly fond of hiking, which was like walking, only you did it up a hill. Byam enjoyed this. In the past 3,000 years it had seen more of the insides of mountains than their outsides, and it turned out the outsides were attractive at human eyelevel.

The mountains were still polite to Byam, as though there were still a chance it might ever become a dragon. This hurt, but Byam squashed the feeling down. It had made its decision.

It was on one of their hikes that Leslie brought up the first time they met. They weren't far off the peak when she stopped to look into the distance.

Byam hadn't realized at first—things looked so different from human height—but it recognized the place before she spoke. Leslie was staring at the very mountain that had been Byam's home for 800 years.

"It's funny," she said. "The last time I was here . . ."

Byam braced itself. *I saw an imugi trying to ascend,* she was going to say. *It faceplanted on the side of a mountain, it was hilarious!*

"I was standing here wishing I was dead," said Leslie.

"What?"

"Not seriously," said Leslie hastily. "I mean, I wouldn't have done anything. I just wanted it to stop."

"What did you want to stop?"

"Everything," said Leslie. "I don't know. I was young. I was having a hard time. It all felt too much to cope with."

Humans lived for such a short time anyway, it had never occurred to Byam that they might want to hasten the end. "You don't still . . ."

"Oh no. It was a while ago." Leslie was still looking at Byam's mountain. She smiled. "You know, I got a sign while I was up here."

"A sign," echoed Byam.

"It probably sounds stupid," said Leslie. "But I saw an imugi. It made me think there might be hope. I started going to therapy. Finished my PhD. Things got better."

"Good," said Byam. It met Leslie's eyes. She had never stopped looking at Byam as though it was special.

Leslie pressed her lips to Byam's mouth.

Byam stayed still. It wasn't sure what to do.

"Sorry. I'm sorry!" Leslie stepped back, looking panicked. "I don't know what I was thinking. I thought maybe—of course we're both women, but I thought maybe that didn't matter to you guys. Or maybe you were even into—I was imagining things. This is so embarrassing. Oh God."

Byam had questions. It picked just one to start with. "What were you doing? With the mouths, I mean."

Leslie took a deep breath and blew it out. "Oh boy." But the explanation proved to be straightforward.

"Oh, it was a mating overture," said Byam.

"I—yeah, I guess you could put it that way," said Leslie. "Listen, I'm sorry I even . . . I don't want to have ruined everything. I care about you a lot, as a friend. Can we move on?"

"Yes," Byam agreed. "Let's try again."

"Phew, I'm really glad you're not—what?"

"I didn't know what you were doing earlier," explained Byam. "You should've said. But I'll be better now I understand it."

Leslie stared. Byam started to feel nervous.

"Do you not want to kiss?" it said.

"No," said Leslie. "I mean, yes?"

She reached out tentatively. Byam squeezed her hand. It seemed to be the right thing to do, because Leslie smiled.

"OK," she said.

After a while Byam moved into Leslie's apartment. It had been spending the nights off the coast, but the waters by the city smelled of diesel and the noise from the ships made its sleep fitful. Leslie's bed was a lot more comfortable than the watery deeps.

Living with her meant Byam had to be in celestial fairy form all the time, but it was used to it by now. At Leslie's request, it turned down the heavenly glow.

"You don't mind?" said Leslie. "Humans aren't used to the halo."

"Nah," said Byam. "It's not like I had the glow before." It froze. "I mean . . . in heaven, everyone is illuminated, so you stop . . . noticing it?"

Fortunately, Leslie wasn't listening. She had opened an envelope and was staring at the letter in dismay.

"He's raising the rent again! Oh, you're fucking kidding me." She took off her glasses and rubbed her eyes. "I need to get out of this city."

"What is *rent*?" said Byam.

Which was how Byam ended up getting a job. Leslie tried to discourage it at first. Even once Byam wore her down and she admitted it would be helpful if Byam also paid "rent," she seemed to think it was a problem that Byam was undocumented.

That was an explanation that took an extra long time. The magic to invent the necessary records was simple in comparison.

"'Byam,'" said Leslie, studying its brand-new driver's licence. "That's an interesting choice."

"It's my name," said Byam absently. It was busy magicking up an immunization history.

"That's your name?" said Leslie. She touched the driver's licence with reverent fingers. "Byam."

She seemed unaccountably pleased. After a moment she said, "You never told me your name before."

"*Oh*," said Byam. Leslie was blushing. "You could have asked!"

Leslie shrugged. "I didn't want to force it. I figured you'd tell me when you were ready."

"It's not because—I would've told you," said Byam. "I just didn't think of it. It's not my real name."

The light in Leslie's face dimmed. "It's not?"

"I mean, it's the name I have," said Byam. It should never have set off down this path. How was it going to explain about dragon-names—the noble, elegant styles, full of meaning and wit, conferred on dragons upon their ascension? Leslie didn't even know Byam was an imugi. She thought Byam had already been admitted to the gates of heaven.

"I'm only a low-level attendant," it said finally. "When I get promoted, I'll be given a real name. One with a good meaning. Like 'Establish Virtue,' or 'Jade Peak,' or 'Sunlit Cloud.'"

"Oh," said Leslie. "I didn't know you were working towards a promotion." She hesitated. "When do you think you'll get promoted?"

"In 10,000 years' time," said Byam. "Maybe."

This was a personal joke. Leslie wasn't meant to get it, and she did not. She only gave Byam a thoughtful look. She dropped a kiss on its forehead, just above its left eyebrow.

"I like 'Byam,'" she said. "It suits you."

They moved out of the city to the outskirts, where the rent was cheaper and they could have more space. Leslie got a cat, which avoided Byam but eventually stopped hissing at its approach. Leslie went running on the beach in the mornings while Byam swam.

She introduced Byam to those of her family who didn't object to the fact that Byam appeared to be a woman. These did not include Leslie's parents, but there was a sister named Jean, and a niece, Eun-hye, whom Byam taught physics.

Tutoring young humans in physics was Byam's first job, but sometimes it forgot itself and taught students the Way, which was not helpful for exams. After a narrowly averted disaster with the bathroom in their new apartment, Byam took a plumbing course.

It turned out Byam was good at working with pipes—better, perhaps, than it had ever been at understanding the Way.

At night, Byam still dreamt of the past. Or rather, it dreamt of the future—the future as Byam had envisioned it, once upon a time. They were impossible, ecstatic dreams—dreams of scything through the clouds, raindrops clinging to its beard; dreams of chasing the cintamani through the sea, its whiskers floating on a warm current.

When Byam woke up, its face wet with salt water, Leslie was always there.

Byam got home one night and knew something was wrong. It could tell from the shape of Leslie's back. When she realized it was there, she raised her head, wiping her face and trying to smile.

"What happened?" said Byam.

"I've been—" The words got stuck. Leslie cleared her throat. "I didn't get tenure."

Byam had learned enough about Leslie's job by now to understand what this meant. Not getting tenure was worse than falling when you were almost at the gates of heaven. It sat down, appalled.

"Would you like me to eat the committee for you?" it suggested.

Leslie laughed. "No." The syllable came out on a sob. She rubbed her eyes. "Thanks, baby, but that wouldn't help."

"What would help?"

"Nothing," said Leslie. Then, in a wobbly voice, "A hug."

Byam put its arms around Leslie, but it seemed poor comfort for the ruin of all her hopes. It felt Leslie underestimated the consolation she was likely to derive from the wholesale destruction of her enemies. But this was not the time to argue.

Byam remembered the roaring in its ears as it fell, the shock of meeting the ground.

"Sometimes," it said, "you try really hard and it's not enough. You put in all you've got and you still never get where you thought you were meant to be. But at least you tried. Some people never try. They resign themselves to bamboozling monks and devouring maidens for all eternity."

"Doesn't sound like a bad life," said Leslie, with another of those ragged laughs. But she kissed Byam's shoulder, to show that she didn't think the life of a wicked imugi had any real appeal.

After Leslie cried some more, she said, "Is it worth it? The trying, I mean."

Byam had to be honest. The only thing that could have made falling worse was if someone had tried to convince Byam it hadn't sucked.

"I don't know," it said.

It could see the night sky through the windows. Usually the lights and pollution of the city blanked out the sky, but tonight there was a single star shining, like the cintamani did sometimes in Byam's dreams.

"Maybe," said Byam.

Leslie said, "Why aren't you trying to become a dragon?"

Byam froze. "What?"

Leslie wriggled out of its arms and turned to face it. "Tell me you're still working towards it and I'll shut up."

"I don't know what you're talking about," said Byam, terrified. "I'm a celestial fairy. What do dragons have to do with anything? They are far too noble and important to have anything to say to a lowly spirit like me—"

"Byam, I know you're not a celestial fairy."

"No, I am, I—" But Byam swallowed its denials at the look on Leslie's face. "What gave it away?"

"I don't know much about celestial fairies," said Leslie. "But I'm pretty sure they don't talk about eating senior professors."

Byam gave her a look of reproach. "I was trying to be helpful!"

"It wasn't just that . . ."

"Have you told Jean and Eun-hye?" Byam bethought itself of the other creature that was important in their lives. "Did you tell the cat? Is that why it doesn't like me?"

"I've told you, I can't actually talk to the cat," said Leslie. (Which was a blatant lie, because she did it all the time, though it was true they had strange conversations, generally at cross-purposes.) "I haven't told anyone. But I couldn't live with you for years and *not* know, Byam. I'm not *completely* stupid. I was hoping you'd eventually be comfortable enough to tell me yourself."

Byam's palms were damp. "Tell you what? 'Oh yeah, Les, I should've mentioned, I'm not an exquisite fairy descended from heaven like you always thought. Actually I'm one of the eternal losers of the unseen world. Hope that's OK!'"

"Hey, forgive me for trying to be sensitive!" snapped Leslie. "I don't care what you are, Byam. I know *who* you are. That's all that matters to me."

"Who I am?" said Byam. It was like a rock had lodged inside its throat. It was hard to speak past it. "An imugi, you mean. An earthworm with a dream."

"An imugi changed my life," said Leslie. "Don't talk them down."

Though it was incredible, it seemed it was true she didn't mind and wasn't about to dump Byam for being the embodiment of pathetic failure.

"I just wish you'd trusted me," she said.

Her eyes were tender, and worried, and red. They reminded Byam that it was Leslie who had just come crashing down to earth.

Byam clasped its hands to keep them from shaking. It took a deep breath. "I'm not a very good girlfriend."

Leslie understood what it was trying to say. She put her arm around Byam.

"Sometimes," she said. "Mostly you do OK."

"I wasn't good at being an imugi either," said Byam. "I'm sorry I didn't tell you. It wasn't like the name. This, I didn't want you to know."

"Why not?"

"If you're an imugi, everyone knows you've failed," explained Byam. "It's like wearing a sign all the time saying 'I've been denied tenure.'"

This proved a bad comparison to make. Leslie winced.

"Sorry," said Byam. It paused. "It hurts. Knowing it wasn't enough, even when you gave it the best of yourself. But you get over it."

You get used to being a failure. It was too early to tell her that. Maybe Leslie would be lucky. Maybe she'd never have the chance to get used to it.

Leslie looked like she was thinking of saying something, but she changed her mind. She squeezed Byam's knee.

"I'm thinking of going into industry," said Leslie.

Byam had no idea what she meant.

"You would be great at that," it said, meaning it.

It turned out Byam was right: Leslie *was* great at working in industry, and her success meant they could move into a bigger place, near Leslie's sister. This worked out well—after Jean's divorce, they helped out with Eun-hye, who perplexed Byam by declaring it her favorite aunt.

A mere ten years after Leslie had been denied tenure, she was saying it had been a blessing in disguise: "I would never have known there was a world outside academia."

They had stopped talking about dragons by then. Leslie had gotten over her fixation with them.

"*I'm* fixated?" she'd said. "You're the one who worked for thousands of years—"

"I don't want to talk about it," Byam had said. When this didn't work, it simply started vanishing whenever Leslie brought it up. Eventually, she stopped bringing it up.

Over time, she seemed to forget what Byam really was. Even Byam started to forget. When Leslie found her first white hair, Byam grew a few too, to make her feel better. Wrinkles were more challenging; it could never seem to get quite the right number. ("You look like a sage," said Leslie, when she was done laughing at its first attempt. "I'm only 48!")

Byam's former life receded into insignificance, the thwarted yearning of its earlier days nearly effaced.

The years went by quickly.

Leslie didn't talk much these days. It tired her, as everything tired her. She spent most of her time asleep, the rest looking out of the window. She didn't often tell Byam what was going through her head.

So it was a surprise when she said, without precursor:

"Why does the yeouiju matter so much?"

It took a moment before Byam understood what she was talking about. It hadn't thought of the cintamani in years. But then the surge of bitterness and longing was as fresh as ever, even in the midst of its grief.

"It's in the name, isn't it?" said Byam. "'The jewel that grants all wishes.'"

"Do you have a lot of wishes that need granting?"

Byam could think of some, but to tell Leslie about them would only distress her. It wasn't like Leslie *wanted* to die.

Before, Byam had always thought that humans must be used to dying, since they did it all the time. But now it had got to know them better, it saw they had no idea how to deal with it.

This was unfortunate, because Byam didn't know either.

"I guess I just always imagined I'd have one some day," it said. It tried to remember what it had felt like before it had given up on becoming a dragon and acquiring its own cintamani. "It was like . . . if I didn't have that hope, life would have no meaning."

Leslie nodded. She was still gazing out of the window. "You should try again."

"Let's not worry about it now—"

"You have thousands of years," said Leslie. "You shouldn't just give up." She looked Byam in the eye. "Don't you still want to be a dragon?"

Byam would have liked to say no. It was unfair of Leslie to awaken all these dormant feelings in it at a time when it already had too many feelings to contend with.

"Eun-hye should be here soon," it said. Leslie's niece was almost the same age Leslie had been when Byam had first come to her office with murder in its heart. Eun-hye had a child herself now, which still seemed implausible to Byam. "She's bringing Sam, won't that be nice?"

"Don't talk to me like I'm an old person," said Leslie, annoyed. "I'm dying, not *decrepit*. Come on, Byam. I thought repression was a human thing."

"That shows how much you know," said Byam. "When you've been a failure for three thousand years, you get good at repressing things!"

"I'm just saying—"

"I don't know why you're—" Byam scrubbed its face. "Am I not good enough as I am?"

"Of course you're good enough," said Leslie. "If you're happy, then that's fine. But you should know you can be anything you want to be. That's all. I don't want you to let fear hold you back."

Byam was silent.

Leslie said, "I only want to know you'll be OK after I'm dead."

"I wish you'd stop saying that," said Byam.

"I know."

"I don't want you to die."

"I know."

Byam laid its head on the bed. If it closed its eyes it could almost pretend they were home, with the cat snoozing on Leslie's feet.

After a while it said, without opening its eyes, "What's your next form going to be?"

"I don't know," said Leslie. "We don't get told in advance." She grinned. "Maybe I'll be an imugi."

"Don't say such things," said Byam, aghast. "You haven't been that bad!"

This made Leslie laugh, which made her cough, so Byam called the nurse, and then Eun-hye came with her little boy, so there was no more talk of dragons, or cintamani, or reversing a pragmatic surrender to the inevitable.

That night the old dreams started again—the ones where Byam was a dragon. But they were a relief compared to the dreams it had been having lately.

It didn't mention them to Leslie. She would only say, "I told you so."

For a long moment after Byam woke, it was confused. The cintamani still hung in the air before it. Then it blinked and the orb revealed itself to be a lamp by the hospital bed.

Leslie was awake, her eyes on Byam. "Hey."

Byam wiped the drool from its cheek, sitting up. "Do you want anything? Water, or—"

"No," said Leslie. Her voice was thin, a mere thread of sound. "I was just watching you sleep like a creeper."

But then she paused. "There is something, actually."

"Yeah?"

"You don't have to."

"If there's anything I can give you," said Byam, "you'll get it."

Still Leslie hesitated.

"Could I see you?" she said finally. "In your true form, I mean."

There was a brief silence. Leslie said, "If you don't want to . . ."

"No, it's fine," said Byam. "Are you sure you won't be scared?"

Leslie nodded. "It'll still be you."

Byam looked around the room. There wasn't enough space for its real form, so it would have to make more space. But that was a simple magic.

It hadn't expected the sense of relief as it expanded into itself. It was as though for several decades it had been wearing shoes a size too small and had finally been allowed to take them off.

Leslie's eyes were wide.

"Are you OK?" said Byam.

"Yes," said Leslie, but she raised her hands to her face. Byam panicked, but before it could transform again, Leslie rubbed her eyes and said, "Don't change back! I haven't looked properly yet."

Her eyes were wet. She studied Byam as though she was trying to imprint the sight onto her memory.

"I'd look better with legs," said Byam shyly. "And antlers. And a bumpy forehead . . ."

"You're beautiful." Leslie touched Byam's side. Her hand was warm. "It was you, wasn't it? That day in the mountains."

Byam shrank. It said, its heart in its mouth, "You knew?"

"I've known for a while."

"Why didn't you say anything?"

"Guess I was waiting for you to tell me." Leslie gave Byam a half smile. "You know me, I hate confrontation. Anything to avoid a fight."

"I should have told you," said Byam. "I wanted to, I just . . ." It had never been able to work out how to tell Leslie its original plan had been to devour her in an act of misdirected revenge.

Dumb, dumb, dumb. Byam could only blame itself for its failures.

"You should've told me." But Leslie didn't seem mad. Maybe she just didn't have the energy for it anymore.

"I'm sorry," said Byam. Leslie held out her hand, and it slid closer, letting her run her hand over its scales. "How did you figure it out?"

Leslie shrugged. "It made sense. You were always there when I needed you." She patted Byam gently. "Can I ask for one more thing?"

"Anything," said Byam. It felt soft and sad, bursting at the seams with melancholy love.

"Promise me you won't give up," said Leslie. "Promise me you'll keep trying."

It was like going in for a kiss and getting slapped in the face. Byam went stiff, staring at Leslie in outrage. "That's fighting dirty!"

"You said anything."

Byam ducked its head, but it couldn't see any way out.

"I couldn't take it," it said miserably, "not now, not after . . . I'm not brave enough to fail again."

Leslie's eyes were pitiless.

"I know you are," she said.

One last time

They scattered Leslie's ashes on the mountain where she had first seen Byam, which would have felt narcissistic if it hadn't been Leslie's own idea. When they were done, Byam said it wanted a moment alone.

No, it was all right, Eun-hye should stay with her mother. Byam was just going round the corner. It wanted to look at the landscape Leslie had loved.

Alone, it took off its clothes, folding them neatly and putting them on a stone. It shrugged off the constriction of the spell that had bound it for years.

It was like taking a deep breath of fresh air after coming up from the subway. For the first time Byam felt a rush of affection for its incomplete self—legless, hornless, orbless as it was. It had done the best it could.

Ascending was familiar, yet strange. Before, Byam had always striven to break free from the bonds of the earth.

This time it was different. Byam seemed to be bringing the earth with it as it rose to meet the sky. Its grief did not fall away—it was closer than ever, a cheek laid against Byam's own.

Everything was much simpler than Byam had thought. Heaven and earth were not so far apart, after all—

"Look, Sam," said Eun-hye. She held her son up, pointing. "There's an imugi going to heaven! Wow!"

The child's small frowning face turned to the sky. Gravity dug its claws into Byam.

It was fruitless to resist. Still, Byam thrashed wildly, hurling itself upwards. Fighting the battle of its life, as though it had any chance of winning.

Leslie had believed in Byam. It had promised to be brave.

"Wow, it's so pretty!" continued Eun-hye's voice, much loved and incredibly unwelcome. "Your imo halmeoni loved imugi."

Sam was young, but he already had very definite opinions.

"No," he said distinctly.

"It's good luck to see an imugi," said Eun-hye. "Look, the imugi's dancing!"

"No!" said Sam, in the weary tone he adopted when adults were being especially dense. "Not imugi. It's a *dragon*."

For the first time in Byam's inglorious career, gravity surrendered. The resistance vanished abruptly. Byam bounced into the clouds like an arrow loosed from the bow.

"No, ippeuni," Eun-hye was explaining. "Dragons are different. Dragons have horns like a cow, and legs and claws, and long beards like Santa . . ."

"Got horns," said Sam.

Byam barely noticed the antlers, or the whiskers unfurling from its face, or the legs popping out along its body, each foot adorned with four gold-tipped claws.

Because there it was—the cintamani of its dreams, a matchless pearl falling through five-colored clouds. It was like meeting a beloved friend in a crowd of strangers.

Byam rushed toward it, its legs (it had legs!) extended to catch the orb. It still half believed it was going to miss, and the whole thing would come crashing down around its ears, a ridiculous daydream after all.

But the cintamani dropped right in its paw. It was lit from the inside, slightly warm to the touch. It was perfect.

Byam only realized it was shedding tears when the clouds started weeping along. It must have looked strange from the ground, the storm descending suddenly out of a clear blue sky.

Eun-hye shrieked, covering Sam's head. "We've got to find Byam imo!"

"It's getting heavy," said Jean. "The baby'll get wet. Get Nathan to bring the car round. I'll look for her."

"No, I will."

"I've got an umbrella!"

They were still fighting, far beneath Byam, as the palaces of heaven rose before it. Ranks of celestial fairies stood by the gate, waiting to welcome it.

They had waited thousands of years. They could wait a little longer. Byam turned back, thinking to stop the storm. Anything to avoid a fight.

But the rain was thinning already. Through the clouds, Byam could see the child leaning out of his mother's arms, thwarting her attempts to keep him dry. He held his hands out to the rain, laughing.

With thanks to Miri Kim, Hana Lee, Perrin Lu, Kara Lee, and Rachel Monte.

Elsewhere

The Earth Spirit's Favorite Anecdote

The year was 3288—the Year of the Qilin. I was born in the Year of the Nian, so I was fifty-three years old. Quite old already, and two eights is auspicious, so that year I left my parents' hole and came to Kuala Ketam.

Our kind can live with their parents their whole lives, from small to big until die, but it doesn't work for everybody's family. I left my parents because they always look Back. Whenever anything new happens, whenever anything changes, they always say: *let's go Back, let's go Back.* Leave hole to go buy thing also, the whole time they keep thinking: *go Back lah, go Back.* How to live like that?

I am not the kind of person who likes to go Back. That's why I'm not so religious. I don't have any problem with the gods, but they got price. Everybody got price one. The gods' price is you must promise to go Back in the end. I never like to make promises—after cannot keep, then how? So I left loh. I wanted to go somewhere where I don't have to do the same thing as everybody else, because everybody is doing different-different things.

Kuala Ketam was like that because of the tin mines. Back then when tin was still important, got all kinds of spirits coming in—gods, ghosts, monsters, all the hantu-hantu also got. And there were people like me: earth people, small spirits who just want to make enough money to send home to their parents, and to save to build up their own hole.

In that kind of society, with everybody new and mix up together and still don't know the rules, got chance to make it if you're smart. I saw that straightaway. I dug a hole in a prime location—high land overlooking the river, and then I settle down and watch out for something to do.

Of course it wasn't that easy to find. I just come from the kampung, got no experience: Who want to hire somebody like that? I was only a small earth spirit some more, no power in myself. But don't think I had nothing to do just because nobody give me a job. Want to set up a hole also have to work like siao. You cannot simply dig a hole where you like—you have to get permission from the forest spirits first. If not they get angry and kick you out, then how?

The forest spirits were the first people at Kuala Ketam, before all the immigrants came. You know what they look like: tall, pointy-pointy ears, their skin grayish-brown like the tree trunk, eyes very big compared to ours. Their faces are harder to describe. Are they good-looking? Depends on who you ask. This kind of thing differs from race to race; different-different people will think their own people only beautiful. It's what you're used to that matters mah. But even so, most races agree that forest spirits are quite sui kuan. Not bad.

Because they come first, the forest spirits are very possessive of the land, and they are the ones who know the land. So there are rules. Before you dig a hole, you must get your freedom of the land from the local forest spirit. Never think you can own the tree you are living in—only forest spirits can own the trees, because they are the true owner of the land. You are only the renter.

The only exception is the rowan tree. The rowan tree got no forest spirit of its own. That's why you must never dig hole near a rowan tree: rowan trees are damn noisy. So many spirits living in the same tree, it's very crowded, and they non-stop fight. "Why your baby so noisy? Why you so smelly? Why your feet pointing the wrong way around?" Everybody shouting like there's no tomorrow. Spirits are like that. They don't know how to serve other people. They don't know how to get along.

But what to do? We're all put on this land together; somehow or other we must learn to put up with each other. That's why you must follow rules, learn to respect other cultures, don't offend the gods if can avoid it. Even if the rules are stupid, even if you're not religious, even if you don't like other people's customs, these things must keep in your heart. Outside must be polite a bit, never mind if you really feel that way or not. That's what we do, we all earth people. That's why we don't get into trouble even though we're not powerful. Even the richest earth spirit knows how to behave, so people don't kacau them. That's how you get through life.

My mother taught me all this, so I knew I must follow the adat. The morning after I finish digging my new hole, I went to look for the forest spirit.

They say deep in the jungle got no undergrowth, because the trees grow very tall and they got a lot of leaves, so the sunlight cannot reach the ground. I don't know if this kind of thing is true or not. Earth spirits don't go deep into the jungle. I walk small way into the trees already I feel nervous.

Because why? Because I know it's not my place. Everybody is like that: the sea spirit must stick to the sea; they live in river also don't like. Their children might get used to it, and for their children the river will become home. But for the sea spirit who is born in the sea, they cannot be comfortable anywhere else. And I was born in the earth.

So in the forest I kept close to myself, kept myself small, show I know I am only a visitor. You don't have to try so hard to look for the forest spirit of your land. The land knows who it belongs to. I just followed the slope of the earth, and it led me to its master.

The forest spirit saw me before I saw it. It was sitting in its tree, very relaxed. Their tree is like some kind of kopitiam to all these forest spirits. They sit there drinking teh tarik all day. Very lazy people.

"Oi, boss," it said. "You going where, boss?"

It jumped down from its tree, landing on its feet. It looked like all forest spirits—tall, pointy ears, big smile. It didn't look male or female. Forest spirits don't have this concept. They say male or female has no meaning. They don't like to follow rules. Like I said, they are very lazy.

We earth people, we all like to have everything clear. I always think the forest spirit's life must be very messy if they cannot even decide whether they are boy or girl.

I admit, I was a bit scared. Forest spirits don't know what are boundaries when it comes to people. Land, yes. But people, they don't know where to draw the line.

The forest spirit looked at me, its head first on one side, then on the other side, moving very fast like a bird. It stood very close. Its eyes were strange to me.

"Sorry I come into your area, sir," I said. "I want to set up hole here. Can I have the freedom of the land?"

I bowed. When you bow to the forest spirit, you must put your hands together and bend your head so your forehead touches your finger. If it is a big forest spirit you can bend your back a bit, but only a bit. You must not respect too much. Only bend to your waist when a god is passing by.

"Ah, hole ah," it said, like it was thinking like that. All forest spirits talk like they are singing. "Hole ah hole ah hole. Hole. Where?"

"In the bank of Sungai Udang, near the mangrove tree there," I said.

"Near the river," it said. "The river goddess like you or not?"

I paused. "I don't know."

It held up one finger. "OK, not to worry. This very easy to find out. You slept one night in the hole already, right?"

I thought I knew what it was trying to say. "Yes, sorry, sir. I only finish digging late at night and I didn't want to kacau you—"

It waved its hand impatiently. "All that never mind. I ask you. Are you dead?"

"Hah?"

I hope you will not say 'hah?' to people like that. I only talk like that because I was surprised. When you don't understand something, you must say, "I beg your pardon?" That is the polite way to say in Occi.

"Are you dead?" said the forest spirit. "Did she try to drown you?"

"No!" I said. "I am alive what. If she drown me I would be dead, right?"

"How I know? Earth can swallow rain. Maybe earth spirit cannot drown." It looked at my face. Then it said, "Looks like the river likes you. Now only left for me to decide."

It smiled.

There's a saying: *never tell a crocodile a joke, never let a forest spirit smile at you.* Both things are equally dangerous, because when a crocodile laughs it opens its mouth big-big, and when a forest spirit smiles . . .

I think you don't know how dangerous that is until you see a forest spirit smile. But by then it's too late.

I thought I was irritated. I don't like people who are all over the place. Like most earth spirits, I like things to be neat, sensible. Of course forest spirits are not sensible.

"I work hard," I said stiffly. "I will be very quiet. I won't make fight with the other spirits or use more than my fair share of the land. If you give me the freedom of the land, I won't misuse it."

"Yalah," said the forest spirit. "All this I can tell from your face. I very clever like that. But earth spirits who work hard and follow rule, everywhere also can find. The question is: Does the land like you?"

This I couldn't answer. I can make friends with the earth. When I dug my hole at Kuala Ketam, the earth was happy; its voices sang to me. But the land is not the same thing as the earth. There are many-many voices in the land: water-voices, air-voices, animal-voices, spirit-voices, tree-voices. The voice of the land is too big for an earth spirit to hear.

"How I know? You should know that what," I said. "It's your land."

"True, true," said the forest spirit, as if it never thought of this before. It wrinkled its forehead and looked serious, but it was like a child pretending to listen to the teacher.

"I think it's not sure lah, boss," it said finally. "Tell you what, I let the land think about you, tomorrow I ask how it feels. Tomorrow you come again. Tomorrow can know."

I was outraged. Forest spirits are so inefficient!

"Tomorrow!" I said. "Meanwhile where I sleep?"

"In the hole lah," it said. "If the river didn't drown you last night, it won't drown you tonight."

"'The river won't drown you!' That's all very well, but what about the land? I got no protection from the spirits then how?"

"I'll tell them not to kacau you for now," it said. It smiled again. "One night is OK. The land won't mind one night. Tomorrow you come, boss."

I should have known from the smile. Two smiles from a forest spirit I never met before! Aiyah, I was very young and innocent. I knew how to make my way in the world, but I didn't know how forest spirits think. I didn't understand that forest spirits are not sensible. They are not like us earth spirits, worry about hole, worry about parents and children and past and future. To them, the only important thing is happiness, and their happiness is different from our one.

Still, I was quite happy with my own happiness when I went to sleep that night. I had my own hole. Soon I would have the freedom of the land, and then I could start working.

That's what I thought.

But the forest spirits have a saying. In Occi, it translates to something like: *tomorrow also can.*

How I know forest spirits have this kind of saying? Because I heard it every day when I went to visit the forest spirit after that. Every day I went and asked: "Can I have the freedom of the land?" Every day, cannot start work, cannot do anything useful—must go to this fellow and drink tea and ask question.

By the second day already I stopped calling it "sir." This kind of person there's no point trying to respect. No matter whether you are rude or polite, they won't change their behavior, but at least you will feel better if you shout at them a bit.

It never said no. It was never so straightforward. Every day: "Sorry lah, boss. I asked the land, but it still not sure."

"Cannot lah, boss, cannot rush the land. The land must make up its own mind. We wait first. You want tea? My mother makes it from her own toenails, it's very good!"

"Come tomorrow lah, tomorrow also can. What's the rush?"

Finally I said, "You ask me what's the rush?"

Earth spirits are not made to drink a lot of tea. My stomach didn't feel so good, and I was losing patience.

"I want to go to work, OK," I shouted. "I have parents! I want to send money Back hole! I want to give them grandchildren! I am not like you. My life is not long. Every tomorrow you give me means another today is wasted. Tomorrow won't do!"

Its face changed, but I couldn't read its expression. The faces of forest spirits are too alien. Their sadness and happiness look different from our sadness and happiness.

"That's true," it said. "Your life is very short." Forest spirits live for long-long time, like their trees, like their land. Otherwise the land would die—the land must have its spirit.

The earth people have a different path. We must have children, so our children can carry on our legacy. We cannot waste time.

"Have you found a husband yet?" said the forest spirit.

"Hah?" I thought the forest spirit was joking maybe, but it seemed quite serious. "None of your business!"

"Don't have yet? Then you're right. Shouldn't waste more time," it said. "Tomorrow you come. Tomorrow sure got answer."

"Chau chibai, go to hell! 'Tomorrow sure got answer' my foot!"

"Yes," said the forest spirit serenely. "Tomorrow sure can one. Tomorrow, boss, tomorrow."

I didn't believe it. I was very angry. When I walked Back to my hole I said to myself: if I stay here with this fellow, I will sure go cuckoo. What the hell, what's its problem? I should just leave.

But for some reason I didn't. I thought: never mind lah. It's a good location. The soil is well-drained; the earth is friendly. The forest spirit even say the river likes me . . . it's not easy to find such a good spot near the water. Probably all forest spirits are like this also. Maybe this time it meant it when it said tomorrow.

Maybe I hoped it wasn't telling the truth, and tomorrow it will tell me again, "Come tomorrow, boss." Usually forest spirits don't talk much to the spirits on its land. Once the forest spirit gave me the freedom of the land, that's it, must say goodbye already. I probably won't see it again. And I quite liked its smile.

But that night I changed my mind. I was sleeping in my hole when I woke up suddenly. I didn't know why I woke up. The earth felt happy and all the night noises were normal. Nothing seemed wrong.

I was about to go to sleep again when I heard it. The hissing.

I sat up and pressed my back to the good kind earth. I could see shapes in the dark. And the hissing, getting louder: *ssss . . .*

They tell stories about the dark. My parents told me. Not to scare me. They told me to protect me, so I would know.

We earth people live in our holes because we have to stay close to the earth. You can only hear the voices of the earth if you live in it, sleep next to it, wake up and say good morning to it every day. And you can only be an earth spirit if you hear the voices of the earth. That is our power. It's not a big power, it cannot even make a god sneeze, but it gives us our rice and our children and our future. We cannot do anything without the earth.

But there are other things underground in the dark, things that belong to the dark, not to the earth or the air or anything good and useful. Spirits we don't know. What they want, we who breathe air and drink water cannot hope to understand. All we know is that sometimes you can have a good hole, you can have the best hole anyone ever have; you can live well and honour the gods and respect your parents—but one night the dark will come, and the next morning your hole will be empty.

These things happen. Nothing can stop it. But you are a bit safer if you have the freedom of the land, because even the dark is part of the land and respects its wishes.

So I pressed myself against the earth and thought, *Fuck that stupid fucker.* "I'll tell them not to kacau you for now" pulak. Nobody can tell the dark what to do except the land. If the forest spirit gave me the freedom of the land, maybe this won't happen. I thought: *If I die, I hope I get reincarnated into a mosquito so I can bite that fucker kau-kau.*

And all the time that *ssss* sound got closer and closer, and the smell of vomit filled the hole. I closed my eyes so I won't have to see.

Then something grabbed my face with little hands. A voice like the wind in a graveyard said:

"Mama?"

I opened my eyes and saw a toyol.

I screamed. Maybe you will think I too pengecut, but I hate toyol. I cannot tahan the way they act like real babies. They make me feel damn geli. This one smelled even worse than toyol usually do, because on top of the smell of rotting flesh, it had vomit on its bib.

I was so angry I didn't even stop to wonder who would put a bib on a dead fetus. I shoved the toyol away. It hit the opposite wall, and I heard the voices of the earth say, *"Eeyer!"*

"Bloody hell!" I shouted. "Who the hell ask you to come here? You think I damn rich, is it? I just come from the kampung, set up new hole, never even get the freedom of the land yet. What kind of stupid spirit so dumb until they think I got treasure to steal? Hah?"

It is OK to say "hah?" in this kind of situation, by the way. You don't have to be polite to burglars.

I think the toyol realized that if it tried to act like a baby, it would kena from me like hell.

"Sorry, ma'am, I cannot say who hire me," it said in a normal voice: a dusty dead voice, but at least with no babyish squeaking. "Union rules."

"You tell me who your boss is," I said, "or I will take you to a priest and get him to bury you right now. You don't think I kesian you just because you're a dead baby. I think all dead babies should be burnt so that something like you cannot happen."

"Sorry lah, sorry lah, I'm just doing my job," the toyol whimpered. "You know my boss. He's the king."

"The king?"

"The owner," said the toyol. "The one in charge. The pengurus. The king."

Then I knew who it meant.

"Go Back to your boss and tell him to go and die," I said. "I'm going Back to sleep. I see you here again, I'll kill you."

"But—"

"You can hear or not? You want me to say 'I'll kill you' louder a bit?"

"No, but—"

"Go away!"

The toyol's lower lip wobbled. "Don't I even get a hug?" it said.

"Go Back now," I said, "or I will cremate your ass."

It went away after that, but I didn't sleep. Like I said, I never go Back. I stayed awake until morning, listening to the earth. The voices were uneasy, but at least the earth never lies.

In the morning, I went to look for the forest spirit when I knew it wouldn't be awake yet. You believe or not? I spent so many days waiting for the forest spirit to give me my freedom, I even knew its habits. You see how dangerous the smile of the forest spirit is?

The forest spirit looked very blur when it came down its tree to meet me.

"Wah, early ah, boss," it said, but I didn't let it say any more.

"From you, right? That toyol," I said. "I cannot stand toyol, you know or not? They're disgusting. Even cockroaches are better."

Its face changed, but it looked alien no matter what expression it had.

"Ah, they're not so bad," it said. "Not like a dead baby's going to do anything else what. Might as well make it useful, right?"

"I cannot stand toyol," I repeated, tight with anger, "and I cannot stand your kind of playing around. 'Tomorrow, tomorrow'—and all the time you just want me to stay so you can steal my money. If you want money, no problem. You should just say, 'If you want the freedom of the land, must pay fee.' Like that I don't mind. I'm not asking you for favor. But day after day you say 'tomorrow.' Day after day, 'Come lah, drink tea with me lah, tomorrow sure can lah.' All because you want to rob me."

"I didn't—"

"You sent your toyol in," I said. "You went in without my permission. Don't you know you cannot go into an earth spirit's hole without asking? But you don't even know respect!"

"Bloody—! You don't even let me explain!"

"Explain what? What's there to explain? You intruded!"

"You don't even have the freedom anyway!" it shouted.

It was right. You don't really own your hole until the land accepts you. Until you have the freedom of the land, your hole belongs to the local forest spirit, like everything else.

But it felt like my hole. I slept so many nights in it; I knew the earth so well. Now it was all spoiled. You cannot go into an earth spirit's hole without asking first. It is like stepping into a person's heart without being invited. For an earth spirit, it is the same thing.

I bowed.

"I'm sorry I intruded so long in your area," I said. "This is obviously the wrong place for me. I will find another place to set up hole."

I bowed again because I was so angry, and then I left.

For the rest of the day I looked for new hole, but I was too damn miserable. Setting up a hole doesn't mean simply digging anywhere, in any mood. When you dig your hole, you must be full of good thoughts. You must be thinking of how happy your parents will be when you send money Back hole; you must think of the children you will have to fill your hole. Then the earth will be happy with you, and you will have a good life in your hole.

But I was too tired and heart-pain to look properly, so finally when it was late and the light was turning blue, I just dug a hole where I was. An earth spirit must not be out when the sun has gone down. There are too many hungry gods and spirits in this world.

But the earth's voices were not happy, and I didn't listen to them. That was a mistake. When I woke up that night, alone in the strange earth, I knew.

There was no sound. That was where I went wrong the night before. There is no hissing, no chittering, no warning when they come. You cannot see or smell anything. But you know they are there. It's the same thing as when your nose smells food and knows you can eat it. I hope you never know the feeling that comes when the dark is near.

This time I didn't try to get closer to the earth. Nothing with a soul can protect you when the dark comes. You realize that deep in your stomach when it actually happens. It was strange earth anyway. It didn't know me, and it was silent in its own fear.

At times like that there is nothing to think. There is just you and the dark, and in a little while you know there will only be the dark left. Want to think also cannot. You can only roll yourself up small and hide far inside your mind.

The things of the dark circled, and I was very alone.

When the hissing started, it was like waking up from a nightmare. I smelled vomit, and suddenly I could see: little baby shapes tumbled into the hole, things with rotting teeth and glowing green eyes. Then I closed my eyes, because it was like waking up from a nightmare into *another* nightmare. This one was not so scary as the first one, but smellier.

Toyol have no souls. Their souls have passed on to wherever the souls of babies go. Maybe they remember what it was like to be a baby—maybe that's why they like to cry and say "Mama": because they feel like that's what they're supposed to be doing. But to be honest I think they do it to be kiampa, to make people want to slap them.

You cannot be scared of the dark if you have no soul, but you can be very hungry. I heard them laugh, and then there was a sound like when you put down an offering of rice and fruit and incense in a holy place and step back. Gods have no table manners. Toyol are like them in that respect.

I opened my eyes again when one of them touched my knee, whining. I kicked out. I wasn't scared anymore. I knew the dark was gone. Not to say I wasn't happy lah, but I wasn't so grateful until let a toyol stroke my leg.

"Aiyah, boss, why you spoil my product?" said a voice. "Toyol not so easy to make, you know. They don't grow on trees. Not like me."

Of course it was my former landlord. There was that chibai, standing at the entrance of the hole like nothing special happen like that. I looked back at the toyol at their feast, and then I looked away again very quickly.

"You got so many toyol," I said. "One less won't make any difference. How the hell you get so many?"

"Hard work," said the forest spirit modestly. "I am setting up a business. I hire out toyol."

I stared at it.

"You are setting up a toyol business," I said. "And it's called what? Toyol Sendirian Berhad?"

"I was thinking of a partnership, actually, not limited company," said the forest spirit. "But you got the idea. Pay fee, get a toyol to come to your house and work for you part-time. No need to find the dead babies yourself, no need to do jampi. All maintenance taken care of."

"And what exactly do your customers do with their toyol?" I said. As you know, when magicians summon up toyol, it is usually because they are too lazy to earn their own money. Toyol have very small hands: good with locks.

"Ah, that one they keep to themselves," said the forest spirit. "No need for us to ask. The business has nothing to do with all that. But don't think it's all just samseng who order. I train my toyol to do all kind of thing. Housewife is our number-two target market. The toyol are very clever to do housework—the customer just have to buy more air freshener lah. The service still very worth it, compared to the local cleaning fairies."

"So what," I said, "the toyol in my hole last night is free promo, is it? Your marketing department damn suck eh. The toyol never clean anything also."

The forest spirit's face changed. This time I knew it was feeling shy. I guess it's just a matter of getting use to the difference.

"No. Ah, no, that one was a security guard," it said. "I, ah—actually the land was quite happy with you already. Technically you already had the freedom of the land. But you are new here. Who knows what kind of pervert might try to break into your hole? I was a bit worried lah, that's all."

"That's all?" I echoed. "That's all? Bastard, if you so concerned until you put toyol in my hole without asking, why didn't you just tell me I had the freedom of the land in the first place?"

"I don't know," said the forest spirit. "My business . . . I can handle the toyol, no problem, but like you said, the marketing side is not so good. The accounting department also. I cannot get anyone to pay their bill. I don't know to manage spirits lah. I no PR skills. You earth spirits are better than me at this kind of thing."

"You string me along because you want a manager for your company," I said flatly.

"Not only that lah," said the forest spirit. "Got other reason also lah."

It looked at its feet, as if got something very interesting to look at.

"You know," it said. "My uncle married a river."

"Hah," I said. I cannot tell you whether it was OK for me to say "hah" then or not. This kind of situation you must figure out for yourself.

"His parents allow, meh?" I said. "Interracial marriage?"

"They're not so happy at first lah," said the forest spirit. "But they got used to it. He was 1,800 years old anyway. Old enough to do what he wanted.

"I'm 2,467," it added.

"Year of the Phoenix," I said.

"Really?"

"I'm born Year of the Nian," I said. "Nian not so compatible with Phoenix."

"I never believe in this astrology thing anyway," said the forest spirit.

"I'm fifty-three," I said. "In another hundred years I'll die already. Hundred fifty if I'm lucky."

"No time to waste, then," said the forest spirit. It smiled.

If I was smart, the first time it smiled I would have run away. But I wasn't smart, and now it was too late.

"Are you coming Back to your hole?" said the forest spirit.

"I never go Back one," I said.

Its face changed.

"But maybe this time I'll make an exception," I said. "Tomorrow lah. Tomorrow I come see you."

"Tomorrow?" it said. "Why waste time? Come lah today."

"Tomorrow," I said. "You come into my hole without permission, you think got no effect ah? I need to rest first. Maybe later I go talk to the earth in my hole, make friend again. I got a lot of thing to do. Tomorrow only if I have time, I'll come. We can talk about what is good manners. Personal boundaries."

"But tomorrow is so long lah," it said. "Come today lah, boss."

"Stop complaining," I said. "You don't learn to wait, you'll never make it in this world. I'll see you tomorrow. Now get out of my hole."

Of course I went to see it the next day. But you can guess what happened. Happy endings are all the same. I'll just say: it's true also, you don't always have to draw line or follow rule. Not being sure whether you are boy or girl or both or neither—it's messy, but then life is memang messy. Once you get use to it . . . but we cannot talk about this kind of things. Let's just say lah. It's quite interesting.

Monkey King, Faerie Queen

Now to be fair, Sun Wukong was already in a bad mood when he arrived at the Faerie Court.

You don't know who Sun Wukong is? You're kidding! You haven't heard of the Great Sage Equal to Heaven, the one who is Mindful of Emptiness, the Exquisite and Most Satisfactory Prince of Monkeys, defier of gods and Buddhas alike, scorner of other people's dignity, and personal inspiration to little monkeys everywhere?

One day a stone cracked and he jumped out: that was the miracle that was his birth. His fur is as silken as your favorite shirt and as golden as the midday sun. He has eyes of fire and the biggest ears anyone ever saw on a monkey. And if you want to look up his name in the Book of Life and Death, forget about it, because he went down to Hell and wiped that shit out himself!

You know who he is? Why didn't you say so? You didn't know his name? That's okay. All gods have more than one name, to give the mortals more chances to swear. You can call him the Monkey God or Monkey King or just plain Monkey, whatever you like. It's the same simian in the end.

This was in the pre-Enlightenment days, you understand, before Sun Wukong mended his ways and became a Buddha. In the days when Sun Wukong was still naughty and enjoyed the occasional punch-up.

This old Sun Wukong had yet to transcend the sin of lust. One day on the Mountain of Flowers and Fruit, where he reigned, Sun

Wukong was trying to impress a pretty monkey. Pretty monkeys with a cynical curling lip are the cause of so much trouble in this world!

"With my staff I can control the tides and whack the sea dragons kau-kau," said Sun Wukong. "And when I am finished, I can make my staff small-small and put it inside my ear."

The pretty monkey was at her most enchanting when she was bored.

"Maybe I am very shallow," she said, "but I always think size matters."

"My staff weighs 13,500 jin at normal size!" said Sun Wukong.

The pretty monkey yawned.

"With my eyes I can see evil no matter what form it takes," said Sun Wukong. "No matter how it tries to hide, it cannot hide from me.

"Once I saw a pink baby dolphin frolicking in the sea. It leapt out of the waves and danced back down into the sea together with its mother. The salt from the water blurred my eyes and at first I smiled upon them. But when I blinked, I saw there was a demon within the baby dolphin! The next time it turned to its mother, it opened its mouth and there was way too many teeth for any dolphin in there!

"I flew down and snatched the demon from the sea and we fought above the heaving waters for eight days and eight nights. On the ninth day he tore out a chunk of my beautiful fur, and as I howled in pain, he vanished into the air. I went down to the sea to tell the mother she was safe, but she beat me for taking away her baby. She gave me two and a half bruises."

"How cruel," said the pretty monkey, frowning. Sun Wukong wasn't altogether comfortable in his mind that she was referring to the dolphin mother, so he hurried on. "Of course I don't really fly. What I do is much more exciting than flying," he said. "My master taught me to travel by jumping from cloud to cloud. For me it's as easy as swinging from one tree to another. In one somersault I can travel 108,000 li."

"Oh, really?" said the pretty monkey, with the most delicate, infuriating inflection of disbelief.

Sun Wukong was getting a little annoyed.

"Yes, see!" he said.

He did one jump, but on the second cloud he stumbled, and to correct himself he made another jump. Now he was tens of thousands of li away from the pretty monkey. He thought of jumping back to see if she was impressed yet, but he was not quite pleased with his last somersault. He tried another one, to see if it would be better. Then another one.

In this way Monkey hurtled halfway across the world. Beneath him snowy deserts unfurled, peopled with bears and wolves. Rivers thundered along their courses and elephants went on parades, shaking their bedizened heads. Sleepy old men nodded off on their doorsteps; women with floury hands molded dough into turtle-shapes. Humans with icicles in their hair sneezed themselves awake. Humans fell asleep under palm-leaf roofs, slapping away mosquitoes. Night and day met each other on their way across the world and shook hands. Sun Wukong tripped on his sixteenth cloud and fell flat on his face in Fairyland.

How could it be so easy to get into Fairyland, you say? But the boundaries of that world are more permeable than you think. Humans are so curious, fairies so easily bored.

Besides, if you are the Monkey King and you are doing the long jump around the world, you are hardly going to land in a petrol station outside Bidor, are you? You're going to land somewhere interesting.

Sun Wukong did not realize he was somewhere interesting when he got up and looked around. He was in a green-gray land, and the air bit at him with freezing teeth. Mist clung to the earth, making a mystery of trees and distant hills.

Sun Wukong observed that the ground was lumpy—the rolling green meadows stretching out beneath his feet were dotted with green-furred mounds. Then he saw that there were people watching him.

This put him in a bad mood. A king never likes to be caught falling flat on his face by barbarians.

For to Sun Wukong's blazing eyes, these were obviously barbarians. Those who wore clothes were in strange, ill-fitting garments, which warped and squeezed their shapes. This barbarian attire was nothing like Sun Wukong's flowing, manly robes, made of silk and richly embroidered with dragons and golden suns.

Several of the barbarians did not wear clothes at all. Of these, many could not have worn human clothes if they had wanted to: they were too small, or too tall, or they stood on all fours and had so much fur they did not need clothes. Some stood on two legs and were broadly human shaped but did not have hair or eyes—at least, not in the usual places. Some of the people you could see through; they were as insubstantial as the mist.

Others were human-looking enough, save that they had nasty pale faces with large tapir-like noses, far more unbeautiful than even the average furless mortal.

The people started chattering to each other in a strange tongue, making a noise like *wo-wo-wo*.

"That's no mortal, by its smell," said a Barghest with glowing eyes and streaming jaws. "It's not the lass we seek."

"But what manner of beast is it?" said a water hag.

"A furred bird, methinks," said a pooka, "to come plunging out of the sky in such fine plumage."

"Whatever it is, Herself will want to see it," said an elf.

Sun Wukong always felt sorry for beings who were less wonderful than he. He decided to be stern but kind.

"Haa!" he said chidingly. "Is this any way to treat a guest? You gossip about them like they are not there, and you don't even offer them something to eat!"

Perhaps they had some modicum of intelligence despite their unpromising appearance, for the people now gathered around him, nodding and smiling. A lovely girl with the big soft eyes and whiskered snout of a seal took his hand with one paw and tugged it gently. With the other paw, she pretended to drink out of an imaginary cup.

"Aha," said Sun Wukong. "That's more like it!"

As they lead Sun Wukong into the hill, let me explain who these people were.

In foreign countries people don't do things the way we do them. Instead of calling nice *nice* and not nice *not nice*, they like to say that what is bad is good and what is good is bad. So this benighted ragtag group of unreverenced lesser godlings were known as the Fair Folk, despite their pinched unpleasant faces. They were the Good Neighbors, even though they soured their human neighbors' milk and stole the occasional baby. They were called the People of Peace, even though their favorite pastime was declaring war and perpetrating grotesque crimes upon each other.

You can imagine how peculiar this would have seemed to Sun Wukong, possessed of such elegant and appropriate titles as "Beautiful Monkey King" and "Stone Simian."

However, as the foreigners could not speak his language, Sun Wukong had no opportunity to learn about their curious naming customs. All he knew of these strangers was that they lived underground like rabbits, and they were trying to press on him a drink that smelled nice.

Sun Wukong drank some. It was not as good as real wine, but it was not bad.

He leaned back in his uncomfortable chair and looked around. The room was larger and finer than he'd expected, considering they were beneath the mounds he had seen earlier. The floors were carpeted and on the walls hung tapestries showing gruesome scenes of battle and ichorshed, as well as happier scenes of weddings between horses and ordinary household objects. Dim corridors led out of the room to unknown places.

A banquet was laid out on the table where Sun Wukong sat, with glowing fruit in silver bowls and a barbecued whole pig laid on a platter. The pig yawned once in a while, but it did not smell any less delicious for it. The place was lit by tinkling winged things like fireflies with faces. "You have funny insects here," said Sun Wukong to the elf. "Our flies are shaped like rice or beans. But your flies are shaped like humans. They wear clothes also. Does it make you feel weird about swatting them?"

"How he chatters on," said the pooka, who was watching the proceedings with malicious interest.

"Did you give him the right brew?" said the selkie. She took the flagon and sniffed it. Her eyes rolled up.

"Your friend doesn't have much stamina," observed Sun Wukong as she flopped wetly onto the floor.

The elf was beginning to have a shiny look about the eyes. He poured more wine into Sun Wukong's goblet.

"Drink more, dear heart, best of strangers," he said. "Drink, drink, and slumber."

"Perhaps you should cradle him to your breast and sing him a lullaby," said the pooka. "That might work just as well."

"It's as if the creature is made of stone," said the water hag. "He's had near the whole flagon!"

In fact Sun Wukong was starting to feel a little drowsy. The glow of the strange human-flies became fuzzy around the edges, and their constant background tinkling seemed to come from far away. Sleep pressed down on his eyelids; its soft velvety darkness started to blanket his brain. His spirit stirred and put on its robes, preparing to go out and wander the world, as your spirit does when you go to sleep.

Hoi! thought Sun Wukong. *Don't go anywhere! I want to stay here and explore!*

His spirit was already pulling on its boots.

You always have all the good times, said his spirit to his waking mind. *You only sleep four hours every night! Why don't you at least give me chance to travel once in a while?*

Sun Wukong got cross. *You already get to travel every night, and you still want to complain! Who is doing all the work around here anyway? I don't see you eating and shitting and brushing our fur. I am the one who has to make sure everything is running properly.*

That is your job, said his spirit haughtily. *I am a poet. You cannot expect me to worry about these mundane matters. Anyway, I'm already dressed and I am going and there's nothing you can do about it.*

Son of a turtle! exclaimed Sun Wukong. *Dare to speak to your big brother like that?*

He threw a punch. His spirit dodged, and the punch landed on the table. The table cracked in half. The pig squealed; the fairies scattered; the fruit bowls grew slim pewter legs and scuttled away.

Dare to punch your own precious spirit? said Sun Wukong's spirit. *If you want to fight, let's fight!*

"What a peculiar beast it is," said the Barghest as Sun Wukong danced around the room, slapping himself.

"I am not certain Herself would like it," said the water hag. "She prefers the biddable type."

"Perhaps we had better put it back where we found it," said the elf. He was tired of pouring wine.

"But what entertainment!" said the pooka. "How he is trouncing himself! If every mortal were like this I'd have nothing to do but sit at my ease and laugh as they each sent themselves to the Devil. What a fool!"

"You'd best not laugh yet," said the Barghest. "It is no mortal, remember, and we know not what powers it may have—"

Sun Wukong decided to try kicking himself. Because he was a trifle tipsy on the wine of Elfland, his aim was poor. Instead of kicking his spirit, Sun Wukong kicked the wall. Fortunately he did not hurt his foot, or even injure the charming tapestry depicting a frog being put under a geas, as the pooka was standing between his foot and the wall.

"Still entertained, coz?" said the water hag to the pooka, but the pooka did not seem to be in the mood for conversation.

"We had best tell Herself of this before the creature has murdered all the fae in Elfland," said the elf.

"Oh, the pooka'll feel better soon enough," said the water hag, but when the elf crept out discreetly, she and the Barghest followed him.

After a while Sun Wukong got bored of fighting.

"Do you still want to be punched, or you want to have a truce?" he asked himself.

There's no use doing this any longer. You have woken yourself up with all this jumping-here jumping-there, said his spirit sulkily. *Anyway we need to pee.*

This was true. The room was dark—all the twinkly tinkly things had fled. Sun Wukong fumbled around, kicking away broken glass and splintered wood as he walked, until he found a place where the wall fell away. In the distance, down the passage, he thought he could see light.

The passage opened on a grand hall. The carpets and tapestries here were eight times as beautiful as the ones in the dining room had been. Veined marble pillars held up a vaulted ceiling, from which hung an effulgent chandelier made of tens of thousands of human-flies imprisoned in crystal.

There was a big wooden chair in the middle of the room, but nobody was sitting on it.

"Haa," said Sun Wukong dubiously.

But he really needed to pee. At least with this light he could see what he was doing. He looked around to double-check that there was nobody there, strolled over to a pillar, and relieved himself.

As Sun Wukong pulled his trousers up, there was a squeak. He peered down. What had appeared to be a patch of shadow behind the pillar turned out to be a terrified lump of human.

"Aiyah," said Sun Wukong. How embarrassing! "Did I splash you?"

But now he thought about it, he began to feel indignant. Who sat around behind pillars in precisely the dark spots where a person in need of the toilet would seek refuge? What kind of uncivilized behavior was this?

"What are you doing there anyway?" he demanded.

But of course the mortal woman did not understand his speech either, any more than her unimpressive gods had done. She shrank back, her eyes round with terror. She had a pale waxen face, speckled like an egg, and tangled orange hair. Her eyes were ringed like a panda's. She smelled terrible.

Sun Wukong withdrew a little, for he was a cleanly monkey, but he felt sorry for the human.

"You are very poor thing har," said Sun Wukong. "Come, don't sit there in the dark. There's a chair over there. You can sit there, be more comfortable."

He took her arm and led her to the chair. It was like picking up a doll: she went along bonelessly, without resistance, until they reached the chair. Then she opened her eyes wide and jerked away, gabbling.

"What?" said Sun Wukong, but there was a loud creaking sound. He looked around to see the large doors at the end of the room swinging open. The human grabbed his arm and pulled him into the shadows behind the pillars.

"She comes!" she hissed. "Be quiet, good monkey, dear monkey. O, why do I do this? Doubtless when she comes, you will deliver me to her. You are an uncanny beast indeed, but I thought you had kind eyes—you were trying to help me. But I am so tired. I do not know my own mind. Sometimes I am even afraid I shall forget why I came. Oh Johnnie, oh my Johnnie!"

Sun Wukong was about to tell her off for venturing to haul the Monkey God around as if he were a mere mortal, but the woman moaned her last words with such unhappiness that he didn't like to do it. Besides, at that point a most interesting scent came to his nose, and his ears pricked up.

Sun Wukong smelled power.

It was a whole stream of people that flowed into the hall, yelping, shrieking, cavorting, gliding, floating, tumbling, crawling, and hopping. Among them Sun Wukong discerned his friends, the elf and the water hag and the Barghest. He pointed them out to the human:

"Good fellers, but no manners."

But his interest did not lie with them. They were mere subjects, he knew now—peons, minions.

In the middle of the crowd stood the big boss, the one he was interested in. The rock in the rushing brook, the still heart of the tornado. A woman built on a gigantic scale, towering above her subjects. Her red curls were nailed to her head by enormous pearl hairpins; her dress was made of rich velvets and patterned silks; her neck and wrists and ears were starred with jewels. Her pale, eyebrowless face shone out of this barbarian luxury like a strange moon.

It was Herself, the Faerie Queen.

She sat down on the wooden chair.

"Hah!" said Sun Wukong. He sprang up and walked out into the center of the room, ignoring the mortal's flailing attempts to stop him. "It's a throne!"

The thrones he was used to had more gold and dragons on them. The kings and queens *he* knew wouldn't have been satisfied with any old chair. But obviously you could not expect equal grandeur in such a poor country as this.

It occurred to him that it might appear impolite to sound so surprised. He modulated his tones:

"Very nice. Very nice. I like things to be simple also. Maybe back on my Mountain of Flowers and Fruit I will call my artisans to make me something like that. Can put it in the garden.

"But I haven't introduced myself. Of course you are the Queen. I am Sun Wukong, the Gallant and Unsurpassed King of the Monkeys."

He bowed. The Queen stared at him with strange pale eyes. A native would have called that gaze eldritch, for the local people had special words to describe the Good People.

Sun Wukong did not know these words, and he was not burdened with any preconceptions. To him the Queen's eyes brought to mind some vicious unthinking animal—pure of purpose, single-minded, and utterly unscrupulous.

"What is this creature?" said the Queen to her subjects. She held out something in her arms for an attending hobgoblin to take. Only then did Sun Wukong observe that she was holding a baby.

A cry broke out behind Sun Wukong. A second later a bad-smelling orange breeze passed him. The human woman threw herself at the hobgoblin, but the Queen held up a hand and she froze.

"Johnnie, Johnnie," cried the woman. "You shall not have him, my darling, my sweet one. Give him back to me."

She might as well have been a mosquito for all the attention the Queen paid her. Looking fixedly at Sun Wukong, the Queen said:

"Who are you?"

Sun Wukong did not understand anything anybody was saying, but he did not have to understand their speech in order to see what they were doing.

Here was a red-haired infant who smelled mortal. Here was an upset red-haired mortal woman who was trying to get to the baby. Here was a powerful ruler with merciless eyes—and the courtier to whom she had handed the infant did not know how to hold a baby. (As a popular king Sun Wukong had kissed many a monkey baby in his time, and he knew you were not supposed to let their tiny heads dangle in that way.)

The human woman began to weep and lament.

In later days Monkey would have to learn to behave himself in foreign courts, but at this time Sun Wukong's head was still unbound. He did not have to obey anybody, or follow any rules. In those days, the only thing he listened to was his warm beating heart.

Sun Wukong is not a thinker; he is a doer. No sooner had his heart moved in his chest than he was in the air, leaping across the court. A punch—the hobgoblin dropped. Sun Wukong scooped the baby up before it could hit the floor—supporting its head, thank you very much—and then he turned to meet the wrath of the Faerie Queen.

Now this was a fight worth traveling for!

The Faerie Queen turned into a great serpent, her scaly coils filling the court and winding around the pillars. She opened her mouth: her breath filled the air with lightning. The Queen's subjects ran, slithered, fluttered, and shambled out of the hall, chittering with fear.

As he ducked lightning bolts with joyful speed, Sun Wukong plucked a hair from his head and breathed on it. Another Sun Wukong sprang into existence, bright eyed and curly tailed.

"Sun Wukong #2, look after this baby!" He thrust the child into his replica's arms.

He tore off seven more hairs in quick succession. Every hair became a Sun Wukong, each lovelier than the last (but none quite as lovely as the original, of course).

"Come, little brothers," he cried. "Let us chop this snake in half and have it for dinner. There is enough for all of us to eat until full!"

"Ah, snake-gall liquor—our favorite!" said his little brothers. They scattered in every direction. One started pulling the serpent's tail. Three were at her head. Everywhere you looked there was a monkey tormenting the snake.

Sun Wukong took a golden needle from his ear and shook it. It grew into a golden staff, longer than Sun Wukong was tall, luminous with power. With a shout, Sun Wukong dived in and hit the Faerie Queen in the eye.

The Faerie Queen roared and vanished. The seven Sun Wukong replicas capered: "Very good, very good! Congratulations, Sun Wukong! How come you are so clever? Who make you to be so handsome?"

It is convenient to be able to summon a clone army, but unfortunately, hairs do not have much brain. The original Sun Wukong did, however, and he saw the air grow black.

"Don't celebrate so fast, idiots! She is coming back!"

But it was too late to warn them. Already the air was full of fleas. Tens of thousands of midges buzzed and stung every monkey. Lice burrowed into their tender monkey flesh.

Sun Wukong's heptaplicates cried out and slapped their heads. Even the first Sun Wukong started itching wildly, but he was not about to be defeated by some bugs.

Scratching himself with one hand, he whirled his staff above his head with the other. Faster and faster the staff spun, until it pulled the air around it into a cyclone. Brighter and hotter the staff burned, until the air around it shimmered like the air above a fire. The fleas were drawn into the wind and burned by the thousands.

"Haha!" said Sun Wukong, but before he could gloat, the fleas melted away. He blinked, and the Faerie Queen leapt for his throat.

Sun Wukong was too caught up in the motion of his staff to ward her off. He hit the floor under the weight of a wolf. She pinned him with her paws, looking into his face with mad eyes, and growled.

"Woi, close your mouth!" Sun Wukong exclaimed. He had a particular horror of bad breath.

The Faerie Queen had an enormous red mouth, full of sharp teeth. For a long uncomfortable second, Sun Wukong wondered whether foreigners liked to eat monkey brains. The next moment seven monkeys hit the Faerie Queen in the side.

With a slash of her paws she ripped them to ribbons. They vanished; seven little hairs came floating down to the ground.

But by now the Queen clearly thought Sun Wukong enough of a challenge that it was worth transforming into her most powerful form. She turned into a woman.

Not the rich woman Sun Wukong had seen earlier, towering in her grand dress and jewels. This was a naked little starveling creature. There was something appealing and sorrowful about it—its face was seamed with wrinkles, like the face of a little monkey baby. The fingers of her small hands curled in like the petals of a flowerbud, and her mouth when it opened was toothless, her gums as soft and pink as an infant's.

But the eyes were wrong. The eyes were like burnt holes in her face, at the very bottom of which was a flicker of blue—the abyssal blue of an empty sky.

When the Faerie Queen reached out, it was like the movement of the tree outside your bedroom window on the day it decides to awake from its vegetal slumber, lean into your room, and enclose you in its bark.

Sun Wukong had been to hell and back again, taking the scenic route each time. He had seen demons of all kinds; he counted among his good friends some quite startlingly ugly monkeys. He had never encountered anything as terrifying as this.

He chortled.

"Good!" he said. "Now we are getting serious!"

Alas for the schemes of mice and monkeys! In the tremendous effort of showing her true self, the Faerie Queen had taken her mind off her other magics. The human woman, forgotten in a corner, suddenly found herself able to move. Sun Wukong #2 was singing the mortal baby a little song about bananas when she tapped him on the shoulder. When he turned around, she kneed him in the crotch.

His shout drew Sun Wukong's attention. The sight of the woman speeding away with her Johnnie clasped in her arms drew the Faerie Queen's.

The Faerie Queen made a creaking sound of fury.

She lifted her twiggy hands and a forest sprang up around the woman. The Queen lifted her hands and the sky was crowded with black crows. They were no longer in a grand hall, but outdoors. Sun Wukong smelled damp air and mulch. Leaves rustled underfoot. The birds were cawing.

Ahead of him the human fell on her knees, got up again, fell. She was still holding her baby close, protecting him from every fall, and Sun Wukong could hear her sobbing breath.

Among the trees lurked fearful shapes. Bright malicious eyes shone in the darkness under the leaves.

Sun Wukong looked at the Faerie Queen, incandescent with power. He looked ahead at the human. She was forging ahead dog-gedly, stumbling over roots, looking at her feet as if they were the only thing she needed to pay attention to, as if she could not see the shadows converging on her. Her thin shoulders shook, from fear or cold.

"Hai," said Sun Wukong.

That human had kicked his poor replica in the balls. Did a Monkey God put up with this kind of thing from mere mortals? Did a Monkey God allow himself even to appear to be running away from a monster as stimulating as the Faerie Queen? Did a Monkey God ever stop fighting before the fight became boring?

"*Hai*," said Sun Wukong sadly.

A Monkey God does not ignore the dictates of his importunate insides. Everything from Sun Wukong's heart to his liver told him the same thing.

He leapt across the room. It was only a room, after all. The Faerie Queen could fill it with the smell of rain on the wind and the squish of deer shit underfoot all she liked. All of this was easy enough to see through if you were a Beauteous and Keen-Sighted Monkey King.

He picked up the woman and her baby, none too gently because they were spoiling the fun. He bounded into the air and hurled himself right through the roof.

They came bursting out of the hill with a sound like the biggest firecracker in the world, earth scattering around them. Outside the sky was full of clouds, ripe to be flown upon. He picked one and jumped right out of Fairyland—

—into the world.

He left the human and her baby next to a flock of sheep, so that if they got hungry, they would have plenty to eat. Of course, they might have to fight the grumpy-looking old man who was slumbering on the stile next to his flock, but if the human was capable of traveling to Fairyland to defy its big boss, then she could deal with an old man. Probably she would knee him in the crotch and he would offer her all his sheep.

As for Sun Wukong, he went back to look for Elfland—but like many other adventurers, he could not find it again. For a while he stood in a damp green meadow and complained.

It would have been some comfort to him to know that the Fair Folk had to move out of the mound where he had fought the Faerie Queen. Sun Wukong had used his head to create the hole in the ceiling, and hundreds of his hairs had got caught in the earth as he went.

Every time the fae tried to repair the hole, the hairs turned into things like monkeys and scholars and calligraphy sets. And the monkeys scratched and howled at them, and the scholars rapped their knuckles with rulers, and the calligraphy sets swept beautiful lines of stinking black ink across their faces.

But he would never know this, because he never saw any of them again.

Fortunately Sun Wukong was an inventive monkey. He could not long face a problem without seeing the solution standing behind it. The answer to his dissatisfaction came to him as he was cursing the sodden sky for daring to rain on such a Well-Groomed and Debonair Monkey King.

If a poor foreign kingdom had been that much fun, what manner of interest and incident must there be in the wealthiest and most powerful kingdom of all? The only court that mattered—the only citadel worth storming—the Heavenly Kingdom?

No barbarian land, that. It would be full of intelligent people who would understand proper speech and recognize the Monkey's multitudinous virtues at once. Also there would certainly be excellent treasure to be admired—or given—or taken.

You should have seen the smile that spread across Sun Wukong's face.

The gods stirred in their beds. In the Heavenly Palace the Jade Emperor sneezed—

But you know the rest of this story. Let us leave Sun Wukong there, hurtling towards his next adventure, intent on getting into trouble—not yet Buddha-like, never yet trapped, but dauntless, immortal, and free.

Liyana

I was the one who found you, did you know? You've heard this story so many times before. But let me tell you one last time, Liyana.

I was looking for chickens' eggs in the garden. Ma was poor growing up; it made her devoutly practical. No useless thing is allowed in our garden. All the trees bear fruit—bananas, mangoes, papayas. Lime plants in pots every New Year, and chickens everywhere.

It's our pineapples that keep beauty in our garden, a row like a bar of golden sunlight on the grass. People stop to stare at them.

They've been here as long as our family's owned this land. The leaves are long and thin, with sharp-toothed edges, like aloe vera. On young plants they're pink as babies' lips.

When our pineapples ripen, they grow big and luminous. The flesh is sweet, the juice smooth on the tongue. Our daughters are always good girls.

It had been so long I almost didn't recognize you when I saw you. I came so close to plucking you out from the sheltering leaves— but God must have been watching me. I touched you, and the tips of my fingers felt the vibration of your beating heart.

Even then I didn't dare believe it, until I parted the leaves and saw you.

Nüguo have thin skin, barbed and purple like the skin of young pineapples. I could see the outline of your body under the shell, nestled in the heart of the fruit. You weren't human yet. Your head was huge; the rest of your body was a tail. Your hands and feet were fins. You were shaped like a peanut or a tadpole.

But I knew who you were straightaway—my little sister.

This time I'd protect you.

I was still little the first time we had a daughter like you. The family must have rejoiced when they found her. Ma would have gone singing around the house. We would have made tiny clothes for her and tried to think of good names, names rich with luck, names promising a happy life.

But I don't remember all that. I only remember the storm. It was the monsoon season and the rain was fierce. The lightning split the sky in half, and the trees bent and touched their heads to the ground.

That day it rained without pause into the night. I was sleeping when a big smack of thunder woke me up. I heard someone crying, a lonely sound in the storm.

When I went downstairs I saw the nüguo sitting on the dining table. Her shell was broken to pieces by the violence of the rain. She was too small to be so unprotected, no bigger than my fist.

Ma was patting her dry with a towel.

I remember I went up to Ma and said, "Ma, I help you wipe your face." I thought her cheeks were wet because she'd gone out in the rain.

After my first little sister died, we thought we'd lost our chance. Everyone knows how rare nüguo are. They come to a family once in a generation, if that. In our family we had been waiting for a long time—there had been no nüguo in Ma's generation.

People left fruits and biscuits at our door when they heard the news. Our friends told us to ask them if we needed help. Without a nüguo they knew our family would be coming on to some suffering times.

You were our miracle. We hid you with a sheet whenever the air smelled of rain. We cleared the soil around you to make sure no weeds were taking your food and water. We made the earth rich at your roots.

Every morning I came and spoke to you. I squatted on the ground, put my hand on the prickly skin of your shell, and felt the tiny repeated thud of your heartbeat.

In this way I learnt to love you. I knew you so well even before you were born.

When you started to ripen we lived in a state of constant fidgets. Ma hovered around the garden day and night. She forgot to serve our lodgers or feed the chickens. Every auntie in the neighborhood visited to dispense advice.

"When your nüguo is going to be born, you must wrap blankets around her to keep her warm," said one.

But another said, "When the nüguo is going to be born already, you must keep her cool. Fan her with nipah leaves and sprinkle her with cold water."

Aiyoh, we were serba salah—no matter what we did it would be wrong. I don't know how we found the courage to decide that you were ready. But finally one day Ma set her mouth and stomped out to the garden.

We harvested you carefully, Ma holding you with both hands as I cut off the thick stem that attached you to the plant with our sharpest parang. Ma carried you to the house, holding you close to her breast. Your thorny shell scratched her arms, but she didn't mind.

Ma is old-fashioned. She thinks too much luck is dangerous. Every happiness must be paid for. Every good thing brings bad things.

Nüguo look like pineapples, but you must cut them as if they are durian. One hack of the chopper along a fault line and the fruit will come open, revealing the treasure inside.

You came out perfect. You didn't scream or wriggle like other babies, red with the indignities of human birth.

You were golden and hairless, your skin covered with millions of tiny thorns only visible up close. The interwoven leaves folded neatly over your fragile skull reminded one of ketupat.

You were a polite baby. The first thing you did was yawn and open your eyes. Such a gentle way of saying hello. The inside of your mouth and the irises of your eyes were pale green.

Ma picked you up out of the juicy shards of the nüguo and put her cheek to your wet cheek. People like us find it difficult to touch people like you. The thorns on your skin catch on our skin, rub rashes into it. The vegetable stiffness of your flesh is strange to us.

But we dried you together, Ma and I, and we dressed you and kissed you even though it made our lips swollen and tender. You were so welcome, Liyana. We'd waited so long for you.

The only nüguo person I knew growing up was our grandmother. But she couldn't tell me about what it was like, of course.

Ah Ma had had a disappointing life. When she was a girl, this house was a gambling den. The people who came here were small-time samseng, or men who didn't like to work—not the kind of men you want your daughter to meet. Her mother and father were too busy to worry too much about Ah Ma. She had to look out for herself, but before she could learn, she fell in love with your grandfather. She was fifteen years old. He was thirty-five.

You don't want to hear about your grandfather. Maybe it's an interesting story. Interesting doesn't mean happy.

But we mustn't speak ill of the dead.

Ma says you're like Ah Ma. She would know—she's the only one who remembers her. Of course Ah Ma wasn't really our grandmother. Ma was her sister's daughter, but the sister went away to work in the city. The sister liked working better than children, but that was all right. Ah Ma loved nothing better than children.

She would have done anything for us. She gave us all she had.

You were like that too—so good, so giving. You cried softly, in hesitant sobs, as if you weren't sure you wanted anyone else to hear. When you got older you followed me everywhere, and everything we did, you wanted to do—making beds, cooking meals, cleaning rooms after the guests left. You learnt quickly. You hated to be spared anything.

In the morning, when the sun had risen but the air was still cool, you'd get up and creep downstairs, quietly, so as not to wake up the guests. Outside in the garden Ma would be hanging up laundry.

You'd step out onto the grass, barefoot, and dig your feet into the ground. You turned your face to the sun and opened your green eyes, and that was how you'd fall asleep. Standing upright, rooted in the earth.

When Ma watered the plants she'd water you last, all around your feet, until you woke up and started giggling because it tickled.

You were so sweet, and we were starved for sweetness. You were so easy after a life of difficult. Ma used to watch you with dazzled eyes, like a woman in love. She loved me too, but not like that. The last time she looked at somebody like that was before our brother left.

You never knew our brother. He was a nice boy, a loveable boy, but not good. The men in our family are always nice but not good. The women are too good. It ends up like that.

You used to ask me so many questions: "What does Ko Ko look like? When is he coming back? Why did he go away?" I felt bad for not being able to answer. Showing you his photograph wasn't enough. That stiff boy in the picture wasn't what I remembered of our brother—in person he'd been brighter, warmer, funnier. When he laughed, his laugh used to fill the whole house, from the floor to the roof.

You helped me write letters to him in your neatest handwriting, I dictating: "Dear Ko Ko, here is the money this time. Please try to make it last longer. Times are hard and the guests are not so many. We have a new white chicken named Pau. We would be so happy to see you again. I hope you are sleeping on comfortable beds. We all love you."

"Can I send my kisses?" you asked. When I said yes, you pressed your lips to the paper, carefully. Golden juice stained the page, smelling of sugar, sticky to the touch.

You should have had a long life. You should have been able to choose when you wanted to go.

Ah Ma was the one who told Ma to put her in the ground. She went because she felt life had lost its luster. The old house was still good, the family could have lived in her for at least another few years. But when Ma protested, Ah Ma said, "Aiyah, living is not fun for me already. Your father passed away, my sons have all gone. I am old. What else can I do for you all?"

When she was buried Ma was sad, of course, but it was a happy time as well. We held a banquet for everybody in the neighborhood, and sang songs as the new house sprouted. When we set fire to the old house the whole family stood outside and held hands around the fire so no bad spirits would disturb the house's passage to heaven.

Ko Ko was only a little boy then. Ma says when he saw the spirit go up from the flames, he thought it was our grandmother. He shouted, "Ah Ma, don't go away!" It made everyone laugh and cry at the same time. Ma explained that Ah Ma was still with us. The bones of our new home were her bones. She would stay and look after us for a long time.

It's not Ah Ma's fault she went bad. In an old house the wood begins to warp. The spirit, restless, dreams of escape. Its dreams make the floorboards buckle and the damp creep up the walls. Fuzz grows in the dim corners of rooms. The house's breath becomes unhealthy, full of spores, so that the air is not good for humans to breathe.

We stood it as long as we could, Liyana. We started wearing slippers inside the house because otherwise the floor drove splinters into our feet. We had always been busy, but we worked even harder, because the house needed so much cleaning. We left the doors and windows open all the time, to clear the air.

But the guests stopped coming. Who wants to lodge in a bad house?

It used to be that we didn't have to take lodgers. When Pa was around we could live on his salary. Ma used to take washing and make clothes for people in the neighborhood, and we sold our pineapples, but that was just for fun—so we could have new clothes, buy treats for the family.

After Pa passed away, we began to struggle. Losing our first nüguo made it even worse. Before, we used to be like other people: all our uncles and aunties lived in the house with us. It's a big house, but it was a tight fit then, because Ah Ma had five children and they were all married and they all had children.

But when the first little sister came and went, the uncles and aunties said it was because Ah Ma was unhappy with us. Losing a nüguo is such bad luck. The uncles and aunties left the house, running from the bad luck, but Ma stayed. She was Ah Ma's eldest daughter. What would be left for Ah Ma if we all went away? What would happen when the house went bad and Ah Ma needed somebody to help her?

Sacrifice creates obligations. Remember that, Liyana. You have rights.

Without the lodgers we could not manage. We killed most of our chickens. We stripped our gardens bare. The rooms stood empty: the air smelled of rot, and any light you lit in the house went out almost at once.

One day early in the morning I came out into the sun. Ma and I were getting very dark because we spent all our time outdoors, away from the house. You were standing in the garden, eating the sunshine with your face to the sky. Ma was watching you, and she had tears in her eyes.

"She's so painful," she said.

I looked at you, but you seemed happy. You didn't notice what was happening to the house. You were still small, and different from humans.

"Not Liyana," said Ma. "Your Ah Ma. She also deserves to be considered. She gave us her whole life and death, and what are we giving her? We are being selfish."

There was a bitter taste in my mouth. "But Liyana is so small."

"We're wrong already," said Ma. "There should have been a nüguo in my generation. Someone my age . . . she would be old enough to decide herself. Maybe she'll even be tired of life, ready to go, like Ah Ma." She put her arms around herself. "Must be I did something bad in my past life. Maybe it's the mistakes I made with your brother."

"It's not your fault," I said.

"Whether it's my fault or not, I'm not the one suffering the consequence," said Ma. She wiped her eyes, but her face was stern. "We owe Ah Ma everything. We must be fair."

So we took you to the garden, Liyana; we didn't have a choice. We kissed your prickly face and we laid you in the ground. It was nighttime and you were sleeping, and the earth is familiar to you, a kinder mother than any human could be. You didn't wake when we started to cover you with soil.

We did it gently, as if we were folding a blanket over your little body. It was only towards the end that you opened your eyes, gluey with sleep, and said, in a faraway voice, "What's happening, Mama?"

"We're saying goodbye to Ah Ma," said Ma. She didn't cry then or later. I was crying silently. I could hardly breathe; the snot was running down my face. I didn't blow my nose, because I was scared of waking you.

"Don't worry, darling," said Ma. "Go back to sleep."

You closed your eyes and you didn't stir even when we began to pat the soil down over your face.

"It's natural for her," said Ma. "When we buried Ah Ma she was awake. She just folded her hands like that and lay there while we threw in the soil. She was looking out at us until the end."

The new house sprouted fast, because you were so young. After a day and a night we could see the new green shoot where we had buried you.

The house will be green at first, Ma said, as green as your eyes were. When it matures it turns brown and hardens. It will last us many long years, as long as you would have lived as a woman.

To push a house beyond that lifespan is not kind or fair. When we had seen the new green shoot we prepared the bonfire. That night we set fire to the old house.

There were not enough people to form a ring around the house—not like the old days when the family all lived together. Ma and I stood in front of the fire and shouted and banged pans to frighten away the bad spirits.

I was watching out for Ah Ma, but my eyes were dazzled by the flames and stung by the smoke. I would have missed her if Ma hadn't said: "Nah—there!"

She gestured at a silver wisp of smoke. It could have been Ah Ma's spirit, or just the smoke from the fire—I wasn't sure how Ma knew it was her. The spiral shivered and vanished. The old house groaned, and the roof came crashing down.

We'll sleep outdoors for now. Luckily it's not the rainy season, but we won't have to do it for long. Already you've put out green creepers over the ruins of the old house.

In a week, maybe two, you'll develop a network of roots, spread over the ground. Up will spring sturdy floors, strong pillars, thick walls. You'll bud rooms and a flexible roof. We'll have to tile the roof ourselves, to protect you from the wind and rain and sunshine. The doors and windows we'll have to carve out of the walls. They will be made of good, young, supple wood, as sound as our daughters always are.

I'll stay with you now, Liyana. Because we're taking your death, you'll have my life. I can't promise to protect you anymore, but when the time comes, I'll set fire to you and let you go. You'll soar up into the dark night sky with a sigh, unshackled from obligation, restored to yourself.

As I sleep under your roof, I'll remember you as you were— when you had a face, when you had eyes, when I could hold your warm prickly skinned body within the compass of my arms and tell you the story of how I found you. When Ma has passed on, I'll still be here, and my daughters after me. As long as you need us, until you can be free again.

The Terra-cotta Bride

Even the housekeeper knew about the terra-cotta bride before Siew Tsin did. Siew Tsin only found out when she ran down the stairs one day, a day like any other, and saw the girl coming in through the main doors in full bridal gear, her ornamented headdress tinkling.

Siew Tsin crouched on the stairs in her old samfu and felt the winds of change raise the hairs on the back of her neck. She had ten seconds before anyone looked at her, ten seconds to rearrange her face so that nobody would know what she felt.

Their husband, Junsheng, took the terra-cotta bride by the hand and presented her to Siew Tsin with an ironic tilt of the head.

"The whole family has come out to greet you," he said to the girl. To Siew Tsin he said:

"This is my new wife. Please look after her."

The girl shone out from her extravagant silk robes like a pearl nestled in a red velvet box. She was beautiful, with skin as smooth as jade and hair like a lacquered black bowl.

Her eyes were black commas, no whites in them. She was not human. She had never been alive.

"You must be like sisters to one another," said their husband.

"What is her name?" said Siew Tsin.

"She can answer questions herself," said Junsheng. "She has a working brain. She is as intelligent as you and me. What is your name, my wife?"

"You haven't given me one," said the terra-cotta bride. Her voice was throaty and surprisingly deep. She spoke without affect.

Junsheng seemed to like this answer. "Precious, we'll have to think of a good name for you," he said. The last time Siew Tsin had seen him so pleased was when he'd been burnt a new car.

Siew Tsin had not given much thought to what happened in the afterlife until the afterlife happened to her. She was young when she died, and it had been sudden. While running across the road, she had been hit by a motorcar and dashed against the curb. One moment she was brimming with life, possessed of ambitions, interests, an affectionate family—the next she was dead.

Hell came as something of a shock. What education Siew Tsin had had was from the blue-eyed nuns at her convent school, with their soft voices and implacable religion. Their lectures, given in warm classrooms on sunny, dozy afternoons, had given her a fluffy idea of the afterlife—all clouds and angels and loving Fathers.

They had not prepared her for the reality. This was strangely like life. Hell was hot and full of unkind people in a hurry, there was far too much red tape, and the bureaucrats were all shockingly corrupt.

It had been a relief to Siew Tsin when she had been scooped up by a long-dead great-uncle. Fourth Great-Uncle had seemed kind enough, though he was preoccupied by his children's lack of filial feeling.

"Why don't they burn me more money? Why don't I hear their prayers?" he said. "Are children's memories so short now? Are they too poor to afford the hell paper, or too miserly?"

Siew Tsin mumbled, "I don't know Auntie and Uncle very well. They live up in Alor Setar. We don't see them often."

She was too embarrassed to explain that they were Christians and did not believe in the rites anymore. They probably thought he was safe in the Christian heaven, kitted out with his own harp and in no need of cash.

She might as well not have tried so hard to save his feelings, because the faithless old man went on to sell her. Again, the procession of events was so fast and illogical that she did not know what was happening until it had happened. One day she was scuttling across the black volcanic floors of hell, trying her best to understand the rules of this new world; the next day she was married off to the richest man in the tenth court of hell.

The marriage worked out well for Fourth Great-Uncle. He got enough money from it to buy himself a house in the tenth court and bribe the officials to turn a blind eye to his continued presence.

The tenth court was the most desirable postcode in hell. The other courts were taken up by spirits busy in the expiation of their sins, and the hell officials who facilitated their moral rehabilitation, using whatever tools were available to them—fire, chains, whips, spears, and hammers for choice. Such work made demons short-tempered and violent in their integrity. What it did to the spirits did not bear thinking about.

The tenth court was for souls who had worked off all their sins, or who had not had sins worth speaking of, or who'd simply had a grand enough funeral—and hence, sufficient hell money—to buy their way out of the torments. It was a waiting room, where spirits waited for their new lives to be prepared for them. This meant that it was a considerably more tranquil place to be dead than every other court of hell. The demons, grown soft from lack of exercise, were as pleasure seeking and corrupt as any human official.

Peace and stability meant the development of a society. The tenth court was where souls could enjoy the hard-earned fruits of their deaths: the mansions their descendants had burnt for them, the incense that floated down from the living world straight into their grateful nostrils. If a spirit was rich, or powerful, or simply intelligent, he could manage it so he went on residing in the tenth court for a long time, avoiding the invitation to tea with Lady Meng that heralded the change to the next life.

Junsheng had been a rich man in life. He had left many children and grandchildren to tend his grave and burn him gifts year after year, so that the condition had persisted after death. When Siew Tsin met him he had been dead for twenty years. This was a long time to have evaded the loss of self entailed by reincarnation, even taking into account the inefficiency of hellish bureaucracy.

Fourth Great-Uncle must have meant well. He must have thought that Junsheng would look after his great niece, give her a better death than she could otherwise expect. After all, Fourth Great-Uncle had been dead for a long while when Siew Tsin came to the underworld. In his lifetime women had had lower expectations. His sister, Siew Tsin's grandmother, had been named Chiu Dai: *come, little brother*.

Siew Tsin had lived in a more modern time. Her parents had wanted her to be happy as well as docile. Resignation to unhappiness didn't come naturally—she had to learn it.

Three months after her wedding, Siew Tsin had run away from Junsheng. She had still had the loved child's belief that it would not be allowed for anything too bad to happen to her. Her plan had been that she would tell a god or kindly functionary what had happened to her and they would somehow restore her to her parents. Perhaps they could arrange for her parents to be blessed with a child in their old age, like Elizabeth in the Bible. The child would of course be their dead daughter, come to them again.

She was not a hundred paces from Junsheng's house when she found the functionary she had been looking for. A fairy from heaven in shining silk robes, standing discontentedly by the entrance of a grand house. A fragrance of sunshine and fresh air billowed from her, cutting through the smell of sulphur and stone. The crowd of spirits and demons that filled the streets left a wide space around her.

A visitation from the Heavenly Court was so unusual that it could be nothing but a good omen. Siew Tsin plunged through the crowd towards the fairy.

When Siew Tsin had explained her situation, she said:

"Can you help me, elder sister? My mother and father live in Klang. Perhaps it is not on your way to heaven."

The fairy had looked on her with compassion.

"It is not, but that is of no account," she said. "I will see that you are looked after."

Half an hour later Siew Tsin was bundled into a sedan chair by four stern hell officials and whisked back to Junsheng's. It appeared the fairy's understanding of what it meant to be looked after was the same as Fourth Great-Uncle's.

Junsheng had not been unkind. He had been extremely definite.

"I am too old and indolent to lecture you," he said. "But you should remember that I have every right to do so, if I wish. Considering the unusual circumstances of our marriage, I cannot be said merely to be your husband. I am your mother and father as well—I have their authority over you, and you have the same obligation to me as you would have had to your parents in life.

"I will treat you as well as they themselves could wish for. In return, you must honour me as you would honour your mother and father. You are young, and I will forgive this mistake. I will say nothing of the inconvenience and embarrassment you have occasioned me. If I had beaten you and thrown you out on the street, or indeed if I had killed you, everyone would have agreed that I was perfectly within my rights. But I am too old, and too fond of my comfort, for this kind of violence. Out of consideration for my feelings, Siew Tsin, you must be a good girl from now on. I cannot countenance any more silliness."

To be fair to Junsheng, he never cast it up to her again. But then again, there was nothing to cast up. Siew Tsin was a fast learner.

"Does elder sister know?" Siew Tsin said to the housekeeper one evening when the terra-cotta bride had gone to bed. The terra-cotta woman did not sleep, but Junsheng preferred her to keep up the pretence of being like the rest of them.

Siew Tsin wondered what she did all night: whether she turned herself off like a wireless, or whether she simply lay unmoving on the bed, her black eyes fixed on the ceiling, until it was morning and she was allowed to get up.

"Mistress Ling'en has not been told," said the housekeeper.

"What will she think of it?" Siew Tsin said.

The housekeeper did not say, *She will not be as angry as she was when he married you.* But there was no need to say it. Even Siew Tsin knew that.

The problem was that Ling'en and Junsheng had once been in love. This was a long time ago, when they were still alive. Junsheng had taken concubines in life, of course, but they had not mattered. It was known that he consulted his wife in everything—in the old days. It had gone sour long before his second wife had arrived on the scene. Ling'en had been living on her own for years when Junsheng married Siew Tsin.

This was unusual. It was hard enough to survive in hell when you were a rich, powerful man with many faithful descendants and the hell officials' favor. There were so many other dangers to contend with— demons promoted from other courts, furiously upstanding and eager to hurry on the cycle of rebirth. The eight thousand terra-cotta warriors who had been buried with an emperor, now lost. Left masterless, the warriors roamed the tenth court, looking for trouble. And worst of all, the dead. In hell, as in every other world, man was man's greatest enemy.

"A woman needs protection," Fourth Great-Uncle had said to Siew Tsin when he'd told her he was marrying her off.

Ling'en had not listened to tiresome old men like Siew Tsin's great-uncle, or to her furious husband. Ling'en lived alone, in a very nice house her favorite son had burnt for her, and so far none of the disasters predicted for unprotected women in hell had befallen her.

Because she found Junsheng tedious and avoided visiting, it took her a while to find out about his second wife. Siew Tsin had been married for several months when Ling'en came to see her.

Siew Tsin remembered her first glimpse of Ling'en vividly. A slender woman, shorter than Siew Tsin, graceful as a willow tree, and youthful-looking despite the grey in her hair. She'd walked into the drawing room where Junsheng and his new wife sat without waiting for the housekeeper to announce her, as if it was still her own house.

Junsheng had said, "So, you finally condescend to visit your husband."

This was when Siew Tsin found out that she was a second wife. It was the start of an unhallowed tradition of her being the last to know anything important.

Ling'en had glanced at Siew Tsin and drawn her eyes away quickly as if she were not worth being looked at.

"This is what you bought to entertain yourself in my absence?" she said. "I would have thought you could afford something more expensive."

"If you had stayed as I had asked, dear wife, I would have consulted your impeccable taste before I made my decision," said Junsheng. "Since you were not here, I am afraid we will have to settle for what my crude judgment told me was appropriate."

"She is young enough," said Ling'en. It was as if she were talking about an object of dubious value that Junsheng had bought at a flea market. "But that won't bring you any sons."

"I did not choose her for that," said Junsheng.

"Then why marry her?"

"She is a respectable girl," said Junsheng. "Her great-uncle was concerned about her welfare and asked me to offer her what protection I could give. He is a learned man, and we have a good relationship."

"You haven't lost your gift for lying," said Ling'en. "How sordid!—But I suppose men feel differently about this kind of thing."

Junsheng did not like this. He liked to think of himself as an honourable man, a patriarch in the good old-fashioned mold. A man of whom Confucius would have approved.

"You are being vulgar. But that is what comes of your unnatural mode of living," he said. "It is no surprise that you have become coarse from having to fend for yourself in such a world. If you could bring yourself to behave with some modicum of propriety, you would not have to struggle. I am not an unreasonable man. I don't think my demands are so outrageous."

"You wouldn't," sneered Ling'en.

"All I ask is that we treat each other like civilized beings," said Junsheng with exasperating patience. "We have been married for so long. I have tried to be a good husband. If you have any complaint about the way I have treated you and our children, you are welcome to express it. All I ask is that you do not work out your grudge in this unseemly way. Feelings are one thing, but think how it makes the family look."

"The family no longer exists," said Ling'en.

"I am trying to be reasonable," said Junsheng.

Ling'en let out what in a less elegant woman would have been a snort.

"Try instead to be intelligent," she suggested. "We are dead and things are different. If you understood this, you would see that I am not coming back no matter how many young girls you marry."

"It was not for that," said Junsheng.

Even Siew Tsin knew this was a stupid thing to say, but Ling'en had apparently made him too cross to be sensible. Ling'en did not bother dignifying his remark with a response, but left the house.

She was not any nicer to Siew Tsin when she saw her later. Their meetings were infrequent, but Ling'en had not cut all ties. Her relationship with Junsheng impressed on one the dreadful lastingness of marriage. They still operated as a team. They met to discuss money, strategies for keeping the hell officials satisfied, and the latest rumours in the tenth court.

They still argued about Ling'en coming back to live with Junsheng, but eventually the arguments grew tired, half-hearted on Junsheng's part. When he realized that marrying Siew Tsin had not insulted Ling'en enough for her to want to return, he lost most of his interest in his new wife. The sex stopped, to Siew Tsin's relief. And she, now an unnoticed part of the household, retreated into herself. Junsheng had a large library of Chinese and English books. There was Chinese chess to play with any servant who could spare the time. If she got really bored, a thoughtful descendant had even burnt Junsheng a piano.

It was a quiet death, but not an objectionable one. Siew Tsin sank like a stone in the river of quotidian incident, ignoring the scent of brimstone that gusted in at the windows. She closed her ears to the stories of the depredations of the terra-cotta warriors, the machinations of the spirits, and the intricate bureaucracies of the hell officials.

She lived, dead, unnoticed by her husband, the household, and even by her own self.

Until the terra-cotta bride came.

Junsheng named her Yonghua, his elegant lady. What Siew Tsin didn't understand was what function she performed.

"Men have their needs," said the housekeeper. In the living world she had been paper, crumpled, folded, rolled, and painted into the form of a woman, burnt as an offering to the revered dead. Here in the afterlife she gave a convincing impression of being flesh, and of possessing all the sad wisdom a real old woman would have had.

"Junsheng is not a man who thinks much about the pleasures of the flesh," said Siew Tsin. Because she had gone to a convent school when she was alive, she did not wonder aloud about how much pleasure a terra-cotta body could yield.

The housekeeper replied, sensing the thought: "You'd be surprised. With Yonghua in his bed, any man would be interested." It was also part of her persona to be earthy.

Yonghua was a marvel of engineering, far more advanced than the Qin-era warriors who looted shops, preyed on spirits, and made death hell for humans and demons alike. The terra-cotta warriors were painted to look human, but Yonghua's creators had coated her in a flexible material that acted and felt like skin. Her cheek was soft and downy, her eyelashes lush and long. Her hair stood out from her head, and the flesh of her arm sprang back to the touch, like fresh dough pressed by a thumb.

Her creators had made her the most tempting of women.

"And seeing as they put so many thoughts into her head," said the housekeeper, "you can be certain they made her for other things as well."

"Who created her?" said Siew Tsin.

The housekeeper flicked a beady-eyed glance at her. Siew Tsin had an odd sense that she had been examined and found wanting.

"Dirty-minded men, as they all are," said the housekeeper, with a lightness that seemed even falser than usual. Siew Tsin would have questioned her further, but the housekeeper went on:

"These busybody men, one day they will make it so it's impossible to tell between the truly dead and the never alive. The girl is forever asking questions. When the servants dress her, it's talk, talk, talk. When we asked her where she'd got all her questions from, she said, 'I was made to be capable of learning. A perfect wife must know her husband.' Now isn't that clever, when she had no mother to teach her?"

"Very clever," murmured Siew Tsin. The last time she'd had this feeling was when she was still alive and her mother and father talked about her cousin Ming Yen, who was brilliant at school, played the guzheng, spoke in a soft voice, took small mouthfuls when she ate, and never answered back to her parents.

When on a dull afternoon Siew Tsin wandered into the music room and found Yonghua sitting at the piano, this seemed like an unpleasant joke played by the gods. Of course Yonghua played the piano. Probably she played it wonderfully.

Siew Tsin backed out of the room, but Yonghua turned and saw her.

"Ah! Second sister," said Yonghua. She stood up. "I am sorry. I have intruded. I should have asked you before touching the piano."

"No, no," said Siew Tsin. Was it embarrassment that made Yonghua bow her head? Did she have feelings, or just reactions? The wild terra-cotta warriors seemed to be animated only by their own lust and rage, seemed to pillage on their own account. But Junsheng said they were driven by pure instinct—that once the enforced bonds of duty and fealty had fallen away, only the dregs of their creators' desires were left to drive the machines, unrestrained by human reason.

"It belongs to Junsheng," said Siew Tsin. "I have no authority over the thing at all."

"But you are the only one who plays it, aren't you?" said Yonghua. "The paper women told me so. That makes you the natural master of the instrument."

"Please do not let me interrupt you," Siew Tsin was mumbling as Yonghua spoke, still hoping to escape.

But Yonghua said, "I do not play. I was looking at it out of curiosity. I had never seen such a thing before."

She paused. "Will you play it for me? I would like to hear how it sounds."

"Oh," said Siew Tsin. Worse and worse! "I'm not sure that I would give you the right impression. I only had a few lessons when I was a child. I am very inexpert."

"As someone who was alive, you will have a better understanding of such matters than me," said Yonghua. "I do not know anything about music or art. Please teach me."

Her directness disarmed Siew Tsin. She sat down and played the only piece she could manage with any respectability—a minuet by Bach. Yonghua watched her all the while, her head bent, her forehead creased, as if she was focusing all her powers on swallowing up the sound.

"That was not very good," said Siew Tsin when she was done. An idea came to her. "Junsheng has a gramophone in his study. I'll play you some recordings of decent pianists. That'll give you a better idea of music."

"Thank you, sister," said Yonghua. There was a glow in her eyes; they were not so strange now Siew Tsin was used to them.

Siew Tsin could not remember the last time she had pleased anyone so much. She found she liked it.

When the housekeeper told them Ling'en had come, Siew Tsin felt an unexpected impulse to hide Yonghua. It was one thing for Ling'en to make unpleasant insinuations about Siew Tsin. Yonghua, blank and innocent as a piece of paper, deserved better. She had no sins to work off, that she should be tormented by restless spirits.

But Siew Tsin could hardly squirrel Yonghua away under the sofa and pretend she was not there. She closed their book and told the housekeeper to bring Ling'en in.

Ling'en gave the room her usual quick once-over when she entered, as if she were casing out the exits. Then she cast Siew Tsin and Yonghua one of her veiled looks, which were like being stabbed by a knife emerging from mist.

"What a charming picture," she said. "The sister-wives studying together. It must delight Junsheng's heart that you get along so well. What have you been reading?"

Yonghua did not look afraid. Siew Tsin was coming to realize that she was not only better at being a wife than Siew Tsin, but better at being a person.

"Second sister is teaching me the poetry of her country," she said.

It was a peculiarity of Yonghua's that she looked people straight in the eye. She did not mean it as impoliteness. It was one of the subtle things that marked her out as inhuman.

"Poetry?" said Ling'en. She laughed. "Did they write poems where you came from, Siew Tsin? I knew our cousins in the southern seas were enterprising, but I had no idea they were artistic. I didn't know you had such an interest in language."

Siew Tsin felt her cheeks warm. It was one of the things that Ling'en liked to torment her about, her odd accent and the occasional awkwardnesses that arose in her Mandarin, when she used phrases they had used in Malaya but nowhere else, or when she translated directly from Malay or English or another dialect.

"I believe there were Chinese poets in Malaya," she said. "But I was teaching Yonghua Malay pantun. She had not heard of the form before and asked if I would show her examples."

"Yonghua speaks Malay, does she?" said Ling'en.

"I'm a fast learner," said Yonghua.

"Of course," said Ling'en. "That is how they would have made you."

Siew Tsin stiffened. In all their days of reading and playing music, she and Yonghua had not touched upon the subject of her provenance. It had seemed to Siew Tsin that it would be indelicate to mention it.

"Junsheng would not have married you, after all," said Ling'en, "if you were not the best technology could offer."

"I am that," Yonghua agreed, "of a certainty."

Siew Tsin could not stop herself from shrinking as Ling'en came over to them, but Yonghua next to her did not so much as twitch.

Ling'en reached out and took Yonghua's chin between slender, sharp-tipped fingers. Yonghua's skin would be cool, Siew Tsin knew, and Ling'en would feel along the line of her jaw, under her fingerpads, a steady pulse, its beat as regular as clockwork.

"What is he playing at?" whispered Ling'en. But though she spoke about Junsheng, she was looking into Yonghua's eyes. Siew Tsin did not know what she saw there.

"Getting to know your new little sister?" said Junsheng's voice at the door. "How nice to have a visit from you, Ling'en. The whole family under one roof, for once."

"In your dotage you are becoming like a woman who cannot open her mouth without reproaching her grandchildren for neglect," said Ling'en.

She dropped her hand. Yonghua's ink-pool eyes were still fixed on her, wide and dazzled.

"Hell is not the most interesting place I have lived either," Ling'en continued. "And old age in death is less rewarding than old age in life. But surely it is going a little far to start trading in blasphemy."

"What could she mean?" said Junsheng. He was smiling with his mouth but not his eyes.

"The thing's an abomination," said Ling'en.

"You are becoming pious in your old age."

"You know I am not generally concerned about appeasing the gods," said Ling'en. "But I'm not in the habit, either, of putting them out. It is none of my business. It simply seems odd that you have spent all these years exhorting me to return for my own safety, only to start playing with fire yourself."

Junsheng shrugged.

"There's always someone who will overthink these things," he said. "I am an old man, and I've worked hard for my pleasures. Don't I deserve some fun at my age?"

"How stupid you must think me," she said. "You used to pay me more respect, Junsheng. This isn't about lust—not for sex, anyway. But far be it from me to meddle in affairs not my own."

"Are you leaving already?" said Junsheng.

"I only came to satisfy my curiosity," said Ling'en.

She glanced at Yonghua.

"It's good you're a quick learner," she said to her. "Make use of your time. You don't have much left."

Yonghua took Siew Tsin's hand and squeezed it. Her fingers were cold.

The press of those fingers gave Siew Tsin a sudden access of courage.

"I will see elder sister out," she said. What was the worst Ling'en had ever done to her, after all? Given her unfriendly looks and implied she was a whore. Well, Siew Tsin was essentially a whore, and looks wouldn't have been able to kill her even if she were still alive.

At the door she said, "What did you mean? About Yonghua not having much time left?"

Ling'en looked surprised. She might have had much the same expression if her pet dog had raised its head and started reciting Tang poetry. For a moment Siew Tsin thought she would not answer, but then she said:

"It's not just Yonghua. You are all at risk. Junsheng is really a fool. He has preserved himself for so long, and now he is throwing it all away for a gamble."

"I don't understand," said Siew Tsin.

"Ask Junsheng," said Ling'en.

Siew Tsin caught her arm before she could leave. "He won't tell me!" she cried. "Junsheng doesn't tell me anything. Nobody tells me anything! They think I'm ignorant. It's true. I don't know anything. But Yonghua can learn anything. Two weeks ago she had never seen a piano. Now she can play everything I can, all the sheet music we own, every piece she's heard on the gramophone. In a few days she will speak Malay as well as I do. What is going to happen to her?"

If the dog had stood up on its hind legs, danced a ballet, and then proposed marriage to Ling'en, Ling'en might have looked much as she did now. But it was an improvement on her looking as if Siew Tsin was something disgusting that had got stuck to her shoe.

"Please tell me," said Siew Tsin. "If it's trouble, maybe there is something I could do to help."

A smile tugged up the corner of Ling'en's mouth.

"Who knew there was a mind in that pretty little head?" she said. She shrugged. "There is nothing you can do."

She would leave without saying anything. Siew Tsin could not bear it. "Please—"

"But you might as well know," said Ling'en. A smile of pure pleasure spread across her face. "It will annoy Junsheng so much. I am going to find a sedan chair to take me home. Walk with me to the main street. I'll tell you."

Yonghua was sitting alone in the room where Siew Tsin had left her. She looked up when Siew Tsin came in.

"Junsheng's gone to his study," Yonghua said. "He seemed—"

She hesitated. Yonghua was exquisitely correct on the subject of their husband, as in everything else. But it was not clear what she thought of him.

"He did not seem happy," she said.

"He and Ling'en can only fight when they are together," said Siew Tsin. "Sometimes they do it through other people."

Yonghua put her head on one side like a bird. "You do not seem happy."

"Do you know why you were made?" said Siew Tsin abruptly.

Yonghua did not seem to think this a strange question.

"I was made to profit my makers," she said.

This was true, of course.

"Do you know why Junsheng married you?" said Siew Tsin.

Yonghua cast down her eyes with the modesty befitting a young girl.

"I believe it is thought prestigious to own me," she said. "I am very expensive."

"Worth more than your weight in gold," said Siew Tsin. Ling'en had said that.

Yonghua smiled. "Precisely."

Ling'en seemed to have decided that Siew Tsin's years of torpor came from an intelligent wish to stay out of trouble, rather than intense shyness. She had said:

"If you have as much sense as you seem to have, you would take care to avoid that machine. If you pretend ignorance, you might have a chance. But better than that, save up, or steal if you have to, and get away from that house. Let Junsheng go to—ah—paradise on his own. There's no reason why you should be dragged into trouble with him."

"Is that why you left?" said Siew Tsin.

Ling'en was so narrow-faced, high-cheekboned, and sharp-chinned that everything she did had edges. Her smile cut like a knife.

"I left because I knew we would be the end of each other if I stayed," she said. "We were always too busy trying to save the other from becoming what we did not like. This way perhaps I'll avoid Junsheng's brand of salvation."

"Yonghua, you are in danger," Siew Tsin wanted to say now, but the door swung open and Junsheng appeared, restored to good humor.

"My precious, why are you sitting here in the dark? I am sorry I was cross. That useless old woman! She has found religion, and it is softening her mind. But forgive me. Come upstairs and entertain your old husband. My useless descendants have exerted themselves for once—we have a new wireless. You can show me how to operate it."

Yonghua rose, murmuring disclaimers. Siew Tsin stayed where she was, just outside the circle of light cast by the lamp.

The light shining in through the windows turned the room a lurid red, smeared with shadows. Outside there was a dim cavern roof for a sky, black volcanic floor for earth, demons and spirits for neighbors. Despite their horse heads and bull faces, the demons of the tenth court were mundane creatures, pot-bellied and often flushed with liquor, courteous enough to the wife of a rich man. But the red light that filled hell made everyone look terrifying—human, demon, or otherwise.

It was not a world Siew Tsin would have chosen to live in. But she did not want to be reborn, either, any more than Junsheng did, any more than all the other spirits showering gold and favors on hell officials so that they could stay where they were. Rebirth entailed a true death, the severing of one's memory and the loss of one's self.

That day she sat in darkness for a long time, and only stirred when a paper maid called her to dinner.

Yonghua heard the attackers before Junsheng or Siew Tsin knew anything of it. They had been reading, Junsheng playing idly with Yonghua's hair, Siew Tsin pretending not to be bothered.

Junsheng seemed to have realized that it pleased Yonghua when he included Siew Tsin. When he called Yonghua to him now he usually asked his second wife to come along, and they spent the evenings together, talking, reading and listening to Cantonese opera on the gramophone. He also seemed to enjoy the pretence of being a family.

Siew Tsin and Yonghua rarely spoke to each other on these occasions. Yonghua because she was the perfect wife and all her attention was on Junsheng. Siew Tsin because nobody could know of their friendship. Nobody could know how much Siew Tsin liked Yonghua.

This was their unspoken understanding. It was a shock when Yonghua breached it. She shook off Junsheng's hand, sat up and said directly to Siew Tsin:

"You must leave now. They're coming."

Siew Tsin stared.

"What?" said Junsheng.

But Yonghua was already on her feet. She put her shoulder against an armoire and pushed it in front of the door while Siew Tsin and Junsheng goggled.

"That will slow them down," she said.

She turned to Siew Tsin, picked her up by the waist, and—moving so quickly Siew Tsin barely had the chance to gasp—threw her out of the open window. Siew Tsin splashed into the ornamental koi pond just as the terra-cotta soldiers kicked the door in.

"Run!" called Yonghua. She slammed the window shut.

There were three attackers, Siew Tsin learned later. It was easy enough to find a terra-cotta warrior willing to be a mercenary—it was one of the few jobs they deigned to do, preferring most of the time to obtain their gold by force—but they didn't take orders at a low price. They were expensive.

It was a rare assignation that could task the abilities of even a lone warrior. Terra-cotta warriors were made for fighting. They were inhumanly strong, nearly indestructible, and subject to none of the restraints that governed the behavior of humans or hell officials. They were built to protect the dead. Nothing frightened them.

Three terra-cotta warriors to murder or collect one rich man was overkill. But of course their employers had known about Yonghua. They had taken her into consideration.

Unfortunately for them, they had miscalculated.

It felt like an eternity to Siew Tsin before she managed to climb out of the pond, but it couldn't have been more than a few minutes. Coughing, tears running from her eyes, she crawled to the window and pushed the shutters open. In her hurry, Yonghua had omitted to lock them.

A red clay face loomed out of the window. Siew Tsin almost screamed, but choked it down. She balled her hand in a fist, raised it—and realized that a large crack ran along the terra-cotta warrior's forehead. She pushed at the head, and the body slumped sideways, lifeless.

Inside the room Junsheng was lying on the floor, his eyes closed. He must have been hit on the head—or thought it wise to feign unconsciousness. And Yonghua—

Yonghua was a blaze of color, a many-layered swirl of fabric, her preternatural silence a heart of stillness in a fluid world of movement. She slammed the heel of her palm into a warrior's jaw, grabbed his arm and threw him. He crashed into the wall with the sound of a vase smashing to pieces.

Yonghua turned around, blocked the descending arm of the other remaining warrior, drew a hairstick from her head, and drove its sharp point into his neck.

The warrior staggered back, groaning. It was a strange noise, like the grinding of rocks. Even stranger were the words that could be distinguished amidst the groans.

"Sister," the warrior said. "Sister, have mercy—"

Yonghua put her fist through his chest.

When she dusted off her hands, Siew Tsin saw that her knuckles were bleeding. She clambered through the window, stepping daintily to avoid the shards of terra-cotta warrior scattered around the room.

"You're hurt," she said.

Yonghua barely glanced at her bleeding hands.

"It's just liquid," she said. "See to Junsheng. Is he hurt?"

But he was stirring. He opened his eyes and gave Yonghua a pallid, pathetic look. She knelt by him, slipping an arm around his neck.

"You are not well," she said.

"I am an old man," he said.

Only 54 when you died, thought Siew Tsin, *and you could pass for 40.*

"In my youth I could have fought off these bandits. But I cannot take shocks like these anymore."

He struggled to sit up. This was what Siew Tsin hated about men, she thought suddenly, to her own surprise. She had not realized before that she hated men. But she did, and this was one of the reasons why: this incessant demand for sympathy and interest from every woman in the vicinity. Junsheng did not like Siew Tsin, he did not even know her, and yet he was extending this appeal to her. It was a sticky thing, his need, with tentacles that would strangle her if they could.

Siew Tsin rejected it.

"You are bleeding," she said to Yonghua.

The look Yonghua gave her was typically opaque, but it felt like a reproof. Siew Tsin was being too obvious.

"That isn't blood," Junsheng said. "It'll be a solution dyed to resemble blood, but its function is almost purely ornamental. It helps oil her joints, but losing some of it won't harm her. You don't feel it at all, do you, my heart-liver?"

"Not at all," said Yonghua. Her eyes passed unseeing over the remains of the terra-cotta warriors lying around them. Junsheng followed her gaze.

"Fools," he said in low-voiced triumph. "You are a jewel—worth every tael I paid for you. They underestimated you. This will have cost them dearly." He turned his head. "See, Siew Tsin, isn't it as I have always said? This is what comes of religious mania—it clouds your vision. The man will succeed who allows neither bodhisattva nor demons to frighten him."

But the self-interested see clearly, thought Siew Tsin.

Siew Tsin had believed that Junsheng had married Yonghua for vanity. She had not wondered why it had occurred to Yonghua's inventor to create her. If you could make something that resembled a human and endow it with every grace and beauty possible, what else would you invent but an exquisite young woman? There would be a sure market.

"You think it is about money and face, and perhaps lust," Ling'en had said the day Siew Tsin had followed her into the street to wait for her sedan chair. Ling'en had spoken amidst that heaving crowd of souls and bureaucrats as if she were discussing haircuts instead of conspiracy and rebellion, her voice unself-consciously clear. "But they are much more ambitious than that."

Think, Ling'en had told her, what could you do with a thing that resembled a human body? Stronger than a human, more beautiful, and most importantly—immortal. Impervious to illness and the persecutions of demons alike. Such a thing was not pinned to the spokes of the Wheel, unlike the bodies of every natural thing. Rebirth did not apply to it.

As spirits, Ling'en and Siew Tsin and Junsheng felt alive. They ate and slept in houses with thatched and tiled roofs, as the living did. But everyone knew the sturdy-feeling walls, heavy doors, and solid roofs were paper. If they were taken out of the fragile unreal world in which they were suspended, every pleasure and pain of the flesh they believed they experienced would show itself to be an illusion. Light their after-lives with a spark and they would burst into flame—and vanish.

"We can last as long as our money and luck hold out," said Ling'en. "But sooner or later some demon or god will take us away from ourselves and flush what remains into our next lives, whether we will or no. Sooner or later, we will die.

"But this man or woman, whoever it was who created our Yon-ghua—they asked themselves: What if we could transfer our con-sciousness into something that is not vulnerable to the demands of the Wheel? If there was something like that, it would render the idea of past lives and future lives obsolete. All lives would become one."

"They want to become Buddhas?" said Siew Tsin.

"Without putting in the work," said Ling'en. "There is a group claiming that they have found the secret of immortality. They have worked out a way to insert their minds into an immortal shell that does not need food or air to live, that is not affected by material things the way humans are.

"Once a person has locked their consciousness into this shell, their memories are sealed in with them forever. Even if the shell drank Lady Meng's tea of forgetfulness, the mind would be untouched. The person could climb up into the living world again and live as them-selves forever. They say to live in this shell is like being human, but even better."

"How do you know about this?" whispered Siew Tsin.

"The revolutionaries asked me for money," said Ling'en. She looked displeased. "Some fool among my servants has been talking too much. It seems people think I am rich enough that I could afford to buy an immortal body to live in. That's why I came to see Yonghua. I would be a fool to buy without checking the merchandise first."

"Yonghua is—"

"A trial. And an advertisement. A few hundred gold taels and my mind could be inserted into a body like hers. I must say she is stun-ning. The chance to have a body like that is very tempting to a woman my age."

"But I don't understand," said Siew Tsin. "Where is her mind from?"

"It's just some script they put in there," said Ling'en. "They have not tried the process with any real mind yet. She is only a prototype."

"And Junsheng has known this all along," said Siew Tsin.

"His brain has grown soft from lack of use," said Ling'en. "If only he'd started a business as I told him to when we first died. It would have kept him occupied. Being kept in style by his descendants has spoilt him. Now he is indulging in conspiracies and plots. We are too old for such things."

"How much danger are we in, eldest sister?" said Siew Tsin.

Ling'en shrugged. "If I were a god, I would be angry at the audacity of mortals, trying to invent a new pantheon. Wouldn't you? But it would be even worse if I were a hell official. It is not just my status that would be threatened. It is my livelihood. What would a hell official do if he did not have spirits to corral into the next life, or to bribe him to refrain?

"Junsheng is well-known enough that they won't simply collect him and toss him into his next life. They don't want the spirits to revolt, and they don't want the rich men to stop paying out. But if they become desperate, they may use other means to get at him and Yonghua. *You* are not important—but they won't notice if their spears pierce three instead of two."

Siew Tsin had asked whether Ling'en was going to sign up.

"Hn!" said Ling'en. "Be tied to this mind for the rest of eternity? That is a worse hell than anything you could endure in the ten courts."

"But . . . you're still here," Siew Tsin ventured.

Some of the old shrewishness returned to Ling'en's voice.

"And you always do exactly what you should?" She shrugged. "Anyway, the plan will never work."

"Why?"

"It's bad theology," said Ling'en. "This fool who created Yonghua was a reanimation engineer when he lived. You'll never persuade me that someone who would do that job could have any understanding of religion."

"A necromancer?" said Siew Tsin, using the English word. "I thought they were only in Europe?"

"This Chen Fei was trained in England. The rain in that country must have washed away all his sense," said Ling'en. "Unlike us, Westerners are not content with feeding their dead regularly and putting in the occasional request for protection. They bottle the vital essence just before it escapes the bodies of the dead and insert this into automata, and put the poor creatures to work doing their drudgery for them."

Siew Tsin's jaw dropped. "But aren't they worried their ancestors will punish them?"

"Westerners have different feelings about their ancestors," said Ling'en. "They say the soul flies from the body at the moment of death, and the vital essence that clings to the corpse is nothing but energy.

"I suppose when Chen Fei died he expected the Devil to greet him in a top hat and tails. Instead he ended up here with the rest of us Chinese. So he has turned his hand to this—perverting the technology of our ancestors for his own vanity. Once he has raised enough funds to fix himself and his followers up with immortal bodies, I expect he will climb up into the world with his army and try to storm the Christian heaven—or the Royal Society, which is much the same thing to him."

Siew Tsin could not imagine Junsheng putting himself out for membership of any society, heavenly or royal or both. She said so.

"No. But for self-interest?" said Ling'en. "My dear sister, who would not move the worlds for that?"

The day after the attack, Siew Tsin shut herself up in Junsheng's library and read furiously.

If she had paid attention, she would have guessed what was going on. The clues were there. Junsheng had a startling number of books on automata, the qualities of terra-cotta as a building material, rebirth, and the soul. There were Buddhist scriptures, anthologies of Taoist tales of the Immortals, and motivational pamphlets on how to win friends and influence people.

And maps. Siew Tsin gave these her closest attention.

When she emerged, her head swam with information—philosophy fighting with topography, folktales entangled with engineering.

It had all been there, laid out like dishes on a banquet table. Junsheng had not even taken care to hide which books he had been reading: they were stacked on the desk and scattered on the floor. He'd written notes to himself in the margins and folded over significant pages. If Siew Tsin had had half the ordinary curiosity of the average sentient being, she told herself, if she'd bothered to peep in one or two of these books, she would have found out what Junsheng was up to.

But she hadn't been interested. Idiot that she was, she had gone into the library and taken down her silly romances, her philosophers, her biographies of great men and women, her Greek and Latin primers. She'd read everything except anything that mattered. She'd told herself that even if nothing was happening externally in her life, at least she was learning. That was something valuable in itself. The nuns at the convent school would have said so.

But the nuns at the convent school had been wrong about death. Why should they be right about anything else?

And Junsheng—he thought so little of her that it had not even occurred to him to hide his research, though everyone knew she spent hours in the library. This was a level of disregard that went beyond contempt. To Junsheng she did not have a brain; she did not have feelings; she did not have motivations. She was a total nonentity and need not be worried about.

The worst thing was that he was right.

Locked in a wordless tantrum, she went to her room and packed her things. Then she went to Junsheng's bedroom and searched his wardrobe. For some reason, when his descendants burnt hell money (which they did with pious fervour and regularity), it always appeared at the bottom of his wardrobe, under the magnificent traditional garments he never wore and the naughty magazines they hid.

There was quite a lot of money this time. Junsheng must have been too distracted by his plans to collect it.

If Yonghua agreed to her plan, they would not have far to go. But where they were going, there would be demons to bribe, as well as gods they would need to hide from. They might have to spend a night or three outdoors. They would need the money.

She put it at the bottom of her bag.

Then she screwed up her courage and went to look for Yonghua.

"She is in the music room, mistress," said a paper maid. The newly awake Siew Tsin noticed the look she gave her. It was a wary look, almost as if she were afraid of her reaction to—what?

She puzzled over it on the way to the music room. It was strange: she had never thought of the paper servants as real before. She had not considered that they might have feelings and thoughts of their own. But weren't they basically the same thing as Yonghua?

People.

We are slave owners, she thought.

The idea was so shocking that she forgot to announce herself when she got to the music room. She opened the door, the words already on her lips to tell Yonghua. But her mouth stayed open and the words never came out.

Ling'en and Yonghua sprang away from each other. Ling'en was looking more human than Siew Tsin had ever seen her, her usually flawless hair dishevelled and her face a fevered pink, as if she had been drinking.

Yonghua was not flushed and her hair was tidy, but the look in her whiteless eyes was dazed.

She had looked like that the first time she had met Ling'en, Siew Tsin realized. And they were here, where Siew Tsin had first played Yonghua Bach. Here.

"I am sorry," said Ling'en. It was an astonishing thing to hear from her, but Siew Tsin barely felt the surprise over the sharp pain at her heart. "Yonghua wanted to hear a folk song from my home region. I can't sing, so I have been playing her scraps. We were—that is—"

She seemed to realize how ridiculous she sounded. She stopped and gathered her dignity around her.

"I should be going," she said. She nodded at Yonghua like a schoolmistress chiding an absent-minded child. "Remember what I told you."

"Yes," said Yonghua. Her voice was a floating thing, unmoored from feeling. She turned her face to follow Ling'en as she left.

Yonghua's creator must not have taught her that people were allowed to smile for themselves, over their own happiness. She had never smiled except when the script in her head told her it was the appropriate social response. As she looked after Ling'en, her face was smooth as a block of silken tofu.

Someone should have taught her that you smile when you are happy, thought Siew Tsin. *Someone ought to help her find out everything she wants to know.*

"Were you looking for me, second sister?" said Yonghua, her eyes still far away. "Or do you want to play the piano? I should not disturb you. I will leave."

"No," said Siew Tsin. "Stay. I am going."

She went back to her bedroom and unpacked her bag. She put everything away. It would be a while before she could bring herself to look at the things again. But she kept the money.

Siew Tsin woke in the morning to confusion. The house rang with raised voices. As she went downstairs, rubbing her eyes, paper servants rushed past her. Distress hung in the air like a bad smell.

Junsheng was sitting in the dining room, drinking black coffee. He had a newspaper spread out on the table in front of him, but he wasn't reading it.

"Good morning," he said when he noticed her.

"What is happening?" said Siew Tsin.

He had clearly been waiting for somebody to ask him this. He took off his spectacles and set them on the table with the deliberateness of an actor following a script.

"It appears it is just you and me again," he said.

Siew Tsin reached out blindly and touched the table. Its solidity comforted her. She sat down.

"Ling'en has outmaneuvered me," said Junsheng. He spoke in an even, detached voice, sounding like an old scholar lecturing on some abstruse topic. "I thought she was angry about Yonghua because she was growing pious in her old age. Ling'en never used to care about what was allowed or not allowed by the gods. We used to be the same. We believed in doing the best one could for oneself and one's family.

"But some people take up religion, you know, when they get old. When Ling'en scolded me about Yonghua, I thought: *Maybe soon she will give up and turn herself in, let them process her into the next life.* I was right about that. But I was not so clever as I thought. I did not predict that she would take Yonghua with her."

"How do you know where she has gone?" said Siew Tsin. "Was there a message?" Wouldn't Yonghua have left her a message?

But that distant absorbed ecstasy in Yonghua's eyes—no. She would not have been thinking about anyone else.

Oh, love was so cruel.

"Where else would she go?" said Junsheng. "She knows she could not evade me if she stayed here, and she would hardly have escaped to any of the other courts of hell. No. She has gone down the bridge."

Of course Ling'en had thought of it before Siew Tsin did. Ling'en had done everything first—married Junsheng, kissed Yonghua, run away with her to find the next life.

"And she just had to take Yonghua with her," said Junsheng. He shook his head. "Ling'en was not spiteful in the old days. I remember her when she was young. You are a nice enough girl, and Yonghua was a work of art, but Ling'en was a real woman. I died before she did, you know, and in the five years after I died our family's wealth tripled under her management. I never met anyone like her. And now we have come to this."

"What will happen to them?" said Siew Tsin.

"Ling'en will die," said Junsheng. "Yonghua will probably get smashed to pieces once the authorities realize what she is. May Ling'en be reborn as a cockroach for this turn. What is it?"

A paper servant put his head in at the door. He was fluttering as he came forward, his face pale.

"Master, we interviewed Lady Meng, as you ordered, and it appears—it appears—"

"Ling'en drank the tea?" said Junsheng.

"Both Mistress Ling'en and Mistress Yonghua did," said the servant.

Junsheng frowned. "That would have had no effect on Yonghua. She cannot be reborn. She is not real."

"Lao Ding told Lady Meng this," said the servant. "Lady Meng replied, 'Then this will make her real.'"

"That is impossible," scoffed Junsheng.

"Master, there is more," said the servant. "At Lady Meng's pavilion, it seems they purchased this."

He opened his hand. In his palm lay a twist of red thread.

Junsheng could not have looked more shocked if the servant had slapped him in the face. He reached out and picked up the string.

When a spirit is ready to go on to the next life, there is one way for it to cling to the things its old self valued. Only one thing may be chosen—the most precious thing. The one person amongst all people in the cosmos, living and dead, it wishes to hang on to, when it becomes necessary to let everything else go.

The spirit and its chosen one bind their ankles together with red thread. They may take each other's hands and smile at each other. When they walk down the bridge into the world of the living, they know it won't be the last time they see one another. The red thread is better than a promise—it's a guarantee. It means they'll meet again in the next life. It means they'll love each other there, too.

Siew Tsin would not have thought of that. She didn't know women were allowed to bind themselves to each other. She would have sacrificed herself and Yonghua on the mere hope that the next life would be better.

There were so many ways in which she was a fool.

"I don't understand," said Junsheng. Siew Tsin recognized the tremor in his voice. That was how she had felt when she'd seen Ling'en and Yonghua in the music room. But they would each have to suffer their betrayals alone.

She got up from the table and walked out of the room.

She kept walking: out of the house, down the slope, into the streets of the tenth court of hell. In her cotton samfu she drifted through the crowd, jabbed by the elbows of busy spirits. Blue-faced demons threw suspicious glances at her. She almost got mowed down by a sedan chair. She kept walking.

Lady Meng's pavilion was on the other side of the settlement. The farther she walked, the emptier the streets became. The buildings thinned out, until the signs of commerce and habitation had dropped away. The road opened out. She saw the end of the line.

It snaked down to Lady Meng's pavilion, perched on the edge of a cliff. Past the pavilion was the bridge, gleaming faintly in the shadows. Siew Tsin's ears filled with the sound of the waves crashing on the rocks below.

The spirits in the queue . . . Siew Tsin averted her eyes, then remembered her purpose and forced herself to look. There were spirits who had been dragged from their comfortable homes in the tenth court when they fell out of favor with the hell officials. They hit out wildly and wept, promising gold, their houses, their women, anything if only they were granted a reprieve.

This was humiliating enough, but worse were the spirits who had come up from the other levels of hell. The inventive tortures inflicted there had left them looking scarcely human. Siew Tsin passed a skinless person who flinched from the touch of the air; a groaning woman whose tongue rolled out of her mouth onto the ground, an unnatural red length; a man whose body had been so distorted by cruelty that he lay on the ground, curled up on himself like a caterpillar, and had to be pushed along by demons.

But there was something odd about these spirits. They were not weeping like the spirits of the tenth court, made craven by prosperity. There was peace in their eyes, a serene understanding of unhappiness.

They had come a long way. They knew themselves better than any living human was allowed to.

Suffering purifies the soul. That was what the nuns had taught her.

But the nuns had been wrong. She put her hand on her chest, as if she could press out the pain in her heart.

The hell officials dourly standing guard along the line did not even look up as she passed. Now that Yonghua had left her, Siew Tsin had become invisible again. Her breath did not stir the air. Her feet left no marks on the ground.

Where was Yonghua? Had Ling'en and Siew Tsin figured out the truth, or was Junsheng right when he said Yonghua could not be reborn? If she was still here, the attempt failed, she must not be smashed to pieces or torn apart by spirits wanting her immortality. Siew Tsin must save her.

If the plan had worked and they had both got away, Siew Tsin would never see Yonghua again. If the pact had failed and left Yonghua alone, she would be in danger, and she would need Siew Tsin.

That was a horrible thought, a horrible thing to desire. It had all gone wrong, and Siew Tsin had gone wrong with it.

A hand touched her elbow. A little old lady smiled up at Siew Tsin.

"You are one of the willing," she said.

"I don't know," said Siew Tsin. But when the old lady said,

"Do you want to see the sea?"

Siew Tsin said, "Yes, Auntie Meng."

They walked arm in arm towards the sound of the waves. Siew Tsin found herself telling Lady Meng everything, from the beginning—when she had died, no more than a girl. She felt very old now. If she were still alive she would be nineteen years old.

"Did it work?" she said. "Did Yonghua escape? Junsheng said she has no soul."

Lady Meng said:

"*This is not mine. This I am not. This is not my soul.* What passes to the next life is the inexorable force of kamma. Someone like you has no more soul than the terra-cotta woman did."

"Ling'en and I thought she could be reborn," said Siew Tsin, mostly to herself. "So we were right."

Lady Meng's eyes creased in a smile.

"Insofar as there is a you," she said. "We are at the bridge. Look."

The bridge arced out into space. At the end of it shone light—light as she had not seen it since she had died—the warm yellow light of the sun. Beneath the bridge lay a dark sea.

The bridge led nowhere. There was no end to it. The brave leapt off it and dived into the unknown sea. The cowardly inched along until the light swallowed them up. But the end was the same. It was a beginning.

It gave Siew Tsin an odd feeling, standing there with the sea breeze in her face and her hand in the old woman's. It made her feel like a child again.

"When I was little, I used to dream about falling," she said. Her own voice seemed to come from far away. "I dreamt I fell from the sky, through the clouds, and it went on for a long time . . . I never hit the ground. I used to wish, when I woke up, that I could do it for real without getting hurt."

"Yes," said Lady Meng.

"Does it hurt?" Siew Tsin whispered.

"By the time they get here, everyone has suffered as much as they ever will," said Lady Meng.

"Don't I need to drink your tea?"

"Not if you jump," said Lady Meng. "The wind takes your memories from you."

"Will I meet her?" said Siew Tsin. "Will I meet Yonghua in my next life?"

"Listen," said Lady Meng. "You will be born again. You will be a baby again. You will smile up at your parents again. You will feel the sun on your face again. You will be young again. Everything you know, you will learn again. You will find love again."

She helped Siew Tsin onto the ledge. She was surprisingly strong for an old lady.

"This time, let us hope you will get to be old," she said. "It is a great suffering to know youth only."

"Goodbye," said Siew Tsin.

"See you next time," said Lady Meng, more accurately.

"Will you remember me when I come again?"

"Of course," said Lady Meng. "I miss you every time."

Siew Tsin closed her eyes and fell off the bridge backwards. She fell forever. The light on her eyelids went from lurid red to warm gold. The smell of seawater was taken over by rain and fresh air. The clouds came up to meet her.

She never hit the ground.

The Four Generations of Chang E

The First Generation

In the final days of Earth as we knew it, Chang E won the moon lottery.

For Earthlings who were neither rich nor well-connected, the lottery was the only way to get on the Lunar Habitation program. (This was the Earthlings' name for it. The moon people said, "those fucking immigrants.")

Chang E sold everything she had: the car, the family heirloom enamel hairpin collection, her external brain. Humans were so much less intelligent than Moonites anyway. The extra brain would have made little difference.

She was entitled to the hairpins. Her grandmother had pressed them into Chang E's hands herself, her soft old hands folding over Chang E's.

"In the future it will be dangerous to be a woman," her grandmother had said. "Maybe even more dangerous than when my grandmother was a girl. You look after yourself, OK?"

It was not as if anyone else would. There was a row over the hairpins. Her parents had been saving them to pay for Elder Brother's education.

Hah! Education! Who had time for education in days like these? In these times you mated young before you died young, you plucked your roses before you came down with some hideous mutation or discovered one in your child, or else you did something crazy—like go to the moon. Like survive.

331

Chang E could see the signs. Her parents' eyes had started following her around hungrily, for all the world as if they were Bugs Bunny and she was a giant carrot. One night Chang E would wake up to find herself trussed up on the altar they had erected to Elder Brother.

Since the change Elder Brother had spent most of his time in his room, slumbering Kraken-like in the gloomful depths of his bed. But by the pricking of their thumbs, by the lengthening of his teeth, Mother and Father trusted that he was their way out of the last war, their guard against assault and cannibalism.

Offerings of oranges, watermelons, and pink-steamed rice cakes piled up around his bed. One day Chang E would join them. Everyone knew the new gods liked best the taste of the flesh of women.

So Chang E sold her last keepsake of her grandmother and pulled on her moon boots without regret.

On the moon Chang E floated free, untrammeled by the Earth's ponderous gravity, untroubled by that sticky thing called family. In the curious glances of the moon people, in their condescension ("Your Lunarish is very good!") she was reinvented.

Away from home, you could be anything. Nobody knew who you'd been. Nobody cared.

She lived in one of the human ghettos, learnt to walk without needing the boots to tether her to the ground, married a human who chopped wood unceasingly to displace his intolerable homesickness.

One night she woke up and saw the light lying at the foot of her bed like snow on the grass. Lifting her head, she saw the weeping blue eye of home. The thought, exultant, thrilled through her: *I'm free! I'm free!*

The Second Generation

Her mother had had a pet moon rabbit. This was before we found out they were sentient. She'd always treated it well, said Chang E. That was the irony: how well we had treated the rabbits! How little some of them deserved it!

Though if any rabbit had ever deserved good treatment, it was her mother's pet rabbit. When Chang E was little, it had made herbal tea for her when she was ill, and sung her nursery rhymes in its native moon-rabbit tongue—little songs, simple and savage, but rather sweet. Of course Chang E wasn't able to sing them to you now. She'd forgotten.

But she was grateful to that rabbit. It had been like a second mother to her, said Chang E.

What Chang E didn't like was the rabbits claiming to be intelligent. It's one thing to cradle babies to your breast and sing them songs, stroking your silken paw across their foreheads. It's another to want the vote, demand entrance to schools, move in to the best part of town and start building warrens.

When Chang E went to university there was a rabbit living in her student hall. Imagine that. A rabbit sharing their kitchen, using their plates, filling the pantry with its food.

Chang E kept her chopsticks and bowls in her bedroom, bringing them back from the kitchen every time she finished a meal. She was polite, in memory of her nanny, but it wasn't pleasant. The entire hall smelled of rabbit food. You worried other people would smell it on you.

Chang E was tired of smelling funny. She was tired of being ugly. She was tired of not fitting in. She'd learnt Lunarish from her immigrant mother, who'd made it sound like a song in a foreign language.

Her first day at school Chang E had sat on the floor, one of three humans among twenty children learning to add and subtract. When her teacher had asked what one and two made, her hand shot up.

"Tree!" she said.

Her teacher had smiled. She'd called up a tree on the holographic display.

"This is a tree." She called up the image of the number three. "Now, this is three."

She made the high-pitched clicking sound in the throat which is so difficult for humans to reproduce.

"Which is it, Changey?"

"Tree," Chang E had said stupidly. "Tree. Tree." Like a broken-down robot.

In a month her Lunarish was perfect, accentless, and she rolled her eyes at her mother's singsong "Chang E, you got listen or not?"

Chang E would have liked to be motherless, pastless, selfless. Why was her skin so yellow, her eyes so small, when she felt so green inside?

After she turned sixteen, Chang E begged the money off her dad, who was conveniently indulgent since the divorce, and went in secret for the surgery.

When she saw herself in the mirror for the first time after the operation she gasped.

Long ovoid eyes, the last word in Lunar beauty, all iris, no ugly inconvenient whites or dark browns to spoil that perfect reflective surface. The eyes took up half her face. They were like black eggs, like jewels.

Her mother screamed when she saw Chang E. Then she cried.

It was strange. Chang E had wanted this surgery with every fiber of her being—her nose hairs swooning with longing, her liver contracting with want.

Yet she would have cried too, seeing her mother so upset, if her new eyes had let her. But Moonite eyes didn't have tear ducts. No eyelids to cradle tears, no eyelashes to sweep them away. She stared unblinking and felt sorry for her mother, who was still alive but locked in an inaccessible past.

The Third Generation

Chang E met H'yi in the lab on her first day at work. He was the only rabbit there and he had the wary, closed-off look so many rabbits had.

At Chang E's school the rabbit students had kept themselves to themselves. They had their own associations—the Rabbit Moonball Club, the Lapin Lacemaking Society—and sat in quiet groups at their own tables in the cafeteria.

Chang E had sat with her Moonite friends.

"There's only so much you can do," they'd said. "If they're not making any effort to integrate . . ."

But Chang E had wondered secretly if the rabbits had the right idea. When she met other Earthlings, each one alone in a group of Moonites, they'd exchange brief embarrassed glances before subsiding back into invisibility. The basic wrongness of being an Earthling was intensified in the presence of other Earthlings. When you were with normal people you could almost forget.

Around humans Chang E could feel her face become used to smiling and frowning, every emotion transmitted to her face with that flexibility of expression that was so distasteful to Moonites. As a child this had pained her, and she'd avoided it as much as possible—better the smoothness of surface that came to her when she was hidden among Moonites.

At twenty-four, Chang E was coming to understand that this was no way to live. But it was a difficult business, this easing into being. She and H'yi did not speak to each other at first, though they were the only non-Moonites in the lab.

The first time she brought human food to work, filling the place with strange warm smells, she kept her head down over her lunch, shrinking from the Moonites' glances. H'yi looked over at her.

"Smells good," he said. "I love noodles."

"Have you had this before?" said Chang E. H'yi's ears twitched. His face didn't change, but somehow Chang E knew he was laughing.

"I haven't spent my entire life in a warren," he said. "We do get out once in a while."

The first time Chang E slept over at his, she felt like she was coming home. The close dark warren was just big enough for her. It smelled of moon dust.

In H'yi's arms, her face buried in his fur, she felt as if the planet itself had caught her up in its embrace. She felt the wall vibrate: next door H'yi's mother was humming to her new litter. It was the moon's own lullaby.

Chang E's mother stopped speaking to her when she got married. It was rebellion, Ma said, but did she have to take it so far?

"I should have known when you changed your name," Ma wept. "After all the effort I went to, giving you a Moonite name. Having the throat operation so I could pronounce it. Sending you to all the best schools and making sure we lived in the right neighborhoods. When will you grow up?"

Growing up meant wanting to be Moonite. Ma had always been disappointed by how bad Chang E was at this.

They only reconciled after Chang E had the baby. Her mother came to visit, sitting stiffly on the sofa. H'yi made himself invisible in the kitchen.

The carpet on the floor between Chang E and her mother might as well have been a maria. But the baby stirred and yawned in Chang E's arms—and stolen glance by jealous, stolen glance, her mother fell in love.

One day Chang E came home from the lab and heard her mother singing to the baby. She stopped outside the nursery and listened, her heart still.

Her mother was singing a rabbit song.

Creaky and true, the voice of an old peasant rabbit unwound from her mouth. The accent was flawless. Her face was innocent, wiped clean of murky passions, as if she'd gone back in time to a self that had not yet discovered its capacity for cruelty.

The Fourth Generation

When Chang E was sixteen, her mother died. The next year Chang E left school and went to Earth, taking her mother's ashes with her in a brown ceramic urn.

The place her mother had chosen was on an island just above the equator, where, Ma had said, their Earthling ancestors had been buried. When Chang E came out of the environment-controlled port building, the air wrapped around her, sticky and close. It was like stepping into a god's mouth and being enclosed by his warm humid breath.

Even on Earth most people travelled by hovercraft, but on this remote outpost wheeled vehicles were still in use. The journey was bumpy—the wheels rendered them victim to every stray imperfection in the road. Chang E hugged the urn to her and stared out the window, trying to ignore her nausea.

It was strange to see so many humans around, and only humans. In the capital city you'd see plenty of Moonites, expats and tourists, but not in a small town like this.

Here, thought Chang E, was what her mother had dreamt of. Earthlings would not be like moon humans, always looking anxiously over their shoulder for the next way in which they would be found wanting.

And yet her mother had not chosen to come here in life. Only in death. Where would Chang E find the answer to that riddle?

Not in the graveyard. This was on an orange hill, studded with white and gray tombstones, the vermillion earth furred in places with scrubby grass.

The sun bore close to the Earth here. The sunshine was almost a tangible thing, the heat a repeated hammer's blow against the temple. The only shade was from the trees, starred with yellow-hearted white flowers. They smelled sweet when Chang E picked them up. She put one in her pocket.

The illness had been sudden, but they'd expected the death. Chang E's mother had arranged everything in advance, so that once Chang E arrived she did not have to do or understand anything. The nuns took over.

Following them, listening with only half her attention on their droning chant in a language she did not know to a god she did not recognize, she looked down on the town below. The air was thick with light over the stubby low buildings, crowded close together the way human habitations tended to be.

How godlike the Moonites must have felt when they entered these skies and saw such towns from above. To love a new world, you had to get close to the ground and listen.

You were not allowed to watch them lower the urn into the ground and cover it with soil. Chang E looked up obediently.

In the blue sky there was a dragon.

She blinked. It was a flock of birds, forming a long line against the sky. A cluster of birds at one end made it look like the dragon had turned its head. The sunlight glinting off their white bodies made it seem that the dragon looked straight at her, with luminous eyes.

She stood and watched the sky, her hand shading her eyes, long after the dragon had left, until the urn was buried and her mother was back in the Earth.

What was the point of this funeral so far from home, a sky's worth of stars lying between Chang E's mother and everyone she had ever known? Had her mother wanted Chang E to stay? Had she hoped Chang E would fall in love with the home of her ancestors, find a human to marry, and by so doing somehow return them all to a place where they were known?

Chang E put her hand in her pocket and found the flower. The petals were waxen, the texture oddly plastic between her fingertips. They had none of the fragility she'd been taught to associate with flowers.

Here is a secret Chang E knew, though her mother didn't.

Past a certain point, you stop being able to go home. At this point, when you have got this far from where you were from, the thread snaps. The narrative breaks. And you are forced, pastless, motherless, selfless, to invent yourself anew.

At a certain point, this stops being sad—but who knows if any human has ever reached that point?

Chang E wiped her eyes and her streaming forehead, followed the nuns back to the temple, and knelt to pray to her nameless forebears.

She was at the exit when she remembered the flower. The Lunar Border Agency got funny if you tried to bring Earth vegetation in. She left the flower on the steps to the temple.

Then Chang E flew back to the Moon.

Acknowledgments

I would like to thank Amir Muhammad of Buku Fixi for first publishing a shorter version of this book; Gavin J. Grant and Kelly Link of Small Beer Press for giving the book a fresh lease of life, as well as my agent Caitlin Blasdell for her help in making that happen; the International Association for the Fantastic in the Arts for granting it half a Crawford Award; Emily Woo Zeller for her painstaking work on the audiobook; Wesley Allsbrook for the amazing new cover; and finally, all of the book's friends—the editors, readers and reviewers who have supported these stories over the years.

Publication History

"The First Witch of Damansara," *Bloody Fabulous*, 2012.

"The Guest," *Expanded Horizons*, November 2010.

"The Fish Bowl," *The Alchemy Press Book of Urban Mythic*, 2013.

"First National Forum on the Position of Minorities in Malaysia," *Fantastique Unfettered*, September 2011.

"Odette," *Shoreline of Infinity*, Summer 2020.

"The House of Aunts," *GigaNotoSaurus*, December 2011.

"Balik Kampung," *End of the Road*, 2013.

"One-Day Travelcard for Fairyland," *Spirits Abroad*, 2014.

"起狮，行礼 (Rising Lion—The Lion Bows)," *Strange Horizons*, March 2011.

"七星鼓 (Seven Star Drum)," *Spirits Abroad*, 2014.

"The Mystery of the Suet Swain," *Spirits Abroad*, 2014.

"Prudence and the Dragon," the *Crossed Genres Quarterly*, February 2011.

"If At First You Don't Succeed, Try, Try Again," B&N SFF, November 2018.

"The Earth Spirit's Favorite Anecdote," *Andromeda Spaceways Inflight Magazine*, May 2012.

"Monkey King, Faerie Queen" *Kaleidotrope*, Spring 2015.

"Liyana," *Spirits Abroad*, 2014.

"The Terra-cotta Bride" *Steam-Powered II: More Lesbian Steampunk Stories*, 2011.

"The Four Generations of Chang E," *Mascara Literary Review*, October 2011.

About the Author

Zen Cho was born and raised in Malaysia, and lives in the UK. Her short fiction has been awarded a Hugo, honour-listed for the Carl Brandon Society Awards, and translated into French, Spanish, Italian, Finnish, Chinese and Japanese. Cho was a finalist for the Astounding Award for Best New Writer, joint winner of the Crawford Award for the Malaysian edition of her collection *Spirits Abroad*, and winner of the British Fantasy Award for Best Newcomer for her debut novel *Sorcerer to the Crown*. She is also the author of the novels *The True Queen* and *Black Water Sister* and a novella, *The Order of the Pure Moon Reflected in Water*.

Cho edited the short-story anthology *Cyberpunk: Malaysia*, a Popular-*The Star* Readers' Choice Awards finalist. She has appeared at events in Malaysia, USA, UK, the Netherlands, Finland, Hong Kong, and Ireland, and co-organised UK convention Nine Worlds Geekfest's first Race & Culture programming track. Cho has spoken about genre and social justice on BBC Radio, Minnesota Public Radio News, and Al Jazeera's online daily TV show The Stream. Her website is zencho.org.

ALSO AVAILABLE FROM SMALL BEER PRESS

Isabel Yap, *Never Have I Ever: Stories*

"Drawing from science fiction, Filipino folklore, fantasy and horror, these thirteen stories are monstrous, scary, joyful, unexpected, inventive, eerie and weird." — Karla Strand, *Ms. Magazine*

Alaya Dawn Johnson, *Reconstruction: Stories*

"Haunting, not just for its vividness, but also for how Johnson writes around felt and imagined absences."
— *Chicago Review of Books*

Elwin Cotman, *Dance on Saturday: Stories*
Philip K. Dick Award finalist
NPR Best of the Year

"Blends humor, emotional clarity, and wild imagination to bring life to stories about identity, power, and human nature." — Arianna Rebolini, *Buzzfeed*

Sofia Samatar, *Tender: Stories*
NPR Best of the Year

"This is a short story collection containing wonder after wonder, done with casual intensity. These are all sharp knives of stories."
— Maria Dahvana Headley, *Electric Lit*